STRAIGHT ON 'TIL MORNING

K.J. SUTTON

ONCE UPON A TIME
books

Front cover image by Giulia Valentini

Typography by Book Covers by Seventhstar

Published in the United States of America

ALSO BY K.J. SUTTON

The *Fortuna Sworn* Saga

Fortuna Sworn

Restless Slumber

Deadly Dreams

Beautiful Nightmares

Novellas

Summer in the Elevator

PART ONE

MISS DAVENPORT

CHAPTER 1

August 5, 1895
London, England

"DON'T BE FRIGHTENED."

The male voice didn't belong to anyone I knew, and fear rushed through me. My eyes snapped open. I saw in an instant the intruder wasn't, in fact, actually inside my room —a face peered through the window.

My first thought was that I was dreaming again, and soon Liza or Mrs. Graham would appear from nowhere, their faces lined with weariness as they tried to wake me.

There was also the factor of how high my bedroom stood above the ground, where no one should have been able to go. There were no trees or rooftops for someone to stand upon, either.

"I'm not frightened," I whispered at last, though the stranger could not possibly hear me. It was a boy, I noted as I sat up. He looked to be my age or a little older, perhaps eighteen or nineteen. Slowly, I pushed the bedclothes aside. My toes touched the rug. It was real and solid, which was unlike any other dream I'd experienced. I paused, hesitating, and felt a quake of trepidation.

"I won't hurt you," my visitor added.

Curiosity got the better of me. I left the warmth of the bed and sent a novel tumbling to the floor, the one I had been reading before I must've succumbed to sleep. I edged toward the window, moving through a slant of moonlight. The boy's eyes flicked to my nightgown, which was so thin the outline of my body was visible—I'd forgotten to retrieve a dressing gown.

Blushing, I halted. We were close enough that I could see my breath on the glass now. The boy's hand was pressed against it. I stared first at the swirl of his fingerprints, then at his face, then toward his feet. They hovered in the air with nothing below to explain how he was there. My eyes searched the space around him, searching for the gleam of strings. Nothing but air.

"It's you," I breathed, awestruck and terrified. But I didn't move, no matter how loudly my instincts screamed to run. After all, none of this was truly happening. "You're Peter."

His eyes glittered. "And you're Wendy."

We studied each other, and it was obvious that Peter was no gentleman. His sun-streaked hair was too wild and his nose was crooked, as though it had been broken several times. There was a mark on his jaw, a darkened patch of skin shaped like one of those countries my brothers had trouble remembering the names of. But Peter had the most riveting eyes, so blue they were nearly silver. His smile drew me in, as well. The curve of his lips held secrets that I wanted to know.

Then there was his clothing. The fawn-colored trousers he wore were faded and threadbare. His shirt was loose, and it had likely been white at one time, but now it was decidedly less so. The ties were undone, allowing me a generous glimpse of his tanned, hard chest. On his feet were a pair of leather work boots. He wore no suspenders, waistcoat, or overcoat. While winter hadn't yet arrived in London, the night wasn't kind to those without layers or fires to warm them.

"This *is* a dream," I said at last. "It has to be."

The boy's grin grew. "Perhaps you're finally awake, and you've been asleep until this moment."

There was something dark and feral in that smile, like a beast weaving through trees beneath the wide, wild moon. I glanced at the latch between us, wanting the reassurance that it was firmly in place. Peter kept his focus on me, and I felt his silent question. Would I let him in?

As if he'd heard the question—impossible, since I hadn't spoken it out loud—Peter tilted his golden head. "I have learned that there are two kinds of people in this world, Wendy Davenport," he informed me. "Those who are brave enough to open the window and those who aren't."

"There's a difference between bravery and foolishness, sir," I retorted, hugging myself.

"Perhaps." He floated there in the air, staring at me, so separate from everything familiar and safe I was tempted to lift the latch for that reason alone. "Do you want me to go, then?"

I opened my mouth to reply, but something stopped me from saying the words. Several seconds ticked past. Satisfaction began to radiate from Peter's starlight eyes. He probably knew, just as I did, that if I didn't let him in I would forever wonder what could have been.

"It's only a dream," I whispered, more to myself than anyone else. No harm could truly befall me, whatever I chose. Peter said nothing. My heart pounded as I reached for that latch. Time seemed to hold its breath.

Then, so quickly I wouldn't have a chance to reconsider, I grasped it and pulled it up.

The window swung open.

I retreated, prepared for anything, and Peter landed soundlessly with another amused expression. The moonlight fell over him, revealing a faint smattering of freckles across the bridge of his nose. Now that he was on the other side of the glass, he was curiously silent. His gaze dropped to my feet and rose again, slowly. The amusement in his face faded. My heart felt like an anvil pounding against my chest. Could Peter hear it? Was my fear as naked as I felt?

Then the boy began to advance. I promptly retreated, breathing faster. *Get out.* The words rose within me, and yet I couldn't say them.

No, I admitted at the same moment my back collided with the wall. I didn't *want* to say them.

Peter put his arms on either side of my body, his palms flattening against the green wallpaper. A rush of scent came with him, and in my mind's eye, I saw a lush, green place of storms and sunlight. Something deep inside me stirred.

We stared at each other some more, and suddenly I knew why I didn't want to banish him—the air between us felt charged in a way I'd never experienced before. Not even with that handsome chimney sweep I'd once met in the alley behind the house, who had pressed such wet, clumsy kisses against my mouth as he pushed his hard length inside me, clutching my thighs with dirty, soot-blackened fingers. Afterward, as we'd both fixed our clothing, our breath mingling in the cold night, I'd glanced at him beneath my lashes and wondered if that's what it was always like. Quick, pleasureless, painful. Everything opposite to what I'd read in my beloved books. That was what I'd risked my reputation for? That was what I'd been longing to experience for so long?

The chimney sweep never came back—despite our weeks of flirting and that dalliance beneath the dark London sky—and I never got an answer to my question.

Until now.

"Do you truly sleep in this?" Peter questioned, lightly plucking the sleeve of my nightgown. His voice was low and heated. My veins warmed in response, along with another part of me that I had only recently begun exploring after the stars came out, when I was safely tucked beneath the bedclothes and no one else could see. When there was no risk of someone discovering my wanton, secret shame.

My voice was faint but steady. "Yes."

Peter's eyes brightened with curiosity—perhaps he'd been expecting a different reaction. That of an innocent maiden, who had never experienced such bold touches and brazen proximity.

This was a dream, I reminded myself, refusing to look away. There were no repercussions in a dream.

Peter must've seen something in my face, something that emboldened him, because his head tilted and he regarded me with unbridled desire. If there had been a charge between us moments ago, the air was practically crackling now.

Without any trace of hesitation or doubt, the golden-haired boy put his fingertips against the hollow of my throat. I didn't move or speak, and after another moment, he skimmed them down my chest, then to my breasts. He dragged the neckline of my nightgown as he did so, and the sleeves slipped off as if they were hardly more than silk stockings.

Now I truly was half-naked. A cool breeze kissed my bared skin, making me realize the window was still open. I shivered, but not because I was cold, and I felt my nipples harden.

Peter noticed, too. He dragged his gaze back to mine and held it with a directness that was startling. "You are magic," he said.

Under any other circumstances, I might've found the words strange. But he spoke them so sincerely, his tone ringing with truth, that I felt myself open to him even further. Something hungry and urgent stole over me. "Kiss me," I breathed.

Peter didn't bend his head or move closer. Instead, he

dropped to his knees. I stared down at him, baffled but not afraid. Slowly, giving me ample opportunity to protest, Peter pushed my nightgown up, and up, and up, until it bunched at my waist in a pool of white lace and cotton, exposing my naked thighs to the air. It felt like my cheeks had caught fire, but I didn't stop him. I just continued to watch, fascinated and aching.

Slowly, Peter leaned forward and pressed his face between my legs. A gasp hurtled up my throat, and I clapped my hand over my mouth to stop it. Dream or not, the instinct ran deep as my bone marrow—to hide, to muffle, to keep any transgression a secret. Then Peter's tongue touched me. The sensation drove out modesty and reason. My head tipped back of its own volition, even though I wanted to watch Peter and see what he was doing. I'd read about this act, of course, but the reality was nothing like what I had imagined.

After another moment, I forgot how to form rational thoughts. Peter's wicked mouth sucked and stroked, so skilled and relentless that I could only make strangled, helpless noises. I was biting my wrist, I realized at some point, probably in a futile attempt to hold onto a solid object as the rest of me floated away. My other hand fumbled at the wall. Peter held my legs tighter, and the movements of his tongue became even more dominant. Demanding.

The rest of the world ceased to exist. *Pleasure*, I thought distantly. That was the feeling building within me like the crest of an ocean wave. It felt like I was on the verge of something, as if I stood outside of a closed door or the edge of a cliff. Peter focused his attentions on one part of me now, sucking it with an intensity that made it difficult to remain upright.

"Oh, God," I moaned, a plea in the words, although I wasn't quite certain what I was pleading for. Peter didn't stop or pull back. Just as my lips parted to cry his name, my body shattered.

I'd never felt anything like it.

Heat and light spread through my entire being. I split apart and soared. I knew I was making a sound of some sort, but my senses had been overtaken by the ecstasy crashing over me. I was powerless, utterly at its mercy, and I didn't care. The wave lasted seconds, yet it seemed like a small eternity, somehow.

Eventually, of course, that wonderful eternity came to an end. I drifted back to the ground, back to London, back to the dim bedroom I still stood in. Sense and reason returned slowly.

I opened my eyes in a daze. My body felt weak, drowsy, as if I'd just run for miles. When I looked down at Peter again, he winked and rose to his feet effortlessly, using his ability to fly. My nightgown fell back into place, but I didn't move. The quiet seemed too loud, too ringing. Words failed me, though, along with any ideas of how to act after such an event had occurred.

I saw something move in my peripheral vision. Expecting nothing more than a fluttering curtain or a cloud passing over the moon, I glanced toward it... then froze. I was slow to comprehend what, exactly, I was seeing. I blinked, stared some more, and blinked again.

"Your shadow, Peter!" I gasped, trying to recoil. I was already pressed to the wall, however, and all I could do was stare. "It's... possessed."

Peter was not concerned. He slipped past me in a rush of warmth and began to touch everything.

"Where I come from, things are different," he said over his shoulder, raising the lid of my music box. Its melody tinkled. I hadn't sold it because it didn't have worth to anyone but me. "If you spend too much time there, your shadow begins to separate from your body. The darkness contains all the parts of yourself you don't want."

My eyes felt wide as saucers. This was, perhaps, the strangest dream I'd ever had. "Extraordinary," I managed.

While Peter explored every nook and cranny of the room, humming beneath his breath, I examined his shadow and wondered what parts of him were within those depths. It seemed to examine me right back. Then, without warning, the thing lunged at me.

Shrieking, I tripped on the edge of my long nightgown and fell against the wall again. Peter's shadow wrapped its insubstantial hands around my neck and began to squeeze. Rasping, I slapped and clawed at it. Nana, the family Newfoundland, barked from the hallway.

Peter wrested the shadow away from me and shoved it back into place. It went still against the floor, as if acknowledging defeat. Straightening, Peter shook his hair out of the way again.

"My shadow has taken a disliking to you, Miss Daven-port," he drawled.

I cowered in the corner, rubbing my throat.

This was no dream. Which meant that all of it—Peter, what we'd done, and everything that had happened during the past few minutes—was entirely real.

It took me several attempts to speak. "My family must have heard that. I think you should leave."

"You think?" Peter echoed, turning to face me. "Or you know? You should be certain of the things you say. You cannot take them back."

I thought of what I did know. For years, word had spread about the boy who could fly and who never seemed to grow older. In the taprooms and over cups of tea, men and women spoke of his allure and his ability to melt with shadows. A girl I knew, Lottie, claimed he had bewitched her. People whispered the words *demon* or *vampire* when his name was mentioned. Mysterious deaths and disappearances were accredited to him. But there were also rumors of how he granted wishes or had the ability to pull one away from the brink of death.

Throughout my childhood I had listened to the tales, wide-eyed, and a secret part of me longed to meet this frightening creature. Just to see him for myself, discern whether there was truth to the myths, and discover whether or not I was brave enough to meet his gaze.

And make a wish of my own.

Somehow, when so many others had been ignored or denied, I was being given a chance to do just that.

Gathering my nerve, I opened my mouth at the same time Peter said, "This broach is quite lovely. Mr. Brooks could probably fetch a high price for it."

Thoughts about wishes faded. I frowned as Peter moved on from the dressing table. "Wait a moment. How did you know that I'm... acquainted with Mr. Brooks? Have you been *following* me?"

A rhetorical question, seeing as I already knew the answer—it felt there was a puzzle piece clicking into place within my head. All day I'd felt a sort of tingling at the back of my neck, as though someone was watching. I felt it at the shop, on the street, in the carriage. I'd dismissed the sensation, blaming it on restless sleep and reading so many fanciful novels.

Raising my gaze back to Peter's, I took a step to the left. Closer to the door and away from him.

"Yes," he answered, unrepentant. He folded his arms and shook some hair out of his eyes.

Transparency was a rare thing in my world. Taken aback, I gave a slight shake of my head. "Why?"

"I heard you this morning. In Whitechapel. You told Liza that you wanted to go on an adventure."

Alarm rushed through me. Though Peter obscured my view, I glanced toward the street, worried that someone could see him or hear what he was saying. He smirked at this. "I'm sure I don't know what you mean," I said stiffly. "I've never been to the East End."

The boy tilted his head. "Well, that's odd. I could have sworn it was you I saw, selling your mother's necklace."

I went rigid at these words. The stillness was so prominent that we could hear Nana's nails clicking on the floor in the hallway. She scratched at my door and whined.

"Please don't tell anyone," I whispered, hugging myself to ward off the sudden chill.

Now Peter leaned even closer. His voice dropped. "I shall not tell a soul, Wendy Davenport."

Once again, a shiver traveled through me that had nothing to do with the cold. To hide it, I lifted my chin and attempted an imitation of my mother's glare. "It's rude to eavesdrop on other people's conversations, you know."

"Is it?" he asked innocently. I just scowled. My mind went back to that morning, standing in Mr. Brooks's shop with Liza.

A grandfather clock ticked loudly as we waited. A chandelier dangled over our heads, and it was out of place in a place grimy as this. Sunlight caught the glass pieces and sent rainbows upon the walls. I wondered if I knew the family that had obviously been forced to sell it.

The thought sent a bolt of sorrow through me. I fixed my attention on the door Mr. Brooks had just disappeared through. It was still difficult to believe my family's circumstances had come to this. That necklace was meant to be mine one day, passed down from mother to daughter. Not sold to a man with yellow teeth and damp fingers.

"Will the price you get for it help things for a while?" Liza asked, keeping her voice soft so we wouldn't be overheard.

I shook my head. "No. Not hardly. Mama says that our only

hope is for me to marry well. Small chance of that, of course, considering I'm already on the verge of becoming an old maid."

She touched my elbow. My friend didn't dare embrace me—not where anyone could see that lady and maid were much closer than decorum allowed—but it was still a comfort. "You don't want to marry?" she asked.

I looked at a map hanging on the wall. The oceans were so blue, the lands so vast. Just that morning I'd read about a phenomenon called the Northern Lights, colors in the sky that were so much more than any sunrise or storm. I ached to see them with my own eyes. Slowly, I shook my head. "No. Not right now, at least. I've barely lived, Liza! I want to see things. I want to meet people and have adventures. Do you understand?"

She didn't. No one would understand. Women were supposed to focus on beauty and stature, not dream about exotic skies or full sails.

Peter gazed at me, and I realized that I had finally met someone who wanted the same things. There was also the painful realization that, if I let him go, my wish would go unspoken. The fact that Peter was here meant magic existed, and if magic existed, why not miracles, too?

I would never forgive myself if I didn't even try.

"My younger brother," I said abruptly, swallowing a burst of nervousness. "He's not well. They say you have the ability to—"

There was a rush of darkness, and vicious hands wrapped around my throat again. I made a ragged, panicked sound and tried to slap at the black figure. Like last time, my hands only passed through air, and I was helpless against the demon's strength. Peter had grabbed hold of it without any difficulty, but he didn't seem able to pull it off me now. I rasped his name, still fruitlessly fighting the mass of darkness squeezing tighter with every second.

Just as the edges of my vision began to go dark, Peter succeeded in getting his darker half away. The moment those otherworldly hands were gone, I was sliding along the wall frantically, my only instinct to put distance between us. I rubbed my throat and breathed hard, willing my heart to slow so I could speak. Peter wrested his shadow back into place and said something I couldn't hear, his voice cold and hard.

"Please leave," I said at last. I'd lost my nerve to bring up wishes—staying alive seemed more important.

Peter straightened, raking his hair back. He flashed me a dimpled grin. "Understandable. I do apologize for his behavior. I'll return tomorrow night, eh?"

Despite all my claims, one evening of daring was enough for me. "No. I don't want to see you again, Peter."

"Of course you do. You just don't know it." With a wink, he alighted onto the window seat and shot into the night sky. The silence following his departure was unsettling.

Nana whined from the hallway again. Still trembling, I went to let her in. The gigantic dog rushed past me, black hackles raised. She sniffed everything Peter had touched and I remained in the doorway, waiting for my family to appear. But it seemed Peter's visit had not awoken anyone—nothing else stirred in the house. Shaking, I closed the door.

A cold nose touched my palm, startling me yet again.

Recovering, I knelt and hugged Nana. It felt like the core of my being had been altered by the encounter with Peter, and her solid bulk was comforting. "Good girl. Good girl."

After a time, I released her and went to the washstand, where I poured water from the porcelain jug and splashed some on my face. Nana watched silently. I crawled back into bed and squeezed my eyes shut, willing myself to think of anything else besides boys who could fly and shadows that could maim. I was not successful.

Heat filled my cheeks as I thought of what I'd allowed Peter to do when I still thought he was a dream. "I'm going to Hell, Nana," I moaned.

Breaking Mama's rules, the dog hopped up and settled onto the space beside me. I buried my fingers into her thick coat and took solace in the sound of her deep, even breaths.

Eventually, the sound lulled me to sleep.

CHAPTER 2

SEEMINGLY MOMENTS LATER, a knock at the door pulled me from slumber. Nana leaped to the floor and my eyes snapped open. Light filtered through the curtains. Was it morning already? Had Peter really been a dream? I searched the room, hoping to spot evidence of his presence, but everything was in its usual place.

No, I realized a moment later, my heartbeat quickening. The window latch. It was undone.

Liza's voice drifted through the wood, asking if I was awake. Though I was not entirely certain, I swung my legs to the side of the bed and stood. "Yes, come in!"

The maid entered with a smile, determined to be hopeful in circumstances that were utterly devoid of it. There was a pile of clothing in her arms, and she set it down on the bed. Nana ran past her and clicked down the hallway. "I trust you slept well, miss," Liza said cheerfully.

"Well enough," I lied, stepping out of my nightgown.

Heat rushed to my face as I recalled how Peter had pulled it off with little more than a tug. I tried not to think of the other things he'd done, not while Liza was here. "Did the bank receive their payment for the month?"

The girl paused, listening for any noise from the hallway. All memories of last night vanished as I waited for her response.

"The money you got for the necklace wasn't enough," she told me, lowering her voice as a precaution. Retrieving my stockings and garters from the pile, she helped me put them on. Then came the drawers. "It won't hold Mr. Pickering off as you'd hoped."

"Blast!" My frustration was so profound that I nearly slapped her hands away when she lowered the chemise over me, but our state of affairs was hardly her fault. I forced myself to be still and think. I couldn't rely on a wish from the infamous Peter to save us. Was there anything else we could sell? Mama had barely relinquished the necklace...

The thought prompted me to ask another difficult question. I looked down at Liza. "How is she today?"

However much my friend tried to hide it, I could still see the pity in her brown eyes. "She was still sleeping, last I checked," Liza answered.

My mother was not ill. Not in body, at least. But when Papa confessed that he had lost everything several weeks ago —I'd listened to their urgent whispers through the bedroom wall—she went into their room and closed the door. She still hadn't come out.

Liza picked up the corset. I braced myself in front of the

mirror, holding the wooden frame as tightly as though it were someone's hand, and winced with every tug of the strings. A new worry presented itself: the person staring back at me looked tired. That would not do. Even the slightest thing could begin rumors, and my family was already undergoing scrutiny. "Do we have any powder left?" I asked the maid.

"I believe your mother has some." Eager to please, Liza hurried out before I could stop her.

To occupy myself and keep thoughts of Peter at bay, I managed the petticoat on my own. I found the skirt and crisp blouse Liza had brought and yanked those on, too. A short jacket completed the ensemble. The mutton sleeves were a bit wrinkled, but I didn't have the heart to point it out. Perhaps I would just stay in today.

"Wendy! I don't want to learn my letters!"

The door rattled on its hinges. I hurried to open it, revealing my pouting brother on the other side. No one had brushed his hair, but at least he was dressed. Eyeing Michael critically, I noted that he was not as pale as he had been yesterday. He'd had scarlet fever weeks ago, and we nearly lost him. Though Michael survived, he was considerably weaker compared to the robust boy he'd been.

"Lower your voice, please. Mama is resting." I knelt to fuss with his unruly curls, now thinking of the large sum we owed the physician.

My brother unfolded his arms to fight with me, his elbows sticking in the air. "Mama is *always* resting. I don't want to spend the day with Sir Gilbert. He smells odd and he won't let me play."

Sighing, I leaned back and gave him my full attention.

"I'll make you a bargain," I said. Michael's eyes lit up, and I lowered my voice to intrigue him further. "If you do well with Sir Gilbert, I'll take you to the park this week and teach you how to fly a kite. What do you say?"

He wrinkled his nose and thought about it. "I suppose."

"There's a good lad. Now join John and Sir Gilbert in the study. Oh, and don't play with Nana under the table anymore or I'll have no choice but to put her outside." I gave his small jacket an affectionate tug and sent him on his way.

Liza soon returned with the powder, and she removed evidence of my sleepless night. "There are strange marks on your neck," I heard her murmur as she worked.

Peter's shadow. I struggled to maintain an expression of indifference. "I must have done it in my sleep."

Liza accepted this explanation without comment, and soon I felt the brush tickle my throat. Once she had finished, I went downstairs with a heavy heart, but at least it was no longer obvious to anyone who cared enough to look.

There was once a time when our family had breakfast together. Now, I took my tea and toast in the parlor, where I was not forced to face an empty table. There was a pile of letters waiting for me next to the settee—undeniably dwindling by the day—but I couldn't bring myself to open any this morning. Instead I dug beneath the chair cushion and found my reading exactly where I'd left it. Chewing leisurely, I consumed a lurid tale my mother would be aghast to discover. Sunlight warmed my skin and offered silent companionship.

Our home was in Belgrave Square, a much-desired neighborhood alongside Hyde Park. Now and then, between pages full of highwaymen and scandalous love affairs, I glanced outside. Noting all the fine carriages and clothing made my thoughts inevitably turn to Mr. Pickering and the bank payment. It felt as if a cloud had passed over, though everything was still bright and warm.

There was one more item I could sell, I thought reluctantly. Papa's pocketwatch.

It required a visit to the club, where my father had undoubtedly spent the night, seeing as his coat and shoes were missing from the foyer. I loathed speaking to either of my parents about our circumstances; both had chosen despair instead of hope.

Restless, I abandoned my reading to pace in the foyer. If I *were* to make an excursion, propriety demanded that a chaperone accompany me from the house. My usual companion, Mrs. Graham, would never agree to such an errand. The old housekeeper was the last of our staff, alongside Liza and the cook. They had far too much to do now everyone was gone. But if the bank didn't get a payment this week, my family wouldn't have a roof over their heads. Michael wouldn't survive that.

Decision made, I fetched my coat from the rack and slipped out the door.

It was unseasonably warm for August. Not even a breeze stirred the air and the sun shone unhindered by clouds. I paused to admire the blue sky, because it felt like I'd only seen it through windows these past few weeks. At that moment, though, a servant hurrying past took notice of me, and I instantly knew why—it was unusual to encounter a lady in the street, unaccompanied by her family, husband, or maid. The woman politely averted her gaze, but it was enough to make my joy fade.

Reminded of my errand, and the need for subtlety, I ducked my head down and turned right.

The club wasn't far. Birds tried to cheer me along the way, and I focused on their song instead of thinking about what I had to ask Papa. Though I stuck to the shadows, sweat gathered beneath my numerous layers of clothing. A drop slid down the small of my back. With a furtive glance around me, I dared to undo the top button of the coat I wore. Even this small action was thrilling, and a tiny smile played about my lips.

Suddenly a sob disturbed the usual morning din. There was a ring of familiarity in the sound, and my smile vanished. *No*, I thought, *please, no.*

To my right, there was a stack of crates. Slumped against them, beside a pool of vomit, was my father.

Containing a gasp of horror, I rushed to him. His face was dark with stubble and his necktie was undone. Someone had stolen his shoes. As I squatted, doing my best to avoid the mess, I shook his shoulder. "Papa! How long have you been here? Are you all right?"

He opened bloodshot eyes, and when he saw who

loomed over him, a grimace twisted his face. "I tried, dear girl. Heaven knows I tried."

Resentment raced through me, darker than ink spilled across a page. I hauled my father up and gagged at his stench. "Stand up straight. People will *see*."

His only response was to sob again. I stumbled beneath his weight—George Davenport was no slight man—and began in the direction of home. As we struggled, drawing stares along the way, my glance skimmed his waistline. I prayed it was there, my purpose for leaving home and our only way to pay Mr. Pickering.

The pocketwatch was gone.

Papa was oblivious to anyone's pain but his own. "Let them see. We're ruined anyway," he bemoaned. I opened my mouth to shush him.

"Is everything all right?"

The reedy voice came from behind. Fear dropped to my stomach like a stone in water. Papa had not spoken quietly; anyone in close proximity would've heard his miserable comments. Slowly, I turned. The stranger was an officer. His uniform was black and stiff, its buttons flashing in the morning light. He had hard eyes and a feathery mustache. Every part of him—his face, his torso, his fingers—was incredibly thin. His cheeks were hollow. But by all appearances, he was a perfectly ordinary man. Why, then, did a layer of ice spread over my skin?

"We're fine, thank you," I chirped. My face felt hot. "Father was feeling a bit dizzy. I'm bringing him home."

"Allow me to assist, Miss...?"

My eyes darted about, desperate for a reason to avoid giving my name. Only the cobblestones and bricks stared back. There was no hope for it. "Wendy Davenport," I said reluctantly.

"I am Constable Bertram Collingwood. Please, allow me." Before I could protest, he took Papa's arm and transferred it to his shoulders. To his credit, the constable didn't flinch at the smell. But now my lie was evident.

"Constable Collingwood, this is very kind, but you really don't..." I trailed off when I realized he wasn't looking at me; something had captured the man's attention above my head. I twisted, following his gaze. There was nothing but empty rooftops and wispy clouds.

When I faced him again, the constable smiled. It didn't reach his eyes. "Which way?" he asked. Helplessly, I pointed.

He stopped asking questions and made no effort at conversation. It would've been impossible, anyway—Papa continued to weep and lament, no matter how many times I attempted to speak over him. Within minutes, we arrived at the house, though I felt years older as I opened the door. I called for help, my voice echoing down the hallway.

"Where would you like him?" Constable Collingwood asked, dragging Papa over the threshold.

"The study might be best," I said. Even a man wouldn't be able to get Papa up the stairs, and at least the study still had books adorning its shelves. Though I tried to block the constable's view of the parlor, which was picked-over and barren, his sharp gaze missed nothing.

There came the sound of heels. Mrs. Graham and Liza

appeared, and if they felt any surprise at the scene that greeted them, both concealed it well. They hurried to lift Papa's legs. As the procession made its way into the study, I patted my hair with shaking hands.

It was not a moment too soon, as Constable Collingwood reappeared seconds later. His hat was askew, and he corrected it with a quick, brisk movement. "I wish your father a speedy recovery. Good day, Miss Davenport," he said.

"Good day, sir. Thank you for your assistance."

With that, he was gone. Even after the door closed, though, unease hovered beneath my skin. I frowned and scratched my arm. I could hear Liza and Mrs. Graham bustling about in the study, ignoring Papa's whimpers and complaints. My conscience pricked at me, urged me to go in.

But I didn't want to see my father like that anymore, so at odds from the kind and composed man of my childhood. Instead, I went upstairs to change my dress. A scent wafted from the material, exactly what I imagined a distillery smelled like.

Just as I donned a fresh gown, the door opened without warning.

"Wendy," a high, familiar voice called. Michael had been saying my name like that from the very beginning—lilting and drawn out, like a lullaby. I poked my head around the armoire, a genuine smile stretching across my face, and Constable Collingwood evaporated from my mind. Michael hopped onto the bed, holding a book in his small hands. Without looking at the title, I knew which story he'd brought to me. *Alice in Wonderland* by Lewis Carroll. His favorite.

Though his lessons couldn't possibly be over, I didn't have the heart to send him back. Not yet, at least.

"Only a few pages," I said, sitting next to him. Skirts be damned. Michael nodded and burrowed into the crook of my arm. Since we had just finished the story days before, I flipped back to the first chapter. "'Alice was beginning to get very tired of sitting by her sister on the bank, and of having nothing to do...'"

A short time later, I closed it again. Afternoon sunlight streamed through the window. "All right, young man. Off to your lessons. Please make sure to put the book back before you return to Sir Gilbert," I instructed.

Michael sighed and clambered down. "Why can't the servants do it, Wendy?"

It was a question I had often asked myself when our troubles first began. Every time Mama called for something, every time Papa fell asleep on the floor, every time my brothers squabbled. I leaned forward to press a kiss against Michael's silky head. "Because we may not always have servants. You must learn to depend on yourself."

His little brow creased. I touched it, smiling sadly, and sent him on his way.

There were some lessons that children shouldn't have to learn so early in life, and as I moved to fix the bedclothes, I allowed myself a wistful thought. A futile imagining of some distant place where children didn't learn such things, not unless they wanted to.

A place where children never grew up.

Night was slow in coming.

I passed the afternoon avoiding my parents and trying to find a solution for the bank payment. I was only successful on one of these counts. When the stars came out, I helped Liza put the boys to bed, then stood impatiently next to the bedpost as she undid the laces on my corset.

"Thank you," I called as she walked to the door, knowing the other girl had sensed my agitation.

Liza hesitated. After a moment, she crossed the room again and took my hands. Her palms were rough. "Everything will be all right, Miss Wendy," she said earnestly. "I know it doesn't seem like it now, but money isn't everything. You're wealthy in other ways."

There seemed to be a lump in my throat; I was only capable of nodding. With a smile, Liza squeezed my fingers and pulled away. She slipped through the door, closing it behind her, and I was alone again. Tears blurred the edges of my vision. To keep them at bay, I readied for bed. Every few seconds I couldn't stop myself from looking to the window. The latch was still undone from Peter's last visit.

I didn't move to secure it.

The moon rose higher. Nana was in the kitchen, where she wouldn't alert the house should any visitors come. I settled on the rug, knees tucked beneath me, surrounded by my father's papers. In an attempt at modesty, I wore a dressing gown. As seconds turned to minutes, and minutes to hours, I still hoped Peter came. I was terrified he would. Fear and anticipation made my veins hum.

Downstairs, the grandfather clock chimed the late hour. My eyelids grew heavy, but I kept on, reviewing the figures again and again. I told myself the only purpose was to save my family, and not to stay awake for Peter. The clock went on, nearing the end of its count, and the sound reminded me of Papa's pocketwatch. I leaned on my hand, once again trying not to cry. My brothers didn't need to see another loved one with red, puffy eyes.

"What are you doing?"

I hadn't even heard him enter. I gasped and sat upright. My gaze went to Peter's face first, which was exactly as I remembered, then to his shadow. That malicious darkness couldn't touch me; I'd made certain the room was too dim. It watched me from a square of moonlight against the floor. The memory of its hands around my throat lingered at the front of my mind, but I managed to remain still.

As he waited for my reply, Peter knelt at the edge of the makeshift circle. A gust of wind followed him and made the pages flutter. I shifted away, remembering that he had asked me a question.

"Going over Papa's accounts," I said. Seeing as he knew everything about my family, there was no need for secrecy. I touched a row of Papa's meticulous handwriting. "I have a knack for numbers."

This was met with silence. I looked up, expecting Peter to be studying the records, but instead his eyes were on me.

Somehow I'd forgotten how beautiful they were, almost metallic in the moonlight. Too often, beauty disguised danger. I stared at him as though he were a wild animal, unpredictable and hungry, while he looked at me as if I were an amusing game of some sort. "Why must you be their savior?" Peter asked, sounding as though he truly wanted to know.

Suddenly there was a voice in my head, insistent and admonishing all at once. *He shouldn't be here. Someone could come. Make him leave.* But the answer was already on my tongue. It felt vital to say it out loud.

"Because no one else will," I whispered. My eyes prickled yet again, and I pushed the papers away. I refocused on Peter, thinking there was something freeing about revealing my innermost thoughts to a stranger. He was still studying me, head tilted. It was the longest he'd gone without moving in my presence.

The instant I noticed this, Peter was in motion again. I tensed as the boy flew past, terrified he was finally revealing his true motives for visiting me, but he just continued the exploration of my room he'd begun yesterday. It was the perfect opportunity to ask him about magic, whether it was real and could save us. He walked past, leaving a perfume of frost-edged night and exotic flowers in his wake. As my nostrils flared, inhaling the heady scent, I heard myself ask instead, "Do you have a family?"

What was I doing?

Peter had taken a book off the shelf and was in the process of flipping through it. At my question, he faltered.

He recovered quickly, putting the book back and picking up an old doll. "I've never found much use, I'm afraid."

"I shall do my best to describe it, then," I murmured, alert to any sound downstairs or sharp movements from Peter. I felt the need to explain further, perhaps not just to him, but to myself, as well. "They are the people you know best in all the world. The ones you share your happiness with, the ones you bear the pain alongside. A bond like no other that can't be found or replaced. The instinct to protect them goes deeper than bones; I believe it exists in the soul. Perhaps it's formed in the womb, in using your mother's own life to survive. Thus, no matter their faults or transgressions, you can't go against it."

Peter turned from the writing desk, his brows raised. "Forgive me, but it seems your parents are missing such instincts."

His blunt words felt like a knife between the ribs. "They aren't missing anything."

Even I heard the feebleness in my voice. Peter seemed to lose interest in this topic and gave no reply. He started moving again, and I went about retrieving my father's pages. I'd just finished putting them back into a neat pile when I heard Peter ask, "What is this?"

My head jerked up. With horror, I saw that he'd found my copy of *The Lustful Turk*.

"Give that back!" I blurted, diving at him. Peter shot into the air and performed a somersault over my head. He landed behind me, and by the time I whirled around, he was already reading.

"Goodness. Heavens. *Gracious.* How scandalous, Miss Davenport! Are you trying to corrupt me?" Peter evaded my attempts without any effort, hopping or flying away every time I got close. Eventually I managed to reach both arms around him, making another desperate grab for the book, but he kept his back to me and his prize at a safe distance. Peter turned the image and tilted his head, studying the text more closely. "Fascinating. Shall we try this?"

He pointed at a passage and glanced at me, eyebrows raised in a silent query, and I sputtered. Without looking away from my face, Peter tossed the book onto the bed. I began to rush for it when he turned around. Since I'd been pressed to his back, my breasts were now against his chest. I was also keenly aware of something hardening between us, poking into my lower stomach.

Suddenly my mouth felt very dry. I swallowed, trying not to think of the wicked things I'd allowed him to do the night before. Things I had only allowed because I'd believed it was all a dream.

This time, I was wide awake. I wouldn't be able to hide behind the excuse of ignorance if I made certain choices.

Peter's eyes had darkened. He trailed his fingertips from my elbow to my wrist, then back again. I stared up at him, breathing harder from the force of want rising inside me. I thought of what I'd said to him yesterday. *Kiss me.* But he hadn't. I still didn't know what it felt like to be kissed by Peter. What harm was there in that? Just once? I raised my face and closed my eyes, every part of me tense with anticipation.

A rush of air stirred the tendrils of hair loose around my face.

When I opened my eyes, Peter was across the room. He finished walking to the window, where his shadow still waited. But he just landed on the sill and turned.

"While I share your taste for danger, there is one flavor best avoided," Peter said abruptly, flattening his hands on both sides of the frame.

I was distracted with worry that someone below would see him. His words sank in a moment later, though, and I frowned. "What are you talking—"

"Constable Collingwood, of course," Peter said, his voice light as air. "You met on the street today. I would advise you to steer clear of him in the future. Did your governess tell you frightening tales as a child, to make you do as you were told? Well, he's the creature she warned you about. He just lacks the fangs and claws she may have mentioned."

Before I could express my indignation at being followed again, or demand to know more about the constable, Peter bowed. "Unfortunately, I must cut my visit short tonight. Errands to run, women to grace with my presence, you understand. Sleep well, Miss Davenport."

With that, he spun toward the street, and I watched his muscles tighten in preparation. My voice stopped him. "Don't come back, Peter."

The boy turned so I could only see one side of his face. He winked, then jumped out.

I hardly slept for the rest of the night.

CHAPTER 3

THE FOLLOWING MORNING, I sat in my usual chair. The parlor was awash in sunlight and the tea service gleamed. Blearily I picked up the tongs and grasped a cube of sugar. With a *plop*, it disintegrated into the brown depths of my tea.

I'd forgotten to bring a novel downstairs, but a penny dreadful was within reach. Despite several readings, I pulled it out to peruse the pages once more. I turned until I reached the drawing. It was a woman, scantily-clad, clutching at a man's bare chest. The first time I'd come upon it, years ago, my first instinct had been to hurriedly flip past. Curiosity made me linger, just as it did now. I studied the man's strong jaw, the curve of the woman's breast, the hunger in both of their expressions. Something inside me stirred. A sensation more powerful than shame.

And I thought of Peter.

Suddenly the doorbell rang. I startled and shoved the penny dreadful beneath my chair cushion. I knew my face was red as Liza walked by to open the door. There was a brief exchange of voices. Supposing it to be the postman, I feigned interest in the world outside, waiting to be alone again. A moment later, Liza rushed into the parlor. An event in itself, because she never interrupted me while I was eating. Her expression was anxious, and I frowned. "Liza, what—"

"Lady Julie Bainbridge to see you, miss," she cut in, her tone a warning.

Before I could react, the lady herself entered the room in a burst of hard heels and rustling skirts. It was unheard of to call so early, unannounced, much less from someone who had never made our acquaintance. I rose to greet her. "Lady Bainbridge! What a pleasant surprise. I was just... rereading my catechism."

An inane lie, since it was nowhere in sight.

The woman stopped, clasped her gloved hands, and studied the room that had grown more stark with each passing day. I shifted self-consciously, wishing I had refrained from selling the painting that hung over the fireplace only days ago. Once she was finished with her perusal, Lady Bainbridge pinned me with her penetrating gaze. It made me think of roiling skies.

"Yes, I suppose it is," she clipped. "I don't make a habit of calling upon strangers, but there's a matter of some urgency that I wish to discuss with you."

I blinked. "With me?"

"Indeed. Pray, are we alone?"

My curiosity was piqued, and I only hesitated for a

moment. "Yes. I believe my father is at the club this morning, and Mama is not feeling well. My brothers are with their tutor. No one will overhear us."

"Excellent," the lady said, and seated herself just as I remembered to offer an invitation.

The movement directed my attention to the half-eaten breakfast still on the table. I had been so intent on the story that I'd let it go cold. "Shall I call for some tea?" I asked, flushing.

Lady Bainbridge waved her hand. The flowers in her hat quivered. "No. There's no time for that, I'm afraid."

I decided to match her abruptness. "Very well. What is so urgent, ma'am? How can I be of assistance?"

Surprisingly, she didn't answer straightaway. Instead Lady Bainbridge pursed her lips and looked out the window. Light touched her face, making her appear younger. It was difficult to ascertain what she was feeling, but I'd heard much about the fine lady sitting beside me. She was a dear friend of the queen, renowned for her flawless decorum and severe manner. The other girls whispered that she was made of stone. For Lady Bainbridge to be here, unintroduced and unannounced, something must be gravely wrong. What possible reason could she have to seek me out?

The stillness stretched and thinned. Her hands were tightly clenched in her lap now, though I didn't think she was aware of it. I was on the verge of speaking when Lady Bainbridge finally said, "First, you should know that you met my brother yesterday."

"Your brother?" I echoed blankly.

"Constable Bertram Collingwood." The instant she said this, I could see him, peering out from her eyes. Lady Bainbridge continued, "When he told me of you, I knew there was no time to waste. Too long we have been waiting for an opportunity like this. With every passing day, the risk becomes greater."

I felt my brows furrow. "I'm afraid I still don't—"

"In order for you to understand everything, I must tell you my entire story," she interrupted, focusing on me again. Any trace of uncertainty had vanished, and she was stone once more.

"Your story?"

She nodded briskly. And without further preamble, this woman I had never met before began. "Many years ago, I found myself in a marriage that was loveless and lonely. My husband was often away, and even when he was home, he barely noticed me. We had a gardener, a handsome man whose voice sounded like poetry. I allowed myself to be taken in by his pretty words, and soon realized I carried his child. Of course, it would not be possible to lie to my husband, for we had not shared a bed in months. So I hid my condition until the time came to give birth. Everything was handled discreetly, and a trustworthy servant left the child on the steps of a church. Years passed, and I thought the incident was buried. I was wrong.

"As you now know, my brother holds an esteemed position at Scotland Yard. He has been in pursuit of the one called Peter for many years." I felt my heart jump at the sound of his name, but she didn't give me a chance to respond. Lady Bainbridge went on, "One night, he was able to get so close that he noticed a peculiar birthmark on the boy's jaw. This may not seem significant, except that Bertram had only ever seen it on one other person. Me."

It was difficult to keep my shock from showing as I fit the puzzle pieces together.

Lady Julie Bainbridge was the infamous Peter's mother.

The room tilted. How could she say all of this so matter-of-factly? Why confess these dark things to me? Such information had the potential to destroy her. I could not stop my gaze from flicking to the woman's jawline. I must not have been the only one to put powder on that morning; it was as smooth and unblemished as the cream in my tea. I was so shaken that I took a sip of it before remembering that it was cold. The cup clattered as I put it down. "Lady Bainbridge, I'm not sure what this has to do with—"

Impatience leaked through her façade, and she cut me off by holding up her hand. "Let's agree to discard any pretenses between us, Miss Davenport. Bertram saw the boy going into your bedroom last night."

The air left my lungs. Words were impossible, though my instincts were screaming to lie. *Lie now!* All I could manage was a strangled sound. Lady Bainbridge saw my horror and sighed. "I have not come here to ruin you. On the contrary, I want to offer you an opportunity."

I felt no relief from her reassurance. Even I heard the caution in my voice as I replied, "An opportunity?"

"After he saw the boy's birthmark, my brother confronted me," the lady continued. "I was forced to reveal the truth about what had happened years before. We realized the boy has the potential to destroy us—the queen herself has seen my birthmark, and should his become public knowledge, she's no fool. She will make the connection."

Lady Bainbridge paused again, but this time, I was wise enough to remain silent. She touched her temple, as if she were in pain.

"There are times I wonder if he is a spirit or a demon, sent here to torment me for my transgressions," the lady murmured, more to herself than me, it seemed. "But my brother assures me that he's quite real."

"He is," I whispered, thinking of the fingerprints Peter left on my window and the warm rush of air as he passed. I also thought of how his lips had felt on the most intimate part of me. Those had been real, too.

I prayed the woman sitting beside me misinterpreted the reason for my burning cheeks.

Thankfully, she didn't seem to notice them at all. Lady Bainbridge's tone hardened. "Which brings me to the reason for my visit this afternoon."

I looked at her, and her eyes had become black, glittering jewels. Wrinkles deepened around her mouth. "Yes?" I said faintly, dread expanding in my stomach like a heavy, over-cooked loaf of bread.

"I want you to kill my son."

∽

Hooves clattered on the street outside. A laugh rang out. Lady Bainbridge waited for me to respond, and once again I found myself wondering if any of this was real.

When I did nothing but sit and stare, she made a sound of impatience. The loose skin below her chin jiggled. "Bertram was quite impressed by how you handled your drunken father," she added. "If he was wrong about your capabilities, perhaps George Davenport will complete this task instead. Although I must confess to disappointment, should this be the outcome. Men are so busy thinking of us as the lesser sex, it was refreshing to think I'd met a young woman who shares my fortitude."

My mind felt dull. "My father? You would ask him to do this?"

This elicited a sharp nod. "It matters little to me which one of you accepts my offer. Regardless, your family will be reimbursed for the trouble. All financial worries would cease to exist."

Keeping our poverty hidden had become so deeply ingrained that my response was instant. "We have no need of—"

"Dear girl, your secret is not so secret anymore. Even my *housemaids* know about your present circumstances."

At this, I stood. Lady Bainbridge had made no threats, but it hovered in the air between us. "Forgive me, ma'am, but I think I hear my mother calling."

She sighed again, as though this was all so tedious. "Very well, I can see that you are determined. Before arriving here today, I made inquiries about your family. The Davenports have always been a respectable lot, but lately there are rumors. Miss Davenport no longer wears lovely new gowns. Their servants have been searching for new positions in the city. Mr. Davenport has been seen with a glass of brandy in his hand more often than not. Mrs. Davenport has not been spotted for—"

"Stop." I swallowed and slowly sat back down. The only sounds were my rapid breathing and the carriages going by outside. Unable to meet Lady Bainbridge's steely gaze, I focused on the streak of silver in her hair. Despite the story she had just told me and the thing she'd asked me to do, she held the power in this room, and we both knew it. Lying was useless. "Even if all of that were true, Peter won't come back. I told him not to."

"Nonsense. Bertram tells me that the boy seems to be following you; I have no doubt that he'll return. Use his infatuation to your advantage."

Her words brought a memory to the surface. The day Constable Collingwood came upon me and Papa in the street, his eyes had fixed on something in the sky. *He must've seen Peter*, I thought numbly.

Now Lady Bainbridge was the one to stand. In a manner eerily similar to her son, she walked the perimeter of the room. She ran her finger along the mantle. We'd dismissed everyone weeks ago, and I knew the dusting had suffered because of it. Shame coiled in my stomach. Humming, Lady Bainbridge rubbed her fingers together.

Dazedly, I lifted my head and listened. "That song. I recognize it."

"Very unlikely. The lullaby was passed down through my family—my mother used to sing it to me every night. *Second star to the right, and straight on 'til morning. A few thoughts with some dust, and soon you'll be soaring.*"

Despite the lady's ugly words, she had a lovely voice. It echoed in my head as I realized where I'd heard the melody before.

Peter.

But Lady Bainbridge's story made it clear that, after giving birth, she'd never seen him again. Could Peter's memory be so extraordinary? Or was there something else at work here?

This was hardly the most pressing matter; Lady Bainbridge still awaited an answer.

I didn't need to think about it. I came to terms with the fact that my family was about to be torn apart, because no matter how much they meant to me, I wasn't a murderer. And the victim wasn't a random stranger or some urchin on the street—it was Peter, the boy with stars for eyes.

I bowed my head for a moment, gathering my composure. A muscle worked in my jaw. When I managed to speak again, the words sounded as rough as the rocks beneath the earth. "Do what you must, ma'am. I won't be party to this."

The *thud-thud-thud* of her footsteps across the floor felt like thunder. She was leaving? I hurriedly jumped up to follow her. In the foyer, Lady Bainbridge frowned into the looking glass hanging beside the door. She adjusted her wide-brimmed hat.

"You're an intelligent girl," she answered without bothering to turn. "Given time, I have faith that you'll come to the right decision. You have until tomorrow evening. If I don't hear from you by then, I'll be sure to whisper about the state of your virtue in the right ear. You know how these things go; all of London will be talking about it by week's end. What man would have you after that, I wonder? And what would become of your family?"

I gripped the wall for balance. As she spoke, my fingers curled, digging into the hard plaster. Fear and resentment accompanied every beat of my heart. "You just urged me to take advantage of my femininity, and now you're using it against me?"

"Indeed. It seems we have one thing in common—both of us will go to drastic measures to protect the ones we love. Good morning, Miss Davenport."

"Good morning, Lady Bainbridge," I said faintly.

There was no butler to open the door, so she did it herself. The woman paused with a hand on the knob and addressed me over her shoulder. "Oh. One more thing. If you think to use this information against me—or breathe a word to someone at Scotland Yard—consider that I am seeking my own son's death. A stranger like yourself would be even less of an obstacle. I look forward to your correspondence, or better yet, proof that the deed is done."

She did not stay to hear my response.

After Lady Bainbridge was gone, it was as if a spell over me lifted. I moved in a burst and rushed toward the stairs, brimming with fury and helpless desperation. It felt as though the walls were shrinking and crushing me. I interrupted Sir Gilbert in the study, offering a flimsy explanation, and took John and Michael to Hyde Park. We were accompanied only by Mrs. Graham.

"What is all this about, Miss Davenport?" she asked crossly, swaying with the motion of the hansom cab. "I have much to do today. There's the washing and cooking and—"

"I realize that, Mrs. Graham, and I'm sorry to keep you from your duties. But I have a promise to keep." I smiled tightly at Michael, who had pressed his face against the window. Feeling my gaze, he turned and grinned back at me. Some of his color had returned. Perhaps she noticed this the same time I did, for Mrs. Graham grumbled but didn't protest further.

We arrived at the park and passed the day running with a kite behind us, hoping it would catch the wind and rise into the sky. The air was still and sweltering, though, and my brother's eyes dimmed with disappointment as the afternoon wore on. I had no words of comfort to offer; sweat trickled under my corset and Lady Bainbridge's visit had stripped away any remaining optimism. The sun touched the horizon, and I knew I was nearly out of time. To think of a solution and to cling to the girl I was. Well, I'd wanted an adventure, hadn't I? Bitterness swelled in my throat.

"It's not working, Wendy," Michael cried, jerking the strings. John had long since given up and was on his stomach, examining something in the grass. He pushed his round, wire-framed spectacles farther up his nose. They were so young. Their lives were so simple. They had no one else willing to fight for them.

Another wave of feeling crashed into me. I backed away, blinking rapidly. Overhead, clouds had rolled in, thick and gray. "Why don't you rest a moment? Eat some of the food Mrs. Graham brought, then we'll try again," I promised.

Needing a respite, as well, I held up my skirts and set off down the path. The housekeeper called my name—it wasn't proper to wander the park alone—but I pretended not to hear. I rushed into a grove of trees and pressed my back against one of the trunks. I breathed raggedly, hearing Lady Bainbridge in the stillness. *I want you to kill my son. The Davenports have always been a respectable lot, but lately there are rumors. I have no doubt that he'll return. You're an intelligent girl.*

Voices drifted to me on a breeze. Two women walked by, pushing a perambulator before them. I heard snatches of their conversation. "...just last night," one of them said with barely-contained glee. "Apparently his travels agreed with him."

"Orville Martin!" the other exclaimed. "Why, the last time I saw him, his head hardly came to my shoulders. How quickly time has passed."

"Indeed."

They continued down the path, and a large tree blocked the women from view. Their gossip usually wouldn't pique my interest, but it had been a welcome distraction—I was sorry to see them go. It was getting late, anyhow. I returned to my brothers, no matter how tempting it was to flee and leave everything behind. Right on cue, a cry sounded from the top of the hill. Following the sound, I saw that Michael had tried flying the kite again and thrown it down in a fit of frustration.

The moment I reached them, Mrs. Graham packed the food. Together we ushered the boys back to the hansom cab, and the four of us rode home in silence. The kite drooped in Michael's arms and John inspected a bug cupped between his palms. Mrs. Graham was the first to speak as she tried to convince him to release it. John argued with her. I was too weary to intervene and drowned their words out.

Halfway to Mayfair, a familiar prickling began at the back of my neck. And I knew, as surely as I knew the moon was rising, that Peter would come tonight. I looked out at the darkening shops and rooftops, expecting to see a glint of fair hair. Only shadows stared back. Now that I knew what they were capable of, it only made the darkness more terrifying.

The cab rolled to a stop. Mrs. Graham and my brother were still quarreling when the driver opened the door. "John," I said softly, accepting the man's proffered hand as I stepped down. "Let the creature go."

My brother got out, heaving a sigh, but opened his hands. A moth fluttered its wings against his skin, unaware that it had been freed. He blew on it gently. Together, we watched it lift into the air and fly away. Once it was out of sight, I wrapped my arm around his shoulders and guided him inside.

Liza was waiting in the foyer. In the absence of a governess, she often helped me with the boys. "Come along, little ones," she bade with a smile, holding her hands out to John and Michael. "Time for bed."

Instant protests arose. Deciding to let Liza persuade them, I went in search of Papa. A glance into his study told me that he was still absent. My stomach tightened with worry. I climbed the stairs to visit Mama—I'd avoided her long enough—and cheer her with talk of our outing. The tray outside her door hadn't been touched. I picked it up and knocked, but no answer came from within. Cautiously, I twisted the knob and strained to see through the darkness. There she was, a lump in the bed.

"Mama? Are you awake?"

Her voice drifted to me. "Hello, darling."

Pushing the door open with my hip, I walked over to her. There was no fire in the grate to show the outline of furniture, so I balanced the tray on my palm and searched for a light. Mama squinted. Her hair shone with oil, and there was a faint odor emanating from the bed that told me she hadn't bathed last night. Unaware of my scrutiny, she propped herself up against the pillows. "Liza told me where you went this afternoon. Did the boys enjoy flying a kite?"

"Yes," I lied, setting the tray on the table. "Michael would have stayed all night if I'd let him."

She scowled and turned her head away. "Why did you bring that in here? Good Lord, the smell is giving me a megrim."

I sat down, telling myself that there was no foul smell and her cheeks were not gaunt. Pretending was what we did best. Me, Lady Bainbridge, my parents. We were fragmented, and it felt as though acknowledging our pain or imperfections would shatter us completely. "You need to eat, Mama,"

I said, touching the side of the bowl to be certain it was still warm. Holding my hand beneath the spoon, I brought it to her lips.

"I'm not hungry."

Yet another surge of helplessness tore through me. I'd tried to be forceful with my mother before and it had gone badly. With Mary Davenport, it was best to coax and plead. The spoon hovered between her and the tray, and I moved closer so she could see my face. "Just a bit of the soup, then. Please."

"Wendy—"

"Please." I didn't move. Mama looked at me for a moment. Then, relenting, she opened her mouth. I didn't give my mother a chance to change her mind and nearly shoved the spoon in. I kept talking to distract her. "You should come with us next time. I know the boys would be ecstatic."

She plucked at the bedclothes. "Perhaps."

The word was barely audible, and I cursed myself for speaking so unthinkingly. Mama was withdrawing again, curling back into the small world she had created for herself to avoid the loss and shame. But I knew what would bring the life back into her eyes. I bit my lip, wavering. "I heard Orville Martin has returned from his travels."

The transformation was instantaneous. She sat up for the first time in weeks, and her voice was stronger as she said, "Mr. Martin? Really?"

I offered another spoonful of soup. "Yes."

Mama gulped it down and clasped her pale hands

together. "Oh, but this is wonderful, darling. You may not be a beauty, but you have the Davenport name. That's more than enough to gain his notice. If Mr. Martin were to propose, everything will be as it was. Don't you think?"

"Yes, Mama."

"You mustn't talk to him of your ships or maps. Men find that sort of thing unseemly. And be sure to wear blue on your outings—it's most becoming on you."

"I will, Mama."

I listened to her plan a future she had given up on. The words held no importance for me, but the smile curving her cracked lips was everything. By the time she had exhausted herself, the bowl was empty. I put it back on the tray and Mama slumped. I busied myself covering her. Just as I reached for the light again she murmured, "I'm so thrilled, Wendy."

She was falling asleep. I kneeled and she ran a drowsy finger down the side of my face. I wanted to promise her that we would be all right. But Lady Bainbridge's voice returned, a taunt, reminding me that this wasn't true. *I'll be sure to whisper the state of your virtue in the right ear. You know how these things go; all of London will be talking about it by week's end. What man would have you after that, I wonder? And what would become of your family?*

Soon, the Davenport name would be worthless. The whole of society would shun us, let alone Orville Martin, and I couldn't see a way to stop it from happening. Even though Peter was no innocent, I couldn't slaughter him.

My mother didn't notice how I clenched the sheets.

"You're so young," she slurred. "But it fades quickly. Remember that."

"Sleep well." I kissed her on the forehead and backed away. The door clicked shut. I smoothed my skirts and walked down the hallway. Knocking gently, I poked my head inside Michael's room.

He was waiting. At the sight of me, my brother sat up eagerly, his teeth gleaming in the lamplight. "I want to hear about Buffalo Bill's Wild West Show tonight. Please?"

"Did you say your prayers?" I asked, feigning sternness.

"Yes, I swear it!"

There were new drawings on the walls. Despite his tender age, Michael was talented. He had covered so much paper with his passionate strokes that the yellow wallpaper was hardly visible. Mrs. Graham worried I was giving him too much encouragement. Once, I had thought there was no harm in dreaming.

Hiding my distress, I sat on the bed and tucked the covers around his frail body. I considered telling him a different story tonight, one that was sensible and dull. But then I saw Michael in my mind's eye, burning with fever, and I could not deny him this. Dropping my voice to a teasing whisper, I leaned in close. "There are cowboys and diving horses and women with aim as good as any man. There are acrobats and jugglers and knife-throwers. It's quite scandalous, I'm told."

"And Chief Blue Horse?" he prodded.

"Yes, he's there, of course. His people perform something called the Sioux Ghost Dance."

I prattled on until Michael closed his eyes, the veins under his skin like blue rivers. Lying there, he painfully resembled our mother.

"I should very much like to see it one day," the small boy mumbled, halfway between worlds.

A lump swelled in my throat. "And you shall."

Michael didn't respond. I lingered for a bit longer, watching his chest rise and fall. Lady Bainbridge's mother may have sung pretty lullabies, but none of them were as beautiful as the sound of my brother's breathing. After another moment, I turned the oil lamp down and left him to his slumber.

The house was silent. Turning, I saw at the bottom of the stairs that a stream of light slipped beneath Papa's study door. I instinctively moved toward it but paused halfway down, gripping the railing with white fingers. What would I say? Would he even understand the intricacies of Lady Bainbridge's offer, drunk as he undoubtedly was?

What if he decided that killing Peter was the right course of action?

Oh, how I wished I could speak to someone older and wiser. Someone that would take this burden from me. But if I entrusted anyone else with what I knew about Lady Bainbridge, it would put them in danger. Her thinly-veiled threat scuttled through my mind. *If you think to use this information against me—or breathe a word to someone at Scotland Yard—consider how I am seeking my own son's death. A stranger like yourself would be even less of an obstacle.* There was no doubt in my mind the lady had someone watching us. She must not suspect I'd betrayed her confidence. I backed away, wincing when one of the steps creaked. Papa didn't emerge.

Rain pattered against the window when I reached my room. I glanced toward the glass, distracted by the sound, and jumped at the sight of Peter. He hovered there, waiting for me to undo the latch once again. This time I only hesitated a moment before doing so—it felt as though I had already stepped into the abyss these past two nights, and now I was in a helpless freefall no one could save me from. The window swung open from a sudden gust of wind.

The strange boy entered, landing softly on the center of the rug. Water dripped off him and gleamed on his skin. Once again the room was tinged in trembling shades of blue and black, making his shadow soft and harmless. That didn't mean I was out of harm's way, though. Peter and I regarded each other, neither of us moving closer, despite the possibilities quivering between us.

You should tell him about Lady Bainbridge, a faint voice said within me. My desire faded in an instant. Peter knew the danger surrounding Constable Collingwood, but I doubted he was aware his own mother sought his demise.

"Well, Wendy Davenport? Are you ready to go on an adventure?" the boy asked as if we were in the midst of a conversation, rather than starting one. White puffs of air marked each exhale of breath.

Pain radiated down my arms, and I realized I'd been clenching my fists so hard, my nails had made bloody crescents. There was something urgent about Peter tonight, an excited glint in his eyes that hadn't been there before.

Thoughts of Lady Bainbridge retreated to the back of my mind.

"What kind of adventure?" I whispered, wondering if this was the part where all the dark rumors and sordid tales came true. My entire body went rigid, like a mouse facing the large, whiskered face of a cat.

But Peter didn't leap at me or unsheathe a weapon. Instead, his expression became solemn and he said simply, "The kind that changes you forever."

He was speaking the truth; I could hear it in his voice. Suddenly I wondered if perhaps Peter and I weren't so different. Both of us so desperate to escape this world of rules and expectations, both of us longing for change and chaos. I continued studying him, absorbed by the way raindrops clung to his eyelashes and how full his lips were in the silvery light.

"Is it true what they say?" I blurted, finally voicing the question that had been living on the tip of my tongue from the moment we met. "Can you grant wishes?"

Thunder rumbled in the space between us. Peter raised his brows, and a roguish grin spread across his face. "Wishes? Is that what they're saying now? Certain ones, I suppose. If you were to wish for a kiss, that would be within my power."

I hardly heard this—all the hopes, all the lies, all the reassurances I had been telling myself for so long tilted and crashed like Michael's clockwork train going off its tracks. Somehow I had convinced myself that an encounter with Peter would return my family to the light and coax color back into my small brother's cheeks. That magic would fix everything.

"You're lying," I said, a note of pleading in my voice that I couldn't help, and I watched Peter's grin fade. There was something in his unwavering gaze that made it obvious he was not.

Pity.

Suddenly there was a knock at the door, and then Liza's jarring whisper, "Miss Wendy? Are you awake?"

A gasp tore from my throat. Forgetting my pain, I made a senseless gesture at Peter, indicating that he should hide. There was no time to see whether he would obey. As I whirled, I caught the twinkle in his eyes. Then I patted my hair and opened the door just enough so that Liza could see my face.

"Yes?" I managed. The sound of my heartbeat was a herd of wild horses. I hope she wouldn't notice my damp skin, my clothes, or how the open window rattled.

Liza didn't notice any of these things.

"You'd best come quick, miss," my friend said, the words low and urgent. She held a candle, which flickered and made the darkness of her eyes all the more prominent. "It's Michael."

CHAPTER 4

FEAR LODGED in my throat like a corset drawn too tight, and all I could manage was a nod. As Liza rushed back down the hall, I glanced over my shoulder, intending to say a hasty goodbye to Peter. But the room was empty. A curtain fluttered, the only indication that he had been there at all.

Setting Peter from my mind, I went to my brother.

His door was cracked open and soft light spilled over the floor. I hurried in. My heart quivered at the sight of Michael, lying there so small and still. The toys he had played with before falling asleep were still nestled atop of the bedclothes. How could this have happened so quickly? I couldn't have left him but an hour ago.

Just like your mother, seeing only what you want to see, that voice in my head hissed. I flinched.

Liza stood on the other side of the bed, hands clasped so strongly I could see the outline of every knuckle. "He was crying out for you," she murmured.

She would never reprimand me, but I saw her confusion —there was a line between her brows and a questioning tilt to her head. How had I not heard his cries in the next room? Shame filled my veins and it felt as though blood had turned to fire.

"Michael," I said softly. The frame of his bed creaked beneath my added weight. His soft curls were matted to his head and his breathing was too raspy. It couldn't be the fever again; there was no shivering or rashes that I could see. As I touched his hand, I thought of our time in the park, all that running and excitement. This was my fault. I should have known better. I gripped tighter so he would know I was there. At that moment, he coughed. Great, wet gurgles that shook his entire body. Still, he didn't wake.

My gaze never left his paper-white face as I asked, "Have you told our parents?"

"Your father wasn't in his study, but no one seemed to hear me knock on the bedroom door."

That wouldn't do. It didn't matter whether Mama was out of sorts or Papa was reeling from his day at the club. I released Michael reluctantly. He didn't stir, but it took all of my strength to step away. "Fetch the Epsom salts," I said to Liza. "I don't think it's the fever, but we can't just twiddle our thumbs until the physician arrives. Has he been sent for?"

She shook her head. "I'll wake Mrs. Graham. One of us will stay with Michael, miss, while you tell Mr. and Mrs. Davenport."

Gratitude made my tongue thick and useless, so I slipped out the door, and hastened down the hall. Flashes of lightning illuminated the narrow space and guided the way. Outside my parents' room, standing in shadow, I held my fist up... and paused. Through the wood came the muffled sounds of sobs. Then the gentle murmur of someone trying to comfort. My chest folded like a used, pocketed handkerchief. I forced myself to speak, loud and clear so there was no mistaking the criticality of my words. "Mama? Papa? Please wake up. Michael is ill."

The voices quieted. The floorboards moaned. Then Papa opened the door, his hair tousled and his clothing in weary disarray.

"Did you say something about your brother?" he asked. His breath touched me, warm and foul. I looked into his eyes and within the depths saw resignation, self-loathing, fear. He wanted me to tell him that he'd heard wrong.

So I looked at his wrinkled forehead instead as I answered, "Mrs. Graham is sending for Dr. Waghorn."

There was a flurry of activity after that. Michael awoke and began crying. Mama and Papa sat at his side and did their best to soothe him. Mrs. Graham bustled around the room and tried to bring his fever down. Liza brought a tray of tea while we waited for the physician's arrival.

Curled up in a chair, I tucked my finger through the tiny handle of the cup. It was hot, even through the glass, making me comprehend just how cold I was. I watched over my family as I had done—albeit poorly—since all our troubles began.

They were strangers when I compared them to the people I'd known so many months ago. Papa's laugh, so uneven and boisterous, hadn't filled my ears once he'd told of us of his unwise investment in a railway company. A glass decanter appeared on his desk in the study. Mama's lectures on posture and decorum became fewer and shorter before disappearing altogether. She stopped leaving her room. Michael, though he'd always seemed to have a cough or a mild ailment, was never still. Now he could hardly walk. And though no one had woken John, I thought of the alterations in him, as well. How he once spoke endlessly of his readings or findings, whether it was at the table or as I tucked blankets around him at night. Lately there was a hesitation in his manner and he retreated more and more with those books rather than tell me about them.

The tinny sound of a doorbell suddenly traveled through the house, putting a halt to my observations. Everyone's heads jerked up. Mrs. Graham was already gone, and it didn't occur to me until it was too late to remind her that she was still in a nightgown. We listened to our housekeeper greet Dr. Waghorn, then there was the unmistakable sound of two sets of feet ascending the stairs. Moments later, the man himself stepped over the threshold. He was a timid person, despite his size, with thick sideburns and pitted skin. He also had a kind voice, which I liked less when he asked all of us to vacate the room, save for my parents.

I refused to go any farther than just outside it. I fidgeted restlessly while he examined Michael, and the usual sense of curiosity I felt toward the physician's work was overpowered by fear. Liza stood beside me. She didn't say that everything would be all right, and I appreciated this more than any pretty lies she could've given me—our house was already so full of them.

After a few minutes, voices floated through the stillness. I strained to hear what they were saying. My mother had told me time and time again that eavesdropping wasn't ladylike, but in this instance, I didn't care. Not one bit.

"Consumption," I heard him say after what felt like hours. There was a clattering sound, and I imagined Dr. Waghorn putting tools back into the Gladstone bag he carried. I longed to watch his every movement, learn for myself what could be done to help my brother. "I have another young patient with identical symptoms. She suffered from the fever, as well. They were already weak. It made them susceptible to other diseases."

"How will you treat it?"

At this, the older man faltered. "Most families leave the city. There's been evidence that fresh air slows its progress. But Michael is in the early stages. Your physician could try pneumothorax. It's a method that injects air into the pleural cavity, which collapses the lung and allows it to—"

"What do you mean, 'your physician?'" Papa demanded. "*You* are our physician."

There was another long, long pause. "I'm afraid I can no longer offer my services in this home."

The saliva in my mouth turned to chalk and my stomach became a clenched fist. Papa voiced the exact words I was thinking. "Are you saying you won't help him?"

"Mr. Davenport, I have already made numerous exceptions when it comes to your family. Your wife and son's health have my deepest sympathies... but there's still been no payment for these visits. Now, there are charitable hospitals and workhouse infirmaries—"

Mama finally interjected, and there was a spark in her voice that made me remember the bright flame she used to be. "You know as well as we do that those places are filthy and overcrowded. Michael could catch an infection or a virus of some sort. He needs to be here, at home, where he can get better. Please, physician. Save him."

The door abruptly opened, and I sprang back. Heat rushed to my cheeks. Dr. Waghorn lumbered past, the lines in his face so deep, it was as though they'd been made by a blade rather than time. But it didn't matter that he felt guilty; all that mattered was how Mama watched him go and then put a hand over her face, her shoulders shaking in smothered sobs. The sight caused something inside of me to throb, like a fresh wound. Papa made a low, helpless sound in his throat as he pulled her against him. We listened to the physician close the door behind him with a soft and devastating *click*.

Michael slept on. Mrs. Graham told us she would tend to him while the rest of us returned to bed. Sniffling, Mama allowed herself to be led away. Papa laid a heavy hand on my shoulder as they passed.

I remained where I was, staring at Michael, terrified that every breath would be his last. My mind went back to that first moment, when I was fourteen and he was just a few hours old. They'd placed him in my arms, and my first thought was that he was very pink. My second was that he was incredibly small. My third was that he was extremely breakable. And my last had been that I would do anything to make sure it didn't happen.

The memory faded, but the fierceness of it never had. While I stood there, the wound inside me bled and bled, and I felt the girl I had been pouring out. There was only one thing left to do. One way to pay Dr. Waghorn's fee and save my brother. There were no more necklaces or paintings to sell.

You would be reimbursed for your trouble, Lady Bainbridge had said this morning. *All your financial worries would cease to exist.*

Peter had to die.

I sent a runner to the Bainbridge residence with a letter clutched in his hand. Written upon it was my answer to Lady Bainbridge.

I accept your offer.

The day passed. During the periods that Michael was asleep, I sat in the parlor, waiting for word from Lady Bainbridge. Or, better yet, banknotes. Her response would come in the evening post, but I couldn't focus on anything else. The penny dreadful hid beneath my chair cushion, untouched.

There was an air of solemnity in the Davenport household that didn't match the rest of London. Outside, the skies were bright and clear. I listened to the cheerful *clip-clop* of horses going by and the relentless birdsong drifting from the tree next to our window. Mama hadn't gotten out of bed and Papa left before any of us even opened our eyes. Both Liza and Mrs. Graham spent the day going up and down the stairs, shoulders tense beneath their uniforms. Sir Gilbert arrived for the boys' lessons and was sent away.

Just as Michael woke again—Liza came downstairs to say that he was asking for me—the lady's reply came, delivered by a runner.

"I'll be up shortly," I told Liza. She glanced at the correspondence in my hands, but her expression betrayed no curiosity or judgment. Without a word, the other girl curtsied and left. I didn't even wait for the sound of her footsteps to fade before opening the letter, and I was so impatient that I nearly tore the envelope in half.

Lady Bainbridge's card was ivory, the edges gilded gold. I flipped it over to read the message written on the back. The handwriting matched the lady herself in elegance and efficiency. *Miss Davenport, thank you for receiving me yesterday. Your home is lovely. I look forward to seeing the parasol cover we spoke about. Your embroidery is renowned within London circles. Please write me upon its completion and I will call on you at your leisure.*

Clever. The lady was leaving no evidence of her involvement. My embroidery was hardly renowned; Mama used to sigh when she saw it. If anything should come to light or the authorities got involved, I would have no one to point a finger at other than myself.

All of a sudden, my stomach grumbled. The sound was

startling, and the card fell from my dazed, limp fingers. I felt strange, unsettled, as though I were wearing someone else's skin. Seeing Lady Bainbridge's carefully-written words forced me to face the reality of what I was about to do. Soon Peter would come, and soon I would kill him.

Could I do it? Was I capable of murdering another person?

There was no other alternative. Not if I wanted to save my brother's life.

I glanced toward the window again. Hues of pink and yellow shone through the glass. *Have any of us eaten today?* I wondered distantly. This led to thoughts of the kitchen—images of all the spices, pots, and knives—and caused an idea to bloom in my mind that had nothing to do with hunger and everything to do with how I might quickly end Peter's life.

I bent and picked up the offending card. After brief consideration, I put it under the cushion with my penny dreadful. It seemed the perfect place for all secret, appalling things.

On soundless feet I went down the hall and cautiously eased into the kitchen. The cook, Mrs. Graham, and Liza were the only ones who used it now that the other servants were gone, but I was still prepared to lie about why I was there. *So sorry, I was hungry. Might I have a bit of cheese?* Usually our housekeeper retired with a glass of sherry. Tonight, however, I had no doubt she was sitting vigil for Michael.

The thought made me stop so abruptly that I nearly lost my footing. I flattened a hand against the door for balance.

Sitting vigil. Michael was dying. Even if Papa did take him to a hospital, there was no cure. Dr. Waghorn said as much. We had no home in the country to pursue fresh air. Any friends who may have offered their own accommodations had long since forsaken us or been shunned for fear of their discovering our fortune. Or lack thereof.

Once again, I was reminded that there were no other options. For them—Mama, Papa, Michael, John—I would become the monster I needed to be. My spine stiffened with resolve and I opened all the drawers. Eventually I found what I was looking for.

The knife's handle was cool and solid. My insides quaked as the blade glinted in the sun's final rays. Glancing around to be certain no one had seen, I returned to my room.

Liza was walking toward the door with a stack of linens in her arms. She paused, giving me a tremulous smile, and I quickly hid the knife in the folds of my skirt. "There you are. The water was getting cold," she said.

I frowned with incomprehension before noticing the copper tub standing in the corner. Liza had set her linens down and was already moving to help me undress. She would see the knife. Panicking, I took a step back and scrambled for an excuse that would force her to leave. "I would like to bathe myself tonight, actually. I only require your assistance with the corset."

She paused, confusion and hurt warring in her eyes. I thought of how she had boiled the water on the kitchen range and carried it up the stairs in buckets. Regret filled my mouth and it tasted like sour milk. Liza was the only friend I had left; I'd had to distance myself from all the rest when my family's troubles began.

But then I pictured her entering my room, seeing me standing over Peter's prone body, the knife in my hand dripping with his red, red blood.

"What are you waiting for?" I asked harshly. Liza blanched and hurried to undo the strings, her fingers clumsy beneath my blouse. I stared straight ahead, comforting myself with the hope that after this was all over, things could go back as they were. A rift was necessary; Liza must not return to my room. There couldn't be any witnesses.

Once the ties were pulled loose, the maid avoided my eyes as she curtsied and left. I listened to her fading footsteps, feeling as though each one was a stomp on my heart. Turning away, I noticed the faint moonlight spilling across the floor. Peter would be coming soon. I bathed quickly, worried that he would appear at the window any moment. Then, smelling like soap and fear, I donned a nightgown and crawled into bed with the knife. I curled on my side and waited.

The moon floated higher and brighter. There was a drunk man in the street who apparently had an intense desire for sheep's trotters—he sang about them in a way one might sing about a long-lost love. He quieted a few minutes later, having probably stumbled into his home or found a hard place to rest his head. I began to think I had been wrong, and Peter would not come. My eyes became heavy.

Just as they drifted shut, there was a light *tap-tap-tap* on the window.

Though I had been expecting it, I flinched at the sound. I sat up, tucking my hand beneath the bedclothes. My fingertips collided with the handle of the knife. I had lifted the latch earlier, and Peter discovered this instantly. He climbed through, his features hidden in shadow.

"You shouldn't have come back," I told him. My voice wobbled.

Drawing nearer, Peter cocked his head. The action made me think of the birds I often fed in the park as a child. "Strange," he said. "It sounds as though you mean that."

He stopped at the foot of the bed. Perhaps his instincts whispered that something wasn't right. I'd seen how fast he could move, and I knew we needed to be closer if I was going to be successful. What if his shadow attacked me again?

There was a roaring in my ears. I swung my legs to the side, trying to hide how badly I was shaking. Then, between one blink and the next, Peter was there. Apparently he'd disregarded any reservations, because he cupped the back of my neck with his rough palm and used it as leverage to pull me backward. I found myself laying down again, staring up at him. There was nothing rough about Peter's movements, but he wasn't being gentle, either. Heat touched my cheeks as I realized that I liked it.

"Why are you here, Peter?" I asked helplessly.

"I'm here because I want you," he said. The directness of it made me blink. In my world, no one said what they were thinking or admitted what they truly desired. I stared into

Peter's bright eyes and realized that, at some point, I'd buried my fingers into his silken hair, abandoning the knife. As the seconds ticked past, I didn't think of my reputation or what anyone else wanted.

"Then take me," I heard myself say.

In response, Peter reached for the button on his trousers. When he wasn't quick enough, I reached to yank at it, too. The boy caught my hand. My gaze flicked up questioningly. He didn't speak, but I nodded to show I'd heard the unspoken words. Yes, I knew where this road led. Yes, I wanted this.

Without looking away, Peter undid the button himself. Just as he started to remove the trousers completely, my thoughts went to the possible scandal. The one secret I wouldn't be able to keep, if we weren't careful tonight. I wetted my lips and fumbled over the words. "Do you... will you be able to..."

The corners of Peter's mouth deepened as he realized what I was trying to say. "I'm not one to make solemn vows, but in these circumstances, you have it. We shall not become parents tonight, you and I."

He gave me no chance to respond. In the next moment, Peter's mouth was on my neck, and he did something with those lips, his tongue, that made my core come alive. I bit back a moan. Then Peter took my hands, which were flat on the bed, and placed them on his broad, warm chest.

"Touch me. Fuck me. Enjoy me," he murmured in my ear, then gave it a quick nip. My hips flew upward in a small, strange bucking movement. Peter grinned before he sat up and pulled his shirt off. I knew I was staring again, but I didn't care. He was... beautiful. Every line looked as though it had been sculpted from clay. His wide shoulders tapered into a narrow waist and a hard stomach. His skin gleamed in the moonlight, not so smooth as it had seemed the first time I saw him—scars marked his body like landmarks on a map. His ribcage, his arm, his hip. I suppressed the strange urge to touch each one.

"I suppose it's my turn," I said eventually. Peter blinked at my words. I liked that I'd surprised him. Giving him a small, mischievous smile, I slid the nightgown slowly up my legs. Peter watched me with eyes that were slightly darker than before. I felt daring and strong in a way I never had before. The nightgown wasn't fully off when I felt his hand between my legs.

When I started to touch the ridges of his stomach, my other hand brushed against something cool and hard. The hilt of the knife, I realized. It was as if someone had emptied a bucket of icy water over me. What was I doing? Why had I allowed this to happen?

Your family will be reimbursed for the trouble. All financial worries would cease to exist.

Consumption. Michael is in the early stages.

Michael. I had agreed to kill Peter to save him. I needed to stop this. Stab the knife in Peter's heart.

But at the same moment I tightened my grip on the hilt, his mouth closed around my nipple and gave it a hard suck, sending sparks of pleasure through me. My determination weakened. *Blast.* I felt like a pendulum, swinging back and forth between denial and certainty.

I forced myself to think of all the reasons why Peter had to die. All those small images that added up to a larger, painful picture. The sweat on Michael's forehead. The soup on my mother's chin. The light beneath the door to my father's study.

"Tell me you were lying. About your ability to grant wishes," I said in a final, desperate attempt to save us both.

Peter paused in his administrations, then pulled away completely. Cold rushed into the space he'd been occupying. Flushing, I sat up and adjusted my nightgown. As Peter straightened, I watched his face closely, hoping to spot anything that might give me hope. The legend of London met my gaze. He pursed his lips and searched my face, as well. Then he said, his voice so gentle, like a feather brushing over my skin, "I don't have the power to save your brother..."

Disappointment burned in my veins and I could no longer look into Peter's eyes. Slowly, I began to pull the knife out from beneath the covers. "Never mind. It was silly."

"...but there may be something else that can."

My mouth snapped shut with an audible sound. My eyes felt huge, like they were about to swallow the rest of my face. The progress of the knife halted. Peter crossed his arms, one brow quirked, silently daring me to ask him what he meant.

Danger, instinct warbled, peeking between splayed fingers like a child in the dark. There it was again, that sense of standing before the window, looking at that latch and frightened of what would happen if I undid it. Terrified of what would happen if I didn't.

But I would ask. Of course I would. If it meant saving Michael, I'd offer my soul. "You know of a cure for consumption?" I said.

I was still sitting, frozen in place, desperate for his answer. Peter ventured close again and knelt between my legs. His fingers trailed along the sides of my thighs, then dipped between them, teasing, exploring, not quite touching the part that ached for him most.

"Come away with me," he whispered, his breath tickling the shell of my ear. I breathed in the wild scent of him and resisted the urge to pull Peter close. "We shall go on an adventure, you and I. You may learn some of my secrets and take them back with you, when the time comes."

As always, everything inside me came alive at his proximity. My heart shuddered, my veins gushed, my bones stretched. But I was thinking of Michael now. Remembering how close he was to death's door. Here was my chance to secure the funding for Dr. Waghorn or a trip to the country. Peter couldn't be trusted and I may never get another opportunity to fulfill Lady Bainbridge's wishes.

I found a firm grasp on the knife and pulled it out from the sheets.

CHAPTER 5

"WENDY?"

At the sound of my brother's voice, I scrambled out of bed, my face and neck burning. Peter, of course, was already gone.

John stood in the doorway, a narrow-boned silhouette. The knife fell onto the rug with a dull *thud* and I prayed no one noticed. "What are you doing in here?" I asked, breathless.

My brother was frowning. As he shuffled forward, his spectacles caught the moonlight. In a small voice he said, "I couldn't sleep. Mrs. Graham wouldn't let me see Michael and we always say good night."

I pushed the knife out of sight with my foot and hurried toward him. "Let's fetch a glass of warm milk, then, shall we? Down to the kitchen with you!"

John obediently turned around, and I seized the opportunity to search my room. There was still no sign of Peter.

Had he left? Uncertain whether what I felt was relief or disappointment—perhaps a little of both—I followed my brother into the hallway. I closed the door without looking back, but my heartbeat felt like a locomotive flying off the tracks.

We made our way to the kitchen on silent, swift feet. John sat at the table while I fetched his nightcap, his dark eyes following me. *He wants to be comforted,* that inner voice said. The words felt like a nudge. But I was distracted, my mind buzzing with thoughts about what I should do if Peter was still upstairs.

A minute later, cup of milk in hand, John didn't argue when I steered him back through the house. I rubbed his back as we climbed the stairs. I sent my brother back into his room with a firm embrace and a kiss on top of his head. Then I returned to my own, thinking quickly. Peter could still be here.

My entire plan had involved taking him by surprise. Now the knife was beneath the bed, where I couldn't subtly retrieve it, and John was awake. What if Peter cried out? For that matter, how would I move his body from my room without anyone seeing? Clearly I hadn't given my plan enough thought, and it was a stroke of luck that someone had interrupted us.

"What is your answer, Wendy Davenport?"

Answer? I shook my head to indicate that I didn't understand, but then I remembered. *Come away with me,* Peter had said. Just before I'd tried to kill him.

Under the weight of his stare, I swallowed and struggled to think. It was difficult with Peter so near, smelling like wind and freedom. The more I considered his proposal, the more I found myself searching for any justification to agree. If I went with him, an opening may present itself and I could do the gruesome deed forced upon me.

But what about Michael and Mama? What kind of sister and daughter would abandon them in their hour of need? Guilt pricked at me, and slowly, I shook my head. "I can't leave them."

"You can't save them by staying." Peter saw the pain in my eyes, the *no* forming on my lips once again. "I told you there might be something that can cure his illness. Come with me and I'll show it to you."

"You're using Michael's life to persuade me?" I said through my teeth. "Why not retrieve this mysterious item and bring it back? That's what a true hero would do."

"I'm no hero. Best get that sorted out right now. This is a bargain."

"A *bargain*?" I repeated, blinking. How ironic. It seemed Peter and his mother shared a common interest in manipulation.

He leaned close. My indignation faded as I prepared myself for his next words. I was beginning to learn that with Peter, the most important things were said quietly. "In exchange for the cure," he said solemnly, his surprisingly sweet breath fanning my face, "I want... your firstborn child."

"I beg your pardon?"

Peter snickered and flew backward, his hands folded

beneath his head. "Come with me, for a week, and I'll give you the cure," he amended.

I swallowed and said, "Michael may not have that long."

This was the hardest truth I had ever said out loud. Peter just shrugged, a movement that seemed distinctly feline. He began doing lazy twirls close to the ceiling. "That is not my concern. Take it or leave it, Wendy Davenport."

There were too many reasons to deny him, even if part of me was tempted to agree. "There's also the matter of a bank payment. My family could be turned out in the time I'm gone," I said.

"I took care of that."

I blinked, certain I'd heard Peter incorrectly. "What are you talking about?"

"I told you the other night that I had errands to run—I fetched the stash I keep in London and paid a runner to deliver it to Mr. Pickering. There was a note, as well, informing him who it was from. As far as that toff is concerned, the Davenports have paid in full."

"Your stash?" I echoed. Hope flared, sending bright flames through me. "Is there more?"

Peter seemed to guess at the direction of my thoughts. "Nothing left for the physician, I'm afraid. I gave everything to Mr. Pickering. What I had in England, at least. The rest is hidden away across the sea. Now what is your answer?"

The ever-looming bank payment was gone. I could feel something fall away, slide off me, like there had been a boulder on my back for weeks. Peter's unexpected act of kindness sent me into a stunned silence. I remembered yesterday's conversation with my mother, pictured the light in her eyes as she spoke of Orville Martin. If I let Peter take me away, it might destroy her. And yet, this adventure was probably the first and last one I could ever have. My only chance to pretend that the future held more than doilies and rules and obligations. I didn't believe Peter about the cure, but the prospect of freedom, however temporary, was temptation enough. It was also a chance to finish what I had begun tonight, regardless of the bank payment he'd made on my family's behalf. Peter had only done it to get what he wanted, after all.

I lifted my chin and met his gaze. The boy hadn't interrupted as I debated, and something told me this was rare for him—it felt as though we were connected by desire and choice in a world that was rife with duty and inevitability.

"Forget them, Wendy. Forget them all. Come with me where you'll never, never have to worry about grown up things again," he murmured.

The look in his eyes sent another wave of heat through my body. How did he do that? Was it his magic?

Magic. Such a thing existed where Peter came from, and magic was all that could save my brother now. All that could save my family, who were unraveling more with each passing day.

"A moment, please," I said at last. Peter frowned, probably trying to ascertain whether I'd agreed or not.

Giving him no chance to ask, I left the room and tiptoed down to Papa's study. I could already feel my heart quickening, its quiet pattern becoming a chaotic crescendo inside me. I left the door cracked open to use the light streaming in behind me. The soft glow fell over the Persian rugs and tall bookshelves. Perched upon one, looking out from its position of honor, was a familiar leather-bound atlas. I didn't allow my gaze to linger on it as I passed. I took what I needed from Papa's desk and began to construct a letter to Lady Bainbridge. My hand was unsteady.

We were interrupted before I could complete the task you gave me. Peter claims to be taking us on an adventure. Rest assured that by the time we return, it will be done.

I didn't sign it. Once the ink was dry, I slid the paper into an envelope and wrote Lady Bainbridge's name on the back. Next I pulled out a fresh sheet, and addressed this one to my parents. No matter how vital the reason for my departure, I wouldn't leave them wondering whether I had been taken or harmed.

I have gone in search of a cure for Michael. I will return in a week's time. Please don't worry. I love you all.

Finished, I folded the letter and put it against my father's tobacco box, where he wouldn't miss it. I started to head for the stairs, but a thought made me pause in the doorway of the study. Clothes. I needed clothes. My petticoats and skirts would be ill-equipped to last where we were bound—it didn't require genius to know that, despite how little information I'd been given.

Another idea bloomed. It had rained today, and yesterday was laundry day, which meant the items on the laundry line were probably hauled inside for indoor drying.

I returned to the kitchen, where my family's clothing had

indeed been hung to dry. I hadn't even noticed them when I was here with John—I must've been lost in thought. No more of that. At least for tonight, when I needed to be at my sharpest.

Knowing John and Michael's clothes would be too small for me, I removed a pair of Papa's trousers, along with one of his shirts. He wouldn't notice, and if Mrs. Graham did, she'd probably assume Mr. Davenport had urgently needed a change of clothes. These days, his were often covered in vomit.

I started in the direction of the stairs when something else occurred to me, and I stopped short. I'd have to dress right here, considering the alternative was the hallway or the bedroom that Peter occupied. While Peter had already seen me in a state of undress, I was far from comfortable at the idea of doing it where he could watch.

Kitchen it was, then.

With rough, anxious movements, I yanked the sleeves of my nightgown down, then allowed the entire thing to slide off me. I stepped out, darting a glance toward the windows. Nothing shifted or fluttered beyond the glass, and I hurried to put the trousers on. After I'd secured the button, though, I slowed again to absorb the alien sensation of wearing pants. Though they were too large, of course, wearing them felt strange yet freeing. A blush spread over my cheeks at the sight of my legs, scandalously outlined and exposed.

And yet I never wanted to take them off.

I shook myself, retrieved my discarded nightgown from the floor, along with a pair of Father's boots, and left the moonlit space behind. On my way back to the second floor, I left my letter for Lady Bainbridge on the silver salver in the foyer and hoped that Liza would still send it, even if I was not there to make the request.

Next I tiptoed into Michael's room. Mrs. Graham was slumped in a chair beside him, a trail of drool gleaming from the corner of her mouth. Carefully, I knelt by the bed. My brother seemed even smaller than usual, hardly bigger than the pillow he rested against. His skin matched the white linens, as well, making his strawberry-colored hair stand out all the more starkly.

"Michael," I whispered, half-wishing he would wake. But I didn't dare speak any louder for fear that it would rouse our housekeeper, as well. "Know that I am not abandoning you. I *will* return with something to make you better. Hold on. Wait for me."

His nostrils flared. Perhaps, wherever he was, in whatever dream, he'd heard me. I memorized Michael's features and kissed his hand. Then, with a sensation as though I were being torn in two, I left him.

In the hallway, I automatically started in the direction of John's room. I slowed as I remembered he was probably still awake, and I couldn't very well say goodbye without explaining why.

I was still hesitating when someone coughed. I spun, spotting my father at the top of the stairs too late. Panic roared through me. *Blast.* How would I explain the fact I was wearing his clothes? Only a fool would believe I'd changed into them while I was sleepwalking...

But Papa didn't even notice my presence. I stood frozen as he passed, and at this proximity, I saw how haggard and gray he'd become. I had assumed he was nursing his sorrows at the club, but the dejected slump to his shoulders suggested something else. Had my father been trying to seek help for Michael, as well?

"Oh, Papa," I said softly. He lumbered into the bedroom he shared with Mama, and I heard the door click shut a moment later.

Seeing my father strengthened my conviction that going with Peter was the right choice. I took a breath and turned away, away from the painful and mundane, toward the hopeful and unknown. The letter I'd written for my family would have to suffice as a farewell to John.

When I opened the door to my own room, Peter was standing by the window. He raised his brows expectantly. I took a breath, knowing that everything was about to change.

"Where are we going?" was all I said, placing my nightgown on the bed. I hesitated, then pulled Father's boots on. My feet were bare, but I wasn't about to fetch my stockings in front of Peter.

Once I straightened, the boy clapped his hands. His shadow, its long shape visible on the floor, crossed its arms in obvious displeasure. "Excellent! As to where we're going, that's a surprise. But first you must learn how to fly."

I stared at him for what felt like the hundredth time. "Fly? Me?"

Peter moved toward me, and I stumbled as I backtracked,

wary of his shadow. Ignoring this, Peter snagged my wrist and yanked me against him.

Before I realized what was happening, his mouth was on mine for the first time, foreign and startling and wonderful all at once. I was so flustered that I didn't immediately push him away. Then... I found I didn't want to. As the kiss went on, the taste of him banished every thought from my mind. I couldn't help but respond. I spread my fingers over his chest, which was wonderfully warm and firm. His tongue asked a question that I readily answered. Every part of his body was pressed to mine, and once again, I awoke in a way I hadn't known was possible before meeting Peter.

He ended it so suddenly that our lips parted with a *smack*. Smirking, the boy crossed his arms in a manner eerily similar to his shadow and rose into the air.

"Why was that necessary?" I asked faintly, hoping Peter couldn't sense how much I longed for him to do it again. He was already far too arrogant.

"It's part of the magic. You must carry my homeland with you, and too much time has passed since I had my face between your legs. The dust will have faded by now," he answered, acting as though he were unaffected by what just transpired between us. Frustration burrowed in my chest.

"Dust?" I echoed, nonplussed.

Peter made a dismissive, impatient gesture. "Now, then. The trick is to think of something meaningful. It doesn't have to be particularly happy or important. Just a thought that makes you feel as though there's more to the world than what everyone sees. Or several thoughts, if you'd prefer to be overzealous in your efforts."

I barely heard him. My mind brightened like a gaslight, realizing why Peter's words were familiar. Dust. Thoughts. The lullaby I'd heard Lady Bainbridge singing! *Second star to the right, and straight on 'til morning. A few thoughts with some dust, and soon you'll be soaring.* Had she been to this place Peter now hailed from? My mind felt like a flurry of leaves scattering down the street.

"Miss Davenport?" Peter's voice came from a long distance.

I returned to reality with a blink. Peter stood in front of me, and he appeared to be waiting for something. He was waiting for me to fly, I realized an instant later, remembering his comments before I'd made the connection to Lady Bainbridge's lullaby.

"A meaningful thought? That's all?" I asked. Peter gave a single nod of his head.

This all seemed so outlandish. Part of me wondered if Peter was playing a grand joke. Well, if this was all a game, at least I would know what sort of person he was. I squared my shoulders as if I were going into battle, because that's how it felt.

Saving Michael, I thought.

Silence pounded at my ears. I wasn't sure what I expected, but there were no dramatic thunderclaps or bursts of light. Hardly daring to breathe, I opened my eyes and looked down.

I wasn't floating, or hovering, or doing anything close to

flying. The floor was solid beneath me. I let out a breath, feeling embarrassed, though I really had no reason to. It was perfectly normal that I shouldn't master a new skill on the first attempt, I told myself. But that didn't mean I was eager to try again.

"I should pack before—" I started, backing away.

"No time for that, I'm afraid. The sun is coming and we don't want all of London to see us in the sky. Now find your thought," Peter instructed.

I was struck again by how impossible it seemed that a single thought would lift me into the air. *Stop stalling, Wendy,* I told myself sternly. I was better than this. Closing my eyes a second time, I thought of my parents. I pictured the ocean. I imagined a vast library.

When I opened my eyes once again, my feet were still firmly planted on the ground. "I can't do it!" I snapped, resisting the urge to stomp like a child.

"The moment you doubt whether you can fly, you cease forever to be able to do it. Try again, and this time, just fucking *believe.*"

Just believe, I repeated silently, too focused to be startled by Peter's language. The notion of this endeavor was simple, and I was an intelligent woman. There was no reason I shouldn't be able to accomplish flight. My lips pursed with determination. Yet again I closed my eyes and thought of the atlas in Papa's study. I thought of my brothers. I thought of Nana. Then, just to be certain I'd considered every possibility, I thought of our cook's delightful lemon biscuits.

When I opened my eyes for the third time, my feet were still firmly planted on the floor.

I uttered the foulest curse word I knew as Peter rolled his eyes. "Very well. I suppose we'll have to improvise," he said.

He moved so quickly that I was in his arms without warning. A shriek escaped me, and we shot out the window. Nana went wild downstairs, doing her best to wake the whole of London. The night rushed past in a blur of darkness and stars.

I clutched Peter's shoulders and stared around us in wonder. My trousers whipped against my legs. The moon seemed so close I could touch it. Far below, the city slumbered like an innocent babe. Nana's frantic sounds grew fainter. Gazing at those gentle lights with the wind in my ears, it was difficult to believe there was any pain or darkness in the world.

"Is this real?" I murmured, feeling as though speaking any louder would shatter the beauty of flight.

Peter glanced down at me. It seemed there was a radiance to his skin I hadn't seen before, proof that he was not quite part of this world. "Does it feel real?"

The boy's arms were solid around me. The air whistling by was cold. My lips still tingled from his kiss. "Yes," I said.

"Well, then, it must be."

I wanted to tell Peter that nothing was so simple. I swallowed the words. Maybe where he came from, it *was*.

"Where are we going?" I asked again.

I didn't expect to get an answer, but then Peter grinned. Dimples deepened in each cheek, and I was struck once more by the impossible realization that I didn't want to kill him.

"We're going to Neverland," he said.

The island was unlike anything I had ever seen before.

It came gradually, like a dream. We soared over city and water and I lost sense of time. There was only Peter, his warm palms, the rush of air. Then morning came. Light leaked through the clouds, as though someone had exhaled near a neglected shelf and sent dust scattering everywhere. Not even the Northern Lights could compare to this. Awed, I looked down... and I saw it. It was difficult to speak or breathe for the awe of it.

Peter lowered his head, and his lips brushed the tender skin of my ear. "Welcome to Neverland, Wendy."

It was paradise. Green trees and white beaches and blue sky. The water was so clear I could see coral reefs, even from this distance. The shape of the island was strange, similar to a handprint, as though God himself had reached down and pulled the land into existence. The ocean surrounding it glittered. I imagined cutting through the water and feeling its coolness on my skin.

Mama would be appalled.

Peter carried me over the island. The air smelled of salt and growing things. I closed my eyes and inhaled. At the same moment, a faint sound disturbed the stillness. Was that... whistling?

Thinking to ask Peter, I opened my eyes. I caught a glimpse of his mouth, forming a word that would make most ladies blush, just as he threw himself backward.

It was so abrupt that my stomach lurched. Something shot past us, leaving a hole in the clouds. I held onto Peter so hard it was a wonder he could breathe. "What's happening?" I cried.

"Cannonballs," Peter snarled. There came that whistling sound again. Peter wrenched out of the way a second time, but in doing so, he lost his grip on me.

Then I was falling.

I flipped, again and again, uselessly clawing at the air as I screamed. My frantic glimpses of the ground showed it getting closer with every second. There was nothing except trees and hard ground. Terror wiped my mind clean of thoughts like an eraser across a chalkboard. I tried to shriek Peter's name, but vomit hurtled up instead. It erupted from my mouth and blinded me as I finally crashed through the canopy, hitting several branches on the way down. I knew I was about to die.

Before I could dread the pain of impact, water was all around, streaming past in bubbles and blue shimmering, which swiftly turned to black as I plummeted toward the bottom. But I slowed at last. I kicked my legs instinctively and drew to a complete stop. Nothing moved around me. I stared through the water without truly seeing it. The silence filling my ears was jarring after that wild fall. It felt like I could still hear the wind roaring past.

Far below the surface, cradled by the warm depths, I felt

my face crumple. I'd never experienced such terror in all my life. Despite all my claims about wanting adventure, it never occurred to me that death was a potential outcome of such choices. I lingered there for a moment or two, allowing myself to cry with painful, unadulterated relief. I kicked my way back to air and daylight.

As I emerged from the water, it only took a moment to see that I had landed in a small lake. I looked around, hardly able to breathe past the violent tremors going through me. I knew it had been sheer luck that caused me to land here, instead of amongst the unforgiving trees. Just a bit farther and I would be nothing more than a pile of broken bones. It was also fortunate there were no rocks within this lake.

Peter had dropped me. *Dropped* me.

As quick as it had come, my indignation faded. I thought of our conversation before leaving London. He'd never promised that I would be safe. He'd never guaranteed that I would come to no harm during my time here. Truthfully, I only had myself to blame.

It might have been helpful to know there was a danger of being shot at with cannons, though.

I continued my appraisal of these new surroundings, uncertain what my next course of action should be. Behind me, cutting a path through wild foliage, there was a narrow river. On the side opposite this was an unbroken line of jungle. That was preferable to finding myself in open sea, should the river current carry me there.

Water lapped at my chin as I started toward shore, and I

resolved to thank my father for teaching me how to swim as a child—a skill most women were denied.

Once I got closer to shore, I dared to move my legs downward, hoping to feel solid ground beneath me. My courage was rewarded when my boots landed on the sandy bottom. Nearly sagging with relief, I stumbled onto the shallow embankment. I knew I should form a plan, decide what to do next, but I seemed to have no control over my body. I dropped to my knees, panting. A wall of jungle loomed over me, rife with sounds I'd never heard before. Something moved, high up in one of the trees, and I realized it was a snake. But it was nothing like the small, harmless creatures I'd seen moving through the grass back home. No, the monstrosity in that tree was a pale yellow and as thick as a man's torso.

Suddenly I wanted to laugh. Giggles did indeed start slipping out of me, and there was a hysterical edge to the sounds.

They caught in my throat, though, when I heard footsteps in the water. Slowly, I turned my head, too terrified to even breathe now. It took several seconds to register what I was seeing.

A black horse stood beside me.

Its mane dripped, as though it had just come out of the water. I could only see one round, dark eye through the tangled strands, and I knew it had to be imaginative thinking that I saw kindness shining from the dark depths of that single pupil. The horse shifted closer, huffing its impatience. *Climb on,* it seemed to say.

Perhaps it would take me to a place where I could signal Peter, or just to a place that was safer. But I'd never ridden bareback before, and this was a wild animal—it could very well try to kill me the moment I tried to climb on. Even so, I felt compelled to push myself up and stretch my hands toward it. The horse only stepped closer, as if to accommodate me. My palm collided with its surprisingly cold side. *Aren't horses supposed to be warm?* I thought absently, tensing in preparation to mount its back.

Foolish, so foolish.

I froze with my hands fisted in the horse's mane, then spun around, searching the trees for whoever had spoken. Nothing moved. Perhaps I'd hit the water too hard upon impact, because for a moment, I could have sworn the voice came from inside my own head. I shook myself and began to swing onto the horse's back again.

Get off, get off, unless you want to be eaten. Yum, yum, yum.

This time, I sensed the voice was coming distinctly from behind, and I whirled again. A jolt went through me when I saw a woman. She stood halfway out of the water, and she wore no clothing. Her bare breasts gleamed in the sunlight, only half-covered by her dark hair, which was so long that it trailed behind her like the train of a gown. There was also a blue-green tint to her skin that didn't fade no matter how many times I blinked.

At the same moment I opened my mouth to say something, the horse lunged. I saw it coming a fraction of a second before it reached me, and I screamed as I dove out of the creature's path. I hit the water and there was no time to recover or flee—my shirt flattened against my chest as the horse yanked on it from behind.

I was screaming again when it dragged me under.

The horse cut through the depths like a fish. I hadn't gotten a chance to hold my breath before falling into the water, and I couldn't think past the cloud of pain and panic. I did have enough frame of mind to notice it was cold and dark now. *We must be near the bottom of the lake.* The grim thought felt like it belonged to someone else, because the rest of me was distant and hazy.

My eyes had started to drift shut when there was a flash of silver, and our downward momentum abruptly halted. I didn't question it—in the next moment, I was kicking and cutting my arms through the water. I made small, panicked sounds deep in my throat as I went, convinced I'd feel the horse's teeth on my legs any second.

But the teeth never came. I broke the surface of the lake for a second time, gasping. I saw that I was on the other side now, far from the patch of shore where I'd just been kneeling. I immediately started for the land closest to me, ignoring my blurred vision. It didn't matter, nothing mattered except getting out of the water.

The ground was not as solid on this side. Coughing and wheezing, I fought through so much mud that it forced me to my knees in order to get across it. I began crawling, and I was faintly aware of the *stench* assailing my sense, but I focused on putting as much distance as possible between me and the black horse. The muck and filth coated my entire body. After a yard or two, I had to stop from the chest pains.

Holding back a whimper, I looked behind me. My heart pounded so hard I felt it everywhere, like thunder under my skin.

The horse had stopped at the edge of the water, its black eyes gleaming with malice. It took a single step closer, its hoof sinking into the earth with a wet sound. I was stiff as a board, terror roaring in my ears. Every instinct shrieked to scramble up and run.

That was when the voice came again, slithering through my mind like the snake I'd seen earlier. *Stay still. Still as a tree, still as a star.*

It took every scrap of self-control I had to obey. The horse seemed to be looking in my direction, and its nostrils flared. *It hunts by scent,* I thought suddenly. That was why the voice had instructed not to move. The mud was probably masking me, as well.

I held my breath, in spite of how much it hurt, and didn't even dare to blink. Time seemed to speed up and slow down all at once. The friendly demeanor had fallen off the creature like snow from a slanted rooftop. Its lips curled back into a snarl, and even at a distance, I saw that its square teeth were coated in something dark. We stared at each other for a full minute, then two.

Finally, the horse snorted and began to retreat. Had I fooled it into thinking I'd gone? Was it a trick? The urge to run gripped me again, but I gritted my teeth and tensed even more, if that was possible. I fought it until the horse's head vanished beneath the water, and all that was left were the fast-fading ripples racing toward shore.

It was gone. My lungs heaved, taking in huge, greedy gulps of air. Remembering the woman, I searched for her and discovered that she hadn't moved. Her gaze met mine, and her voice invaded me again, undeniable this time. *That was a kelpie. Naughty, naughty, they are. It would have taken you to the bottom of the lake and drowned you,* she said.

A kelpie? What on earth was that? Mingled with the dim shock was the realization that she had saved my life. Words of gratitude rose to my lips, but all that emerged was a ragged breath. I couldn't ignore the instinct that had taken form as a tightness in my chest, the certainty that I shouldn't acknowledge a debt between me and this strange woman. Perhaps it had to do with how she was staring. She looked... *hungry.*

I cleared my throat. "Would you happen to know—"

The speed with which she moved was like nothing I'd seen before. In stunned horror, I watched her come at me in an explosion of fins and sharp teeth. Then there was a biting pain at my wrists, and I found myself being dragged through the mud so quickly that I left a trail through it, like a worm tunneling through the earth. I screamed, over and over, and I'd instinctively begun struggling against the creature's hold, but there was something preternatural about her strength. It was like there were manacles on my wrists, and the truth of my situation struck just as I was pulled into the water *again.*

I had survived a kelpie only to be killed by a mermaid.

I'd caught a glimpse of her tail when she shot out of the water, and it had none of the pretty green scales I'd described in my stories to John and Michael. Water filled my mouth and lungs. My hair streamed behind me. I struggled more this time, trying to yank free.

We hadn't gotten far when she screeched.

Something dark marred the water around us. Blood, I realized, but it was darker than a human's. I followed it to the source and spotted an arrow jutting from the mermaid's side now. My next realization was that she'd released me when she was shot. Reacting instinctively, like a mouse escaping a cat's paws, I kicked my way back to the surface.

As I emerged a third time, there was a lone figure on shore, a lanky boy with brown hair. He held a bow in his hands, another arrow notched and ready. I should have been alarmed at the sight of him, but all I could summon was relief. Anything was preferable to drowning. I moved with limbs that didn't feel like mine. *Not fast enough*, instinct hissed. I kicked harder, biting my lip to hold back a terrified sob.

Before I could reach solid ground, fingers clamped around my ankles. I screamed as the creature pulled me back down.

Wendy belongs to Peter, does she? her silken voice hissed against my ear, no, my mind, bubbles surrounding us. I wanted to break free, to tell her that I didn't belong to anyone, but she was so strong and I was swallowing water again. She clutched me tighter, our cheeks smashed together. *Give Serafa a taste of his blood—tasty, so tasty—and she will grant you a wish.*

The mermaid let go.

My head pounded and my chest ached, but I forced

myself to swim to the surface once again. Giving Serafa no time to change her mind, I paddled back to shore. Over. It was over. I almost collapsed before I'd reached solid ground. I lifted my head, which felt heavier than usual, and found the boy again.

"Do you know Peter? Is he all right?" I asked hoarsely, sloshing and stumbling back up the bank. The stranger's next arrow was still ready, but it seemed the mermaid had retreated.

"Peter is waitin' for you. Best avoid this place from now on," I heard my hero advise. "It's connected to Mermaid Lagoon."

"I'll remember that next time I'm falling from the sky," I muttered. Before either of us could say anything else, my stomach gave a lurch. I stumbled into the foliage, bent over, and emptied its meager contents onto the ground. Most of it was water.

Once the nausea had subsided, I stayed where I was, panting with my palm pressed hard against a tree. Save for chittering insects and a chorus of birdsong, silence permeated the jungle. Then, from behind, the boy cleared his throat. It was a light in the dark, guiding reason back to me. I faced him again.

Expressionless, the boy shifted his bow to the other shoulder. "Are you ready to 'ead back?" he asked before I could apologize for my revolting display.

I frowned. "Back?"

"Like I said, Peter will be waitin'. Lad is probably getting impatient, since it took me a while to track you. Sometimes the island likes to play games."

It took me several moments to comprehend the island had a mind of its own. "How is this possible?" I breathed.

Kelpies. Mermaids. I'd known Peter was extraordinary, and that magic existed in the world, but I had never imagined anything like this.

The boy with the bow and arrow stopped waiting for an answer. He stepped past me, assumably to lead the way, and he moved as if his bones were made of liquid. I hesitated for an instant, comprehending that this boy could be lying about knowing Peter. But when it became apparent he was about to leave me alone, I decided to risk it.

He talked as we walked. "I was worried the mermaid wouldn't let go, even after I shot 'er," he said casually. "The hunger drives 'em mad, you know. Makes 'em miraculously strong. I've seen mermaids kill crocodiles with the toughest hides you can imagine, I have."

I was so tired that I tripped over a tree root and nearly smacked into a branch. I regained my footing and resisted the urge to scream in frustration. "It sounds as though you admire them," I said through my teeth.

The boy hadn't slowed, forcing me to break into a run to catch up. The jungle was so thick that every step was an effort to navigate vines, roots, or tangles of plants. "Well, mermaids 'ave their uses. For instance, they can grant wishes," he said over his shoulder.

"How interesting," I murmured. He said nothing about the kelpie, and at the moment, I had no desire to speak of it.

I studied the back of the boy's head, a thousand questions crowding in my throat but no strength to voice them. For now, I was only capable of concentrating on my feet. One in front of the other. Never had I missed my own bed so badly.

For minutes or hours—I wasn't sure which—we trudged through the jungle without a word.

The boy broke the silence exactly once. A sound had echoed through the humid air, not a roar or a howl but something between the two. "That's a barghest," he remarked, his voice floating back to me. "You don't want to run into one of those."

I couldn't contain a shudder, and only the fact that he hadn't stopped gave me enough nerve to keep going. "I'll take your word for it," was all I said.

We marched on. I managed to match the boy's pace and follow him through the jungle for at least another two hours without complaint. Eventually, though, I had to stop. The boy noticed straightaway that I'd halted, and this time he did, too. He put his back to a tree and pulled something out of his pocket. An arrowhead, I concluded after a lingering glance. He began sharpening its edges with a small stone.

Following the boy's example, I pressed my spine against a tree. I hadn't been this sore in my entire life. I swallowed a quiet groan, reaching up to rub the back of my neck.

Suddenly, out of the corner of my eye, I noticed something bright and vibrant. Curious, I peered closer. When I realized what it was, a cry escaped me.

My companion pushed off the tree and had an arrow notched in a moment. "You all right?"

That spot of brightness was gone. I was so exhausted that I wasn't certain it had been real. I blinked rapidly, swaying on my feet. Nothing appeared or emerged. I swallowed and started walking again, eager to put this place behind us. "Yes. Sorry. A bit jumpy, is all."

Even as the words left my mouth, I looked behind us.

Because I'd sworn, just for an instant, I'd seen a pair of yellow eyes staring back at me.

CHAPTER 6

My rescuer went by the name of Nose. It seemed cruel, like a mockery of his own, which was admittedly large compared to most people's.

When I asked him what his real name was, Nose shrugged. "Don't remember," he muttered.

Good manners dictated that I shouldn't pry. But I still had so many questions I longed to ask, building within me like steam in a teapot. How had the boy gotten here? How had he met Peter? Even if I were to give in to my curiosity, even if I had the strength to make conversation, I suspected I might not get any answers. There was a wariness about this boy that matched my own. Someone that knew fear and held its hand in the dark.

Thinking this, I decided to spare Nose from my questions and turned my bleary attention to the jungle. Moonlight wriggled through openings in the green chaos above us —we must have been walking longer than I realized—and touched the ground in defiance. Without it, I would not have noticed the clearing we entered.

I also would not have been able to see the boy leaning against a large tree, his arms crossed, grinning at us as though we were returning from a picnic.

"You lot certainly took your time! Got lost, did you?" Peter said by way of greeting. He appraised me as Nose left us to our own devices. Peter raised his hand toward my cheek. "You've got some mud on—"

I slapped it away. "Do *not* touch me."

Unperturbed, he shrugged and looked upward. "Miss Davenport, I'd like you to meet the children of Neverland."

I frowned and followed his gaze toward the treetops. Nothing moved. The only sound was a breeze whispering through the leaves. But that crawling sensation had returned, moving beneath my skin, and I knew we were being watched. "Where are they?" I asked.

As an answer, Peter strode to the center of the tall grass. He halted beneath a slant of moonlight. His shadow appeared, brought to life by the glow. Though it didn't have features, I knew it was looking at me. My spine went rigid. Oblivious, Peter spread his legs, planted his fists, threw back his shoulders. He tipped his head and released a feral sound. Part beast, part boy. I shrank from it. Nothing seemed to happen afterward. Then a creaking sound disturbed the stillness, like ancient hinges that hadn't seen oil in a long time.

Lanterns swayed and flickered, revealing the faces hidden in the leaves. Their countenances were filthy and their bones pronounced. There were at least a dozen of them. The children of Neverland, Peter had called them.

"Where are their parents?" I whispered, forgetting everything I'd just endured at the sight of so many faces peering down.

"They have none," Peter replied, watching me. "Over the years I've found them. Some were hungry, some were alone, some were dying. And I always gave them a choice."

A choice? I thought. It was like a page from a fairy tale book. I imagined it, one of those boys—no, I was startled to see there were several girls amongst the ones peering down —lying on a grimy London street. Carriages rolling by, voices shouting over them, eyes flicking past. Then, like an apparition, Peter appeared. To them he was a lighthouse in the distance, after being tossed and taunted by a storm for so long in one lonely boat. He offered adventure and new lands. He promised life when all they knew was a place that took it. I wondered if Neverland was what they expected.

"Why do they sleep in the trees?" I asked, angling my face away so Peter couldn't see my anger.

"'Twould be foolish to let ourselves get eaten in the middle of the night." He shot upward and vanished into the trees.

"Peter!" I shouted, knowing it was useless.

Someone tugged at my sleeve. Shrieking, I spun to face this latest threat. A boy much taller than Peter stood there, his eyes fixed on my feet. He was a handsome lad, though his dark hair was too long and his fair skin smeared with dirt. He had the broadest shoulders I'd ever seen.

"My name is Housekeeper, miss," he rumbled in a voice deeper than roots traveling through the earth. "There are some empty branches next to mine. I can show you."

My chest heaved with uneven gasps. *Did he say empty branches?* I swallowed and managed to rasp, "I would be most grateful, thank you."

Without another word, Housekeeper went to a particularly large tree across the way and stepped behind it. The murky jungle swallowed him whole. Despite my reluctance to reenter that darkness, I hurried to circle the trunk. The boy had disappeared, but a sound came from above. I glanced toward it and spotted him through the leaves and vines, climbing branches like an enormous monkey.

I started to demand that Housekeeper come back down —I'd never climbed a tree in my life—but something squawked in the distance. No bird outside my window sounded like that, and I envisioned something with a vicious beak and cruel talons. Swallowing my protests, I quickly hauled myself up.

Despite his size, Housekeeper was agile and bold. On numerous occasions he had to wait for me. Most of the lanterns had gone out and the handholds were precarious or difficult to find. I felt the others staring, but I couldn't stare back. There were only leaves and bark and vines everywhere I looked. My clothes clung to me from sweat. Finally the boy stopped, squatting with his back to a trunk. At his feet— bare, I noted, and one of his toenails had been torn off—was a gigantic leaf. I balanced on a branch and my arms trembled with effort.

"Good night," my guide said after an uncertain pause.

I gaped at him. "You mean for me to sleep here? On *this*?"

He just shrugged, and I got the distinct impression I'd insulted him. "Sleep where you like. But I don't expect you'll live to see the morning. And sunrises are quite lovely in Neverland; it would be a shame."

With that, he lifted his brawny arms and climbed out of sight. I knelt there, thinking that I'd made a mistake leaving London. Soft sounds floated through the darkness. Frogs, birdsong, hushed conversations. Someone coughed nearby. I wasn't sure what I was waiting for—the leaf was hardly going to transform into a bed. I exhaled through my nose in a quiet sigh. Still on my hands and knees, I edged forward and hopped experimentally. The branch bobbed a bit, but it seemed safe enough.

After some maneuvering, I tucked myself within the leaf. It had a softness to it that made me think of velvet. My very bones ached, but I couldn't bring myself to fall asleep. One of the boys had started snoring and the sound was comforting in its normality. I listened to it and found myself staring at a lantern Housekeeper must have left alight for my sake, which gently swung back and forth on its handle.

At long last, I was able to truly think about the events of the day.

In spite of my encounters with Peter, part of me hadn't truly believed in magic, creatures, or anything mystical. Now it was undeniable. Everything I knew was being torn apart and tossed into the wind, like someone plucking petals off a flower and letting them go.

I hadn't expected there to be children here, either. How much did they depend on Peter? Would his death affect their survival? What if one of them witnessed it when I killed him? Too many questions, too many possibilities, too many tasks. I buried my fingers in my hair and bit back a sob.

"Wendy."

He spoke quietly, but I still jumped. Peter hovered beside the branch. His expression was serious. It reminded me of the night we met.

Don't be frightened, he'd said.

I'm not, I'd answered.

What a fool I was. That girl hadn't been to Neverland or known there were real monsters in the world. She should have been afraid. She'd wanted adventure, and that's exactly what she'd gotten.

Feeling the sting of more tears, I clenched my jaw. "What do you want, Peter? Why was I shot out of the sky by a cannonball today? Do you know what I've been through?

"Those are very complicated questions, Wendy Davenport. And Nose might've mentioned a mermaid, yes." He held out a pile of clothing. There was a pair of boots atop it.

I accepted with a frown. At first glance, the offering appeared to be multiple shirts and trousers. Mama would be horrified at the sight of me wearing any of it, and imagining her pale dismay gave me a vicious thrill.

"Where did you get these?" I questioned, noting the tears and stains in the material, evidence that I would not be the first to wear them.

"From a boy who no longer needs clothes." Peter's implication was clear, reminding me yet again of the danger all around. I twisted a loose thread between my fingers and refused to meet his gaze.

"Why didn't you come to find me yourself?" I whispered, hating how vulnerable I felt around him. In spite of my efforts, a tear escaped and fled down the curve of my cheek.

Peter tracked its progress with interest, as though it were one of John's insects. "I had other matters to attend to."

"I could have died." Now my voice was tight and hard, like a fist. A moment later, the thread broke. I didn't bother asking where he'd been again; it was obvious Peter had as many secrets as I did, and I was no longer sure I wanted to know them.

He grinned. My fear of the boy returned in a rush. He was a thing that had never—would never—be tamed.

"Fortunately, you didn't," he countered. As though my death would have been nothing more than a momentary disappointment for him. "There's so much more to show you."

"Take me back to London, Peter. Right now." The words spilled out like my mouth was a crack in a teapot. Pain and fear had overtaken any logic or bravery I might have had.

Peter cocked his head in a way that was already becoming familiar. One brow rose in a question. No, a challenge. "What of our bargain? Don't you want the cure for your brother?" he purred.

Fury filled me. I had no more patience for lies and false hope! Just as I was about to burst, the boy's expression changed. He raked his hair back and visibly swallowed a sigh. He opened his mouth, closed it again, then glared at me. "Do you know why swallows build in the eaves of houses?" he demanded.

I blinked. "What? Swallows? Peter, I'm trying to—"

"It is to listen to the stories." He held my gaze for another moment, but he didn't continue. Those lovely eyes of his dropped. I looked down, too, and discovered there was nothing much to see. The fire still crackled below, but it was smaller now, and its light was hardly more than an occasional flicker through all the branches and leaves. The jungle around us was bits of green, moonlight, and darkness.

Why are you telling me this? I was about to say.

Then, all at once, I understood his meaning. Peter was the swallow. But what did that make me, then? The house? The storyteller? One of the stories themselves? Why couldn't Peter just say what he felt without making it into a riddle? Feeling cross, I raised my gaze, every question crowding on my tongue.

But of course the boy was gone.

I slept fitfully. Dreams chased me like they were hounds on the hunt and I was a fox, leaping desperately over fences and through thick woods. Behind my eyelids I saw closing doors, a gloved finger on the mantel, beads of sweat. A fluttering curtain, outstretched arms, houses far below. A wide moon, silvery water, blood all around.

Then there was Peter. We were in my room, everything

soft and night-touched. He stood before me, unafraid and unmoving. The knife was in my hand. I could end it. All it would take was a moment, a single moment. If I was strong enough. "I have to save my brother," I said to Peter.

"I know," he replied.

Our eyes locked and I stepped closer. Placed the tip of my weapon at his throat. Still, he didn't move. I willed myself to draw the knife across that smooth, sun-darkened skin. Part of me even wanted to. Seconds ticked by.

And I awoke.

The world around me was green and utterly foreign. I experienced a tilting sensation of disorientation and panic until the events of yesterday came trickling back. My terror slowly ebbed. I found the courage to peek over the edge of the leaf. Fog hovered above the ground, obscuring every-thing from view. No sign of the lovely sunrise Housekeeper mentioned. But the children were there; I could hear them talking, laughing, working. I must have slept longer than I usually did.

Taking advantage of the mist, I dressed quickly, glad to discard my ruined clothes. My mind worked as I pulled on the clothing Peter had brought the night before. Somehow I needed to fulfill Lady Bainbridge's wishes and, afterward, convince one of the other boys to fly me home. *Before* they realized what had happened, as I very much doubted anyone would be willing if they knew I'd murdered their leader.

Which brought me to another obstacle. *How will you kill him? You don't have the knife anymore,* logic pointed out.

Perhaps it was only a matter of luring Peter to the water and letting the mermaid do it for me...

The smell of food made me realize how ravenous I was. My stomach grumbled while I climbed down the tree.

Fog swirled with my every movement. I headed for the fire crackling in the center of the clearing. It was tended to by a small boy. There were a few others scattered about, but not as many as I'd seen last night. One seemed to be sharpening the end of a stick with a rock. Another was tying knots with a bit of rope. I could feel every last one of them watching me.

A boy I noticed straightaway—his hair stuck out in every direction and was starkly orange—rotated a crisp, dead animal over the flames. The smell of meat permeated the damp air and my mouth watered. I approached. At first glance, I thought the boy's face was spattered with dirt. Upon closer inspection I saw that it was not dirt but freckles that covered his skin.

At the sight of me, he jumped up. "So you're the one Peter can't stop going on about!"

Beaming, he stuck out his free hand. His body hummed with vitality. I hadn't shaken someone's hand in my entire life. I hesitated, torn between what I had been taught and what I wanted. The boy wasn't bothered by this; his smile didn't waver. As I finally took his hand, and he pumped it up and down, I realized the boy was still waiting for my reply.

"Yes, well, I'm sure he's always excited about new arrivals," I mumbled.

"Not just since your arrival, miss. We've had to listen to

him babble about you for *months*." He'd been poking the meat with a knife while he spoke. Apparently it wasn't ready, because the boy turned to me again, still smiling. His cheer was relentless and it started to thaw the icy wall of mistrust I'd built.

An instant later, his words penetrated. Months? Peter had spoken about me for months? I was so surprised, so baffled, that I didn't know what to say. The meat popped and the boy leaped to rotate it. The reprieve allowed me to manage, "What is your name?"

"I'm Freckles," he told me with a hint of pride. Once again, he put his face next to the roasting animal and examined it critically. "Usually Housekeeper is the one who cooks, but he thought it would be good for someone else to know how."

Nose, Housekeeper, Freckles. I frowned. "Do none of you have real names?"

"They are our real names, miss. The ones that are given to us once we've proven ourselves in Neverland. Whoever we were before doesn't matter."

I had never heard of such a thing. Earning a name rather than being given one. Freckles continued to inspect the meat, seeming unaware of the peculiarity of what he was saying. "And how do you prove yourself?" I asked.

The boy didn't answer this time. Instead, he poked at the animal some more. After a moment he nodded to himself, lifted the entire thing off the flames, and jammed the end of the stick into the ground. He put his hands around his mouth and bellowed, *"Food!"*

Suddenly the clearing was chaos. They came from the treetops and the jungle beyond. I tried to count and estimated there to be over twenty. The children snatched at Freckles's animal like vultures over a carcass and scurried off to consume their tiny portions. Grease stained the ground around the stick. Soon there was nothing left but bones.

Freckles brought a bit for me, using a leaf for a plate, before plopping down to enjoy his own portion. His hip brushed against mine, but I didn't move away; I was too busy staring at my food longingly. Steam rose from the meat, a warning that it would still be too hot to touch. This didn't seem to stop any of the others, though, and I wondered whether they had any feeling left in their fingers and tongues.

"Why is no one flying?" I asked in hopes of distracting myself.

Freckles tore into his meal so messily that Mama would have gasped, if she were here. He answered while his mouth was still full, hardly sparing me a glance. "Because that takes a bit 'o magic, it does, which none of us have. None of us besides Peter, that is."

Hearing this, tension coiled in my stomach. *Blast.* There went my hope of one of them flying me back to London. How would I get off this island once Peter was gone?

I prayed another option would present itself. In the meantime, there was nothing left to do but eat. As I carefully took a piece of meat from the shiny leaf I was holding, I sat very still—which was unbelievably easy to do in the trousers Peter had given me—and observed the activity around us.

Some of the children were smiling and boisterous, rough and playful. Others were solemn and silent, guarded and watchful. Voices filled the gloom.

"Strange fog," I heard one of them say. "Island must be in a mood."

Movement drew my gaze to the edge of the clearing, which had been empty moments ago. Someone stood alone, half-hidden, clutching the bark of a tree. It was a girl, though she was difficult to see through the grayness. Tendrils of near-white hair blew into her face but she didn't brush them away. She was so lovely that my heart twinged with envy and longing. Was she one of Peter's children? No. Somehow, I knew she wasn't part of this ragtag band. There was something about her that seemed separate and... wistful.

Then, before my eyes, she faded into nothing.

CHAPTER 7

My heart stuttered in shock.

I stared so intently at that tree, waiting for the girl to reappear, that my eyes stung. She'd been real, I was sure of it. But how could she be there and gone? Had she simply taken a step back? I told myself it was the fog making things seem unnatural. There was no such thing as ghosts.

You're in Neverland now, a voice reminded me. A shiver wracked through my frame.

"Is something wrong?" Freckles asked, sitting to my left. He scrunched his forehead, the picture of concern. The corners of his mouth shone from the meat.

I grappled for something to say. My gaze fell on a boy venturing near the picked-over stick. He was shirtless and so thin that I could see the outline of his ribs. His hair was matted with filth and twigs. "Who is that?" I asked, nodding in his direction.

My new friend looked at the boy, who was squatting and

searching the dirt for scraps. I felt a pang of pity. Freckles did not seem to share the sentiment.

"No one," he answered, his gaze skittering away. His smile had departed, as well. Curious.

"Well, that's nonsense. Everyone is someone."

"Not him. He doesn't have a name. And he'll never get one, either."

I felt a line deepen between my eyebrows. "Why not?"

But Freckles was finished, it seemed. He hopped to his feet and ran to another group. I kept my eyes on the boy with no name. I wasn't the only one who'd noticed him—the other children were throwing small bones, jeering and calling out insults. Nose and Housekeeper didn't participate, I saw, but they did nothing to prevent what was happening. *Don't make a scene,* Mama used to say, over and over.

I was still about to intervene—I couldn't watch needless brutality, no matter how strange the land or how deep my mother's teachings went—when Peter landed in the clearing.

The reaction was instantaneous. As though they'd been given one of Dr. Waghorn's bottles of laudanum, every child stilled. The nameless boy was nowhere to be seen now. Peter strutted like a rooster, his hair glinting in the firelight. A girl giggled. He winked at her and announced, "As you can see, we have a new arrival! Let's make her feel welcome, shall we? To the plains!"

"To the plains!" they chorused. Everyone burst into motion again, climbing tree trunks or submerged into the jungle as if it was water.

Peter approached the place where I still sat. The wispy fog made his eyes and hair darker, his features more celestial. "It's your first day in Neverland. You shouldn't be sitting in the dirt," he said.

I tipped my head back and gazed up at him. "Where should I be sitting, then?"

"Well, Miss Davenport. Might I have your permission to accompany you upwards?" Peter bent into a sweeping bow and flourished his hand through the air, mocking the formality that was all I knew. Somehow, though, a smile tugged at my mouth. I failed to suppress it and Peter grinned back. The tension that had bound us together like a chain started to rust.

Even so, I wasn't ready to trust him. "I can walk," I said, gesturing to the children who were swiftly disappearing.

"It's a long way." Peter's manner was matter-of-fact. "Much farther than you've ever walked in that park of yours."

My gaze narrowed. How long had Peter been following me, exactly? If what Freckles said was true, then it was far longer than I'd been aware. But to what purpose? What could Peter possibly stand to gain from me?

Does it matter? practicality demanded, seeming more vicious than usual. *If all goes well, he'll be dead soon enough.*

At the reminder, nausea trailed my stomach and throat with teasing fingers. Peter was again awaiting my response. As I had yet to find the thought that would enable me to fly, depending on him was the only viable option. I pursed my lips, resenting the uncontainable rush of anticipation going through me. "Very well."

With a cocky smile, Peter moved in a blur. He scooped me up as though I were no more than a spoonful of sugar. This time I was prepared for it, and I arched my neck to watch the sky loom closer. We left darkness and fog behind. It was as though someone had yanked me from a terrible dream and this, the infinite air and distant mountains, was the safe bedroom one opens their eyes to and realizes none of it was real.

I was shocked to see the sun had begun its descent. Splashes of pink and gold made everything seem like we were inside a painting. "How is this possible?" I demanded. "It was just morning."

Peter didn't look away from the horizon as he answered. "Neverland doesn't follow silly rules like time."

Trees gave way to rolling hills. I could see the ocean beyond them, and for the first time, the sight of it didn't drown me in longing. My grip tightened around Peter's neck and the world had never felt so vast, so savage, so beautiful. In the distance, to the left, a thin column of smoke rose to greet the clouds. The children on the ground were running toward it, shrieking and imitating animal calls. Were those *cottages* near the cliff edge? I looked up at Peter, unable to resist. He flashed that grin again, teeth shining in the twilight. One incisor was slightly crooked.

"That's the village," he told me.

We drew nearer and I was able to discern the source of

the smoke—an enormous fire, burning in the center of everything. "Has it always been there?"

"Not always. The islanders are Welsh, English, Dutch, Irish, French, African, and so on. They're mostly descendants of those who came here by shipwreck, marooning, or pure happenstance. Some of them continue traditions from their homelands, but for the most part, the Neverlanders have become their own people now."

A gust of wind blew a strand of hair across my face. I tucked it back, asking hesitantly, "Are they... friendly?"

"Quite. They'll do their best to convince you to stay there."

"Stay? Why?"

"The Neverlanders value children over everything else. And to them, the Neverwood isn't an ideal place for us to live."

There was no chance to react to this; we were close enough to the village that I could make out its inhabitants now. Laughter rang from a pair of dark-skinned women who appeared to be hanging a bedsheet on a clothing line. On the outskirts of the cottages, two towheaded boys scuffled in the dirt.

A young girl with an armful of firewood spotted us. Beaming, she dropped her burden and raised her voice to alert the others. I couldn't make out the words, but one was unmistakable, the syllables high and trembling with joy. *Peter!*

The islanders gathered, smiles crinkling their eyes. We landed in front of them like actors appearing on a stage. I slid out of Peter's grasp. Once I was firmly standing on my own, he moved to my side. The part of me that existed in empty rooms and silent moments missed the sensation of his skin pressed to mine. In hopes of banishing it completely, I lifted my chin and took another step away from him.

Peter was oblivious. He walked toward a wizened man who clutched a torch in both of his hands, using it as a cane, of sorts. But it was the flame I noticed most, because it was like none I had ever seen before, with colors of the sea instead of yellow and red. It had to be magic.

Still deep in conversation, Peter gestured to me. The Neverlanders' expressions continued to be kind and welcoming. I wasn't sure how to properly greet them—curtsies and handshakes struck me as out of place here—so I gave an inane wave. Nearly all of them waved back.

After another minute, Peter called my name. Trying to hide how nervous I felt, I closed the distance between us. Peter introduced the Torch Bearer, which was apparently what the villagers called their leader, the gray-haired man who carried those beautiful flames. Then the other children arrived, and the village was chaotic with movement and sound and bodies. There was an air of familiarity between the two groups that spoke of many warm nights together. A man clapped Nose on the back and the girl who'd dropped the firewood clasped one of Peter's children to her.

I stayed where I was, uncertain what to do or how to act, my shirt flapping forlornly in the wind. A young girl had dragged Peter away. I couldn't see her face, but she gestured with enthusiasm as she spoke. Peter nodded now and then, his expression courteous and affectionate. He'd never looked at me that way before. A stab of jealousy made me grimace. I looked away and found myself staring into a pair of wide hazel eyes.

"Please join us," a woman said in French.

"Thank you," I replied in the same tongue, and I was immediately rewarded with a huge smile. Despite the lack of interest I'd always shown, my governess had made certain I possessed a working knowledge of French. For the first time since meeting Miss Parker, that sallow-faced creature with a fondness for rulers and withholding meals, I was grateful to her.

As if we'd known each other for years, the woman tucked my hand into the crook of her arm and led me away. Near the large fire, which had been getting taller and fiercer with every passing minute, a gathering of musicians started to play. I spotted a drum, a fiddle, a tambourine. The flames crackled in frustration as they grappled at the sky again and again. There were some islanders seated around it—they were far enough away that the heat wouldn't be uncomfortable. Amongst them, piles of fruit rested on pieces of wood.

Every single person I saw had a shadow firmly attached at the feet.

"Hello, Bashira," the woman said, stopping when we reached a girl who looked to be my age. "This is Wendy. She is Peter's guest."

Startling me, the girl replied in English. "Hello, Élise. It's nice to meet you, Wendy. Would you like to sit with me?"

Flashing a dimpled smile, the girl patted the grass beside

her. Her hair cascaded down her back in a thick, dark curtain, and she wore a simple gown the color of the sky. I glanced at Élise, a question in my eyes. Would she be offended if I left her? The woman gave my arm a squeeze that seemed to say, *It is your choice.*

"Thank you," I said to Bashira with a tentative smile. Someone called Élise's name. She nodded at us both and moved away. I settled onto the ground, noting how much easier it was to move about in trousers rather than cumbersome skirts. After a moment of hesitation, I crossed my legs. I'd never sat like this before, and something about it felt indecent.

"I'm so glad Peter brought you here, since I've decided we should be friends," Bashira informed me.

I returned her smile. Until that moment, I hadn't realized how much I missed Liza, and this girl's warm manner reminded me of her. "I would like that. Perhaps you can show me more of the island before I go home."

She frowned and tilted her head. "Home?"

"Back to London," I clarified.

Bashira seemed mystified, as though returning was a notion that had never occurred to her before. "But why?"

"Because I must..." I frowned. The reason was there in my mind, just out of reach. The girl watched me with obvious concern while I dug my fingers into the dirt and struggled to remember, desperate for the piece that I knew was vital. Then, suddenly, it clicked back into place. As though someone had been holding it away and playing a vicious game. "My brother. I must return to my brother."

I breathed hard, so relieved I couldn't say anything else. The girl could see I was shaken by the momentary lapse of memory and put her hand over mine. "Don't worry. It's easy to forget things here."

She meant to comfort, but if anything, her words only served to agitate me further. Michael's life depended upon whatever happened on this island. I couldn't forget him again, not even for a moment.

Desperate to change the subject, I searched for the man holding that remarkable torch. "I've never seen flames such as those," I said.

Bashira followed my gaze and smiled proudly. "It was a gift from the island's original inhabitants," she told me, answering the unspoken question. "The one who cares for it is also the one who leads us, for however long they decide to live."

"'Decide to live?'" I echoed with a frown. "What do you mean?"

"The island is generous. Anyone who walks upon it receives its gift of magic. Immortality," Bashira clarified when I probably looked as mystified as I felt.

Already I had dozens more questions I longed to ask her. Only years of my mother's and governess's teachings kept me from asking every single one. There would be time enough for that, I told myself firmly. "I must say, your English is flawless," I said after a brief struggle.

The girl beamed at my compliment and twisted to retrieve some fruit from the makeshift tray. Turning back, she presented it to me. It was a color I had never seen before, something that made me imagine the depths of ocean no one but mermaids and fish had been to. "You've come on a special night, did you know?" she asked.

As I started to answer, her glance flicked to something behind me. A moment later, a familiar scent filled the air—boy and wind and earth. Once again, I had trouble recalling whatever I'd been about to say. Peter flopped down beside me, exclaiming, "Bunch of cheats, the entire lot. Don't know who taught them that."

With a knowing look that went from me to him, Bashira got to her feet. "I should visit my grandmother. She's too old to join us and I do not want her to think we have forgotten her."

I didn't want to be alone with Peter, to further know the person I would be killing. "No, please, stay and—"

She had already drifted away. Peter made a joke I didn't hear, shifting so that we sat even closer. I felt unexpectedly nervous and watched children frolic around the flames. "They speak well of you here. However did you manage to fool so many people?" I asked airily, rotating the fruit in my fingers.

Peter laughed, and I decided it was a beautiful sound. I would rather die than admit that to him, though. I couldn't help noticing how he put his entire body into it, as though Peter felt it in every part of himself, down to the tiniest toe. His head tipped back and that lovely hair rippled like a lion's mane.

I was so busy admiring it that at first I didn't see Peter's shadow, which stretched toward me with incorporeal hands.

At the very last moment, just as they were about to wrap around my throat, I realized what was happening and scrambled to my feet. The fruit fell from my grasp. Peter's laughter died.

"None of that," he chided, his face transforming into a surprising scowl. The shadow shriveled like a dog tucking a tail between its legs.

I stood a safe distance away and gasped for breath. "Why... why does your shadow loathe me so much, Peter?"

He shrugged and patted the ground next to him, just as Bashira had done. "No idea. Does it matter?"

Somehow, I knew it mattered more than anything else between us. Neither of us were about to admit it, of course; that required trust and friendship and I had no idea what Peter was to me.

But I wanted to find out.

Slowly, against my better judgment, I returned to his side. No one seemed to have noticed what almost transpired, and I concentrated on the activities in front of us again, sitting stiffer than before. My hands rested against my knees in white fists. Peter didn't attempt conversation, and we allowed the shrieks of the children and the hiss of the flames to fill our silence. After a time, one of the islanders caught my eye. Her clothing was thin and worn, revealing the jutting bones beneath. My instincts told me her appearance was deceiving, but I wasn't certain why. It was something about the way she held herself, I thought.

"That girl," I said suddenly. "The one you were talking to

earlier. She's in the middle of everything. They all move around her and look at her and watch her."

He followed my gaze. "Her name is Lillian—she prefers Lily, these days—and I believe she'll lead these people one day."

The girl couldn't be more than fifteen or sixteen. Her brown hair ended at her shoulders in ragged, sun-touch wisps. She was thin, her body more gangly than willowy, as if Lily hadn't finished growing into it yet. But she was already quite tall, and that seemed unlikely.

She looked ordinary enough, I thought, and she wore no crown or fine clothing to make herself stand out.

"Is it her birthright?" I questioned, intrigued in spite of myself.

"No. That's not how things are done in Neverland. Here, you claim your power." Peter shook hair out of his eyes. The honeyed strands caught the fading sun. "The islanders watch their children grow. They train the ones that possess strength or cunning. Then, once the Torch Bearer dies, those contenders must battle each other until a victor emerges."

My eyes widened. "To the death?"

"To first blood. Like I said, they value children here. They don't cast them aside as it's done in London."

Though Peter's expression remained impassive, his shadow betrayed him—it was quivering with suppressed rage. For the first time, I saw that Peter felt the pain of his mother's abandonment. He always wore a mask of indifference, and a glimpse of the face beneath it was startling. "As you were?" I dared to say, so quietly no one but him could possibly hear it.

Peter said nothing. He kept his attention on Lily, and I peeled my eyes away to watch her, as well. Eventually she left the fire to stand amongst her friends.

The beat of the drum changed, becoming slower and heavier. Two figures moved to stand in front of the fire. A boy just on the cusp of being a man and a girl with seemingly endless limbs. They faced each other. They began to move as though there was something connecting their bodies, string or air or something infinitely more significant. The dancers didn't touch, but there was an intensity in their eyes that was just as powerful as a brush of the hand or lips. I felt as if I were intruding on something intimate and private. My cheeks flushed and I forgot about everything else besides them.

Peter leaned over and his breath tickled me. It smelled of sugar and every sweet thing. "This is a mating dance. Every month, they are given the opportunity to choose."

"It makes me want to laugh and cry all at once," I murmured without looking away. Silence met this. When I glanced at Peter, wondering if he'd heard, he was watching me instead of the besotted pair. Abashed, I ducked my head. "But that doesn't make much sense, I suppose."

He nudged his shoulder against mine. Like magic, the fruit I had dropped was suddenly in his hand. He held it out and replied, "The best things never make sense."

A shock went through our hands as I took it from him. Peter's eyes were the lightest of blues today, like bright parts of sky peeking between fluffy clouds. Clutching the fruit—my nails punctured the skin and cool juice spurted down my wrist—I made myself blink and pretend to be absorbed by the dancers again. My stomach reminded me that I hadn't eaten since that morning, so I raised the piece of fruit and took a small, timid bite. The flavor was wonderful and immediate.

"It tastes like a candy cane!" I exclaimed. Images from my childhood returned in a rush: roaring fires, beautifully-wrapped gifts, green trees.

Peter grinned. "I wondered what you would say. For me, it tastes like the spice cakes I used to steal from one of my favorite street vendors. It's different for everyone."

"Truly? Well, I'll never eat anything else for as long as I live!"

He laughed again and I found myself smiling, too. Peter's manner was so open and friendly; the space between us no longer felt awkward but amiable. I wanted to take advantage of it and ask him about the silver-haired girl I'd seen vanish. Whether there was such a thing as ghosts in Neverland.

Instead I heard myself swallow and say, "I spoke to Freckles. He said... he said that you've been talking about me for months. Strange, since we only met days ago."

I waited for Peter to fly away or completely ignore me, as he usually did when I said something he didn't want to answer. "I took an interest in you last spring," he admitted.

The delicious fruit stopped in my throat and I coughed. "But why?"

Peter plucked a blade of grass from the earth and began

tearing it into pieces. Without looking at me he said, "You left your window open one night. I heard you telling a story to your brother and I stopped to listen. Londoners put so much importance on houses and marriages and clothes. But none of that matters—the important thing is what you do with your life, not how you look going about it."

What a strange and freeing notion, I thought. Even in my daydreams, I'd never pictured a life that didn't include worrying about the rules of propriety or whether my gown was in fashion. It felt as though my mother's voice had always been in my head, controlling me even when she wasn't there. *Fix your hair. Adjust your skirt. Mind your posture. Smile at that gentleman.* But at Peter's words, the idea that none of it truly mattered, she withdrew. The quiet, however brief, was blissful. My eyes fluttered shut.

I felt something inside me shift, like a dam struggling against a great pressure.

At that same moment, something *roared*. Birds took flight in a burst of panic, wings beating at the air like a laundress on a sheet. The dancers froze. I tensed, prepared to run, and the fruit hit the ground a second time. It rolled away as the islanders dove for weapons. We all waited, but nothing appeared. The grass around us stirred in a breeze, making a sound that was strangely soothing.

When I turned back to Peter, he was looking at me with a speculative twist to his lips. I glanced toward the plains again, where I could still feel the fading echoes of whatever creature had called out. "What *was* that?"

But all he said was, "I think Neverland may change you as much as you change Neverland."

Just like we had in my dream, Peter and I stared at each other. *You have to kill this boy,* my heart warned. But why hadn't I tried again? Why did I keep putting off the inevitable? "Your island only has a week with me," I reminded him, my voice tight. "What can change in a matter of a few days?"

"Everything."

He spoke so certainly that it had the effect of a wall appearing in my path, halting all momentum. I could only stare. Then, saving me from fumbling for a response, Peter did a little hop and presented his hand. His meaning was clear. They weren't doing the mating part anymore, and the children had rejoined the fray. Dancing was one activity from my old life I'd actually enjoyed. There was no harm in it, was there?

I would've liked to tell myself that it was an impulse, reaching out, accepting his silent invitation, but it was every bit a decision as it was opening my window that first night. Our fingers curved into each other and my skin prickled with awareness. The sensation felt like more than attraction. I turned my head and spotted Lily. The lovely girl stood in the center of it all, unmoving, glaring at me so blatantly that it felt as though I were about to face her in the bloody battle Peter had spoken of. Did she sense the intent in my heart?

"I should return to Bashira," I stammered, pulling away from him.

"She's there." Peter aimed his chin. He spun me around

and I caught a glimpse of my new friend as though she were the flash in a camera. Then I was facing Peter's chest again and there was no one but him.

"Tell me the names of the other children," I said desperately.

We continued our odd waltz. Peter didn't seem to mind the change in topic. "You've met Nose," he began, nodding at the boy restringing his bow in the grass. "He's the oldest and quietest. I found him dying of fever in an alley. He's got a knack for walking through the Neverwood without making a sound and shooting an arrow into a creature far away.

"That's Housekeeper, of course," Peter continued, and I followed his gaze. Housekeeper towered over even the tallest islander, so broad-shouldered that he could probably seat both my brothers upon them. "One day I was observing the gang he was part of, and he fought the other lads to save a lady. They disowned him and I came forward. He's a big fellow, but he's always fussing and clucking.

"There's Tootles." This one sat on his own, legs tucked against him, watching the gathering with a glazed expression. "He's been in Neverland the longest, besides me. I took him from an orphanage. He's always been a bit mad—you won't get much sense out of him, but he's saved my life more than once. Seems to know when things are going to happen before they do. He predicted Lily's triumph, you know.

"Across the way is Nibs." The girl had a scar along her cheek and was so slight I worried one strong gust of wind would carry her into the mountains. "I stumbled upon her while she was on the run for stealing a loaf of bread. She's got the quickest fingers I've ever seen and she's smarter than she lets on.

"Then we have Slightly." Peter directed my attention to a towheaded child hardly more than a toddler. He had attached himself to the women. His cheeks were round and dimpled as he smiled shyly at the one fussing with his hair. "He's the youngest of us. I discovered him wandering the streets, crying out for his mother. It was clear he'd been on his own quite a while. Though he came with me willingly enough, he's always telling us that she'll come looking for him. He clings to his memories more than anyone else on the island."

With that, it seemed Peter was finished. There were more children he hadn't spoken of, which meant these were probably his favorites. It seemed there was some truth to the rumors in London, but as always, they'd become blurred and distorted—Peter *was* responsible for disappearances, but there'd been nothing malicious in his actions. The parties had gone of their own volition.

I observed each child thoughtfully. They all emanated wariness in the lines of their faces and how they moved, despite all the time they'd spent in this supposed paradise. Peter had painted this place on a canvas of wonder and enchantment, but it had only taken me a lingering look to learn the pretty strokes of his brush disguised much, much more.

Suddenly a familiar, urgent need gripped me and interrupted all thought. I stopped, trying to find the proper phrasing. "Peter, where do the women of the village... that is to say, is there a place they go to..."

Understanding tilted the corners of his mouth upward. He stepped away to let me pass. "I'm afraid you'll have to squat in the grass like the rest of us, Miss Davenport. I did promise you an adventure, didn't I?"

I huffed. There was a copse of trees not far off, and I marched toward it. Merriment rang in Peter's voice as he shouted something unseemly about the many uses of leaves. No one else paid any mind. I hurried into the shadows and looked for the thickest tree trunk to hide behind. A few moments later, I discovered yet another reason to be grateful for trousers.

I'd hardly buttoned them back up when large hands clamped around my shoulders and yanked me back. I screamed and lost my balance, falling against a barrel-shaped chest. The back of my knuckles met with the stubble of someone's jaw. A hoarse voice cursed in my ear before I was pinned.

"What is this?" I demanded, squirming. The man smelled of hot sweat and oily skin. "Unhand me or I'll scream again!"

"Now, none of that, miss. We mean you no 'arm." In a single, swift motion, my captor clamped a stained handkerchief over my face. Its scent was cloying and unnatural. Maybe some part of me had thought this was a joke orchestrated by the other children, but now I wrenched back and forth in his grasp more violently, trying to cry for help. Any sound I made was smothered. Only a few seconds ticked by when the trees tipped and the nearby drum became a slow, uneven sound. My bones melted and I swayed, now trying to fight against the effects of whatever drug he'd put on the handkerchief. The man took advantage of this; he grabbed my waist and hauled my entire body over his shoulder.

As he carried me away from Peter and the islanders, I caught sight of those yellow eyes again amongst the trees. They were like two candles at the end of a dark hallway.

"Do you see them?" I attempted to ask. Gibberish was all that escaped. Some drool slid out of my mouth, as well. A rumbling went through my ear, but I couldn't make out the man's answer. It didn't matter, anyway.

I had already succumbed to the hallucinations.

CHAPTER 8

THE TREES WERE SPEAKING to me.

They had strange voices, the likes of which I had never heard before. Creaks and groans that made me think of settling walls in a new house, restless spirits during the night, a ship holding ground against a storm. Their words did not penetrate my ears. Rather, they eased through my mind like moonlight creeping across the floor. *Man... there's a man... does not belong... stole the girl... running, running...*

I wanted to tell them to intervene, grow branches so long and low to the ground that he would have nowhere to go. But my tongue was a slug, slimy and slow. All I could do was allow the man to carry me away and listen to his feet tramp through the underbrush. His footsteps were like earthquakes.

No, those weren't his footsteps. Groggily I realized that it had begun to storm; it was thunder making the island shake. The moon had been shoved to the back of space like a child in a crowd. Neverland had turned to gray and rain pattered on my skin. I flopped against the stranger's back—my face and arms repeatedly collided with the coarse, rank material of his shirt—and moaned.

I had no sense of time. Leaves blurred past and they were all I could see, when my eyes were open at all. They were too dizzying, changing from green to black to blue. Vines were living things with aspirations and roots were animated creatures with intentions. I could still hear the trees, just beneath the fury of the sky. Attempting to recognize the exact words made my head pound, so all I could do was endure the aftermath of whatever chemical the man had smashed against my face.

Then, quite suddenly, the ground slanted and came up to meet me. I felt a solid object at my back and, an instant later, a face appeared in my line of vision. The man was made entirely of harsh edges and peppery whiskers. His scowl seemed as though it had been carved, a statue transformed to flesh. There was something peeking out beneath his collar, a spot of color that didn't belong. A tattoo. I would've expected a woman or a remnant of sailing to be his choice of permanent decoration. Instead, a spiderweb peered up from his skin.

As I gaped, the man said something that held a reassuring note in it. Immediately after, he straightened and walked away, down the beach I was just noticing. It took me quite some time to understand that the man had sat me by a tree and left to fetch a dinghy—the small boat was moored close enough that I could see him straining to push it to the restless water. I rested there, slipping in and out of consciousness. Some faraway part of me knew I should use this chance, but it felt like I no longer had a body.

The wind strengthened. It blew hair across my face and blinded me. I blinked again and again, powerless against even this. Just as I was about to scream, the strands of hair parted and I could see again. A face loomed before me. I cringed, thinking it was the whiskered man, and raised my gaze.

The silver-haired girl knelt in the sand.

Her colorless eyes were frantic. *This is no ghost*, I thought faintly. She looked more real than anything I'd ever encountered, more real than the blue diamond I'd relinquished in Mr. Brooks's shop, or the candle wax dripping off the table in Mama's bedroom, or the beads of sweat collecting on Michael's white forehead.

But there was something strange about her skin, I thought. Something I couldn't define...

"...you step onto that ship, you won't return," she was whispering. I made a valiant effort to hear the words clearly and comprehend them. Her hands hovered around my face, not completely touching, but I imagined it would be slight as a feather trailing over skin. She bent so our faces were level. "I see that you understand. *Save yourself*, Wendy."

The girl glanced over her shoulder and stiffened. Once again, she became vapor and memory before my eyes. The man was coming up the slope, his mouth puckered in agitation. He was muttering to himself; his lips formed Peter's name.

As if I were a ragdoll or an invalid, he picked me up in the crooks of his arms. I protested, mewling like a newborn kitten. My head lolled painfully to the right, giving me a perfect view of the storm above us. The man hurried to the dinghy and gently lowered me into it. Lightning streaked through the roiling clouds. He was going to risk it, I realized dimly. He was more frightened of the boy who could fly than electrocution.

Soon after thinking this, I lost myself again. All I knew was the violent rocking and the volatile rain. On several occasions the man cursed. I saw him fumble with an oar and nearly lose it. It drew my attention to his arm, which was covered in birds. They fluttered their wings and blinked at me with beady eyes. I wasn't sure whether I was dreaming or not. A day or a second later, a sea monster rose over us. Rivulets of water ran down its heaving sides. *No, not a monster,* I thought. *A ship.*

This was what the girl had been trying to warn me about —whatever waited for me inside those wooden walls would be my undoing. For a wild moment I considered using whatever strength I had left to roll myself out of the boat and into the sea. But the hungry, frothing waves would consume me, and I still had so much living to do. Resigned, I closed my eyes again and waited. Spotting the tiny boat, men began to shout. There was much bustle and commotion as they brought us up to the deck. I was no more than a sack of potatoes, being transferred from sailor's man's arms to another.

Their main concern was the storm, however—it was relentless. The ship became slick and treacherous. I listened to the crew bellow about ropes and sails as I was rushed through the chaos. Then there came the sound of a door slamming and darkness suddenly enveloped us.

Now that there was some semblance of silence, I could hear the man again. He was disgruntled, muttering swear words I'd never heard before. Another door soon whined on its hinges, and in whatever room we'd entered, I was unceremoniously dropped onto a bed.

With that, the man left. I was alone in this place with just the rain lashing against the windows for company. My limbs wouldn't move, but I was in a state of numbness, unable to try or care. All that mattered was the nausea shuddering through me like thunder.

Even more time passed. I drifted in and out of awareness like the eternal war of night succumbing to day and back again. At some point, the storm finally abated, leaving a dismal sky in its wake. My mind felt like a child just learning how to walk, pushing itself up on wobbly legs. I blinked at the ceiling above me. And I thought, *I'm alive.*

The skin around my nose and mouth burned. I was also certain that I was going to vomit. But I was alive—for now, that was all the encouragement I needed. Slowly, I took stock of my surroundings. A cautious glance made it obvious I was in the captain's quarters. I'd never been on a ship before, but I had read enough books to know. There was the great bed where I rested, a dressing table, shelves, cabinets, and a desk. The chair before it was mammoth and ornate.

I'd turned my head on the pillow to look at the room, which led me to notice a scent clinging to the sheets.

Though there was nothing repugnant about it, they undeniably belonged to a man. Reason began to ebb back, and with it came heart-pounding fear. Who did this ship belong to? Why had I been taken? Was Peter searching for me?

Just as I was about to scramble from the bed, the door opened. A slender form stepped inside and saw me. "Oh, gracious," the man said, bowing elegantly. "Hello, there. Strange to see you with your eyes open. I've been checking on you throughout the night. My name is Mr. Starkey, the ship quartermaster. I see the chloroform is finally wearing off."

I rose too quickly and swore, using one of the new words I'd learned. I pressed a hand to my face and sank down. "Why... why am I..."

Mr. Starkey smiled serenely. He tucked his hands behind his back. "Don't worry, the effects aren't permanent and Mr. Jukes didn't give you much. At least he was instructed not to, the lout. You'll feel like yourself again in a bit."

The light streaming through the glass was as withered and pale as an old woman, but I was still able to study this stranger. He was mild-mannered and normal in appearance —nothing striking or memorable. It would've been easy to believe he was about to give me a history lesson or test my French. Still, there was something about him that made the tiny hairs on the back of my neck stand on end. I sat on my own hands to hide their trembling and forced myself to speak in calm, measured tones. "If you think to hold me for ransom, I should tell you now that my family has nothing."

The man laughed at this, as though I'd told a grand joke.

He shook his head. "I'll inform the captain you're awake. Ransom," I heard him repeat, almost merrily, just before closing the door. It clicked as he locked it, and the sound left no room for doubt that I was a prisoner here. But *why*? What could I possibly have that they wanted?

Images were returning to me now, fragmented and strange, similar to the sensation when one opens their eyes in the morning and tries to recall a dream. I remembered talking trees, a girl with eyes like stars, a great sea serpent. *Save yourself, Wendy,* the girl had urged. Did that mean there would be no rescue from Peter?

Panic took a step closer and I felt its hot breath on my skin. I clutched the sheets and concentrated on my own breathing. Right. Well, if no one was coming, I couldn't sit here a moment longer. First I had to search the room and see if there was anything that could be used to defend myself. I would worry about how to escape later.

Having this to focus on helped as my legs rebelled at standing. I used the bed for support as I walked to the desk. The drawers slid open without resistance; most of them held nothing but documents and maps. There were no pens or quills. I gritted my teeth and continued to explore. At the window, I paused again.

Through the glass, I could see there was a second ship. It was impossible to make out the name along its side. Beyond that, the darkened shape of Neverland loomed. From this vantage point its outline looked strange, like someone on their hands and knees. Whether they were praying or begging for mercy, I couldn't be certain. Maybe both.

"That one belongs to my financer. You won't see him, though; Mr. Ashdown never leaves his cabin."

The voice came from behind. I turned so swiftly pain shot through my neck.

It was not Mr. Starkey this time. The stranger standing in the doorway was not so threatening. Instead he was... delicate. Lashes long and black, just like his hair, which curled over the back of his neck. His nose was narrow and his cheekbones high. There was a tiny mole just above his lip. His body was a straight line, even his hips, but he carried himself well. There was a scabbard hanging from his waist and it held a curved sword.

I realized I was gawking. Flushing, I brought my gaze back to his. The man's eyes were gray, I noted. Like furious stormclouds or aged steel. There was something distinctly familiar about him, as though we had met before.

This was the captain?

Like the other man had moments before, he bowed courteously. It was so at odds from what I'd been expecting that I could only stare. "Good evening, Miss Davenport," the captain said, seeming unaffected by my behavior. "Welcome aboard the *Jolly Roger*."

I heard nothing but my name. I gripped the sill tighter and rasped, "How do you know who I am?"

He entered slowly, closing the door behind him. He took exactly four steps—I tensed more and more with each one—and halted beside the closest bedpost, leaning his hip against it. His manner was relaxed and cordial, but I didn't miss the fact that he kept himself between me and the corridor.

As I tilted my face up, the captain's brow furrowed; he must've just noticed what the chloroform had done to me. "First, I would like to apologize for the manner in which my men brought you here," he said. "It's not how I would've preferred to do so, but I weighed every outcome, and this seemed the most efficient way."

Again, I was at a loss. I'd anticipated violence. Blood and bruises, demands and disparagements. Not this charismatic individual speaking to me as though I'd invited him to take tea in the parlor.

"You don't speak like I imagined a pirate would," I managed, hoping he took my glance around the room as avoidance. But my captors had done a thorough job of ensuring I would be helpless—there was absolutely nothing I could use to defend myself.

"A pirate?" the captain repeated, raising his brows. "What tales has Peter been telling you?"

Apparently, none. He'd made no mention of anyone else on the island besides islanders and children. *More secrets*, I thought. I wasn't sure how much to reveal about the nature of my journey to this man; I refused to give him anything to use against me. My only reply was, "Only a pirate would shoot cannonballs at two people in the sky."

I'd seen the cannons on deck. It didn't require much intelligence to understand what had happened upon the day of my arrival. The only thing I didn't know was why these men were after Peter.

The man in front of me winced, as if I'd injured him with my words. "I owe you an apology for that, as well. Those shots came from Mr. Ashdown's men, I'm afraid. Peter has killed members of their crew and there's bad blood between them. They've now been made aware that any repeat of the incident will land them in the brig. I assure you that my intentions are honorable, Miss Davenport."

"You know Peter?"

He pursed his lips and nodded. Ignoring the way I stiffened, the young captain fully came around the bed and pulled the huge chair out for me. I remained where I was. He settled on the edge of the mattress and folded his hands between his knees. "Right. No time to waste. I'm going to tell you everything, Miss Davenport. All I ask is that you trust me."

At this, I snorted, the most unladylike thing I'd ever done. Well, besides the things I'd done with Peter. Despite its volatile nature, being in Neverland had caused something inside me to bloom, like a flower long-held in winter's frosty grip finally opening to sunlight. "That's *all you ask*? Trust isn't given upon acquaintance, like a name or a handshake."

"What made you trust Peter, then?" the captain questioned. There was nothing confrontational in his voice; he truly wanted to know.

Sincerity was hard to deny. Maybe that's why the truth came from my lips. "Whatever gave you the impression that I do?"

Now he studied me anew, as though I'd surprised him. His steely eyes were fathomless as they bored into mine. We were so still I could hear waves lapping at the ship and men shouting on the deck.

"I was born into a family of privilege," the captain told me abruptly. He spoke in a rush, as though he wanted to be finished with what he'd just begun. "My parents valued reputation over everything else. Even land and titles, though we have plenty of those, as well. To this day, we are considered one of the finest families in London. Which is why, when my uncle confided to me that my mother had hidden an... indiscretion over two decades before, I could hardly believe it. He was worried the secret would come to light. That it would bring us ruin and destroy everything we'd built. He wanted my assistance in destroying the evidence, not just burying it."

The story had a certain note in it, like a song I'd heard before. Questions were piling in the center of my brain, climbing and clicking like a horde of beetles had found their way inside and were building a nest. Suddenly I realized who he reminded me of. "It can't be," I whispered.

"I searched my soul," the captain continued. His voice was distant, as though he were back in London, making the choice between family and decency all over again. "It didn't seem right that a sibling should pay for Mother's mistake. So I secretly conducted my own investigation. It took me months to search all the orphanages in London. But eventually, I found him. The child my mother had hidden and abandoned."

I shook my head. "You don't mean..."

The captain focused on my face again. This time, his eyes

didn't waver. "They brought him to me and I knew he was the one when I saw a familiar mark on his jaw. Since my mother left no note all those years ago, they'd chosen a name for him. He was called Peter."

Captain Bainbridge shares his mother's flair for storytelling, I thought dimly.

I didn't remember sitting in the chair, but then it was solid beneath me. Two boys. Two sons. The thought went around and around in my head, like the horses I'd watched race at the track once. Captain Bainbridge waited patiently.

After a few minutes I raised my gaze and demanded, "How is it I've never heard of you before?"

And do you know what your mother asked me to do? I added silently, uncertain how much I should reveal.

There was another storm outside and wind slapped at the windows. *Let me in*, it seemed to say.

A wry smile curved the captain's lips as he answered, "When I was twelve, Mama caught me in the garden with the neighbor's boy. It wouldn't do to have a son like me about, tarnishing that precious Bainbridge name and reputation, would it? So I was sent away to school and eventually forgotten about. I returned years later, fully grown, and Uncle Bertram immediately enlisted my help in finding Peter. I think it was a way to make sure that I would stay occupied and quiet."

The neighbor's boy. Of course I'd heard of such things,

but I'd been so sheltered that I had never encountered it before. I cleared my throat and fumbled for a response. "You like... men?"

"I like people, Miss Davenport," Captain Bainbridge corrected. The ship swayed. "Individuals who are kind and intelligent. What body they happen to possess makes no difference to me."

His frankness was disconcerting and refreshing all at once. It made me realize that, at some point during our conversation, I'd lost my fear of this man. That wouldn't do—he'd still taken me against my will and not divulged the reason why.

"I see," I said faintly, recalling my earlier efforts to find a weapon. I noticed the sword again, glinting within reach. My insides quivered with apprehension. Did I dare?

"Might I conclude my story?" Captain Bainbridge asked politely. I nodded and he went on, "Seeing no other alternative, I rented a room above a tavern and kept Peter there. He was bright and curious. I showed him how to read and write. How to speak properly. I also taught him how to use a sword. And the boy began to trust me. Many peaceful months passed. I must've become too compliant in our attempts to find Peter, however, because my uncle discovered the rented room. One day, while I was out, Bertram arrived and tried to kill him. By the time I returned, the place was in shambles, Bertram was injured, and my brother was gone. Thinking that I had utterly betrayed him, as it turns out. When I found him again, I tried to explain. I offered to take him home, along with the other children he's brought here. But the encounter ended violently."

This still bothered him—it was obvious in the way he stared out the window, flashes of light highlighting the frown playing about his mouth. I watched the captain for a moment, searching for Peter in his features. There was nothing definitive, but he was there nonetheless. Perhaps that was why I felt drawn to him.

"How on earth did you find Peter again?" I asked when the silence became too long.

The captain seemed to shake himself and return to the present. "I was only able because Peter wanted me to," he replied. "Despite his absence, I kept that room above the tavern. I went there once a week to see if he'd come back. He never did, but a year later I opened the door to discover something on the floor. A map. Though it wasn't marked by a note or a symbol, this island was the only place Peter could be, considering Neverland doesn't exist on any other map I've seen. I immediately started preparations for the journey, making it a point to secure funds that weren't from my family."

The mention of family made me consider, once again, whether or not I should tell the captain his uncle wasn't the only one seeking Peter's death—that his own mother was making efforts, as well. But that would reveal my involvement, and I wasn't sure how that would affect my present circumstances. Best to wait and assess, I decided. "Did you ever tell Peter the truth about his mother? About who you really are?"

At this, Captain Bainbridge hesitated. He turned back to the window, as though Peter might be hovering there, listening to our conversation with malice in his eyes. "I told him that we were brothers, yes. But he believes our mother is dead and we have no other family in the world."

"Why would you lie about that?"

"What good would it do for him to know?" the man countered, clenching his hands tighter. The skin over his knuckles whitened. "He'd only long for a mother who abandoned him and an uncle who wants him dead."

The revelation planted a seed of compassion in my chest, and I fell silent. Yes, Peter was frightening and thoughtless, at times. There was so much about him and his world that I didn't understand. But no child should feel unwanted. Whatever their flaws, my parents had given me a sense of belonging. All my life I'd had a place, a part. What did it do to a person, I wondered, to be kept from that?

"Forgive me," Peter's brother said abruptly. He stood from the bed to bow. "We've yet to make a proper introduction. I'm James Bainbridge. How do you do?"

"Wendy Davenport. But you already knew that, somehow." The words were automatic, distracted; all my focus was on the sword at his hip, which was so close now I could see a scratch on the handle. The possibility of escape made my control unravel like a runaway spool of thread. I wanted off this ship. I wanted away from this island. I wanted to fly back to the safe world I knew.

Before I could worry or reason, I flew forward and wrenched at it. The sword's unexpected weight made me stumble and the blade hit the floor with a clatter. Captain Bainbridge and I simultaneously dove. The cabin was so confined that the side of my head collided with his shoulder and the ship lurched at that same moment. The force of both events sent him backward. The captain's spine slammed into the bedpost—I caught his pained grimace—before wrapping his hand around it and regaining balance. I'd grabbed hold of the desk and thrust my other arm out. By the time the captain recovered, the tip of his sword was pointed directly at his throat. My chest heaved. He appraised me, undeniable admiration in his eyes, and wings fluttered inside me.

When he spoke, though, his tone was affable as ever. "Have you ever killed a man, Miss Davenport?"

"Have *you*?" I countered, curious to know the answer. Perhaps it would tell me what sort of person hid behind this impeccably polite façade.

Something akin to amusement lit his gaze. Slowly, Captain Bainbridge released the bedpost. He edged to the side and I followed his movement. We circled each other in a way disturbingly similar to the mating dance from the plains, although there was a darker feel to this. Not a joining of souls, but a clashing of them. Thunder rumbled through the water, the wood, our bones. I'd acted rashly, I knew. I darted a glance at the door, then the windows, trying to decide which would lead to freedom.

"The windows don't open," the captain said. "You wouldn't survive the water anyway, considering it's infested with crocodiles. Better them than the mermaids, though."

"What do you *want* from me?" I hissed. Spittle flew from my mouth. I despised his confidence, my powerlessness, the strange effect he had on me. The sword trembled in my grasp as I searched the room yet again for an escape that didn't exist.

Captain Bainbridge stepped so close that the sword touched him. My gaze snapped back to his. Those stormy eyes didn't flinch or waver at the feel of cold metal against his skin, and his voice was unexpectedly earnest as he said, "I want to speak to my brother again. To be in his life. To regain his trust. I can't do any of that without you."

Instant denial rose inside of me, and I glared at him. "I don't have any influence over him."

"But you do. I have an ally on the island; it's how I learned of you. Peter watched you back in London. He uses your Christian name. And I'd bet my life that he won't make you participate in the—"

"None of that means *anything*," I growled. Frustration made my movements jerky as I shoved my hair back, tangling fingers in the snarls. "Do you truly believe I can change his mind about you with a simple conversation?"

Captain Bainbridge paused, clearly experiencing some sort of inner struggle. That was the moment I noticed I'd lowered the sword; my arm and shoulder were shrieking in pain and I didn't know if I had the strength to lift it again. The captain could have taken advantage of this; instead he continued to bare his soul.

"That's not the only reason I'd have you return to him," he replied tentatively.

Every part of him—his posture, his expression, his tone —emanated vulnerability and sincerity, pieces that most of us dropped along the way to growing up. Suddenly I could see that boy in the garden from long ago, risking his home and family for a few seconds of bliss. Some might call his choice impulse or selfishness.

I called it bravery.

"Go on," I said.

The door opened, startling both of us. I tensed as, for a wild moment, I thought about bolting through it. I could feel Captain Bainbridge watching me, but he made no move to prevent my escape. Because he knew I wouldn't get past all the other men on board, I realized, my stomach sinking. The tension seeped from my limbs as I accepted I wasn't going anywhere.

Wordlessly, a man carried in a small table. He didn't blink at the sight of his captain having a confrontation with a swollen-faced girl clutching a sword. He just put the table in the corner and left. Over the next minute, he casually entered and exited the room, bringing chairs and then steaming dishes. He had a decidedly round build, his head only reaching my shoulder, I'd guess. The top of it was balding. The only adornment on his person was a pair of crooked spectacles perched on the end of his nose. In spite of the man's simple appearance, he set items upon the table deftly, as though he'd done it a thousand times before. He even lit a candle.

Beside me, Captain Bainbridge cleared his throat. "You must be famished. Would you join me for dinner?"

The smell of food was my undoing. Rich and succulent, spiced and fresh. Was that beef? Saliva coated my tongue; it felt as though I hadn't had a proper meal in days. I relented completely, the sword touching the floor with a hollow sound. The captain took it from me, caution evident in his taut muscles and sharp gaze, but I didn't protest. He re-sheathed it and hurried to pull out a chair. I sat like an automaton, devoid of hope or character. The legs creaked as though bemoaning my defeat. I stared ravenously at a loaf of bread.

While Captain Bainbridge was preoccupied with seating himself—humming the lullaby he must've learned from his mother, which Peter learned from him—I slid a knife off the table and into my lap.

"That'll be all, Mr. Smee," I heard Captain Bainbridge tell the other man. I prayed neither of them had seen my thievery.

But all the silent cook did was retreat, leaving Captain Bainbridge and I alone once again.

Every instinct and voice in my head screamed for food. All I wanted was to tear into it with my teeth, swallow it whole. Yet somehow, there was still a drop of dignity in my blood, rushing along with all the chloroform and anxiety. I left my utensils untouched. "You said there was another reason you want me to use my supposed influence over Peter. What is it?" I asked.

Ever the gentleman, Captain Bainbridge leaned back from his plate; he wouldn't eat until I did. "I haven't been in Neverland nearly as long as Peter has," he began, "but I've met its inhabitants over time. There was... one in particular that gave me as much incentive to stay as earning my brother's forgiveness. Her name was Bell. Somehow Peter discovered our courtship, and as punishment for my betrayal in London, he took her. She's hidden away somewhere on the island. I don't know whether she's trapped, suffering, or dead."

So I was to be a spy.

Another brick of distrust was placed on the wall between us as I wondered whether it was truly Peter's friendship he wanted or this girl. I appraised the captain again. All I could see in his face was optimism. My nostrils flared as the smell of cooked meat taunted me, but I still resisted. To do so before things were settled felt like another show of weakness or acquiescence.

"Why should I help you?" I challenged. Everything had a price—his mother had been the one to teach me that.

The captain didn't hesitate, and his tone rang with confident finality. "I'll give you safe passage home."

Silence rushed through the cabin, filling it like water. Captain Bainbridge probably believed I was considering his offer; truthfully, I was constructing a new plan. Weighing the facts. His desire to reunite with Peter contended with the fact that I was to kill him. There was also the same obstacle as with the other children, in that the captain wouldn't want to help me once he knew I'd murdered his brother. Without Peter's death, however, there would be terrible consequences.

I kept searching for the solution. And there it was, tucked

away amidst a hundred discarded ideas, like a dusty trunk in an attic. What if Captain Bainbridge departed the island believing Peter was still alive?

Yes. If I was quick enough, clever enough, I could survive this. Go home. Resume life with my family. No more eyes lurking in the dark, unanswered questions, or being the rope in another family's game of tug o' war. Before fear overtook me, I stuck out my hand. It hovered over the table, warm from the steam rising off the beef. "We have a bargain."

Peter's brother didn't smile or make a sound of relief. His hand was solemn around mine, and I pretended to be immune to the wings within me taking flight. "Meet me every sunrise," he instructed. "At the edge of the Neverwood. I'll come for however long it takes, whether it's a week or a month. If you arrange a meeting with Peter or obtain information about Bell, I'll be forever in your debt."

A week? A month?

I won't be here that long, I almost told him. "Until tomorrow, then."

When I tried to pull my hand away, Captain Bainbridge didn't release me. Instead, his fingers tightened. Thunder vibrated through the walls. The candle dipped and sputtered. "A word of caution, Miss Davenport—Neverland and Peter are inexplicably linked. When he's angry, it storms. When he's excited, the sun is hotter than I've ever felt it. Last year one of Mr. Ashdown's men trapped my brother in a net. Before he could so much as touch Peter, the poor soul was crushed by a falling tree."

The captain waited a moment after speaking, perhaps

waiting for my reply or to be certain I understood the danger of crossing Peter. Slowly, my fingers slipped from his. Captain Bainbridge made no more efforts at conversation and focused on cutting the beef in front of him. Since it was now evident I'd need him for the journey to London, I raised the knife I'd stolen and put it to the meat. It slid through like butter. Unbidden, I imagined cutting Peter open instead. My stomach turned to lead and suddenly my appetite was gone. How could I kill someone if the very notion of it made me ill?

I squared my shoulders and faced the captain again. My fork clinked, bringing his gaze back to mine, away from that ruined beef. "If I'm going to risk Peter's wrath by mentioning your name—not to mention searching for Bell—I should know how to protect myself. Will you teach me?" I asked, steeling myself for mockery or disbelief.

James Bainbridge didn't laugh. He didn't frown. He didn't hesitate.

"Of course," he said.

CHAPTER 9

Waves pounded at us as the dinghy struggled back to shore. I gripped the edges to keep from tipping into the water. A cloak clung to me, the hood raised over my head. If I were spotted coming back from Captain Bainbridge's ship, Peter's trust would vanish more quickly than my family's fortune. Still, it seemed an unnecessary precaution in the face of this storm. No one would be able to see us.

The sea and wind and rain, coming together like a great, dark hand, reached up to capsize the boat. The men—Mr. Jukes and one I hadn't met, a dark-skinned man wearing an eyepatch—fought against it with their oars. As I strained to hold on, I stared at the outline of the island, feeling as though it were smirking at me.

Miraculously, our ragged company landed on shore. Drenched but alive. Gasping, I stumbled toward the trees. The sand sucked at my boots. Captain Bainbridge's men let me go; they were too preoccupied with the boat to shout any threats or words of warning. But I wouldn't soon forget the image of their leader, standing on deck as we were lowered, his gaze unwavering despite the chaos all around us. Rain lashing, men calling, sky flashing. Those words echoed through my head, like the clang of church bells after a sermon. *We have a bargain.*

I batted at branches and leaves, squinting in the downpour. The village should be nearby, and from there I hoped Bashira would be willing to show me the way to the Neverwood.

The storm did everything in its power to stop me. As I drew closer to the village, I remembered to remove the cloak, bunch it up, and hide it. Then I turned, preparing to emerge from the trees with some wild tale of how I'd gotten lost or confused.

And there he was.

Peter stood in the spot where I'd been taken, utterly soaked. His shirt was so wet it was transparent. The sopping material clung to every part of him. Every sharp ridge and hard plane. He seemed to be examining the ground, but any signs of my scuffle with Mr. Jukes had long since washed away.

I wondered what had drawn Peter here. His head seemed to be tilted, as though he were listening. To my own ears, there was nothing but howling wind and angry thunder.

It was evident he was unaware of my presence. The perfect opportunity, I realized. I didn't have Captain Bainbridge's knife or sword, but there was a cruel, sharp-edged rock on the ground. My breathing was shallow as I bent to pick it up. I could do this. He was not a boy, he was a means to an end. Not someone who I'd kissed or danced with. Just a stranger that stood in my way. I raised the rock, willed myself to bring it down.

In that instant, it felt as though the rain transformed into needles. They fell glinting from the clouds and pierced my skin. I stared at the back of Peter's golden head, gritting my teeth. *Just do it. For your family. For your own survival.*

The rock fell from my fingers.

Peter spun so quickly that water went flying. When he saw it was me, his eyes widened.

"Blimey!" he exclaimed, pushing his hair back. It was so wet that it stayed slicked, as though he'd put oil through the strands. The muscles in his arms flexed. "Been a while since anyone's snuck up on me like that! What happened to you? We looked everywhere. I nearly went mad!"

It was obvious Peter hadn't meant to shout this last part, because embarrassment flickered through his features before he schooled them into nothing. What I felt, though, was frustration. Twice I had tried. Twice I had failed. There would not be a third.

The swelling in my face must've gone down, because Peter asked no questions about this. Just as I began to reply, the story of my whereabouts perched and ready on the tip of my tongue, the storm abated. Clouds scattered like a bored crowd and rays of light appeared around us. The suddenness of it was unnatural. I looked at Peter and took in his wide grin. "So it's true," I breathed.

Clearly puzzled, Peter scratched his cheek. "What are you—"

A sound interrupted him, similar to thunder. I frowned. *Another* storm? Then the ground began to shake, as though Neverland was a giant teapot left on the kitchen range too long. Peter stepped toward me, but his gaze was elsewhere, searching the darkness and the air above.

"The island is angry," he murmured.

Dread wrapped its arms around me at these words. *Neverland and Peter are inexplicably linked*, Captain Bainbridge had said, and suddenly it was easy to believe a piece of earth possessed a mind of its own.

Well, if it *was* sentient, the island had just witnessed me poising a rock over Peter's skull. Now it knew what I'd come here to do. As if it could hear thoughts, as well, Neverland's enraged growl made my bones rattle.

To hide my unease, I stared at Peter's shoddy boots. "Can we go back now?"

Though he probably knew something was amiss, he asked no questions—in the next moment, we were flying. Over the village, past the mountains, toward the Neverwood. Already the horizon was clear, the sun able to find its way again. The wind smelled fresh and damp. Inhaling, I allowed myself to nestle against Peter's chest. To pretend that this island was as idyllic as it seemed from up high.

When I moved my head to watch a hawk and a bird lock in a deadly battle, I caught Peter staring at me. There was a twist to his lips that hinted of something wanting to be said. I raised my brows questioningly.

"This is my favorite place," he blurted, much in the way my brother answered his tutor whenever he was uncertain the man would be pleased or displeased.

For a moment, I looked at him blankly. "The sky?" I guessed.

"Yes. I feel like... myself. Down there I'm someone different. So many expectations, so much magic." Peter faltered. His grip on me tightened, but it wasn't painful. "When I'm up here, all that falls away. Like a second skin or an old costume."

Though there was a part of me that wanted to clap my hands over my ears, forget what he'd just told me, a larger part wanted to know more. Glimpse more of what hid behind the red, velvet curtain. Peter was no longer a story that had arrived at my window one night. He was flesh and his favorite place was the sky.

There was no expectancy in his face. He was shifting our course, preparing to land in the children's camp. His hair fluttered in a strong gust. Yet I felt an urge to give him a glimpse of me in return. The voice in my head tried to stop it. I grabbed it and shoved it into a dark room, closing the door firmly behind me. "My favorite place was my father's study," I said.

If he was startled, Peter didn't show it. "Was?" he prompted.

Funny, I hadn't even noticed putting it that way. I shrugged and suddenly found myself unable to look away from a cloud. It was shaped like a dog. "I suppose that changed when he started to drink. Then the room smelled like sweat and brandy. But before that, during the happy days, there was a corner I loved. It held a large chair. The material wasn't comfortable—leather, which squeaked every time I moved—but the arms curved and made it feel as though I were being held. And next to the chair, on a shelf, was an atlas."

Out of the corner of my eye, I saw a soft smile. "Now the truth comes out."

"I'd trace the lines of continents and rivers with my finger, try to imagine traveling them. My grandfather was an explorer. He died in India before I was born. Maybe that's where I inherited this... restlessness. Maybe that's why I can't be normal."

Peter wrinkled his nose. "Normal? Do you mean like the other society girls?"

"Being like them—wanting the things they do—would be easier. For my parents, for me." I remembered Mama's delight when I'd mentioned Orville Martin. It was difficult to recall the details of her face, but I could see her hair fanning out on the pillow, hear the animation in her voice as she made plans. If I were like the other girls, I would be able to save my family through other means. Not with bargains or blood. I blinked rapidly and turned my face away from Peter. "I started reading novels after that, perhaps to distract myself from the maps, but those only gave me hunger of a different kind."

Realizing what I'd just admitted out loud, a searing heat filled my cheeks. I waited for Peter to tease. His response traveled through his chest and into me as he said, "When something is easy, that doesn't mean it's better."

I was so surprised that I couldn't think of anything else to say. We were approaching the camp, anyway. There was a scent of cooked meat around us and smoke rising from the treetops. "You're remarkably wise for someone so young," I commented, knowing our time together was at an end. For now, at least. I could only hope the memory would fade with all the others, for I didn't want to think about Peter's fondness for the sky as I watched the light fade from his eyes. *Soon*, I promised myself. *I'll do it soon.*

Peter descended into the Neverwood. Darkness immediately enveloped us. The children shouted and grinned at the sight of their leader. Freckles was cooking something over the fire again. Upon closer inspection, I saw that it was the largest rodent I'd ever seen.

"*Food!*" he called, ignoring the commotion.

Suddenly I was grateful for the meal I'd eaten with Captain Bainbridge, else I would've gone hungry tonight. I retreated to the edge of the camp. Seconds later one of the children sat beside me. Tootles, Peter had called him. There was a scar on his left cheek I hadn't noticed at the village, running from the corner of his eye to the corner of his lip. The line of his mouth was naturally downturned, as though he was unaccustomed to smiling. Without preamble he said, "You can trust him, miss."

He sounded young and old at the same time. *Seems to know when things are going to happen before they do*, Peter had told me when we first spoke of Tootles. Unease lodged in my throat, making it hard to breathe. "What do you mean? Did you... see something?"

But he didn't answer; we were no longer alone. Peter hovered in the air, cross-legged, chewing his supper leisurely.

"Now," he said around a mouthful. A piece of skin fell from the bone. "Tell us where you went. Did the island take you on an adventure?"

As if he'd cast a spell, the rest of the children ceased their conversations and listened. Some came closer.

They waited, and it was clear what everyone wanted. Like a fluttering curtain, an image moved in my mind. It was a boy resting against a pillow, his eyes wide and rapt. He seemed familiar. Like a face from a dream. And, thinking of him, I told a story. One of a playful island and a lost girl. A violent storm and a forest of shadows. I made exaggerated gestures with my hands and my voice rose and fell like music. There was no mention of pirates or perplexing captains.

It made me notice the boy with no name again, who snatched the bit of food Peter had dropped and scuttled back to the darkness.

Once I was finished, my audience regarded me with admiration and awe. Peter wore a small, self-satisfied smile, as if he'd known all along what I was capable of. I excused myself to slip into the jungle. As I found refuge within a thicket of leaves and vines, I heard the children saying my name. The warmth of acceptance filled me, and I felt like a fool, smiling while I squatted there.

When I came back minutes later, the clearing was empty, for the most part. Even Housekeeper and Freckles had gone, which probably meant they were hunting, bathing, or washing clothes. I instantly spotted Slightly squatting at the edge of the clearing. A boy I didn't recognize was beside him, speaking in hushed tones. As I watched, the boy shifted and a splash of color caught my eye.

They were staring at a flower. It was lovely, made of unfurled petals and a pink hue that rivaled the sunset.

"Don't touch that," I warned instinctively, rushing toward the children. I reached to yank them away. Just as my fingers closed around Slightly's small shoulder, the plant lifted its face.

Horror slid through my veins when I saw it had teeth, sharp and dripping. I dragged both children back, and the flower struck so quickly I didn't comprehend anything had happened until Slightly began screaming. Fabric ripped. Once we were safely away, I released my hold and circled the boys, uttering a silent prayer that the wound was small and Slightly was simply in shock.

My stomach dropped.

Too much blood, I thought faintly, staring at the child's torn skin and the jagged imprint of the flower's bite. *There's too much blood.*

Slightly's screams jarred me from my terrified daze, and I knelt in front of him. My smile was so wide it hurt. "There, now. I'm going to make it better. Just be very still and try not to cry. Can you do that for me?"

I showered him with praise and reassurances as I tore the

bottom of my shirt and wrapped it around his leg. What few children remained in the camp had either scattered or kept their distance, so there was no one to help. I knew from eavesdropping on Dr. Waghorn's visits that the bite needed to be cleaned, but my main priorities were to stop the bleeding and avoid drawing more attention to our presence in the Neverwood.

Once I had secured the makeshift bandage, I lifted my head again. Slightly had lost consciousness but the other boy was still there. He'd been utterly silent during my efforts.

"I need you to find Peter," I told him.

The boy nodded and, still without uttering a word, got to his feet and ran into the jungle. With the tips of my fingers, I pushed Slightly's sweaty bangs out of his eyes, leaving a red smear. Once again I cursed my lack of knowledge and abilities. Peter was our only hope.

I couldn't think of anything else to do as we waited. Though Slightly wasn't awake to hear me, I prattled on about London and other places of the world. When I ran out of facts and tidbits about those, I told him stories. Beautiful, bloody stories about bespelled princesses and hungry wolves. Not the most comforting of tales, perhaps, but neither of us were really listening to the words spilling out of me.

Overhead, through the few gaps in the canopy, I saw the sky begin to darken.

An eternity later, Peter finally appeared. Freckles was behind him, followed closely by Housekeeper. I swallowed hysterical demands about their whereabouts and backed away to watch him place oddly-shaped leaves over the teeth marks. Slightly's thrashing halted. His panting slowed. More years passed until his eyes opened.

I released a strangled sound, and the taste of salt burst in my mouth. Suddenly grateful for the gloom, I rested my cheek on Slightly's greasy head and let the tears fall. *He's a child, just a small child,* I kept thinking. When I still wouldn't release him, he squirmed.

"He'll be fine," Peter said, more for Slightly's sake than mine, I thought. "The Pink Lady may have a vicious bite, but the remedy is easy enough to procure."

My relief was so profound, so overwhelming that I didn't think to ask about this mysterious treatment. My grip loosened and Slightly seized the opportunity to escape. It was as if he had no recollection of what happened. Or maybe it was the resilience of a child.

"He's fine? He'll live?" I dabbed my wet cheeks, belatedly realizing that there was still blood on me.

"Show us a bit of gratitude, eh?" Peter flashed a wicked grin. Dimples deepened in his cheeks. I barely heard him; I couldn't take my eyes off Slightly. He laughed at something his friend was doing, the boy I'd sent to fetch Peter. He looked no worse for wear after his wild flight through the jungle. More children poured into the clearing, returning from wherever their adventures had taken them.

"I remember the first time I thought I would lose one of my brothers," I whispered. I couldn't stop picturing him now, my youngest sibling. Slightly's brush with death had jolted the memory back like a rough shake or an unforgiving slap. "It started as a cough. We hardly noticed. That may seem... selfish or unloving, I know. But my family was busy. We didn't have time to notice. And that might be harder to think about than my brother suffering. Because it feels like we let it happen, you see? Eventually the cough became more and, well, you know the rest."

Peter was silent. Maybe he was thinking of his own brother. Under normal circumstances, it was a good opportunity to finally bring up Captain Bainbridge. All I did, though, was let out a weary sigh. I stepped closer and kissed Peter's cheek. He went still.

"You saved a child's life tonight. I won't forget that," I said. I bid him goodnight and walked away.

As I approached Slightly, my thoughts were a London street, full of overwhelming clamor and bustle. It couldn't be coincidence that the island saw me try to smash Peter's head with a rock, then a carnivorous flower appeared in the camp hours later. How was I supposed to kill him when he had an island for a protector?

"Would you like to sleep beside me tonight?" I murmured to Slightly, holding out my hand.

His only response was to tuck his small fingers in mine. A testament to how exhausted he was, I thought. We climbed up to my strange bed and nestled beneath the leaf. The rest of the children seemed to follow suit. Slightly fell asleep instantly, snoring softly, but despite my own fatigue I stayed awake.

The moon rose higher and higher. Insects clicked. All

the while I lay next to Slightly, restless and unsettled. Eventually I realized there was something I had to do before sleep came.

Flickering light from the dying fire guided me. I climbed back down to the clearing and landed with a jarring thud. No one sounded the alarm. Relaxing, I squatted to pat the ground. Moments later a stone greeted my fingertips and I lifted it with a grunt.

I carried the stone along the edge of the trees. The object of my search was easy to spot, even in the darkness. It was a shout of color in a place of silent black. The flower, sensing my presence, began to awaken. I waited until it lifted its head and saw me before dropping my burden on top of those pink petals.

The flower didn't utter a sound, but I didn't leave as it died. Not yet. I stood there and watched the thing twitch and slow. I watched until the life left it completely.

CHAPTER 10

DAWN ARRIVED with heat and whispers.

Slightly was snoring when I opened my eyes. Between each deafening inhale, snatches of conversation rose through the canopy. The others were talking about the moon. It was hard to imagine the coolness of night, picture that round orb in the sky, when it was so hot I could feel my skin melting. Sunlight beat down on my arm, which rested in a spot where the leaves offered no protection.

I sat up, wincing, and peeled my shirt away from sweat-soaked skin. Hunger gnawed at me, but the sight of perspiration on Slightly's temple made it insignificant. Was it a fever? I quickly lifted the leaf to peer at his wound. There didn't seem to be any infection or sign of pus, just torn flesh that was already scabbing over. The weight I carried on my shoulders lightened a bit, and my breathing slowed.

Suddenly I wanted nothing more than to get away, and I remembered that Captain Bainbridge would be waiting for me on the beach. *Perfect.* I had nothing new to report, of course, but there was no harm in meeting him. Perhaps I could learn more about Peter.

Somewhere overhead, a bird squawked. I scooted down to touch a freckle on Slightly's cheek. The child stirred and mumbled intelligibly. "I'm going to fetch some breakfast, love," I told him.

He didn't wake up, and I took his silence as acquiesce.

Today there was no fire or roasted animal waiting when my boots settled on soil—instead, the children had collected fruit. A boy emerged from the wild to add a banana to their bounty. I felt a prick of guilt, seeing this. What had I contributed to this camp? Was this another exception Peter had made for me? If so, it was no wonder some of them resented my presence.

Tentatively, I approached the vibrant pile of food. Housekeeper was sitting by it, arranging each piece precisely, as though they had assigned spots and it took all his concentration to find them. My mouth watered. "Good morning," I said.

His lips were a thin line. "Morning," he mumbled back.

I studied the other faces in the clearing. The tension was palpable. Somehow, though, I sensed it had nothing to do with me. Not the heat, either.

"Why is everyone talking about the full moon?" I asked, fanning myself.

"You'll see soon enough," Peter's voice replied. A moment later he dropped gracefully from the sky, bringing a rush of air with him. "Oh, my favorite. This is lovely, Housekeeper."

"We had to go farther today," the other boy said. "Almost to the lake."

Unperturbed, Peter plucked a mango from the pile and bit into it. My stomach made such an envious sound that he bent and retrieved one for me, as well. It was utterly foreign, shaped like an exploding star, but I didn't hesitate. Peter waited until I'd eaten the entire thing, my face and fingers sticky with juice, before saying, "Now, would you like to do something dangerous and terribly thrilling?"

Housekeeper had put his focus back on the fruit. I tore my gaze away from his placid face to Peter's, then shook my head. A drop of sweat slid down my neck. "Slightly is still healing. He shouldn't be alone."

Another lie, considering I'd fully intended to sneak away for the rendezvous with Captain Bainbridge.

"Freckles and Housekeeper will be here. I'll tell them to watch the lad." Peter raised his brows at the larger boy, who glanced up from his work long enough to grunt. Wavering, I shifted from foot to foot.

"What's so thrilling about it?" I asked finally.

"That's a surprise."

Of course it was. I thought about it some more, and just as a second denial was rising inside me, a small form dropped from one of the trees—it was one of the boys whose names I hadn't yet learned. He came and took two pieces of fruit for himself. Housekeeper's head slowly turned and, when he noticed, the boy froze. After brief deliberation, he put one back.

Unable to hold back an amused smile, I turned to Peter.

Captain Bainbridge would have to wait until tomorrow. "Shall we go, then?"

Peter grinned back. He held his arms out, elbows bent. He waited. This time, when I went to him, it was entirely of my own volition. Peter arched his neck back, all his thoughts on flight, while I stared at him. I admired the line of his jaw, the hint of stubble there. My hand formed a fist, to stop myself from tracing the edge of that jaw, from discovering the feel of his hair and skin. As we rose, the children cupped their hands around their mouths and howled. The sound followed us into the blue sky.

Up high, the heat wasn't as stifling, and I hoped whatever surprise Peter had in store for me didn't return us to the jungle. Curiosity fluttered in my chest as I tried to discern which direction we were going. I swallowed my questions, though, and reclined in Peter's grasp. Like a great, languid whale, Neverland drifted by. It looked as though more trees had sprouted overnight. The mountains appeared taller, half-obscured by clouds, when yesterday I'd been able to imagine standing atop them.

Peter stayed well away from the side of the island where his brother was anchored. I searched for a glimpse of sails, but all I could see were trees and blue skies. How often did ships pass the island? Did any of them come ashore?

I looked up at Peter to ask him, but his attention was fixed somewhere below my face. I followed his gaze down to the exposed, creamy tops of my breasts—some buttons must've come undone when he picked me up. At the same time I noticed this, something brushed my bottom in the lightest of touches. There was no mystery in what it could be, and every thought about ships and potential ways to get home left my mind.

"Is that all it takes?" I murmured, and only our proximity kept my words from being snatched away by the wind. "A peek inside my shirt?"

But Peter didn't smile. "That's all it takes," he said.

I felt a familiar stirring deep within me. Hardly able to believe my own daring, I held my hip away from Peter's body, creating ample room to reach down with both hands. I used one to undo his button, then the other crept into his trousers. After a beat of nervous hesitation, I wrapped my fingers around Peter's shaft. It was longer than I remembered from that brief touch in my bedroom.

As I pulled it out into the open, I glanced up at Peter through my lashes. His eyes were latched to my face, and though I couldn't read his expression, I sensed his fascination. My thumb brushed along the tip in a gentle, teasing motion, and I heard the swift intake of breath he took.

Emboldened, I grasped Peter's cock more firmly now, and slowly, just like the audacious heroines in my novels, began to move my hand up and down. At first, I kept the motions strong and steady. When Peter didn't make any more sounds, I changed tactics and implemented some creativity, adding a subtle curve to the strokes. His breathing quickened. *Interesting,* I thought, then adjusted my method once again by going faster.

"You are either an angel," Peter said, a small catch in his voice, "or a very, very wicked woman."

The corners of my mouth tipped upward. My confidence increased with every stroke. Peter was so distracted that we were barely moving now, but I paid no mind to our surroundings—I was too enraptured by the expression on his face. Peter's eyes were half-lidded, his lips slightly parted. Then he startled me by leaning forward and kissing my temple. He didn't pull away, and my shoulder moved against his chest, his lips warm against my skin as I pleasured him.

Suddenly Peter shuddered, our forward momentum coming to a complete stop, and I knew he was nearing his release. His groan was so deep that I felt it rumble through him. Liquid spewed from his manhood and plummeted toward the island far below. My hand finally went still, and though there was an unfulfilled ache between my legs, I looked at Peter with a feeling of satisfaction.

He opened his eyes a moment later, and they cleared as he focused on my face. "You've ruined flying for me," he said, brows raised. "Now I shall always prefer to do it this way."

I stared at Peter in shock, then I burst out laughing.

His mouth twitched as he watched me. I laughed until my sides ached, and by the time the sound had subsided, we were nearing the island. Knowing we probably wouldn't be alone much longer, my mirth faded and I hurried to put Peter's cock back in his trousers. My face heated from the intimacy of it. I pretended not to notice the merry twinkle in his eyes, and once I'd secured the button, I refocused on our journey.

I must have been half-expecting to visit the village, because when we swerved away from it, I glanced at Peter, hoping his expression would give something away. This time, it held an anticipation that had never been there before, not even when I'd opened my window to him that first night. His hair was bright as a halo. I caught myself staring again and averted my gaze, which made me notice the fast-approaching ground. It seemed our journey was finished.

"Here we are," Peter chirped. I nearly fell out of his arms in my eagerness, looking around excitedly.

We were in a field.

"Peter, what..." I trailed off. He was already striding off through the golden grass. Huffing, I ran to catch up. There was an outcropping of rocks nearby and Peter began to climb, his bare feet slapping on the hot surfaces. I clambered after him. My tongue felt like a desert, void of water or sensation. Vivid colors marched across my vision but I pressed on. A gust of wind filled my ears.

One of the rocks was large and flat. By the time I'd caught up, Peter was stretched across its surface, lying on his stomach. "Come to the edge," he bid me.

His words penetrated the haze of thirst and dizziness around me and I nearly gasped—it was a cliff. The outcropping dropped without warning, and anyone who wasn't paying attention could fall to their death. The sea glittered in the distance. I halted, my chest heaving. Peter was absorbed in something below. He paid me no mind while I got on my hands and knees.

I crawled forward, my palms dampened with sweat. I could hear my heart hammering in my ears. A breeze went past, carrying a briny scent on it. I dared to lean over, eager to see what had Peter so enraptured.

There were hundreds of them.

Gigantic, winged creatures with feathers of a hue that couldn't be compared to anything I'd ever seen. Not blood, not fire, not dye. They cut through the air like scissors. Others observed from enormous nests tucked into the bluffs. Their movements were so swift, my eyes had difficulty following them.

"What *are* they?" I breathed. The creature closest to us was particularly striking. It flew in stern, purposeful circles. Suddenly its black beak parted and a sound shattered the stillness. It was the call of a living thing that had never known walls or reason. To them, there was only endless sky and simple instinct. The enormous animal tucked its wings and dove. We watched as it mercilessly killed a seagull.

"Birds, of course. I call them Neverbirds," Peter informed me.

Well, they were the largest birds I'd ever seen. Their wingspan was as wide as the drawing room at home. Tracking one with particularly bright feathers, I leaned over. The drop was even farther than I had pictured, so far that the frothing waves seemed like restless clouds. My fingers collided with a small rock and sent it soaring over the cliff-side. Though it made no sound, the birds began to shriek. Dozens of golden eyes swung our way. Even the ones in nests took flight. I froze.

"Their eyesight is impeccable," Peter said calmly. "They know we're here now."

The Neverbirds were fluttering their wings, circling, staring up at us. My mind foolishly rushed back to a childhood memory, when I had snuck into the kitchen to play with some kittens. The runt of the litter had been more wild than the rest. It liked to pounce at my hands and skirt. The Neverbirds reminded me of that kitten, when it had fixed its round gaze on me, hunkered to the floor, rippled its shoulders. I always knew when I'd become prey.

"Should we run?" I asked, trying not to show my terror.

"Only if you want to get killed."

"What do we do, then?"

Peter tensed. Then, like a billow of smoke, the flock rose. We scrambled back. When I tried to flee, Peter grabbed my hand and yanked me back around. "Stand your ground!" he shouted.

The Neverbirds tried to snatch us with midnight talons or impale us with those hooked beaks. Every time Peter ducked, slapped, and bellowed. Timidly, I did the same. There were a few instances I wasn't quick or forceful enough and I cried out as cuts and gouges opened across my skin. Blood dripped to the rocks. Gradually, though, the Neverbirds lost interest or gave up, until only a few remained.

Suddenly I noticed that Peter wasn't fighting next to me anymore—instead, he stood off to the side, where a Neverbird was nearly touching him, its shoulder pressed to his. There was a glint of recognition in its bottomless eyes. I swung away, frightened and confused, and found myself facing the last Neverbird. It was the one I'd first seen, the one that swooped and killed a seagull in a matter of seconds. For the length of a breath, we faced each other.

Then it struck.

I reacted on instinct, throwing my body to the side. I cried out as I fell on my arm. The Neverbird was upon me in an instant, pecking at the ground like any other bird in search of a morning worm. I rolled again and again, hardly having a chance to breathe, much less shriek for Peter's help. Grass and dirt embedded in my skin. I was getting dangerously close to the edge.

"It's a bit like the bull riding they do in America," I heard Peter call, laughter in his voice. "Jump on and don't let go!"

Fury sizzled through my veins as I realized that, once again, he had put me in danger without any regard to whether I would survive. Now I was determined to survive just to ensure Peter was punished.

In the instant before I'd be forced to roll again, I curled my fingers around a small rock and wrenched around to throw it at the Neverbird. Surprisingly, my aim was true, and the stone bounced off the bird's cheek. Its head snapped back in surprise. I hadn't harmed it, but the seconds the creature took to recover were enough to stand again. Panting, I stood up and faced the Neverbird. It screeched, flapping its huge wings. The gust sent me sprawling, and somehow I landed on my stomach. Air left me in a *whoosh*.

Fire licked through my lower back. I released an ear-splitting scream—the bird had torn its beak through my flesh. The pain was crippling and my vision blurred, but somehow I managed to scramble up yet again, turning to keep the bird in my line of sight. In a halting, deadly dance, it stepped forward and I stepped back. We did this once. Twice. When my heels were dangling off the drop, I stopped. The heat, the pain, and Peter melted away. Nothing else existed but me and the Neverbird. Its round, gold eyes burned into mine. Its muscles bunched. I subtly readied myself, knowing I would either succeed or die.

I wasn't sure why, but suddenly this moment felt very important. For reasons that had nothing to do with my potential doom.

This time, when the Neverbird lunged, I leaped out of the way and managed to stay on my feet. Then I darted past the dark, twisting head and ran the length of its wing. The Neverbird was already recoiling, but I grabbed fistfuls of feathers and hauled myself onto its back. It screamed its rage, hopping violently. When I didn't budge, clamping my legs even tighter against it, the bird spread its wings and jumped off the cliff. Peter's victorious howl followed us.

Tears slid from the corners of my eyes and into my hair. The Neverbird moved beneath me, and I had never known such power. It brought us past the nests and crags, rushing toward a part of the island I hadn't seen yet, on the other side of the mountain. There was more jungle, more wind, more ocean. To the right, there appeared to be a second, smaller island. Before I could wonder what sort of creatures lived there, the Neverbird tilted, one wing pointed to the earth. I clenched my fists harder, likely leaving crescent-shaped marks on my palms. Bile clogged my throat as I tried not to think about how far the fall would be.

Maybe the Neverbird sensed this. Without warning, it tucked its wings. We rushed headlong toward the hard, unforgiving ground. The wind tore at my hair and my scream, tossing both into the sky. I wanted to squeeze my eyes shut—avoid the pain and shock of my life ending—but found I couldn't. So I watched, mute and wide-eyed, as the ground came closer in a blur of rock and grass. Then, at the last possible second, the Neverbird swung its body up and away. We came so close that I could've reached out and touched a wildflower. I gasped with relief, my heart a hammer against the walls of my chest. My grip slightly loosened.

"You're smiling."

At the sound of Peter's voice, I jumped. He and his Neverbird flew alongside us. "What?" I called, the wind threatening to snatch it away.

He didn't repeat himself, but he didn't need to. I touched my curved lips with the tips of my fingers. The girl I once was would have been mute, trembling, or fleeing. And yet I felt more alive than I ever had before.

The Neverbird had ceased fighting me. Flying on it was still terrifying, but now I was able to admire its glossy feathers. Close scrutiny revealed that they weren't a single color, either. Earlier, from the edge, they had looked red. Now I saw that they were every shade of red discovered and undiscovered. From the burnt orange of autumn leaves, to the scarlet of a parrot's feathers, to the deep maroon of a rose.

Eventually we soared over the Neverlanders. They shouted and pointed. I searched the upturned faces and waved at Bashira. Her teeth glinted in the sunlight and she adjusted her hold on a basket to wave back. The islanders were saying our names, but mine sounded strange. Different. The Neverbird shifted its course, removing the wind from my ears, and suddenly I could hear it. *Wendy-bird*, they were saying. *Wendy-bird!*

Pride swelled in my chest. I was more than a daughter, a sister, a lady. More than a reflection in the mirror or other people's eyes. More than a marriage prospect or the children I would bear. I had a name and I'd earned it.

It was dusk by the time we returned to the ground, and I'd seen all of Neverland. The lines and landscapes were drawn in my mind like a map. Now we were at the edge of the Neverwood, a short walk from the camp. When I slid off the bird, my legs felt weak, as though I'd been on a ship. Despite this, I moved quickly to put some distance between me and the great bird after dismounting. Our battle was still fresh in my mind, regardless of the incredible flight we'd just taken through the clouds. When she didn't instantly take her leave of me, I felt a warm burst of surprise.

While Peter murmured to his Neverbird, I stretched. The sight of blood on my shirt startled me—I'd completely forgotten about the gouges in my back. As soon as I remembered them, the pain returned. I winced and thought of how uncomfortable it would be to sleep in that tree tonight.

As if to apologize, the Neverbird shoved her head against my chest so hard that I stumbled back. I put my hands on her beak, still wary of being bitten in half or impaled, but the enormous bird merely made a sound that reminded me of a cat's purr. "She'll never forget your face," Peter said, observing us.

I raised my eyebrows at him. "How do you know it's a female?"

"Because unlike other birds, when it comes to these beasts, it's the fairer sex that gets all the beauty."

I ran my hand down the bird's cheek and, as if the gentleness of the touch startled her, she went still. "Do you bring everyone here? The others in the Neverwood?" I asked, avoiding Peter's gaze as I voiced the question.

"No."

"Why not?"

This time, Peter didn't reply. As I continued to pet the bird in front of me, I glanced at him sidelong. He was seemingly preoccupied with removing something from his creature's feathers, and my lips pursed in silent speculation. I thought of Captain Bainbridge's story. Then I thought of how Peter had sought me out in London. If he showed the others how to fly, it meant they could leave at any time. For someone who had made every effort to ensure he wasn't alone on this island, it stood to reason that he shouldn't want to make it easy to be betrayed or left again.

I knew if I said any of this out loud, Peter would probably fly away. Away from my questions and the truths he was pretending didn't exist.

"I should give her a name," I said abruptly, narrowly dodging the bird's talon as she shifted. Her burning eyes flicked toward the sky, and she shrieked without warning.

The sound rang with a deep restlessness I understood better than anyone. "What did you name yours?"

Peter shrugged, then sent his Neverbird off with a light shove. My braid blew back from the force of its beating wings. "I didn't. Truthfully, it didn't even occur to me. Seems a bit like naming a wild horse."

"They're not completely wild now," I argued. "We've changed them. That creature may be free, but she's no longer untouched. She knows how it feels being bent to someone else's will, she's heard what joy sounds like, she's begun to understand what a bond is."

There was a pause. Peter angled his head and pursed his lips, regarding me and the Neverbird with a speculative air. Eventually he said, "How interesting. I've never thought of it in that way before. Very well, Wendy Davenport, what shall you call this changed Neverbird?"

The Neverbird ruffled her wings, as if she was anxious to be unfettered again. I gazed at her and thought of beauty, wild things, dreams. I also thought about the Northern Lights. What I'd read about them was imprinted on me like a birthmark or a scar—those lights were christened after the Roman goddess of dawn, along with a Greek term for the north wind. The goddess had always stuck in my mind most, though. The syllables of her name felt like light themselves. Of distant shores and sights unseen.

"Aurora," I whispered. "You are Aurora."

Like a newly-made shoe, the name fit perfectly. I didn't explain it to Peter and he didn't ask. This knowledge belonged purely to me, just as the Neverbird's freedom belonged to her. To give it away would be to give away something priceless and irreplaceable.

The creature seemed unaffected by her christening. With a pat, I released her. She seized her chance and returned to the sky with an ear-splitting scream. The grass flattened with the force of her momentum.

"They're so different from the seabirds I've seen," I commented wistfully, already missing the feel of Aurora's feathers in my hands.

"I don't think they were meant for the sea. I think they were driven out of the mountains."

"Driven? By what?"

His eyes gleamed with a light I didn't understand. A sort of... excitement that only became brighter when he looked at me. "By something far more deadly. Are you ready?" was all he said.

More secrets. Rebelliously, I sat down in the grass and crossed my legs. It was becoming habit, and I tried not to think of the inevitable day I'd be wearing a skirt again. "There was a girl I knew," I said abruptly. "Her name was Lottie. I saw her at every coming out ball. She would always tell other girls about her encounter with the mysterious Peter. I was sure she was making it up. She claimed she was in love with you."

"Most women are," the boy agreed solemnly, sinking down beside me.

He didn't elaborate on the nature of this visit to Lottie. I hid my jealousy and plucked a flower off its stem. Two of the petals detached and blew away. "But I'd like to believe there's more to love than that. It's a choice, isn't it? One you make once you've learned about the person. Who they are, what they want, what they think about. And it's a choice you continue making every day after."

I couldn't help thinking of my parents as I said this, and I wondered if what they shared was truly love. Each of them had been drowning, in their own way, whether in darkness or drink, and neither had done anything to help the other.

Unaware of the direction my thoughts had taken, my companion leaned his chin on his hand. His expression was tragic. "Are you saying you're not in love with me?"

Though I knew he spoke in jest, the words made me bristle. "We're not even friends, Peter. You're handsome and exciting, I'll give you that. But I can hardly love someone based on that alone. Unlike Lottie."

For once, it seemed as though Peter didn't know what to say. Silence rode on the breeze like a brave soul and a Neverbird. There was a line between his brows, and he looked flummoxed. Hadn't anyone rejected him before?

"Wendy," Peter said. But he wasn't looking at me.

I twisted, following his stare. When I saw where his attention had gone, it felt like my stomach dropped out of my body. I wasn't sure if what I felt was horror or something else entirely.

My shadow had a mind of its own. It moved against the grass, wrenching back and forth, struggling as if it were bound by rope or chain. As we watched, it finally stepped away, no longer attached to me. Its eyeless face seemed to turn in my direction, and the shadow gave a deep, mocking curtsy. I felt stirrings of panic, the same sensation I experienced opening my bedroom window or meeting the gaze of my Neverbird.

The darkness contains all the parts of yourself you don't want, Peter had explained.

"I predicted that Neverland would change you, didn't I?" he said now. I barely heard him. What swirled in that darkness? What had I lost? Did it mean I was becoming more like Peter?

The boy next to me stood, brushing his hands together in a jarring, sudden sound. Blades of grass floated away on a breeze. "We really should go," he announced. "The full moon is a dangerous time. Well, more dangerous than usual. Beasts emerge to hunt and more intelligent creatures come out to play. And there's the drawing, of course."

"The drawing?" I asked faintly, not moving or looking at him. My shadow was dancing what appeared to be the polonaise.

As a response, Peter lifted me in his arms. His touch was almost... tender. I was too dazed to wonder at this. Too dazed, even, to notice the vibrant sunset streaking across the sky like the work of a paintbrush or the fragrant wind that somehow soothed the pain in my back.

Then I was being set on my feet again, blinking at the fire. Slightly noticed our return and toddled over, his nappy clearly in need of washing. My shadow appeared on the ground, still independent, hovering around the child as though he were a daisy and it was a bumblebee. Curiously, the worry I'd felt for him was gone, along with any inclination to ask about his health or examine the state of his makeshift bandage.

Dread hung in the air like mist. Nibs was approaching every person in the camp, showing them something in her hand. Sticks, I realized. They were pulling sticks out. A boy drew one and started to cry. All at once, my mind went back to a conversation with Freckles, when we'd been speaking of the strange things they called each other.

They are our real names, miss. The ones that are given to us once we've proven ourselves in Neverland. Whoever we were before doesn't matter.

And how do you prove yourself? I had asked him.

Before I could finish this line of thinking, Nibs walked toward me with a smug smile. Her scar looked darker than usual, making it look as if she had two mouths, two smiles. A small hand slipped into mine, and I looked down at Slightly. His brown eyes were wide and frightened. I frowned.

Just as Nibs was about to present the drawing to me, Peter spoke from above. "No."

Though the word was said quietly, every other conversation stopped like an ax going through wood. Forceful, splintering, permanent. The children's expressions were shocked. They stared at the boy in the air. One dared to venture, "But, Peter, it's—"

"No initiation. She is Wendy."

"Every one of us 'as 'ad ter do it!" Nibs protested. "Why does—"

"I said," Peter cut in, his tone disarmingly calm, "she is Wendy."

With that, he flew over to a tree and settled on one of the thick branches. Several pairs of eyes glared at me, as if I was to blame for his displeasure. I felt my chin jut defiantly. After a moment, some of the children huddled in a circle, muttering amongst themselves.

After a moment, Nibs stalked to the gathering crowd and spat something. I heard my name. A few glanced toward me and Slightly, their expressions varying from resentful to furious. A girl with two braids made a gesture that I suspected was meant to be obscene. I stared back, bewildered. The incident with my shadow retreated to the back of my mind.

Nibs finished the drawings, and a black boy drew the next short stick. His face crumpled for an instant, chin quivering, before he straightened and wiped it clean of all feeling. I felt as though I'd just witnessed a child cease being a child, and become something else entirely.

The other short stick was drawn by a boy who almost rivaled Housekeeper in size.

Filmy beams of moonlight lit the clearing, shining upon the children as they formed a circle—no, a wall, impenetrable as it was. Almost simultaneously, everyone looked up. Peter was still sitting in the tree, his legs swinging. He held a piece of fruit, and his left cheek bulged with his last bite of it. No one breathed as they waited. For what?

"Begin," Peter said.

Shouts instantly ripped through the air and filled my ears. I heard bets, goading, and a useless bid for order. Seconds after that, there was the sound of fist meeting flesh. Alarmed, I pushed through the mass of bodies. The stench of sweat and filth permeated the air. Nibs noticed my approach and sneered. Her arms shot out to shove me. I reeled back, recovered, and tried a different way that was out of her reach. Finally I stood on tiptoe to look over someone's shoulder, a girl who was as tall and thin as a reed.

The two boys that had drawn short sticks were in the middle of it all, facing each other. In the time it had taken me to get closer, one already had a smashed nose and the other cradled his arm. There were two knives jammed hilt-up in the dirt.

Freckles was watching nearby. I snagged his sleeve. "What *is* this?"

The boy looked at me with unhappy eyes, saying nothing, and it was obvious he was only a pawn in this game. Thinking of the king, I glared at Peter, who still sat above it all. I ran to climb the tree. Pain shot through the wounds in my back—at least the discomfort in my foot had eased—but I gritted my teeth and kept going. Though Peter must have felt the branch bend under my added weight, he just leaned forward, never taking his eyes off the fight. Strangely enough, his shadow was cradling its head and rocking. I watched it for a moment or two, frowning.

"I first got the idea from the islanders," Peter said matter-of-factly. One of the boys yelped. "The Proving is so effective. Of course, ours goes much further than spilling a drop of blood."

"The Proving?" I echoed, sounding as bewildered as I felt. This time, Peter was too absorbed in the fight to respond.

Something niggled at the back of my mind like a worm trying to dig its way through earth. It was the conversation I'd had with Captain Bainbridge in his quarters. *I'd bet my life that he won't make you participate,* he'd said. How had he known? About the drawing, or that Peter wouldn't require me to play a part in it?

The smaller boy had both knives in his hands now, and he brandished them frantically, moving faster than I thought possible. The din grew louder and filled my ears. "Peter! Stop this!" I begged.

He examined his fingernails. "How else do you suggest I thin them out? There's not an abundance of food on the island, and if we acquire too many children, pirates or other hungry things will find us. They knew the risks when they chose to come to Neverland."

"You have money, I know you do," I insisted. "Why not bring back food every time you fly to England?"

Peter's brows rose. "I do. But there's only so much weight I can bear and remain airborne. Considering I had to carry you last time, food is in even shorter supply at the moment."

His logic was cold and terrible. Turning, I watched the boy with the knives slice them across the larger one's stomach. He dropped to his knees, sobbing, sounding for all the world like a child Michael's age. If someone didn't intervene, he would die.

I spun back to their king, my voice full of beseeching now. "It's *wrong,* Peter."

"You care too much. There's a high price for morality and sentiment. It's going to cost you someday," he informed me. I was speechless. The two of them—Peter and his shadow—watched me. When I didn't respond, Peter quirked a brow. "Was there something else?"

"You're every bit the monster London believes you to be," I hissed.

Peter rolled his eyes. Rage swelled in my chest and made me remember why I'd come to Neverland. In return for saving Michael's life, I would make sure Peter's death was quick and painless. But there *would* be a death; the thought of killing him was not so unbearable anymore. I left the perch, resolving to step into the circle myself. Peter let me go.

Once again I fought to the middle. An elbow hit me in the gut and vicious fingers pinched the delicate skin of my wrist. Desperate, I stomped on someone's bare foot, and suddenly there was a temporary opening, narrow but still enough to fit through.

A meaty arm thrust out in front of me as I surged forward, blocking the way again. I implored Housekeeper with my expression. He gave me an impassive glance and rumbled, "If you're sure."

His arm fell.

I was too late. The cheering reached deafening heights, and I felt something hot splatter me as I watched the smaller boy bury a knife in his opponent's chest. The big one swayed for a few seconds, eyes wide and disbelieving, as if he'd thought this was a bad dream. Then he collapsed face-first in the dirt.

He was instantly taken by both arms and dragged away to the darkness.

At some point, the cheering had stopped, leaving the camp in utter silence. Everyone stared at the boy who had fought and survived, his scrawny body heaving, his eyes sparking with defiance. *A child no longer*, I thought, realizing that it was one more lie Peter had told us about Neverland. Our bodies might not age here, but our souls certainly did. What use was eternal youth without the joy to go along with it?

The stillness shattered like glass when someone called, "One of us."

Within moments, everyone in the clearing took up the chant, like a trickle of water becoming a stream. "One of us, one of us, one of us!"

Children jostled me in their rush to congratulate and clap the victor on his back. He still showed no remorse or regret—there was only the hardness that I'd been seeing in all the other children during my time here. As the others recounted the fight, tones stained with excitement and reverence, he clutched that bloody knife and took it all in. I was frozen, too. Unable to accept that I hadn't stopped it and unwilling to believe that Peter would orchestrate it.

A calloused palm touched my arm. I looked down at Freckles, thinking distantly that I needed to bathe.

"Peter does everything for a reason, miss," he told me. But his dirty features were contorted, as though he'd felt the knife, too.

"He's not a god, Freckles. You needn't follow him so blindly." I hadn't spoken harshly—it was a wonder he'd heard me at all, in fact—but the boy still flinched. Cowed, he looked down at his toes.

The chatter behind us had begun to wane. As the excitement eased and spectators dispersed, I searched for Slightly. Somehow I'd forgotten him. There he stood, across the camp, small and still. During the commotion, he hadn't moved. Guilt pricked my throat, as if I'd swallowed a dozen thorns. While Housekeeper barked out orders, giving the bloodthirsty children tasks to occupy them, I knelt in front of the young boy. I didn't ask if he was all right, because there were some questions that didn't need to be voiced to know the answer.

His eyelids fluttered. Silently, I offered my hand, and he took it.

Together, we climbed the tree. Almost like an atonement for what it had brought about, the moon filtered through the leaves so brightly we had no trouble finding our bed. Slightly and I huddled beneath the leaf and waited for it to go quiet.

The quiet was slow in coming, but it did come. Once their bellies were full and their ritual finished, the children withdrew. Murmurings floated upward, then silence. Bugs and birds called to each other and worshipped the moon. After making sure Slightly was settled in for the night—the act rankled me, oddly enough, and I slipped away before he'd truly fallen asleep—I retrieved the tattered shirt I'd discarded days ago and went to the boy who'd survived the drawing.

My shadow stayed with Slightly.

The boy sat near the fire, back to a tree, knees hugged against his chest. That frightening hardness in his countenance was gone, replaced by pain. His shadow was no longer part of him, either. It sat on his other side, brought to life by the dwindling flames. My heart cracked a little when I saw it was holding what looked to be the same knife the boy had used to take his first life.

I approached noisily, to avoid startling him. But he'd known so much fear tonight that I doubted its taste would ever fade on his tongue. It would hold his hand for the rest of his life, a companion as constant as a shadow or a heartbeat.

Though the boy didn't speak or twitch, I sensed his awareness. He knew I was there. "What's your name?" I asked, kneeling.

He said nothing. A log on the fire shifted and sparks flitted through the air. They reflected in the darkness of the boy's large pupils. Wordlessly I tore a strip from the bottom of my ruined shirt and dabbed a cut on his lip with it. The boy's eyes closed, and I wondered how long it had been since someone had touched him with kindness.

When he still didn't protest, I shifted so I was in front of him, then went on to wrap his torn knuckles in a feeble attempt to prevent infection. The bleeding had stopped, at least. I cast a subtle glance down the rest of him as I secured the strip with a knot. There were no other injuries that I could see, but I suspected the worst ones were somewhere I couldn't reach.

Once I'd finished, the boy lowered himself to the hard

ground and curled on his side. He closed his eyes, the muscles in his face tense and lined.

Gently I said, "Don't blame yourself for what happened tonight. We all do horrible things to survive."

My only response was the crackle and spit of the flames. After a moment, I sat beside the boy. One of his hands was tucked beneath his chest, but the other rested palm-down on the dirt. Another minute passed before I dared to rest my hand on top of it. His eyes were closed, but his body was tense and coiled like an animal prepared to bolt.

The moon and stars watched us. All around, the island stirred in its sleep. Things moved in the darkness and muggy breezes sighed through plants. I stood with reluctance, thinking of Slightly, all alone up in the tree.

Sleep well, I almost said to the boy. But he wouldn't—his dreams would be swollen with images of shouting children, a wall of glinting teeth and sneers, knives, his own blood-covered hands. I'd learned better than anyone that ghosts weren't the only things that haunted us.

Instead, all I said was, "Until tomorrow."

I walked away, thinking that was the end of it. Just as I put one foot at the bottom of the tree, bracing myself for the climb, his drowsy words drifted to me.

"Good night, Mother."

CHAPTER 11

CAPTAIN BAINBRIDGE WAS true to his word.

The next morning he stood at the edge of the Never-wood, his back to me, one hand draped over the handle of his sword. Color leaked across the horizon like blood seeping from a cut. A long-legged bird walked along the shore and the captain seemed to be watching it. A dinghy bobbed in the nearby water.

Instead of announcing myself, I lingered in the murky jungle to study him as closely as he'd studied me when we first met. His shoulders were broader than I remembered, and a sort of calmness emanated from him, even from a distance.

Where Peter seemed to be caught in that place between a boy and a man, this was no boy. During our encounter on the ship, I'd been so disoriented and suspicious. Captain Bainbridge had been my captor, then Peter's brother. But now I wondered who he was, truly. This man who loved a person for their mind, regardless of gender or station. Who didn't blink at my request to learn a male trade.

Thinking this, I stepped into the light. The change was so drastic, so bright that I squinted, and I could only hear the captain as he greeted me. "Miss Davenport. You look well."

My eyes adjusted to the day, and I saw my shadow perform the niceties expected of me. It was still disarming to watch. "I apologize for not coming yesterday. I was otherwise engaged," I said coolly.

He waved his hand in dismissal. "I understand you may not be able to slip away every day. I just appreciate any effort you make to repair the rift between me and my brother, no matter how small."

I searched his expression and found nothing but sincerity. James Bainbridge was an open door while his brother was tightly locked, every thought and bit of kindness kept prisoner behind it. "Let's get on with it, then."

If he was startled by my behavior, the captain didn't show it. He adopted my briskness and began our first lesson. Though we weren't using weapons yet, I noticed that he'd brought two crudely-made wooden swords. Had he made them himself, after our conversation? I was concentrating on his instructions and there was no opportunity to ask. But it remained at the back of my mind, growing like a creature in a cocoon.

Eventually Captain Bainbridge took a step back to examine my stance. "Legs spread apart," he ordered.

I obeyed and hoped he wouldn't notice my blush. Sweat dampened my back and neck. "Like this?"

He nodded curtly, all the praise I would receive, it seemed. "Balance is vital. As well as always keeping the blade close to your body. But the most important things are speed and control; never let your emotions get the best of you, Miss Davenport."

It went on like this until the sun was halfway finished with its journey across the sky. We even fit in a lesson on knife throwing. I'd told the children that I was off to bathe, and God willing, no one would be searching for me. The more I learned, though, the more my worry faded. There was so much to remember! *Slide your feet, don't lift. Keep straight posture. Chest and torso forward. Elbows bent.*

"Have you spoken to Peter yet?" Captain Bainbridge asked abruptly.

The sound of Peter's name shattered my concentration. I lost my balance as I moved into one of the positions he'd taught me, and my still-healing back gave a shout of protest. Captain Bainbridge rushed forward.

"Are you all right?" he asked, forehead wrinkling with concern. I ignored his attempt to assist me and got to my feet, stalling by brushing the dirt off my backside. The captain watched, still waiting for an answer to his question about Peter, but I didn't want to think about Peter.

The place he'd claimed in my heart—no, the place I had foolishly and recklessly given him—was made of light and shadow. The boy himself was a walking contradiction. He carried me over London, then abandoned me in a terrifying jungle. He introduced me to new people and ideas, then I discovered his involvement in a girl's kidnapping. He offered to help save my brother's life, then forced children to take one on the full moon.

"No. Not yet," I finally muttered.

A dark curl fell into Captain Bainbridge's eye. Impatience glimmered in the other. "It hasn't been long, granted, but—"

As he spoke, I'd been bending to pick up one of the wooden swords. The movement caused another jab of agony along my back. Captain Bainbridge heard the intake of breath and forgot Peter.

"Are you hurt?" he questioned, reaching for me again. "Miss Davenport, there's blood on your shirt!"

Perhaps he wasn't thinking, either, for he lifted my shirt without hesitation. My head was too clouded with pain to stop him. *No, don't, I'm fine,* I tried to say at the same moment his fingers traced the skin surrounding the wound. The captain said something, but his words were a hum to my ears. I sucked in another breath—this time for another reason entirely—and everything seemed to stop for an instant. The wind, the water, our lungs.

The spell broke when Captain Bainbridge dropped my shirt like it had burned him. I could feel that sensation again —the same one Peter had awoken when we met, the same one I felt again in meeting his brother. A tingling that made the gouges in my back seem inconsequential.

I cleared my throat and turned to face him. "I had an encounter with a Neverbird. You needn't worry. A few more days and I'll be right as rain."

As though he were a stranger, the man bowed. His

expression was smooth, like a freshly-ironed tablecloth. "Forgive me."

I could still feel the trail of sparks his fingers had left on me. "Yes, well, I should be going now."

It was the truth. Slightly's wound hadn't fully healed yet, and the dressing needed to be changed. Admittedly, my concern was a forced thing, like a curtsey or a corset. In this moment, however, it was a welcome distraction. I adjusted my stained shirt and avoided meeting the captain's gray eyes. "Shall we continue tomorrow?"

"I gave you my word, didn't I?"

Rolling waves filled the silence between us. I didn't know what to say; something had changed and neither of us knew what, exactly. After another stilted moment, I turned away, back to the Neverwood. I felt his gaze with every step, until the dark hands of the jungle wrapped around me and hid me from view.

Frogs croaked into the stillness. I wove through a tangle of vines, praying that the island was feeling generous and would allow me safe return to camp. Earlier, I'd left a trail to follow, impermanent markings in bark with my nails. They appeared sporadically, but I was encouraged by each one— Neverland wasn't playing its vicious games today.

The second I thought it, the air shifted.

A swath of fog enveloped everything. I knew from its speed that more was at work than science or nature. I tried to stay on the path I'd made, but soon the trees were unfamiliar and it was painfully evident that I was lost. Again. Gritting my teeth, I stopped and tried to decide which tree to climb. The best course of action was to find the camp from above, away from this clinging mist.

In the midst of my efforts, I tripped over something on the ground.

It sent me sprawling, and I twisted irritably to see what it was. Empty eye sockets stared back. I recoiled, jamming my heels into the dirt. Horror congealed in my throat, blocking all air and sound. It was the body of a young girl. Animals had picked it clean. Her bones were sprawled on a bed of moss, her gown in tatters.

Distantly I thought that I'd never seen a corpse before—it was not as thrilling as novels and my own imaginings made it out to be. The fog swirled around us and all I could think about were the things she would never do. What words she would never say, what choices she would never make, what life she would never have. Had the girl been killed after one of the drawings? Had Neverland taken her in a fit of impulse or boredom?

Though she was decomposed, part of me expected her to move or speak, clacking those chipped and yellowed teeth. Shuddering, I scrambled up and ran, desperate to find the camp. At least there, everything was living.

Minutes later, I spotted a bit of sunlight through the trees. Thinking I'd found the camp, my heartbeat quickened. Before emerging, I paused in the shadows to tuck my shirt in and hide the blood from the children.

Why should you hide it from them? a snide, resentful voice demanded. But I still did, perhaps more from habit than kindness. A monkey shrieked as I parted the leaves.

Disappointment settled on my chest, heavy as a stone—this wasn't the camp. The clearing in front of me was much smaller, the size of our drawing room rug at home, and there were only two people here. I recognized them both instantly, and I smothered my gasp just in time, hurriedly retreating behind a tree.

It was Peter and the silver-haired girl.

Cautiously, I eased into a better vantage point. They were so absorbed in each other that I needn't have hidden so quickly. He had his arms around her, and they were pressed together in a way that made their relationship unmistakable—this was no friend or relation. She was plainly not the ghost I'd believed her to be, either. The sight of them made simple things suddenly difficult to accomplish, like blinking and breathing. I wasn't even capable of lying to myself, saying I didn't care. I did. Oh, I did.

Suddenly the cause of the fog was obvious. Peter cast a furtive glance around, revealing that this meeting was meant to be secret. He returned his focus to the beautiful girl leaning against him. The jungle was so silent that I could hear his words as if he were standing beside me. "Bell, I..."

There was a sorrow in his voice, a rare glimpse of vulnerability, but I hardly noticed. *Bell*, he'd said. I heard nothing after that. It was the name of the girl that James Bainbridge had claimed was taken against her will. The one he'd fallen in love with. Yet here she was, unbound and unharmed. Nestled in Peter's embrace as though it were the safest place in the world.

Wanting to know more, no, *needing* to know, I edged closer. A stick snapped beneath my weight.

Peter and Bell sprang apart. I abandoned all pretense, stepping on another infernal twig as I backed away. Mist filled the space I vacated. "Is that you?" Peter snarled in my direction. Had he glimpsed my face? I saw his muscles tense, preparing to lift into flight and investigate.

In a whisper of fog and fear, I fled.

No one noticed my arrival back to camp.

Housekeeper had already assigned tasks to the children —every eye was focused, every pair of hands occupied. Though ill feeling toward me had eased since the drawing, I was still eager to atone, so I passed the afternoon foraging for food. Minutes into my self-imposed task, the victor of the drawing appeared silently at my side. He'd been named Nimble, a reference to how quickly he'd moved during the battle for his life. Though neither of us spoke, the silence between us was comfortable.

It was one of the longer days in Neverland, and by the time darkness fell, I was sticky with sweat and fatigue. I barely managed the climb up to bed.

Peter never returned.

After witnessing the scene between him and the silver-haired girl, I thought sleep would be impossible. But the instant I laid my head down and nestled beneath the downy leaf, I was gone.

Hours later, I opened my eyes. It was the first time I wasn't startled by all the green, the tittering of sounds, the abundance of unknown scents. A dream began to withdraw, and I did nothing to convince it to stay. I didn't want to remember the shock in Peter's eyes as he looked down and saw the knife I'd put in his gut.

There was a butterfly resting on the underside of the branch above me. Its design was like no other, a warning to any that thought to trifle with the tiny creature. So many jagged lines and violent colors—just another reminder that everything was dangerous here. Sighing, I turned on my side. Slightly slept on, his eyes moving back and forth beneath closed lids. He was curled into himself. Light fell over the place on his leg where the Pink Lady had bitten him. I traced the new scar absently. In the blue-black shadows of morning, it looked faint, like a distant memory. I relived those terrifying moments again. The tearing, the sobbing, the bleeding. Then Peter's nonchalant rescue. I'd been so delirious with relief that I'd never thought to ask how he'd done it. I remembered leaves...

Urgency suddenly gripped me. If I didn't ask Peter about the remedy soon, I would forget. Neverland stole memories as often as it stole lives. And though I couldn't quite recall why knowing such a thing was important, I knew it was.

Slightly didn't stir as I left. I felt no guilt at the prospect of him waking up alone, but my shadow tarried to lovingly pet his arm. I ignored whatever feeling this stirred in me— along with any confusion at seeing my shadow, still separate and independent—and found the first mushroom to use as a foothold. Someone coughed nearby.

During my rush to the ground, the sun started to awaken, sending timid streams of light down like swinging legs to the floor after hours in a warm bed. It made the grooves in the bark and the lines in the leaves seem soft and supple.

It even altered Peter, who was there when I climbed down.

He stood next to the pile of ashes that had been a fire, daybreak slanting over his face. His shadow was there, stretching against the ground. I saw it turn, and I stopped just beyond its reach. Peter, however, didn't move at the sound of my approach. I wasn't entirely certain he knew I was there. His head was angled, chin pointed. It reminded me of audiences at the opera house, intent on hearing every note of the music.

I could still taste the bitter words I'd flung at Peter two nights ago. We hadn't spoken since the drawing. The island had allowed me to outrun him yesterday, and I returned to camp long before he did. Throughout supper, he didn't seem to suspect I was the one who'd spied on him and Bell.

I watched him now, reluctant to speak. He still hadn't opened his eyes. "Tell me again," Peter murmured.

Suddenly I knew what he was doing, what occupied his every sense—he was listening to the trees. Of course the boy who could fly and befriend islands and embrace ghosts would be able to hear them. My own interaction with the trees felt like a story I'd read a long, long time ago. Part of me wondered if it had happened at all.

A small form dropped from the canopy at the far edge of the clearing, interrupting my thoughts. It was the nameless boy. He instantly spotted Peter and paled. He ran, but not before I noticed the fresh bruise on his cheek. I took a step toward the jungle he'd disappeared into.

"Don't bother," Peter said, finally rousing. "He knows better than to interact with anyone here."

I faced him. The snoring above us was a reminder that others were still sleeping. "What has he done to deserve this?" I asked through my teeth.

From the moment we met, Peter had dodged numerous questions, avoided countless answers. I felt my eyebrows go up in surprise as he replied, "I caught him conspiring with the pirates. They're moored here, near the island. And a more bloodthirsty lot you'll never meet. That git is their eyes and ears. I allowed him to stay here because I hoped he would prove to be useful. His usefulness may have run its course, though."

"Why?"

"He sees too much," Peter said shortly. At first, I was bewildered by this. But his hostility reminded me of the encounter in the Neverwood, when I'd come upon him and Bell. *Is that you?* he'd said.

The strings came together like an embroidery pattern, forming a complete picture. I'd been so relieved he hadn't suspected me that I hadn't considered whether Peter would place the blame on someone else. Even if the boy *was* in league with Captain Bainbridge and his crew—which would explain how the man had known about me, the drawing, and so much else—that bruise on his cheek should have been mine.

Captain Bainbridge. He'd be waiting at our spot again. But after seeing Bell, my once-ailing distrust of him was strong and thriving. I didn't want to meet him, not when I knew so little and hadn't decided what to reveal. Well, I *mostly* didn't want to meet him. There was a small part of me that still longed to steal away.

Belatedly I realized that Peter was addressing me again. "...find you yesterday. The others said you went off by yourself. Did some exploring, eh?"

"Our time together is nearly at an end," I said, ignoring this. My voice was cold. "Soon, you fly me back to London."

Peter went still. I noticed because he was a being constantly in motion, ever fidgeting or exploring or flying. He was only silent for a moment, but a moment had never been so long. "I was hoping you'd forgotten," he replied at last.

His tone was playful. I didn't believe it. All that mattered, though, was the feel of Slightly's scar under my fingertips and the implications it held. I told myself to forget the rest. Especially the way Peter's eyes caught the morning. Like fresh-cut sapphires.

"How did you save Slightly's life?" I asked bluntly. My head hurt as I strained to recall why it was so important. No, the island wouldn't take my memories, I wouldn't let it.

Peter pursed his lips and considered me. "I have something else to show you."

"There's nothing you could show me that I would possibly want to see."

Maybe Peter saw that charm wouldn't work this time. His expression lost any mischief or merriment and radiated sincerity instead. He shoved his hands in his pockets. "Be angry all you want," he said. "Hate me, even. But if you're truly leaving, this is something you'll regret missing."

The words gave me pause, as Peter knew it would. I thought of the Neverbirds. If I hadn't gone with him that day, Aurora would still be soaring over the white-tipped waves with no knowledge of my existence. Her feathers untouched and her wild heart untamed. And I'd be the lesser for it, as well.

Replying felt indicative of forgiveness, so I merely made a gesture that said, *You may pick me up now.* Peter didn't smile or joke. His hold was loose and courteous, like a stranger's. We rose, and I had a fleeting thought of Slightly waking up alone before the sight of Neverland's horizon blotted it out.

On this, the final adventure Peter and I would share, he brought us toward the Neverbird nests again. This time we shot past them—Aurora appeared and flew alongside us, shrieking—and traveled lower, just over the water. I squinted. There was a tiny opening in the cliffside ahead, the sort of thing you'd only spot if you already knew it was there. Peter headed straight for that bit of darkness. If we were inside when the tide came in, we'd undoubtedly drown. Once again I thought of Aurora and the black terror I'd experienced facing her across the rocks. It was all worth it, in the end.

Peter carried me inside and landed on wet, uneven rock. My forehead brushed his wind-chilled cheek as I tried to see where we were. The nearby water was glassy and tranquil. It was impossible to ascertain its depth and I refused to wonder about what sort of creatures lurked there. Deeper within, the darkness was absolute. Light was only able to reach the cave mouth and a bit beyond. Unconcerned, Peter strode down the rocky shelf. He didn't let go of my hand and I didn't pull away. He stopped at the edge of the darkness, moved closer to the water, and unbuttoned his trousers.

I gasped and turned my back on him, despite the intimacy we'd already shared. "What are you *doing*?"

"Swimming."

"But you can't..." I started to protest. Without thinking, I glanced toward Peter and caught a glimpse of his firm backside as he shed the rest of his clothes. Though he wasn't facing me, I also saw the tip of what hung between his legs. Suddenly I felt unbearably hot.

"Haven't you learned yet?" he called back. "We can do whatever we want."

But something else had my attention now—there were drawings on the walls. Time and sea had made them fade, but I could still discern shapes. One was meant to be a Neverbird, judging from its vicious beak and the size of its wings. Another was a mermaid, her hair long and her fin sensuously curved, as if to beckon.

It wasn't so much the images the lines created, but the

idea of them. I couldn't help imagining the person who had stood here and pressed something hard onto this surface. The image evoked something that felt like a memory. A boy bent over paper. Had I known someone who enjoyed such things?

Peter said my name. I blinked and turned toward the sound of his voice. He was in the water now, moving his arms to stay afloat. My shadow looked at me and shook its head—ladies didn't swim. Like an ember, my hesitation dimmed, then winked out completely. With trembling fingers, I removed the shirt and trousers Peter had given me. I expected cold air to race over my skin, but the warmth was no trick; the atmosphere felt balmy, as if we were in a place with palm trees and white sand.

My toes curled over the rock. I was as naked as the day I was born, and two instincts warred within. One wanted to cover myself in mortification and the other yearned to revel in the new, thrilling sensation.

I didn't allow myself to be timid anymore. Taking a breath, I stepped off the edge and plummeted into the water. It closed over my head, and just like that, I was back in the darkness with Serafa. Then Peter was there, pulling me back to the light. He attempted to speak as I sputtered and flailed. For a few dizzying seconds, he wore the mermaid's face. Her black eyes, her smooth skin.

"Breathe. Just breathe. In and out, slowly, slowly. Good."

I closed my eyes. Peter's voice was like the markings I'd left on the trees, leading me back. The nausea and terror ebbed until I was able to relax in his grip, focus on him again.

"Thank you," I managed. It irked me, needing assistance, expressing gratitude to Peter of all people.

He didn't answer because all his attention seemed to be focused downward. Following Peter's gaze, I realized that the tops of my breasts were peeking above the water. A fire ignited in me, stoked by the heat of his gaze.

I'd been kicking my legs, unwilling to depend wholly on Peter to stay above the surface, and now the movements became rough and agitated. Water lapped against the rocks. "Why did you bring me here?" I asked after an obvious pause.

Peter adjusted his hold so that he had me by the waist. Our bodies pressed together, skin-to-skin. I felt his undeniable arousal against my pelvic bone, and a breath caught in my throat. "We need to swim farther in," he said.

Curiosity crowded in with the desire. I imitated how he swept his arm, much like an oar, and we were swallowed by the darkness. Trepidation slowed my progress. Was I foolish to trust him? What if this was a trap? I waited, hesitant to even breathe for fear I'd miss some sound to give Peter away, but nothing happened.

Just as I was about to voice my impatience, the ceiling came alive.

The transformation felt audible, as if it were possible for light to contain sound. Thousands upon thousands of them, like a star-filled sky. They clung to the rocks and cast a phosphorescent glow. "Oh," I breathed, forgetting to swim. Peter's hold tightened. "It's... it's just..."

Beautiful wasn't adequate enough.

"They're glowworms," Peter murmured. I glanced at him, an instinct, intending to gawk at the strange stars some more. But it was my turn; I couldn't stop staring at *him* now, admiring the planes and angles of his features. The way his lashes cast intricate shadows over his cheeks. Peter felt my gaze and looked down at me. I didn't look away. Our toes kept touching in the water. We floated there, in the darkness that was no longer frightening, two people with no pasts or futures. We simply were.

"You see? There are good things in Neverland," Peter whispered. The freckles over his nose were stark in the blue light. I couldn't speak, even if I knew what to say.

Somehow my hands were on his shoulders. I tried to think about what I'd witnessed just hours ago, tried to picture the passionate embrace I had stumbled upon in the jungle. It was this place, I told myself. It was the beautiful lights all around us that made it impossible to resist him. I succumbed to the yearning and leaned in.

Peter kissed me back instantly, and I wrapped my legs around his waist. He gripped the rock shelf on either side of my head, trapping me between his arms, but I felt no fear— only desire. The desire to taste him again, to finally feel him inside me, to lose myself to the rhythm and sensation I'd been longing for since meeting Peter. The sensation that no book or penny dreadful had come close to adequately describing, but that didn't stop them from trying.

"We can't," I forced myself to say. Although I had been ready to risk such things the last time we'd touched like this, I'd thought about it since then. Realized how reckless and foolish my behavior had been. "There could be a child."

"The women in the village have contraceptives. They would be glad to share with you," Peter told me, his voice low and heated.

Hearing him speak of such things so freely made me blink. Contraceptives? Here? Available without judgment or risk?

My kiss must have been all the answer Peter needed, and this time, he was the one who drew back. There was a cautious light in his eyes, and I understood it. Despite all we'd done, we hadn't crossed this final boundary yet. Doing so now had the potential to change everything. "Wendy, are you—" Peter began.

"Yes," I said. "Yes."

In response, he hauled himself out of the water, the tendons in his arms standing on end. Peter settled on the rocks, his manhood fully erect. Without a word, he reached down and pulled me out, too. As if I weighed nothing, he arranged me so that I was sitting in his lap, my legs resting on either side of his hips. His arousal pressed against my entrance now, but he didn't move to enter me. "What are you—" I started, breathless.

"Water makes it difficult to do this," he said, his voice a low growl. He licked his fingers and ran them up and down his length. Then, gripping my hips, he lifted me up and onto it.

His cock filled me, and I gasped, my core clenching in response. Peter groaned. The sound only made what I was feeling more urgent. Then Peter opened his eyes and stared into mine. He didn't make a request or offer any guidance, and for a moment, I felt foolish. Inexperienced. I started to rise, instinctively shying away, but Peter let out a breath at the movement. His expression was rapture and hunger all at once, and I knew mine matched it.

Slowly, my uncertainty melting like frost in springtime, I sank onto Peter a second time, earning exalted exhales from both of us now. No wonder so many girls risked ruin for this, I thought as our lips met in a hard, hungry claiming. No wonder the bitter people of the world had deemed it a sin.

Breaking our kiss, I braced my hands on Peter's shoulders, which brought my breasts close to his face. At the same moment I began to move my hips, following a quiet instinct —with every moment, though, it got louder—I felt Peter's mouth close around one of my nipples and give it a hard suck. Something about the action made my core tighten. "Peter," I moaned.

His palms skimmed down my bare back, then landed on my backside, where he cupped the cheeks and urged me even closer to him, until every part of us was fused together. I buried my fingers in his hair and moved faster, harder. Peter matched the pace I'd set. A familiar pressure built within me, and I knew I was on the verge of feeling that blinding burst of pleasure again.

Suddenly Peter let out a groan and his body shuddered

beneath me. I watched his throat work, strangely satisfied by the sight.

Afterward, Peter's hands slid off me and he rested his palms on the rock behind him. His skin gleamed with perspiration, and when I saw that, I finally noticed the sweat clinging to my own. I started to get off him, intending to slip into the water and wash off.

"What are you doing?" Peter demanded, his hands moving in a blur. He gripped my hips again and kept me in place. "We're not finished."

My voice was breathless as I said, "We're not?"

In a single, deft maneuver, Peter gently lowered me onto my back. I watched his face, noting the gleam in his sky-colored eyes. I felt his breath against the sheath between my legs, a warm puff of air that sent a delicious heat through me.

Then he lowered his head completely, and pleasure exploded through my body.

I started to bite my wrist again, thinking to muffle the sounds crowding at the back of my throat. Peter reached up, his fingers wrapping around my wrist. He did the same to my other one, then held both against the rock beneath us.

"I want to hear you," he said, his lips moving against me. I couldn't contain a moan, and the sound echoed over the water, bouncing off the stone walls. The glowworms went out in a startled burst, enshrouding us in darkness, save for the faint light pouring inside the cave mouth.

That light felt far, far away. Peter explored me as if I were a map, and his tongue was tracing every river and coastline.

All-too soon a familiar sensation gripped my lower stomach, a tightness that demanded release. My mindless squirming came to an abrupt halt, and I let out another moan, this one so loud and long that it seemed to fill the entire cavern.

My sense of self drifted back in pieces, like driftwood landing on a stretch of shore. As my vision returned, Peter grasped my hands and pulled me upright. My core was still trembling, and I felt both exhausted and invigorated, though I didn't understand how that could be. I was about to share this with Peter when our gazes caught and held. Just like that, I forgot whatever I'd been about to say. We sat there and stared at each other, our wet skin aglow from the hundreds of small lights all around. The water lapped softly beside us. As the silence lingered, and neither of us looked away, I felt something shift inside me—something that had nothing to do with the part Peter had just sucked and licked.

His guard is down, a voice blared through the stillness. I hesitated, my lips so close that I could feel Peter's breath. Today it smelled of honeysuckle. The possibilities wracked through me like a cruel cough. I could try to drown him or smash my fist at the side of his head. Quickly and quietly, then all of this could be over.

"Wendy?"

A glowworm flickered to my left. It made one side of Peter's countenance darken. He was frowning, watching the indecision claw me apart like a beast trying to burst from my chest.

"I'm cold," I said. And it was true. Despite the friendly breeze and tepid water, bumps had risen all over my skin and I was shivering. Peter brought me back to the rocky edge, where I hauled myself up, too shaken to be embarrassed about my nakedness. He must've sensed the discord within me, because Peter didn't tease or peek as he retrieved his own clothing. The glowworms began to wink out.

As I pulled my trousers on, I saw the drawings on the wall again. So wistful and alone, like a child lost in the street. A monkey peered out from the stone with wise, drooping eyes. All at once, I realized why the drawings were so familiar—I knew someone who had done the same, with paper and pen. Someone I'd come to Neverland for. Someone I was trying to save.

Bits of memory came back, like shells and misplaced objects in a tide. My brother needed the cure. *That* was the bargain I'd made with Peter. *That* was why I felt such urgency at every waking moment.

But why was I so certain that I couldn't leave this island while Peter was still alive?

My musings were interrupted by the boy himself. Almost roughly, he put his arms under me. I grabbed his shirt to maintain balance. Then, swift as a gust of wind, Peter flew out of the tiny cave. I blinked in shock when we emerged—it was already nighttime, though we couldn't have left the others more than an hour ago. Real stars twinkled and the waning moon sighed.

Maybe Neverland was bringing the days to an end faster in its keenness for me to leave. Strangely enough, I didn't share the feeling. Not anymore. Remembering the reasons for this journey hadn't brought me relief, only more pain.

Like something held me by every limb and was pulling them in different directions.

Air rushed past as we ascended into the inky expanse of sky. My hair and clothes began to dry. Now, thinking of the brother we'd left behind, I asked it again, raising my voice to be heard over the wind. "How did you save Slightly's life, Peter? When he was bitten by the flower?"

He kept his gaze on the faraway mountain, which looked like a forbidding, hulking giant from a story. His reply was too offhand, too casual. "Bravery, cunning, and stunning good looks. What else?"

"We had a bargain. I'd come to Neverland for one week, and you'd give me the cure."

"I thought you didn't believe there was one," he challenged.

When I said nothing, Peter relented. We dropped into the field above the Neverbird nests and he held my waist to steady me. Dew shone in the grass. I stepped back, leaving a damp trail between us, and waited. I didn't entertain the thought of calling for Aurora, not when a conversation this vital was taking place.

"Tell me about the cure, Peter," I said.

The boy raked a hand through his hair, which was still damp from our time in the water. Grudgingly he told me, "Your brother just needed some leaves of the Fire Tree. It's painful but effective. Burns away fever and infection. We only use them in dire need, since they grow back rather slowly."

Crickets sang while my thoughts went around and

around like a broken toy. The Fire Tree was the cure. Peter had been telling the truth all along. *Maybe I don't have to kill him*, I thought

The revelation made me feel as though I'd been underwater, holding my breath for too long, staring up at the bright, unattainable surface.

Memories or not, I knew saving my brother had been tied to destroying Peter. Yet here he was, offering me another way. If I were to do as I originally planned—to kill him and go with Captain Bainbridge—the voyage would take time. Time I didn't have, I now realized. Obtaining the cure and returning to London with Peter was the most logical solution. It was likely I would have an opportunity to carry out my task after we'd arrived.

"Take me to it," I ordered, so desperate that I started running toward the trees.

But Peter didn't move. I stomped back, exhaling noisily through my nostrils. A wet strand of hair fell into his eyes and he jabbed a toe at the dirt. Annoyance tugged the corners of my mouth down, and I was on the verge of reminding him about our bargain when he mumbled, "I wish you would forget about returning. Forget London. Forget everything but what we could do together."

Surprise rooted me in place. "Peter—"

"You belong here." He raised his gaze and pierced me with his earnestness. "The others are beginning to accept you, too, I've seen it. You were wrong in saying bonds can't be found or replaced; you could be part of *our* family."

"Family?" I echoed. The surprise swirled away on a gust

of anger. Peter winced at the unadulterated disdain in my voice. "You think this is a *family*? Do family members normally slaughter each other, then?"

"No. They do worse."

That telltale muscle in his jaw twitched. Noticing it, my ire faded and my conversation with Captain Bainbridge elbowed its way in. To Peter, the ragged children in that jungle were his only option. The only way to avoid being completely alone. The family he'd been born with had, in his mind, either died or betrayed him. In his mind, the events of the full moon were probably part of Neverland, part of the darkness that lived here and slipped into our lungs and hearts and heads like air.

I didn't pardon it, but I understood it.

In the grass, fireflies flared and faded, bringing me back to that cave where it had felt so simple before memories and motives crowded in. I watched them and slowly shook my head. "I can't live here, Peter."

He came to stand beside me, and our arms touched. A Neverbird screeched. "Then stay just a little longer. Don't make me bring you back tomorrow. Give us another day."

The seconds ticked by, and in a place where time stopped or sped up, I felt each one as if it were a poke or jab. Peter didn't ask again, but his longing was so palpable I could taste it like a kiss. Now my thoughts turned to the first words we exchanged. *Don't be frightened*, he'd said. That was when I'd told my first lie to him. Admitting fear felt shameful or weak. But maybe it simply meant that you were about to do something very important.

So I agreed for a thousand reasons. Really, though, I only needed one. "Very well."

Peter's smile was radiant. He gave a small whoop and snatched me up, hurdling us into the stars. My arms looped around his neck and I arched my neck back, the sound of our laughter coming together to create a lovely sort of music. When I lowered my face, thinking to speak to Peter, the words faded when I saw his expression. For the first time since meeting him, his eyes shone with... hope.

Forgive me, I thought to them. The ones I'd left behind.

Agreeing to Peter's request was the most selfish thing I'd ever done. I wondered if I'd regret it. I reassured myself that soon, we would return to the city I had always known. Soon I would carry the leaves of the Fire Tree in my pocket and pull my brother back from the brink of death.

The brother whose name I still couldn't remember.

PART TWO

WENDY-BIRD

CHAPTER 12

ON THE MORNING of my seventh day in Neverland, I awoke and immediately knew something had changed.

The sun streamed down in bursts. An empty spiderweb glistened in the leaves. I lay smiling, arms flung over my head. I felt lighter, as though the bones inside me were hollow. I'd done something by telling Peter I would stay. A brick hadn't come off my wall of resistance—it had come crumbling down entirely. There were no voices or memories or feelings to make things dreary. I couldn't recall what I'd been doing before coming to Neverland and why I'd been so adamant about leaving it.

"Wendy-bird!"

More voices chimed in, calling for my presence. *Wake up! Join us! Come play!* Slightly scampered after me as I rushed to the ground. His nose ran and his voice was shrill as he said my name. My shadow tried to give him a consolatory embrace.

I was already gone.

The extra day I gave Peter turned into two. Then three. Then four. After that, they blended together. I was wildness and chaos. My own mother wouldn't recognize me, but I didn't care. I ran through the jungle with my torn trousers and loose hair, shrieking and giggling with the rest of the children. I flew through the clouds and over the hills on my great bird's back, my fair skin darkening by the day. And all the while I felt Peter's eyes on me. Every time I looked toward him, our gazes caught like two stars aligning in the sky, shining bright and briefly. Then I remembered how tightly he'd held Bell in his arms when I came upon them in the jungle, and I looked away.

Though we hadn't touched each other since the night Peter took me to see the glowworms, I still asked Bashira for the herb the village women consumed to avoid becoming with child.

I continued to meet James Bainbridge, but I didn't make the mistake of trusting him; either Bell had lied to him or he was lying to me. My appearances were always sporadic and late. The captain never uttered a single complaint, though—every morning he waited outside the Neverwood, staring at sky and ocean, his lean form dark against the vivid skyline.

There came a day when, during our lesson, the captain's wooden sword pounded against mine and kept coming. Usually, when I tired or fumbled, he took pity and stepped away. But now he was merciless, swinging again and again, moving so swiftly my eyes had trouble following him. A small stone dug into my heel, penetrating the thinning sole of my boot, but I didn't flinch. Panting, I met him blow for blow. Sweat made my skin slick. My shadow sat nearby, primly perched on a rock.

Just when I felt I couldn't stand anymore, a surge of strength went through me. I ducked and spun, slicing my makeshift blade in an arc. The action caught James by surprise, and it collided with the side of his neck, certain death if we'd been truly sparring. Air hissed through James's teeth as he exhaled. Heat shimmered around us and neither of us spoke. My chest rose and fell. We stared at each other, uncertain whether it was the lesson or something else entirely stirring our blood.

"Good. Very good," he said after a long, long pause.

I swallowed the apology rising in my throat and removed the sword. "Again."

But Captain Bainbridge didn't reposition himself. Instead, he cupped the reddening skin at his throat and glanced down. "You're limping, Miss Davenport."

"What are you—" Discomfort spread through my foot, brought on by the reminder. Impatiently I sat on a fallen tree to dig the stone out.

For a minute, the captain watched me. I pretended I was oblivious, that the stone had become the sun I orbited. It dropped to the dirt. Putting my boot back on also took all of my concentration.

"You're doing unnaturally well," he said suddenly.

"What do you mean?" Finished, I set my elbows on my knees and peered up at him. The sword rested beside me, and a fervor that matched my own seemed to emanate from it. All I wanted to do was grip that splintered hilt and fight so fast, so hard that nothing else mattered. Until my palms bled and the stars cowered and I was more weapon than girl. But I forced myself to be still and wait. Above us, the sun went slowly along, like an old horse pulling a gilded carriage. Today, the hours had no end.

"In the world where we come from, it should take years to learn the sword," Peter's brother informed me matter-of-factly. He retrieved the waterskin he'd brought and ripped it open with his teeth. Water slipped out of the opening and down the tanned column of his pulsing throat.

I tracked its progress with my eyes, not comprehending what he was saying. When I did, though, a new worry presented itself—Neverland was a place of magic and the unexplained. Everywhere else, I knew, was not.

"Suppose... suppose I should lose the ability if I return?" I asked, my voice soft. "I know the island is taking my memories. I haven't fought against it, really. Like our shadows, you lose what you don't bother to hold onto. But does it take the things I do want, as well?"

Once I return, I'd meant to say. If the captain noticed this wording, he chose not to acknowledge it. He met my gaze again, and there was understanding in those gray depths. Gently he answered, "I suspect we leave Neverland with more than we arrived with, my dear. Not less."

A faint, bittersweet smile curved my lips. "It's a very pretty thought, sir."

Captain Bainbridge appraised me, his head slightly tilted, just as Peter liked to do. The similarity was so jolting that I went still, trying to breathe as guilt flooded me. During these lessons it was easy to forget that every moment I spent with this man was another secret, another betrayal to the boy I'd left in the jungle.

It felt as though Captain Bainbridge's voice came from a distance as he asked, "If I may ask, why did you wish to learn the sword?"

I forced myself to meet his gaze. The sun beat down on our heads as I thought about his question. "Whatever our differences," I said slowly, "we do have one thing in common. Society has placed limits on who you can be, and it's no different for a woman. We are taught to write, not for the sake of penning novels, but for the art of letter writing. We learn arithmetic to run a household, but heaven forbid we venture into advanced algebra. There's no practical use, after all, and then we'd be able to challenge our husband's expertise. We're expected to be proficient musicians, for the sake of playing and singing to potential suitors, but of course our choice of instruments is limited. Mustn't have our faces turning red, after all, or raise our arms in an unseemly fashion. We are helpless, and we are kept helpless, because we would be too much of a threat otherwise."

This time, there was nothing sweet about my smile—it was bitter, through and through. I said nothing more, because that was my answer. That was why I'd wanted to learn the sword.

Silence trembled around us. Captain Bainbridge took a step closer and offered a drink. He looked unsurprised when I shook my head. He set his waterskin on the rock, then motioned that I should stand with a wave of his elegant fingers. "Now, there is one more thing I must teach you."

He didn't remark upon what I'd said, and his manner had returned to its instructive briskness. I wasn't sure why, but it made me like him even more. I got back to my feet and faced him, but the captain made no movement toward our swords. I frowned. "What are we doing?"

His attention went to something over my shoulder, and his generous mouth puckered with displeasure or perplexity. I turned to see what it was. Peter? A Neverbird?

Without warning, Captain Bainbridge's fingers snagged my wrist and he yanked me backward. It was so sudden that I lost my footing and fell against him. Before I could react, the false blade held me in place. His chest heaved against me. His body was hard and hot. His lips, damp from the waterskin, tickled my ear.

"There will be opponents who fight without honor. Never forget that," he murmured. I felt something hard and long against my backside, and in that moment, I wanted nothing more than to wrap my hand around it and face him. A fire started in my belly, and the heat spread downward.

For an instant, neither of us spoke or moved. I could feel Captain Bainbridge's heart against my back, beating as hard and fast as my own. Perhaps he expected retaliation or vile insults. Instead, I relaxed in his grasp. The sword's pressure eased.

A feral sound burst from my lips. I wrenched free, barely avoiding his responding jab, and jumped on the rock. Blood dribbled down his chin—my skull had smashed into his nose.

"You may be even more dangerous than he is," Captain Bainbridge observed, the statement muffled from his hand, which rose to stem the flow.

I acted as though I hadn't heard, but it felt like my veins were singing. I leaped off and bounded toward the Neverwood, tangled hair flying.

"Wendy!" the captain called. I paused at the edge of the brush, turning my head to indicate that I was listening. "One girl is more use than twenty boys."

Something fluttered inside me. "Thank you," I said.

As he nodded, I turned and plunged into the jungle. I wasn't sure why I felt the need to run, to fly, to put as much distance between me and the captain, but I did. I weaved through the tangles and threats as though I'd been born here. The sound of my pounding feet was drowned out by whispers; the trees were conversing, and I was close, so close to understanding them. Grinning, I stopped to stroke the bark of a particularly large one, the trunk so wide and thick that my arms couldn't encircle it. The whispers grew louder.

The beast... the great beast... watching from the shadows...

Time slowed. My heartbeat faltered. The birds quieted. Even without the trees' feathery remarks, I could feel it. A presence. A threat. My skin tingled from the force of its scrutiny. Telling myself to show no fear, I faced the beast they spoke of.

It stood amongst the vines and thorns and leaves, a cat that was like no other. Its impossibly bright, yellow eyes were steady and unblinking. Its paws were so large I knew they could kill me with one blow, and those curved, black claws looked sharper than any knife. Behind the creature, a tail flicked, deceptive in its playfulness. We stared at each other like statues, forever carved in this moment.

I think they were driven out of the mountains, Peter had said of the Neverbirds once. I'd undoubtedly discovered what had been powerful enough to do so.

After an eon—or perhaps just a smattering of seconds— I couldn't stop myself from swallowing. Even though the rest of me didn't move, the cat's round ears perked, as if I'd said something. What language did this wild thing speak? Would it respond to terror or courage? I didn't have a rock or a wooden sword, just my fists and my wits. Both were still frozen.

While I debated what to do, the cat seemed to reach a decision of its own. With a growl, it backed away. The jungle swallowed it whole. But I didn't budge from that spot, even when it was apparent the great beast was gone. I strained to hear the trees again. They'd gone silent, as well. It felt like I was alone on the island, with nothing but the aloof clouds for company.

Finally something moved. Thinking the amber-eyed cat had returned, I jerked. It was only my shadow, rocking back and forth on the ground. The sight of it filled me with contempt, and I was finally free.

I ran like the Devil himself gave chase.

A line of perspiration streamed down my temple as I

burst into the camp. Everything was so ordinary, so calm. I leaned over and wheezed.

Housekeeper was preparing supper. The air smelled of meat, due to the boar roasting over the spit. Its snout was shriveled and its face was twisted in a final grimace. A few children smiled in greeting. Slightly sat on the outskirts, next to Tootles. He noticed me but stayed where he was; he'd clearly given up on receiving any sort of care or comfort days ago. Part of me knew I should feel guilty about this, but when it came to caring for any of the children here, it felt like someone had crushed chloroform against my face again —my feelings were distant and hazy. There was only a slight puzzlement at why things had changed.

And perhaps a touch of regret.

All at once, every head in the clearing popped up. It wasn't me they were looking at, but the boy who'd emerged from the trees seconds after me. I recognized him from the village. I'd come to expect unwavering serenity from those on the plains, but this visitor drooped from heat and sorrow.

"What's wrong?" Peter had appeared, his expression tense and alert. He hardly spared me a glance and I mustered an equally indifferent façade.

We waited for the boy to speak. He did nothing to hide the extent of his grief; it ravaged his young features and made him ancient. There were tears in his voice as he told us the news.

"The Torch Bearer is dead."

Our party was solemn and silent upon arrival to the village.

Peter immediately went to the cottage that belonged to Lily, but I was too distracted to be bothered by this—the field was chaotic. All around, islanders gathered and cooked and arranged. I stood off to the side, watching the preparations. The rest of my companions had run off, too, playing a game that belied the gravity of this day. I thought to offer my help to someone, but I felt like I was in a hurricane, picked up and swept along with nothing to grab hold of.

Finally one of the women noticed me. "Go see Bashira. You must dress!" she said urgently.

Dress? I frowned in confusion, but she was already preoccupied, reprimanding a shame-faced boy who was covered in mud. Grateful for the excuse to visit my friend, I slipped away. Shouts filled the air with as much tangibility as wind, blowing this way and that. Someone was demanding more firewood. A child holding a tray of meat hurried by, and the tantalizing scent of it followed me all the way to the cottage.

I entered in a rustle of gladness and apprehension. Bashira was applying makeup to a girl's face with a small brush. At the sound of my arrival, she turned. I nearly didn't recognize her. Her eyes were outlined heavily in some kind of thick, black substance and her hair was pulled back in lovely, intricate braids.

"Wendy-bird," she said, beaming. "I wondered if you'd come today."

"Is that all right? I don't want to intrude."

She waved the question away. I knew I was staring, but

Bashira didn't seem to notice. She said something in her tongue and the other girl gave me a brief, shy smile before hopping to her feet. She brushed past and rushed out. I listened to her walk through the grass, a sound like the swishing of a skirt, and soon silence prevailed in the confined space. My friend was searching through a pile of clothing now. I watched her, mesmerized by the quick, hummingbird movements. Then I heard myself blurt, "Bashira, may I ask you a forward question?"

She looked over her shoulder at me. Her brow lowered. "Forward?" she echoed.

My cheeks heated. I cleared my throat once. Twice. "That is to say, I'd like to ask you something that isn't... entirely proper."

Bashira giggled. She'd selected something from the pile and brought it with her as she knelt in front of me. She set the garment down to clasp my hands. Startled, I didn't pull away. And after a moment, I didn't want to. Her palms were rough and warm, reminding me of something... or someone. The feeling was like tasting fresh bread after eating loaves that were crusty and stale. "I've never known anyone who acts the way you do!" she said, squeezing. "Like you're in a cage. We're *free*, Wendy-bird. There's no need to ask for permission here."

She waited, her dark eyes gleaming and expectant. My mind went back to the day before, beneath that hot, hot sun. The hard line of Captain Bainbridge's body against mine, the sweat beading on our skin, the way my rapid breath moved with his.

"I think there's something wrong with me. When I see certain pictures or spend time with particular people. Is there someone in the village who makes you feel..." My words slowed and staggered like a child learning to walk.

A huge smile had stretched across Bashira's face. "There is *nothing* wrong with you. I know this feeling you speak of."

"You do?" I said, and I was so relieved that there was a familiar sting in my eyes. For an instant, Bashira's face blurred.

"There's a bird in Neverland—I don't know its name in English—and come mating season, it pursues as many members of the flock as it wants," she told me. "Male or female, it doesn't matter. Beauty and desire have no limitations here. But sometimes the other bird does not feel the same, and it will deny every gesture or advance. Sometimes, if this happens, the admirer literally bursts."

"Bursts?"

"Yes," Bashira said solemnly. Then she laughed with a heartiness that was strange coming from someone of her size. She released me and stood. "We're not exactly like those birds, of course, but I understand it. Like I could shed my skin from being so full of wanting!"

There was nothing wrong with me. I was so relieved that I joined her in laughter. It was short-lived, though, when my thoughts continued to linger on the man I met at the edge of the Neverwood. "And if they want you back? The one who makes you feel such things?"

"It is as I said. We are free."

She made it sound so easy, so simple. I twisted my lips in

consideration. A slug the size of my index finger oozed its way up the wall. My eyes didn't see it, really; I was seeing another now, a boy with hair like the sun and a grin just as bright.

"What if... what if people are like that bird, and there isn't just one mate for us?" I ventured. Asking the question out loud felt frightening and daring. An acknowledgment rather than a possibility. It was no longer the cracked music box in my head; I'd opened the lid and let its music tinkle through the air.

Still, Bashira was unruffled. She shrugged and reached for the clothing she'd picked out earlier. "I have desired more than one in this village. But I think there is always one whose feathers are a bit brighter, don't you?"

Before I could answer, she shook the material out. It unfolded to become a dress, long and lovely in its elegance. My mood instantly darkened at the sight of it. The shadow next to me reached for the creation with eager fingers. "No," I snarled, gipping the legs of my trousers, bunching it in my fists. "No dresses."

The other girl regarded me thoughtfully. I felt naked and exposed beneath her gaze. "There's no need to fear what you are, Wendy-bird."

Though I didn't know why, exactly, I bristled at this. "And what am I?"

"That's something only you can know."

"Then I'm doomed," I muttered. Bashira's lips twitched.

"We will keep your trousers here. You can put them back on the moment the celebration is finished." But I still didn't move. Her tone gentled as she added, "It does not take away your strength or your character. Humans do that, not clothes. You're a woman. Be proud of this."

The words struck me with the voracity of a physical blow. I remembered my first night at the village, what Peter said about these people. *Here, you claim your power.* What if I did the same? What if there was more than one meaning to power?

When I uttered no further protests, Bashira gestured for me to remove my clothing. I did so, reluctantly. I wasn't bashful—it had the feel of something I'd done many times before. In a disorienting flash, there was suddenly a different girl standing in front of me. She had anxious brown eyes and wore the wrinkled uniform of a housemaid. Her name touched my tongue like the faintest of tastes, gone before I could truly define it. Then Bashira was there again, smiling as she dropped a gossamer gown over my head.

Once settled, it clung to every part of me, feeling wrong and familiar all at once. Bashira was already fussing with my hair, but I was still preoccupied by the dress, fingering the material, which seemed to be made of feathers and spiderwebs. Eventually, Bashira made a triumphant sound and stepped away, forcing me to lift my gaze. There was no looking glass; all I could see was the colored and translucent rocks clinking in the tangled strands of my hair. Bashira beamed as she told me she'd found them on the beach. Her expression was so pleased, so approving, that I mustered a smile to match it. Oblivious, my friend strode to the door.

"Oh!" she exclaimed, peeking through the crack. "It's begun!"

We hurried out of the cottage. The islanders had crowded at the cliff's edge, taking care not to crush the bright wildflowers growing there. The tiny things seemed like onlookers themselves, stretching proudly on their stalks, vibrant splashes of color against the fading horizon. The air was strangely, eerily still. It felt like a hushed church just before the reverend appeared. No wind, no murmurs, no music.

Short as we were, Bashira and I made our way to a spot near the front. Peter was there, with just a few people between us. As always, I sensed his presence, but the scene taking place held all my attention. My heart quickened with anticipation.

There were seven people at the front of the crowd. They stood in a circle, facing the torch that burned brightly in the middle. They varied in every way, from sex, to age, to build. The majority were boys—although most were so brawny it hardly felt right calling them that—but there were two girls. One was startlingly tall, her yellow hair a long braid down her back, her exposed arms defined with muscle.

And Lily was the other.

Peter moved to stand at my side. I pretended not to be affected by the fact he'd sought me out, but suddenly I felt warmer. "What are they doing?" I asked, noting that all seven individuals held a weapon of some sort.

He kept his gaze on them, too. "I told you, Wendy-bird. They must battle each other to first blood."

"Already?" I blurted. They hadn't even buried the previous Torch Bearer yet.

We were looking at each other now, and Peter must've seen this thought in my eyes. "The Neverlanders grieve when one of their own dies, of course, but it's different when the Torch Bearer departs peacefully. After the torch has been passed to the next one, they throw a party, of sorts. A celebration."

A black-haired woman began speaking to the seven warriors, her back to the crowd. They all shouted something in unison. I considered asking Peter for a translation, but then Lily caught my attention—she was engaged in what looked like a private conversation with the older woman, nodding at something she said. Their voices were too low for anyone else to hear, but Lily's dark eyes were hard with determination.

Terrifying as the idea was, I liked that nothing was being forced on the young girl. This was something she'd fought for, something she wanted. What was it like, to want something so badly? To dedicate your very life to it?

"Penny for your thoughts," Peter remarked.

I opened my mouth to respond just as three of the warriors moved. They walked a few steps, then turned to face the other three, effectively pairing off. From the farthest edge of the gathering, a drum began to pound. *Boom. Boom. Boom.* The black-haired woman gave a shout, and quick as a blink, every warrior on the hill was in motion.

Shouts and sound rose around me. Each fight was mesmerizing, a dazzling display of skill and training, yet I found myself only watching Lily. The dark-skinned boy she fought was quick on his feet, but within a minute, she opened his arm with a long cut. Lowering his weapon, the boy put a fist on his chest and bowed his head. Lily inclined her head in acknowledgment.

The yellow-haired girl was waiting off to the side, the tip of her blunt sword dripping red. The broad-shouldered warrior she'd beaten was already making his way through the crowd, probably off to tend to his wound. The instant Lily turned to her, the other girl was a blur of movement. Lily raised her sword quickly, and there was a clash of silver and steel. A cluster of young people nearby chanted, "Aisling! Aisling! Aisling!"

Aisling lasted a little longer than the other warrior Lily had faced—her talent rested in deflecting and dancing. But Lily must've been trained by someone with more knowledge, more skill, because suddenly she lunged and spun her wrist. Within seconds, Aisling's sword went flying through the air. It landed on the ground with a dull sound. Lily's arm moved again, and suddenly Aisling was holding her shoulder to staunch a tide of red.

But her face revealed no pain or bitterness. Just as the other boy had done, Aisling smashed her fist against her bosom and lowered her head. Once again, Lily returned the gesture, and the yellow-haired girl left the hill like the others had.

There was only one other warrior standing now.

Lily spun to face the sinewy one I'd heard someone call Roan. He had been locked in a skirmish all this time with a red-haired boy, but I saw no sign of him now. There was a stain in the grass where Roan stood waiting, and his face was void of all expression, his fair hair shifting in a sudden breeze. Something about him made my stomach twist.

But Lily was no coward, and she wasted no time. With a loosed breath and swing of her sword, she instantly put Roan on the offensive. Again and again, he barely managed to block her ferocious strikes. She was like a snake lashing out with its bright fangs. Her leather breastplate gleamed in the fading sun, as though she'd buffed it with oil before all this. Her braid whipped this way and that as she moved. I couldn't take my eyes off her, and neither could Peter, a swift glance told me. Not wanting to miss a single moment, I refocused on the two Neverlanders battling for blood. For the torch. For their people.

Lily was better than him, I thought, surprised by a surge of satisfaction that followed the observation.

Roan knew it, too. A vein stood out in his forehead, and there was a frantic light in his eyes. He was even faster than Aisling, but it wasn't enough—it was only a matter of time before Lily found her opening. The shouts and calls from the villagers were almost deafening now, all of it a meaningless hum in my ears. I leaned forward, wanting to see the moment Lily claimed her victory. Though I didn't consider us friends in any capacity, her triumph had become important. I needed her to win, needed her to prove something to us both.

I couldn't tell if it was desperation or planning, but in a movement so swift my eyes didn't catch it, Roan swung his leg and planted his booted heel in the center of Lily's chest. It looked as though he'd put every bit of his substantial weight behind the blow. Lily stumbled back, and it felt like my heart staggered with her, afraid that even one misstep would cost her the torch.

I was right to be afraid—still moving extraordinarily fast for someone his size, Roan took two long-legged strides forward. He was going to cut her, I thought with a rush of disappointment. Lily had lost.

Instead, Roan plunged his sword into her chest.

CHAPTER 13

EVERYONE on the cliffs was mute with horror.

Peter stood rigid beside me, but I couldn't look away from Lily long enough to see his expression. My mind refused to accept it. She was supposed to win. Tootles saw her triumph in one of his visions, hadn't he? She would recover from this. She had to.

And yet the blade in her chest said otherwise.

The silence was so prominent that the only sound was the whistling wind. We all waited for her to collapse. My heart was already hurting for Peter... and for Lily, too.

But instead of dying, the young girl grasped the hilt of the sword that was still inside her and pulled it out without even blinking. I watched with a baffled frown. Letting out a feral cry, Lily launched at Roan. He'd clearly thought she was on the verge of death, as well, because he didn't raise a hand to defend himself. The bulky warrior toppled backward with all the grace of a newborn horse.

Lily swung a sword in each hand now, sunlight bouncing off the metal. There was no blood. No stain on her shirt. No hole in her breastplate. As she placed the edges of both swords beneath Roan's jaw, I realized what had happened in a rush of certainty—Roan's sword had merely gone through the space between her arm and side.

He stared up at her now, tight-lipped, his nostrils flaring. Neither of them said a word, their chests heaving into the stillness. Every single person on this hill knew he had tried to kill her. Seconds passed that felt like minutes, and I saw a change come over Lily. The hate in Roan's eyes burned hotter than the torch he fought for, but suddenly the face looking back at him was calm. Calculating.

The face of a queen, I thought.

I waited for Lily to lower her weapon and speak words of mercy. Instead, her arms moved, finishing the cross of her swords. I closed my eyes just in time to avoid seeing her cut Roan's throat open. But I heard the squelch of flesh, the undeniable sound of blood spurting. My stomach heaved, and I waited for the burn of vomit to come surging up. After a few moments, though, the sensation passed. Slowly, I opened my eyes again.

I hadn't expected that. I hadn't expected her to kill him.

Lily didn't step back from the body or clean her sword. Instead, she faced her people and thrust her weapon into the air. "*¡Yo quemo!*" she shouted, her teeth gleaming red. "*¡Yo quemo!*"

Wild cheers rose into the dimming sky. It was over, I realized faintly, still seeing that moment Lily had struck the killing blow. Despite the grueling ordeal she'd just been through, the Neverlanders surrounded their new Torch Bearer and gathered her up on their shoulders. They began to move away from the place where she'd fought. Only three people stayed behind. A young boy, who bore a striking resemblance to Roan, a woman with gray streaked through her hair, and an old woman with a stooped back. They gathered around the body on the ground, and I heard one of them release a long wail.

The sound was overpowered by singing, which now filled the night from corner to corner. Still reeling from what I just witnessed, I trailed after the crowd. They carried Lily up, and up, and up a grassy slope. I followed at a distance, keeping my eyes on them. Now and then, I saw a golden head catch the fading sun.

At the very top, the islanders finally set Lily down. They gathered a second time, and the joyous shouts faded into a solemn silence. I stopped beside Bashira.

"What's happening?" I asked under my breath.

My friend flashed me a swift, dimpled smile before fixing her attention toward the front of the crowd. "Lily is making her vows to us."

I turned, too. Like a lone rock facing a hundred rushing, frothing waves, Lily stood before her people, her back to the open sky. She held the torch aloft now, and the firelight shone upon the uncertainty in her expression.

When she opened her mouth to speak, however, everything changed. Her spine straightened and she grew before our eyes. Her voice was loud and unwavering—not even the wind could snatch it away. I couldn't understand what she was saying, but it didn't matter. I felt the meaning of her words. Through the rivers of my veins, inside the hollow of my stomach. She was making a vow, a promise, an oath. Even if we could not see it with our eyes, it was strong as any document or ring.

Warmth tickled my ear. Bashira leaned close to whisper, "She is offering herself to us. Once we accept, her leadership is sanctioned."

Suddenly Lily raised her fist and shouted. Spittle flew. In a flurry of movement, the crowd around me shouted back. It was more than a marriage, I realized. This girl was giving herself to them. I wanted that. To be so consumed, so impassioned by something it was a simple choice to completely hand myself over to it.

In my musings, I'd missed the final moments of the ceremony. The islanders were trickling back toward the village, led by their new Torch Bearer. Bashira began to follow. She noticed me lingering at the edge and smiled questioningly. I waved her on. As they gathered around the fire, the music started. Platters of food were passed around, and the smell of it beckoned.

Just as I started toward them, Peter appeared. It was so soundless that I wasn't quite certain whether he was boy or spirit. I faltered, and something in his expression prompted me to stay. Peter stood next to me, hands shoved in his trouser pockets. He didn't comment on the dress or Lily's ascension. He didn't say anything. From a distance, we watched the islanders laugh and belong. The moon and stars drew closer. We thought our own thoughts and felt our own feelings. Then, hesitantly, Peter laced his fingers through mine. And I let him.

He didn't let go as we joined the others. Only one noticed our presence; Lily's glance flicked down to our entwined hands. She scowled. I wanted to tell her that she needn't be so protective—if anyone was going to be hurt in this, it was me. She was surrounded by her friends, though, and now a man was blessing the food. He spoke in a language I didn't know, but it was obvious he was praying when I noted how everyone restrained themselves from touching the feast. Élise and several others, both men and women, started dispersing plates laden with meat, greens, and fruit.

I released Peter's hand to accept one, and when I turned to him, he was gone. I rolled my eyes. *Of course.* Bashira was nowhere in sight, and after brief deliberation, I settled beside Freckles. A smile of greeting stretched across his greasy face. Before I could say anything, he tore into the meat again. I decided to match his enthusiasm as we ate.

After a time, Lily left her circle. I knew, because I couldn't seem to stop staring at her. She went from person to person, her demeanor respectful and gracious. The smooth tenor of her voice was more intriguing than any crackling fire or beastly howl, and I listened to the conversations carefully— the Neverlanders were offering her pieces of wisdom and well wishes.

When Lily reached us, I expected her to brush past and continue on to the next group. But she shocked me by sitting, and our knees nearly touched. The bite of food I'd just taken stopped in my throat.

Lily didn't strike me as one who fell prey to uncertainty, yet she kept her eyes on the dirt and said nothing. So, I asked the question that had been fluttering in my mind since the moment we'd heard the news. "Aren't you frightened at all? Of the responsibility?"

I cringed at the desperate curiosity in my voice, but she didn't seem to notice. Her answer was slow in coming. It was the first time she'd spoken directly to me, and the words were thick with resentment. "I'd be a fool if I weren't."

No one else heard this—Freckles had jumped up and gone to speak with a girl near the bonfire. We were alone, in a way. At Lily's words I paused, mulling over my reply. Finally I told her, "Everyone says that you'll be the greatest Torch Bearer this island has known."

I thought it would be reassuring, hearing of these people's confidence in her. But she pursed her lips, looking as though she'd taken a bite of something and couldn't decide whether it was wonderful or revolting. Lily looked toward the sea, toward the horizon, and the final dregs of sunlight tinted her skin golden. "I'm not interested in standing amongst the great," she murmured. "I want to be known for sitting amongst the weak."

Then she hopped to her feet with such fluid grace it was obvious her skin contained waterfalls and air instead of muscles and blood. Before I'd truly comprehended what she'd just confided, the girl ran to the fire, where the dancing had begun. Lily closed her eyes and moved to the music with abandon, a sort of violent rhythm I'd never seen before. It was beautiful.

Breathless, Bashira came to me. She offered her hand, the meaning clear. I smiled and shook my head. Instead of returning to her friends, she flopped down and observed with me. One of the dancers had gone still and was looking at Lily with unabashed desire. I recognized him from the Proving.

"Who's that?" I asked, disliking him instantly. The possessiveness in his stance, the intelligence in his black eyes.

"That is Drystan. He's a very skilled warrior, as I'm sure you saw today." She nudged my shoulder with hers. "Do you think him handsome?"

I thought he was dangerous; even my shadow cringed from him. On this island, men and women were equal. But I could see that Drystan had a different perspective and nothing would alter it. It had the feel of a battle I'd been fighting for years, like I'd been rolling in the muck and cold, and now I was covered in blood and wounds made from unheard words and dismissed dreams. Wherever I came from, there were more like him.

Why would I ever go back to that?

I remembered Bashira was waiting for me to speak. Drystan was undeniably appealing, with his strong jaw and hard lines... but here, I had eyes for only one boy. The endearing tuft at the back of his head. His gangly limbs. His impish smile.

As though my thoughts had conjured him, Peter was

there in a rush of gold and vitality. He grabbed hold of me and hauled me to my feet. "No, Peter, I don't—"

"Too late!" he chirped. It was true. We were already surrounded by a mass of whirling, jumping, happy people. Bashira remained on the crushed grass, urging us on. Amidst my protests, Peter gripped my waist and dipped me back. Caught off guard, I laughed and clutched at his shoulders. His hold on me was tight as the ground loomed so close I could touch it. My rock-studded hair streamed behind me, loose and long. The drum became faint, other voices a hum. Our gazes met. His was laden with so many emotions, so many secrets that I couldn't pick one any more than I could pick a favorite star.

My delight faded. I wasn't supposed to laugh, I wasn't supposed to enjoy his company. He was devoted to another, no matter how often I conveniently forgot that fact. She had silver hair and magic. And I... I couldn't allow the vulnerability that caring for Peter meant. It seemed like I'd only recently recovered from a long illness, and he was a drop of the poison that had weakened me.

I stepped away.

I'd forgotten about the dress. It nearly tripped me, and I yanked angrily at the material. Peter frowned, reaching for my hand. I evaded his touch and bolted, shoving through the throng, heading toward Bashira's cottage.

By now the celebration was affected by the cups that had been passed around at the start of the meal, full to the brim with a bitter, bubbly liquid. Slurred words and sharp laughter filled my ears. I walked faster, eager to be out of the dress, and glanced at the sky. Nestled in their velvet blanket, the stars peeked down at the ceremony taking place. As I kept staring at them, I heard an odd sort of melody in my head. Something about dust and soaring...

I was at the door of Bashira's cottage now. Putting the strange thought from my mind, I hurried inside. The fire in the grate had nearly burned out. Shapes quivered on the wall of the cottage, like creatures underwater. If I was still enough, maybe I'd hear the moan of a whale.

"Wendy!" Peter burst into the ocean and it evaporated. He'd followed me.

"Go away," I snapped, and bent to snatch up my trousers. He didn't. I spun to face him. "What do you want, Peter?"

He fidgeted, looking more frustrated than I'd ever seen him. I glanced downward, searching for his shadow as I always did, but the room was too dim. Oblivious to my fear, Peter raked his hair back. The gesture was achingly familiar now. Then his eyes fixed on me, bewitching as a love spell. Or a hex.

"It's just... I didn't say it earlier. You look..." He cleared his throat. "I wish I knew a better word than 'beautiful.' Never been much for reading, me."

In all the time I'd known him—sometimes it seemed like days, others it felt like years, and on certain occasions it was just a smattering of seconds—Peter hadn't been kind. Agreeable, maybe, and certainly passionate, but not kind.

And it wasn't just the compliment. I thought of how he'd held my hand during the blessing. How warm his fingers had felt around mine.

For the thousandth time, I forgot to hate him. The dam already had so many holes, had become so debilitated, that a rush of feeling broke through. And I was forced to admit to myself what I'd been resisting from the night we met.

I wanted Peter.

Not just physically, but all of him. His heart, his essence, his mind. I wanted to consume him the way it felt he was consuming me. Peter was the sea and I was the shore, gradually crumbling and disappearing beneath his relentlessness.

What was it Bashira had said? *I think there is always one whose feathers are a bit brighter, don't you?*

He stood on the far side of the cottage, waiting for me to say something, firelight quivering across his skin. Frustrated, wistful, I dropped the trousers, stepped over them, and crossed the space. I cupped Peter's face. Stubble tickled my fingertips.

His throat bobbed. "What are you doing?"

"Claiming my power," I whispered. Then, after giving him a chance to turn away, I kissed him.

It was different from our other kisses—this wasn't a rough exchange between strangers. It was uncertain and exploring, like stepping into a lovely, winding garden. His hands were feathers on my neck, there and gone, only to lightly press against my lower back and pull me closer. Instinctively I deepened the kiss, hungry for more. He tasted like the bittersweet drink in that cup.

Suddenly it wasn't uncertain anymore. Nor gentle. I gripped his hair without restraint, and every part of him was crushed against every part of me. Peter made a sound, almost a growl but not quite, and it vibrated through me. I couldn't think, couldn't reason, couldn't concentrate on anything but him and this. His knee nudged between my legs, and I opened them wider. Without breaking our kiss, Peter picked me up and guided my legs around his waist. Once I'd crossed them behind him and put my arms around his neck, he walked forward and set me on the edge of a table. Herbs and flowers fell to the floor.

I was on the verge of undoing his trousers when Peter broke away. "I want to see what's underneath that dress," he said thickly.

He pulled it down, baring my breasts to the air. Then he lifted the skirt and held it against my waist. The gown bunched around my middle, leaving the rest of me naked. Peter took his cock out, positioned it against me, and thrust inside with a smooth jerk of his hips. I gasped. The table shook with every movement, more green bundles and bursts of color making their way to the floor.

There was a moment, as I was moaning beneath him, that I had a queer feeling. There was something I was supposed to do, I thought faintly. Something I was forgetting. *Oh, what does it matter?* Nothing else mattered but this.

Peter went utterly still, and I opened my eyes to see that he was in the throes of ecstasy. A subtle warmth filled me. I sat up and saw that some of it had slipped out and trickled onto my skirt.

I would need to wash this gown before returning it to Bashira.

Just as Peter started to speak, a shout rang out. Both of us froze. We realized at the same time that it was only a child sprinting past. Still, it felt like we had both woken from the same dream.

"We should return," I said quietly. Peter's expression was fathomless as he nodded. We pulled apart, and I shakily straightened my dress.

"Wendy..." I waited for him to go on, but Peter faltered. For a moment or two, he just stared at me, his lips deliciously red and swollen. He was going to mention Bell. Tell me that what we'd done was a mistake.

Desperate to avoid hearing the words out loud, I blurted, "Race you!"

I was a bullet from a pistol, shooting into the night. Peter couldn't help his own nature, and soon I heard the sound of his pursuit. Within seconds we were back in brightness and noise. When I reached the bonfire, I slowed and looked over my shoulder. But Peter had stopped chasing me—without looking in my direction, he ran at Lily and swept her into a galloping dance. She shrieked with girlish pleasure.

The hot acidity of jealousy filled my heart. I wasn't certain why it upset me, that he was acting so casually. We weren't courting and Peter was not the sort to dote upon anyone. I'd known all that before I kissed him and I couldn't pretend otherwise, no matter how much I wanted to.

Clearing my throat, I looked away from the pretty picture he made with Lily and took stock of my surroundings. The celebration was in full swing. The musicians played in their place near the fire, which was even bigger than the last time I'd seen it lit. Bright fingers of flame reached for the sky, leaving behind wisps of smoke. Trays of food were laid out, here and there, and most of the dishes had been picked clean.

I searched for Bashira. I soon found her at the base of the hill, and she seemed quite taken with a young man I hadn't seen before. He had skinny arms and a shy smile. I didn't want to interrupt their conversation, so I was about to fix my gaze elsewhere when Bashira spotted me and beckoned. I smiled and closed the distance between us.

"Wendy-bird, this is Juan," she said once I was within earshot.

"I'm glad to finally meet you, Wendy-bird." Bashira's beau stepped forward and kissed my cheek, a standard greeting here in Neverland. At first, I'd been unnerved by it. Now I didn't bat an eyelash. Juan stepped back again, returning to Bashira's side. I heard him say something, but I had glanced to the side, and my eyes just happened to move past the place where Peter stood.

He was looking back at me.

"I beg your pardon?" I said finally, tearing my gaze from Peter's. With notable effort, I gave Juan my full attention.

"I asked what it's like to fly on a Neverbird," he repeated.

As the night wore on, more and more islanders joined the dancing. Eventually Juan asked Bashira for a turn. The girl accepted, of course, and off they went. I stayed where I was, trying my damndest not to watch Peter.

It was because of my avoidance that I noticed Tootles. The boy was a spot of stillness, surrounded by writhing bodies and endless commotion. He sat by himself.

Since the night of the drawing, when Nimble had called me his mother, I'd tried to keep my distance from the other children. But I could see that something was wrong; Tootles's jaw was clenched and he stared at the festivities with glazed eyes. His hands were limp and palm-up on the ground.

I hurried over and knelt in front of the boy, nearly tearing the blasted skirt again. "Tootles? What is it?" I asked with quiet urgency.

Nothing. Not so much as a twitch. I looked for Peter, thinking he would know how to help.

He stood with Lily and her friends again, shrouded in shadow, but I felt his gaze on me. I couldn't make out the details of his features, only the hair glinting on his crossed arms as the flames flickered. I blinked, and suddenly he had me on that table again, his muscled body filling my vision as he plunged, again and again, claiming my body and everything else. Then I blinked again, and we were separated by several yards and a thousand unspoken words.

Suddenly Tootles moved his head, and my concern for him returned in a rush. When I turned, he was looking directly at me. This time, his eyes were clear. "Tootles?"

"Peter is going to die," he said.

CHAPTER 14

WE FLEW BACK to camp in silence.

Peter's touch was brisk, and he made no effort at conversation. I hardly noticed. Even with the wind in my ears and the stars whispering overhead, there was only one sound I could hear. Over and over again, incessant as a ticking clock. Tootle's voice saying, *Peter is going to die.*

The moon was locked in a fierce battle with the clouds. Breaths left my mouth in thick, swirling gusts. In the time since we'd left Bashira's cottage, the night had chilled. The air itself seemed to glitter with frost, as if the sky was wearing a diamond necklace. Though the cold had begun to numb my thoughts, a few survived, crackling hot as any campfire. Should I tell Peter what Tootles saw in his vision?

Everything was different now. All my fears of rejection had abated, along with the niggling sense that I should resist loving Peter. Even with my memories retreated—there was no part of me that wanted to pull them back—it seemed like all I'd done since meeting him was lie. The truth was water running through the spaces between fingers, and I wanted to keep one. Just one. That's what mattered most after hearing Tootle's dire outcome.

"It was me," I told Peter abruptly. My voice was stark against the razor-edged night. I watched his focus shift back to me, and though it felt like his eyes pierced my courage as easily as a needle through paper, I forced myself to go on. "The other night, I mean. *I* saw you and that girl together in the Neverwood. It wasn't that boy you despise so much."

It took a few seconds for Peter to understand. When he did, his face visibly hardened, and he changed direction without warning, hurtling toward the canopy of trees. My insides fluttered but I stayed collected, the only sign of the apprehension I felt hidden as fists against my sides. Leaves and vines blurred around us. The moment our feet touched the ground, Peter abruptly let go of me as though I'd burned him. I stumbled on the wretched skirt I still wore—in my shocked daze, I'd forgotten to take the trousers back from Bashira—then caught my balance as Captain Bainbridge taught me.

In the night's luminous glow, Peter looked like a statue, smooth and cold and unfeeling. "What do you know, Wendy Davenport?" he asked, his tone low and even.

Danger, instinct whispered. But I raised my chin and met his gaze squarely. Thunder rumbled. In the distance, a brief flash of lightning. "Nothing, it turns out. When I disappeared—the day you thought I'd gone off exploring—I met a pirate. He told me that you'd taken Bell against her will. But she hardly looked like a captive, which made me realize that I'd been listening to the word of a *pirate*. Silly, really."

This babbling explanation didn't make Peter soften or waver, and I wasn't sure why I stopped myself from saying James's name. Distrust hovered between us, loud as the crickets and frogs singing their night ballads. Rain began to patter against the green roof above. It couldn't touch us yet.

"Why didn't you say anything before?" Peter demanded. One of the raindrops found its way through, landing on his forehead. It slid down his nose and hung off the end like someone grappling at a cliff's edge.

He wanted to know why I hadn't said anything? Quite simply, I never wanted to know the answer. To hear him speak her name and be unable to deny the feeling there. Maybe I wasn't ready to reveal every truth, for I just gave an inane shrug and mumbled, "I suppose I decided it was none of my business."

Peter scowled. He didn't know that he was asking the wrong questions, that the real curiosity was why I'd admitted all of this to him now. He stalked away, rubbing the back of his neck. With his attention diverted, his shadow lunged for me, but I stood in a spot of darkness that was safe from its vicious grasp. I watched its frenzied movements, wondering why Peter's shadow still found me so abhorrent after all this time.

Suddenly, like water to a dry, dry seed, a tiny idea sprouted.

Before I could coax it to grow, Peter returned. His spine was stiff with resolve. There was also something in his eyes that captured my attention—for once, he was not all games and fun. There truly was a soul behind the flesh and bones. I stopped breathing so I would hear every syllable that came out of his mouth.

And the boy who kept a thousand secrets finally entrusted me with one. The galaxy shuddered as he said, "Tink wasn't taken. She was killed."

Peter and I sat in the highest tree of Neverland. We looked out at the jungle, our legs swinging back and forth. The skirt didn't hinder me now, making me wonder if my body remembered something I didn't. The clouds had hurriedly departed, allowing the moon and stars to shine. I counted them in my head, aware that it was impossible to get them all, but counting all the same. Even knowing something was impossible shouldn't deter one from trying it, at least once or twice.

"Stars are beautiful, but they can't take part in anything. They must just look on forever," Peter remarked, his tone absent. Lazy. As if we had all the time in the world. At that moment, it felt like we did.

The words struck a chord within me. I frowned at the sky, peering more closely at the glowing bits hanging there like tinsel and ornaments on a Christmas tree. Why should Peter's comment make me feel such kinship with them?

"I don't agree," I said impulsively, "Some stars never

change position, and that's how sailors are able use them as a compass. I'd hardly call that looking on, would you?"

Peter raised his eyebrows. Now he studied the stars anew, and there was a speculative tilt to his head. "You're right, Wendy-bird. I'd forgotten that some things are more than they appear."

"Imagine how much else I might be right about," I replied without looking at him. Peter's shoulder nudged mine, and from the corner of my eye, I saw that he was smiling. After a moment, I realized that I was smiling, too.

As our companionable silence stretched, a bat flitted past. It had something wriggling and squealing in its mouth, and within seconds, the unfortunate sound stopped. Once, I might have trembled at this.

"Why do you live in the Neverwood?" I asked Peter abruptly. He turned his head. "Freckles told me that a child disappears every few days, dragged away by animals or killed by something else. It seems like the most dangerous part of the island."

"That's exactly why. No one else dares to enter it."

Like the drawing, this made sense in a terrible way. It reminded me of the unchecked ferocity that existed within Peter. His compliments, his touches, his confessions had made it easy to forget. And I couldn't avoid speaking of Bell forever. So, with his gaze lingering on mine in a way that made it tempting to forget all over again, I took a breath and plunged. "Why do you call her 'Tink,' Peter?"

At this, it seemed as though shutters closed over those eyes. Clouds moved in like someone closing the drapes, using darkness to hide their pain. Peter looked out at his kingdom, shifting so that his hands dangled over his knees. He seemed to be preparing himself, just as I had. An insect settled on his skin while I waited. He didn't brush it away, and it flapped glowing, transparent wings.

"Her proper name is Bell, it's true," Peter said finally. Disturbed by the puff of his breath, the winged thing departed into the teeming night. "But amongst her people she's odd, always building a contraption or wondering how something works. 'Tinkering again?' I used to ask her."

There was a catch in his voice, and I pretended not to notice. With deliberate lightness I remarked, "Death doesn't seem to have come between you."

"If you don't consider being unable to touch each other an obstacle." His voice was hard, and I felt a flutter of apprehension when I heard it. Usually when Peter sounded like that, bad things followed.

I felt my brow lower in confusion. There was a picture of Peter and Bell in the corner of my mind, framed and ready for inspection whenever I passed it. Because of this, I would never be able to forget the moment I came upon them. "But I saw you holding her."

"You saw me wishing I could hold her," Peter countered. He acted detached, but I could sense his anguish. The lump in his throat moved. Would he accept comfort if I were to offer it? Or was his heart, his mind so full of Bell that no one else could ever hope to reach him?

Somewhere nearby, a creature began to chitter. The tension between us abated slightly, as though the sound were a signal of some kind. "Was Bell one of the islanders, then?" I ventured.

Peter didn't answer. He reached over my head, and his alluring scent wafted past me. I dug my fingers into the branch to keep from touching him. Peter's arm lowered, and I saw that he held a flower. It was white and violet, the petals long and stringy. They tickled my wrist as Peter held it out and bowed, as if he were any other gentleman with a bouquet.

"She's the one who first brought me to Neverland," he said, watching me smell the flower. "I'd been injured during the fight with Constable Collingwood, and I collapsed in Cornwall Gardens. It was wintertime, so the cold would've killed me if the blood loss didn't. Tink brought me to the Fire Tree... and I never left. Not for a few years, at least. I only returned to London because of the stories I heard at the village. I'd completely forgotten about my time there, you see. Then the dear captain took it upon himself to find Neverland and bring those lovely memories back."

Peter fell silent again. I looked at him, wishing words existed that would help ease his pain. As I lowered my gaze, I noticed that his hand was very close to mine, and every part of me yearned to entwine my fingers in his. Neverland felt it, too. The leaves themselves leaned closer, as if to cradle and comfort.

Something kept me from reaching out. I spun the flower stem between my fingers and said, "I'm sorry, Peter."

He didn't shrug, fly off, or say something flippant. Instead, Peter just continued to sit there with me. The clouds rolled and shifted again, and the tiniest bit of moonlight broke through. I was able to watch his grief give way to fury. All traces of vulnerability vanished. His mouth was a thin line, a dark slash across his face. "It was his fault. Bainbridge," he growled.

I almost told Peter another truth, then. About what I knew of his past and the bargain I'd struck with his brother on board the *Jolly Roger*. But I thought of the betrayal I would see in his face, how the trust he'd displayed tonight would be gone forever. If Tootles's vision came to pass, Peter would leave this world despising me, and the thought was unbearable. "Who's that?" I asked instead, hating myself enough for the both of us.

Peter plucked a leaf off its branch and ripped it into tiny pieces. He opened his hand and let the breeze take it. "He's captain of the pirates."

"Did... did this man kill Bell?" I held my breath, fearing the answer. That the person who was teaching me to fight, whose touch ignited me quick as a light, was capable of such a hideous act.

"Not with his own hands, no. But he may as well have. It was his men that done it." A trace of an accent slipped into Peter's voice, betraying the depth of emotion there. He still wouldn't meet my gaze. In the closest tree, something stirred. A monkey. It crawled into the open, and there was an oddly-shaped lump on its back—its offspring, I realized a moment later. It noticed us and swung out of sight.

Peter didn't say any more. Speaking of the captain was unnerving, anyway; if I wasn't careful enough, I could give something away. Seeking to change the subject, I mentally walked by that picture again and resented Bell for her loveliness. But she'd tried to help me the day Captain Bainbridge's man had clamped that chloroform-covered handkerchief over my face. I owed her compassion at the very least.

"So there are spirits in Neverland?" I asked next, thinking of how often it felt like I was being watched.

But apparently our conversation was over. Peter stood and pushed some hair out of his eyes. He looked down at me like I was a stranger. Like we hadn't gasped together in the dark, hands roving and exploring over the hills and plains that were our bodies. Reluctantly, I pushed myself up and stepped closer, still holding the flower he'd given me. In a practiced move we had both become used to, he placed his arms behind my back and knees, then carried me into the stars. Bashira's dress fluttered around my legs, eliciting an image of a window with gauzy curtains. I focused on that instead of spirits or ill-boding visions.

It wasn't until we were nearly to camp that Peter spoke again. His voice was hushed so as to avoid waking those slumbering in the trees.

"I will always love her, Wendy," he said. It was unexpected, yet somehow not. I wished it didn't matter so much. My only reaction was a bleak nod. He put me in the middle of the clearing and left without another word.

As I watched him go, clutching my flower a bit too tightly, it occurred to me that I didn't even know where he slept.

I was about to step onto the first mushroom and begin

the climb when the fine hairs on the back of my neck prickled—someone was watching me. One of the spirits? Or, even worse, the yellow-eyed cat with the huge, flesh-tearing claws? I tensed, sweeping my gaze across the clearing. Relief swept through me when I realized it was just my shadow.

It stood in the trampled grass, given life by the moon. We looked at each other, and for once it was without impatience or resentment. She tilted her head, as if to say, *Would you like me to take it?* I knew she meant the ache, the tightness in my chest put there by the knowledge of Peter's fate and that he was Bell's, dead or no.

"No," I told it. "This, I will keep."

It gave off an air of surprise. I couldn't name the reason why this was important to me, feeling such pain. But it was, and I'd already relinquished too many parts of myself. Any more and I wouldn't be Wendy. I'd just be... nameless. No one. A shadow of a shadow.

And so, with my aching heart and mournful thoughts, I climbed toward the sky to join the other sad children of Neverland.

CHAPTER 15

THE SUN ROSE, and I was awake to greet it.

My slumber had been dream-filled, restless, and brief. I sat on the leaf that served as my bed and watched the play of colors reflecting off the jungle walls. I didn't run to meet Captain Bainbridge. Not today. A listlessness had stolen over me, and I had no desire to go anywhere or see anyone. I couldn't stop thinking about what I'd learned of Captain Bainbridge's lies, Bell's violent death, or Peter's inevitable end.

Halfway through the morning, though, my stomach would no longer tolerate my self-imposed isolation. Reluctantly, I slunk downward. Most of the others were off hunting or gathering, playing or wandering. There was no food save for a piece of fruit no one wanted, lying dejectedly in the dirt. Housekeeper was building a fire, his face set into an expression of concentration.

I sat beside him and picked the fruit up, examining it for

any insects or rot. My thoughts drifted back to yesterday, and all that I'd learned. There had been several vital pieces of new information. Why, then, did I keep returning to those final moments when I'd watched Peter fly away?

"Where does Peter sleep?" I asked without preamble, glancing at Housekeeper sidelong.

The boy lifted one shoulder in a shrug. "Nowhere near here, that's all I know. Peter has terrible nightmares, he does. Used to wake us up every night with his crying. When there got to be more of us, he stopped sleeping where we could hear him."

It seemed Peter and I shared another thing in common—he was plagued by his dreams, too. Although, strangely enough, I hadn't walked in my sleep once since arriving to Neverland.

With a thoughtful frown, I bit into the fruit's pulpy skin and gazed about the camp. Everything looked different now that I knew what would happen to the one that ruled over it all. The fire was nothing more than a pile of drenched, smoldering wood. The children were not spontaneous and free, but rather desperate and abandoned. The sounds of the jungle were grating, an omen of frightening things to come. I gulped the bitterness down and, once it had been stripped bare, let the pit fall from my limp fingers. It rolled through the tangle of vines and dead leaves, leading my gaze to two young girls.

Near the remains of the Pink Lady, they played with ugly dolls constructed from sticks and mud. Their voices were unnaturally high-pitched in an attempt to animate the makeshift toys. And very mischievous toys they were. I found myself watching them. It was so entertaining that—for the space of a few blinks or a deep, deep breath—my lethargy lifted.

Stories. I used to tell stories. I'd found solace in weaving fantastical tales of magic, princesses, and other worlds. I couldn't quite see the upturned faces in my memories, but I remembered how it had felt as I spoke of them. Every bad thing had ceased to exist. The invisible weight on my shoulders had completely slid off, at least for a short while.

The beginnings of an idea took hold.

Need swelled in my veins, an all-consuming urge. I approached the girls, trying to contain the frantic excitement rolling off my skin like mist over sea. Their names escaped me, and I pasted a friendly smile on my face to hide this fact.

The playmates sensed me coming and went still. Both wore wary expressions, and I felt a pang of regret, that they should look at me so. Since my arrival, I had done little to gain their trust or friendship. Why would they agree to anything I proposed?

Because this is Neverland, the lonely voice that lives inside us all whispered.

"What do you want?" one of them demanded when I didn't speak. Her companion had a kinder face, and it encouraged me to try. Heavy with hope, I told them about my idea. They listened with cautious interest, and once I was finished, I was amazed at how quickly they took to it. Neighing like stallions, the girls galloped into the trees to find others who would participate. They soon returned with three boys in tow, and we set to work.

Throughout the day, more children trickled into camp, noticed the bustle around me, and edged closer to investigate. I explained our purpose. Some lost interest and took positions far away from us. Others asked if there was a role for them. And there was, every time—I made sure of it. There were mutterings that I'd gone mad or belonged in an asylum. Maybe we all did, but at least we'd walk through the doors laughing.

Once everything was in place, there was nothing left to do but wait. Dusk painted the horizon in hues of pink and orange. The orphans of Neverland ate their supper with eyes cast upward. Conversation was scattered and tense. And eventually, Peter came in a blast of wind and sighs. His feet touched the jungle floor with a dull thud, and I noticed a streak of mud covering one cheek. Spines straightened and gazes brightened with anticipation. "Ready yourselves," I urged under my breath.

Peter noticed them crowding together. The moment the sun was low enough and his shadow effectively eliminated, I went to him.

"What is this?" he questioned, sounding more tired than curious. He accepted a leg of meat from Housekeeper.

"A surprise," I said, with a hint of satisfaction. See how *he* liked annoying, ambiguous answers. "Will you sit?"

As a reply, Peter settled next to me, biting into the leg. Grease dripped from it and stained his trousers, unheeded. We waited. The children I'd recruited put on their costumes or made adjustments. A mosquito hummed in my ear, and I swatted at it impatiently.

Housekeeper took this as a signal and lumbered to the center. Our tiny audience quieted.

"We give you *Alice's Adventures in Wonderland*," the large boy droned. Anyone who didn't know him would believe he was incredibly bored with the entire affair, but I had learned to look for the glint in his eye. There it was, a moon behind clouds. Then Housekeeper surprised us all by giving a deep, graceful bow and adding, "Enjoy your trip down the rabbit hole."

And so it went.

For only having an afternoon to memorize their lines, the children did magnificently. Throughout the play I silently recited them, too. Whoever I'd been before, I must have read Carroll's book dozens of times, because the words were engraved on my mind like a message on a love token.

It was obvious that the young ones weren't the only one enjoying it; Nose chuckled behind me. Warmth flickered in my chest, better than any campfire.

Soon the White Rabbit made an appearance. It was the nameless boy, the one who everyone gave a wide berth because of Peter's decree. I'd sought him out earlier, and he'd been so frightened, so guarded, I'd barely been able to keep him from bolting. Getting him to agree to this was an even greater challenge.

His voice came out nervous and high-pitched. Perfect for the part I'd assigned him, knowing that he wouldn't have to act very hard to achieve the façade. We'd made him ears out of leaves and string.

"Oh my e-ears and whiskers, how late it's g-getting!" he stammered. Scattered laughter sounded throughout the camp, some of it mocking, and the boy flushed. He didn't abandon his act, however, and I knew it wasn't wishful thinking when the audience began to look at him with the same interest they'd given the others.

Peter glowered.

The actors improvised for what we didn't have. Arms moved through the air as if there were water when Alice cried and cried and cried. Everyone cowered when she was meant to have grown so tall her head touched the ceiling. The caterpillar was just a boy lounging on two stumps we'd place beside each other, but his fingers were pinched as if he held something between them.

It was magic. Magic that had nothing to do with Neverland or the boy beside me. We'd created this all on our own.

A stocky girl playing Alice—she didn't look at all as I'd envisioned the character, but she was doing well—speculated, "I wonder if I've been changed in the night?"

She paused, longer than she should have, and it was obvious she didn't know the next part. More laughter. The girl rolled her eyes, and they flicked to me. I mouthed the words. Her face brightened. "Oh! Right. Was I the same when I got up this morning? I almost think I can remember feeling a little different. But if I'm not the same, the next question is, 'Who in the world am I?'" She forgot the rest of the line but didn't bother to try remembering this time. With undisguised relief, she looked to the Mad Hatter.

Who was none other than Slightly. The child stepped forward with a ridiculous smile stretched across his face. He bowed to us, much less smoothly than Housekeeper had, and tipped his imaginary hat as I'd shown him. Everywhere I looked, there were delighted smiles.

The tea party was my favorite scene. I'd managed to convince Tootles to let me smear whiskers over his cheeks for his role as the Cheshire Cat. Another role that I had chosen well; I'd never noticed before, but he moved in such a delicate, deliberate way. Instead of watching Tootles, though, I constantly looked to the audience so I could gauge their reactions. Bask in what I'd managed to accomplish. For once, I was not only entranced by the island—I was entranced by them.

Just as I was about to turn for the umpteenth time, Peter leaned closer, and his breath tickled my cheek. Heat of a different sort spread through me, and I twisted forward again to hide it. "Why did you do this?" he asked quietly.

For you, I almost said. But that wasn't true. I'd done it for myself, too. For the lost boys and girls around us, with their dirty faces and earned names and murky memories. Peter was their light, and if he was put out, there was nothing to keep the darkness at bay. I knew, God, I knew, that even if we couldn't recall the reasons for our pain, it was still there. Nestled in our ribcages and in our hearts, where it couldn't be removed or examined. And what would distract us from that pain when Peter was gone?

Swallowing, I kept my eyes on Tootle's antics now. My voice was also low as I answered thickly, "They deserve a few minutes of happiness."

"Off with her head!" The boy playing the red queen—I hadn't been able to coerce another girl into the project—sounded almost as disinterested as Housekeeper had. His colorless knuckles betrayed him; we had found a long stick to use as a scepter, and his grip on it looked unrelenting. He glanced at me, and I nodded encouragingly.

When the tip of Peter's finger subtly stroked the length of mine, my forced concentration dissolved. I stared at him. He smelled like sunlight and breezes, felt so solid and summery. Sensing the intensity of my gaze, he turned. Our eyes said a thousand things, but his mouth only one. And the next question Peter asked was the last thing I would have expected.

"What about you?" he breathed, unsmiling even when everyone else was laughing. "What would make you happy?"

Longing exploded through my body. Peter didn't touch me again, but he may as well have, for all the effects the fire and ice of that look had on my most secret of places. *I don't know,* I wanted to say. Another lie. I wanted Peter. I wanted him to live. I wanted to tell him the truth of why I'd come to Neverland. I squared my shoulders, a soldier against an onslaught of shouting, writhing, endless fears. "I'd be happy if—"

A voice shattered the glass sphere that had formed around us. "We're all mad here!"

I jumped, realizing Alice's adventures hadn't ended yet. I

couldn't remember whose line that was, or who had even said it, but one of the actors was trying to get my attention. I turned away to pinpoint which line he was meant to be reciting. After a moment, Peter did, too. My chest was tight; I couldn't breathe. I focused on that. In and out, in and out. The boy remembered his line without my assistance, and continued on.

The play was nearly finished. A good thing, since daylight was leaking past the planet, drop by drop into the great beyond, and leaving night in its place. Sensing the end, Alice let out a long sigh. "It would be so nice if something made sense for a change," she said.

Silence permeated the clearing, disrupted only by the fire and a single cough. Then I clapped. So hard and so long that my palms stung.

Everyone else followed suit. We made our own thunder, strong enough to shake the air. Those at the front either blushed, scowled, or pretended as if they hardly cared about any of it. The girl who'd been Alice picked up Slightly, propping him on her tiny hip. Freckles beamed as he took a bow of his own, arms flourishing through the air. Nibs grinned and ruffled his hair, to which he responded by shoving her playfully. I'd never seen Nibs smile before —it transformed her entire face. Into someone who had never wielded a bloody knife or seen death. For the first time, I wondered about who she was before coming to Neverland, and whether she ever wished to be that girl again. Not the girl who'd been starving or forced to steal for survival, of course, but the one who hadn't known the nightmares of an island that existed by following the second star to the right, then flying straight on 'til morning.

What an odd thought. Second star to the right? Straight on 'til morning? Frowning now, I stood there and tried to observe the joy and listen to the praise. The audience had surged forward and I lingered at edge of it all, contemplating. Peter slung his arm around Tootles and his voice floated across the clearing, complimenting the show.

Something touched my back, pointed and painful. It was so sudden that I instinctively started to turn. "Not a peep," a familiar voice muttered. I froze. "Come with me."

I kept my eyes on Peter, trying to alert him with my expression. He snickered at something Nibs was saying, wholly immersed. Slowly, I retreated into the jungle, careful of the knife still at my back. A leaf brushed my cheek. "What's the meaning of this?"

"The captain wants ter see you," Mr. Jukes said. He lifted his hand where I could see it. Despite the dim lighting, I made out the chloroform-covered cloth clenched in his palm. Understanding made my vision hazy; he was giving me a choice. Go willingly, or go unconscious.

"Lead the way," I said flatly. Mr. Jukes moved from my line of sight, never easing the pressure of the blade, and gestured that I should walk. I imagined him dying in every painful, horrifying way.

When I didn't immediately leap into motion, Mr. Jukes jabbed his weapon. "Get a move on, then!"

Pain radiated through me. Blood, hot and wet, trickled

down my back. Breathing hard, I looked back at Peter one last time before plunging into the darkness.

In the captain's quarters, I paced back and forth.

The floorboards grumbled at me. My fury made everything strange—I could feel the walls breathing. Shrinking. Smothering. Outside, however, all was serene. Night wasn't quite upon the island yet, I saw now that the jungle wasn't jealously hunched over us. There was a final gasp of light, like someone on their deathbed, futilely struggling against it. My glance went again and again to the clock on the shelf, anxiously tracking the seconds. Outside the window, the other ship floated, and I could finally make out the name across its wooden side.

The Fountain.

"Miss Davenport. Thank you for your patience."

The door squealed open and I whirled to face Captain Bainbridge. Any of the fondness or gratitude I'd felt for him had streamed out of the wound in my back. "Why did you bring me here again?" I hissed. "I'm not a whore or a servant you can summon."

Peter's brother calmly strolled to the desk. I stayed where I was, dried blood making my shirt stiff and my hands fists. A safe distance from me, he stopped and fiddled with a book on the desk's surface. He lifted the pages with his thumb and they made a fluttering sound as they settled again. Then the captain seemed to shake himself. He faced me. I denied the stirring his gray eyes caused down, down, down. "I understand you've learned some things. I wanted to have a conversation without being overheard," he said mildly.

Instantly I knew what he meant—what Peter had told me about the men killing Bell. How could anyone possibly know that? I pictured us sitting in that tree, our legs swinging, no one else but the stars and the animals to overhear. Could the captain have been there, or one of his men?

No.

Peter's words echoed through me. *I caught him conspiring with the pirates. That git is their eyes and ears.* The nameless boy must have been eavesdropping below the tree Peter and I had chosen to discuss our secrets.

The realization only made me angrier. Under that, like a river beneath the ground, was hurt I was desperately trying to bury. Somehow, I'd allowed myself to trust this man. I focused on him again, and a sneer curled my lips. "What a fool you must think me. Listening to your story and actually feeling *sorry* for you."

With that, his mask shattered. The pieces fell around our feet. "Yes, I lied," he said doggedly, moving his hand from the book to the handle of his sword. "I hoped your search for Bell would lead you to the answers I need. But I still want to earn Peter's forgiveness, as well."

The ship shifted and groaned, ignored by both of us. Using the windowsill for balance, I scoffed. "*Forgiveness?* I think not. That was the biggest lie of all—you only wanted Bell. I just don't know why, because I no longer believe there was any courtship between you two."

The captain had no trouble staying on his feet. He heaved a sigh and dragged his hand over his mouth. In that instant, I realized how weary he looked. It was as if he hadn't slept in weeks, no, years. There were smudges beneath his eyes. He was drawn and pale. His hair was long and tousled, not in the boyish way Peter's was, but as someone who hadn't had time to cut or brush it. And I wondered what could possibly be so consuming.

As if he could hear my thoughts, the captain said, "There is much you still don't know, Miss Davenport."

"Then tell me. The truth this time."

He tapped the sword. It made a clinking sound in the stillness, in time with the ticking of the clock. I couldn't stop myself from looking at it again. Thankfully, Captain Bainbridge didn't see this. He was at war, a soundless chaos inside him, as though the soldiers were in his stomach, shooting and jabbing without restraint. *Clink. Tick. Clink. Tick.* "Has Peter told you of the faeries?" he announced.

Faeries? In Neverland? My expression must've told him everything he needed to know. The captain pursed his lips and nodded. "I thought not."

But I was not as surprised as I might've been a few weeks ago. This new revelation absorbed into my brain like water to forest. It was only logical, really, in a place where there were mermaids and Neverbirds and days that only lasted an hour. Why shouldn't there be faeries? Curiosity flitted through me. Whatever they were like, faeries must be the quiet sort—I hadn't heard or seen anything. Not a giggle in my ear or the flash of a wing.

"So you were after them?" I clarified, frowning at Captain Bainbridge now. Trying to understand how this fit into the story of him and Peter.

"Not for my own gain. Finding the faeries was just to buy time and appease Mr. Ashdown. I did mention him before, didn't I? He's here because I needed a financier in order to reach Neverland and find Peter. Everyone in London knows the tales of my brother and how he never ages. Mr. Ashdown is ill and only has a few more months to live. I told him that I knew the whereabouts of a legend, a way to save his life. Have you ever heard of the Fountain of Youth, Miss Davenport?"

This was more startling than the talk of faeries. I blinked. "You think it's on the island?"

He took a step closer. Perhaps he believed I wouldn't notice. But it helped me to finally discern how he and Peter were alike, something that had been bothering me from the moment we met.

It was the allure.

There was nothing else to tie them together. One brother dark, one brother light. One brother volatile, one brother sincere. One brother buoyant, one brother pensive. And yet, despite all the differences, I was drawn in the same way. To look, to know, to touch. I would be able to find them even if they were standing across a cramped ballroom, a hundred faces and swirling dresses moving between us.

Over the captain's shoulder, I glanced at the clock yet again, but the tone of his voice made my gaze snap back to his. It was distracted, pondering. He seemed wholly focused on the details of my face rather than the vital information he was giving me.

"...the beginning, I thought the Fountain of Youth was nothing more than a child's tale," he said. "I simply needed Mr. Ashdown's ships. But then one of my men was gored by a boar, and a compassionate faerie saved his life with a few drops from her veins. He came back, raving about the potency of her blood. We doubted him, but after that day, the man had a spring to his step. He could run faster and work longer. He emanated such life. It became apparent that, if consumed, faerie blood will have similar effects as the Fountain."

"And that's when you found Bell," I stated.

The distraction was gone from Captain Bainbridge's eyes —now they were clear and bright. He swallowed, and there was anguish in it. "That's when we found Bell."

My nostrils flared. I felt indignation for the girl they'd killed, sorrow for the boy who loved her. The air thickened and, sensing this, the captain spoke in a rush. "I did everything I could to control the men and remember the reason I'd come. They were like hounds on a hunt, especially when their encounter with her revealed another secret of the fae— the gold dust on their skin holds the power of flight."

With these words, I solved another mystery of Neverland. Neverland and Peter, who possessed more secrets than there were stars in the night sky.

First I thought of the song he was always humming. *A few thoughts with some dust, and soon you'll be soaring.*

Then I remembered the night we'd left... wherever I had

come from, right after Peter had kissed me for the first time. The question I'd asked echoed through my mind again. I heard the breathless quality in my voice. *Why was that necessary?*

It's part of the magic. You must carry my homeland with you, and too much time has passed since I had my face between your legs. The dust will have faded by now, Peter said.

No wonder the other children couldn't fly. Being so close to Bell, Peter probably knew where to find the faeries. He had access to their magic while the orphans did not. But why hadn't he told me about them when we'd been discussing what really happened to Bell? He'd dodged it when I asked after her people, assuming them to be the villagers on the hill.

I thought of her now, the girl he would always love. Thought of the strange sheen to her skin that I'd noticed after being drugged. Later, I had dismissed the memory. Blamed the things I'd seen on the chloroform. Now I knew it had been dust, as golden as Peter's lovely hair. Magic.

The captain didn't seem to notice how I had gone still with shock. "I swear to you, Miss Davenport, it was not supposed to happen that way," he added.

In his imploring, he took yet another step toward me. I promptly retreated, and my back pressed against glass. "How?" I asked, cold as a mermaid's touch.

There was a long, long pause, full of such shame and regret it was like an overwhelming perfume.

"She'd gone to the beach to gather something," Peter's brother whispered. The clock ticked. "We weren't normally on that side of the island, and the men caught her unawares. They were mad, wanting a bite, a taste. One of them dealt a fatal blow. She managed to pull free and stumble into the jungle. Smee shot a few of the crew as a warning and it stopped the rest from running after her. But by the time I found Bell, she'd died. I buried her under a tree and marked the grave with a cross, so her people would know."

Pity him, my heart murmured.

Hate him, my mind ordered.

But it was hard to hate him when he was standing there, guilty and tired and alone. He'd lied to me, it was true… but I had lost count of how many lies coated my own tongue.

As I speculated, the ship groaned and sobbed. The sound made me think of the passing seconds again, and I twisted to peer out the window, take in the red eventide. It looked as though the *Jolly Roger* was floating on a sea of blood. Was it my imagination, or were we lower to the water's surface?

When I said nothing about his confession, Captain Bainbridge shrugged ruefully. "Well, it seems all for naught. Soon Mr. Ashdown will die and I'll go back to London, never to see Peter again."

I scowled, tense with anticipation. "If you think all of this will—"

He silenced me with a kiss. At least, he attempted to, in a burst of soft lips and hesitant hands. I recovered quickly and grabbed his face to shove it away, much more violently than he had touched me. "No," I said. "I get to choose."

The captain waited. I left the window to edge around

where he stood, appraising him along the way. His lashes were damp, framing dark, unhappy eyes. There were red lines on his cheek, marks my furious nails left behind. Then my attention went to that delicate mole hovering at the corner of his lip, and I succumbed to the inexplicable urge to put a finger on it.

And I did make a choice. My hands tangled in the material of his shirt, pulling him to me. Just like that, his lips were on mine. It felt strange when all I'd known was Peter's of late. I explored the captain's mouth. He was gentle at first, always the gentleman, but I yanked him even closer, impatient. Captain Bainbridge made a sound of surprise and deepened the kiss. His hand formed a fist in my hair while I ran my fingertips over his stubble, his neck, his shoulders. With every moment, though, I could hear that voice inside me. It grew louder and louder, like the clanging of a distant bell, until I could finally make out what it was saying.

Wrong.

I put my hand on his chest and lightly, so lightly, applied pressure.

He was gone instantly.

Captain Bainbridge sat on the bed. I used the chair for support. We both trembled. My shadow was livid, wanting him, wanting more. She stomped her foot and pointed insistently. For once I understood why—she was drawn to the safe choices, the logical solutions. Loving Peter would lead to heartbreak, we both knew that. But loving this man would lead to another sort of brokenness, which was not something I could easily explain to a shadow.

"I had to know what that was like," the captain cut in, a glint of obstinacy in his eye that I'd never seen before. He stared at a painting on the wall, his chest rising and falling more than storm-driven waves. "Just once. I meant to do it before I told you the truth, before you despised me."

My breathing was also uneven. I touched my swollen lips. *I don't despise you*, the secret places within me whispered. But all I could manage aloud was, "I shouldn't have done that."

"Do words like 'should' and 'shouldn't' belong in Neverland?"

His words gave me pause. Maybe Captain Bainbridge was right, and I was a fool to cling to old ideals. Any sense of decency I'd come to the island with had long dissipated like steam from a bath, hadn't it?

No. As with most things, he was a little of both—partly right, partly wrong. Beside us, my shadow continued to seethe. I watched it and thought about how much we lost and how much we gained on this island. Slowly I said, "I've learned so much here. But the lesson Neverland has taught me again and again is that anything can change. Even Peter."

Suddenly the floor we stood on tilted, and I grabbed the desk for balance. The boards shuddered as something wrested with the ship. I felt the vibrations through my boots an instant before a thin layer of water slipped through the crack beneath the door. It reached our feet in a burst of cold. Whatever I'd been about to say to the captain scrambled to the recesses of my head and cowered.

We were out of time.

"What's happening?" Captain Bainbridge demanded, leaping out to grab hold of me. But he already knew, just as I did.

The ship was sinking.

My mind flashed to the smears of blood I'd left on the wooden slabs as Mr. Jukes and I were lifted in the dinghy. Easily accomplished, as he'd left a gouge in my back that offered blood freely to my seeking fingers. Despite how much I'd forgotten, Nose's warning about the mermaids had never faded. In my anger at the captain's lies, not to mention being kidnapped *again*, it had been a shout in my skull. *The hunger drives them mad. Makes them miraculously strong. I've seen them kill crocodiles with the toughest hides you can imagine.*

When Mr. Jukes turned his back, I didn't hesitate. Not for a moment.

As I hoped, they must have been chewing and smashing their way toward the bloodstains. Admittedly, I hadn't been entirely certain it would work. Now I watched the mermaids' handiwork unfold, as water rose from beneath the floorboards. Noticing this at the same time I did, Captain Bainbridge sprinted out of the cabin and up the stairs, taking them three at a time. His urgent shouts were drowned out by the struggles of the ship.

I began to follow, to seize my chance and slip through the door and up to freedom, when a figure filled the passageway.

Mr. Starkey smiled at me as he closed the door.

I knew before my hand wrapped around the knob that it would be locked. I'd never learned to pick one, and there was no time for that anyhow. Cursing, I spun and faced the room again. The only possibility was the window. The *Jolly Roger* was already substantially submerged, and the water was up to my knees. Panicking, I sloshed to the chair in front of Captain Bainbridge's desk. It was heavier than I expected, and the thin tendons stood out in my arms in the effort to lift it. I grunted as I ran at the glass. The chair bounced off without leaving so much as a scratch.

By now the water was at my thighs and the cabin was dimming. A map floated past, the lines of the world blurring together. Bedclothes tangled about my waist. A picture frame bumped into me. Ignoring it, I hurried to retrieve the chair—there was nothing else solid enough—and used the last of my strength to hold it over me. And again, it ricocheted off harmlessly. I screamed my frustration. I searched in vain for a tool or something else I could carry. When I turned to ransack the cabinets, my gaze darted past the half-submersed window. Then darted back in disbelief.

Something moved in the deep. A shimmer. A flutter. Eyes.

A mermaid emerged from the dark.

Not Serafa. This was a creature I had never encountered before, with wider features and yellower teeth. I was frozen, but the sliver of reason inside me was inherently grateful that her voice could not reach my ears. Since I wasn't fighting for my life, I studied the new mermaid in a way I hadn't been able to with Serafa. She had two slits in the center of her face instead of a nose. No hair, no eyelashes, no lips. The webbing between her fingers was veiny. Despite all this, she had a strange, enthralling beauty.

I was abruptly jerked from my reverie when the mermaid started to bang the window with her fist. She did it again. And again. A dozen cracks spread through the glass like spiderwebs. Her white eyes devoured me. There was nowhere to go, to hide, and I could only huddle against the shelves and try not to whimper. Cool waves lapped at my stomach. A school of glowing fish drifted past. I refocused on the mermaid, preparing myself for what I would do when she came through that window and attempted to eat the flesh from my bones.

Instead, she retreated.

I breathed raggedly, straining to see anything in that black water, but the creature didn't return. There was no opportunity to wonder at this.

The glass gave way in a burst of water and sound.

And a crocodile poured inside the cabin.

It was the biggest reptile I had ever seen, as long and wide as a dining room table. I shrieked and reacted on instinct, snatching the nearest object within reach. Still ticking, the clock ricocheted off the crocodile's teeth and into the darkness of its yawning, endless throat. The beast was startled, and it paused in its forward progress. Past the roaring terror, I comprehended that I now had an opening by which to escape—the hole in the window was big enough for me to fit through. But the crocodile advanced again, a dark and soundless shape. Briefly I considered climbing the shelf, until I realized it was hardly tall enough to carry me out of the beast's reach. There were no swords, no knives, no pistols. I couldn't fly.

My Neverbird could, though.

It would only work if she was nearby, and she could still arrive too late. Knowing this, I sucked in the mightiest gulp of air I was capable of and released it. *"Aurora!"*

The water pouring inside swallowed the syllables—there wasn't even an echo. But it seemed to puzzle the crocodile, as it faltered at the sound of my voice. For a breathless moment, it felt like I could hear our two heartbeats, mine wild and thundering, the beast's steady and calculating. If I didn't do something, I would drown before it could take its first bite. The water level was rising more rapidly—it was at my chest now—and cracks continued spreading through the remnants of the window. The gap of air near the top of it was shrinking. Every muscle in my body went rigid, readying to scramble over the crocodile and leap. For good measure, I climbed as many shelves as I could, until my head brushed the ceiling.

At that moment, as though God himself were watching, a familiar bird landed outside, blocking out whatever light was left. Floating on the water's surface, Aurora's head poked through the jagged opening, her amber gaze blazing with curiosity. She spotted the crocodile straightaway. With an excited scream that split my ears and made the cabin shatter like a porcelain doll, my Neverbird clamped the beast's tail in her beak and dragged it out with her, flapping her wings through the water without any difficulty.

I reached the window just as the ship completely sank.

The sea tried to suck me back. I grappled at the glass, my eyes and throat and lungs flooding with ocean. Blood clouded in front of me; I'd wrapped my fingers around the sharp, broken shards. Somehow, in a span of seconds that felt like star-filled eons, I hauled myself out and planted my boots on the ship's side for leverage. Bubbles streamed upward. Then, lungs howling, I pushed myself off. For an instant, I was certain the *Jolly Roger* would still pull me down with it. I kicked my legs, used my arms, did all I could to fight the tide. Its force gradually eased, but I'd still been dragged too far from the surface.

While Aurora battled the crocodile in the cold, blue depths, I made my way to air and sky. They beckoned welcomingly. Everything was becoming hazy, though. There were spots of color that didn't belong. My frantic efforts slowed. And, after another minute of struggle, I gave up the air and the sky. I convulsed as water rushed into every pore and vein. Then, peace. I floated into oblivion, arms outspread. Death loomed. My eyes began to slide shut, and I dreamed.

In my dream, hands tightened around me. I felt myself surge upward. Then I exploded into the night.

After another handful of seconds, I became aware that I was being cradled close. Lips brushed across my forehead in a kiss so tender, it was as though I were something infinitely precious.

"Wake up, Wendy," someone said.

It was as if the words were underwater, garbled and distant. There was a semblance of lucidity still tucked away inside me, and I obeyed. Or tried to, at least. Water dribbled down my chin, then spewed from my stomach. I gagged, and the voice kept speaking, offering comfort and encouragement. When it was done, I licked my lips and swallowed, trying to croak out gratitude. My throat wouldn't work.

"You're in your father's study," the voice said in my ear now. "Can you see them? All those books? That wretched chair you love so much?"

"Peter, wait!" someone else shouted.

At the sound of Captain Bainbridge's voice, understanding slammed back into me, like a spirit re-entering a body. Both Peter and I stiffened. My eyes opened, and the lines of Neverland solidified. Slowly, so slowly, Peter turned toward his brother. The captain stood in a dinghy, several of his men sitting behind him. It rocked precariously. Beyond them, the *Jolly Roger* was gone. All that remained was horizon. Horizon and Aurora, who was flying in wide circles around us, her eyes fixed on me.

I mustered a small, reassuring smile for her. Her beak parted to release that familiar, wild cry.

The sound echoed in my ears as I returned my gaze to Peter. His expression was pitiless—only a likeness of his true self—and his returning shout echoed over the white-capped waves. "What do you want?"

"Haven't I done enough penance for my sins? Haven't I proven myself?" Captain Bainbridge pleaded. He didn't seem to care that they had an audience.

"No," Peter said simply.

"But what can I—"

"*We were brothers!*" A rumble of thunder accompanied Peter's cry. The sky was gray now, and every ray of light had turned to shadow. He glared at Captain Bainbridge through a sheen of tears, shaking so violently that I worried he would drop me. Pain flew off his skin like sparks. His face was etched with every feeling, every memory. "Don't you understand? In that cold, filthy orphanage, I prayed for someone like you. Then lo and behold, the brother I'd always dreamed of came along and I trusted him. But even if I were to forgive you for sending Collingwood to the tavern, there will never be a price high enough or a deed pure enough to forgive you for Bell. *Not for Bell.*"

Everything was still. The sea, the men, the moon. Captain Bainbridge made no excuses or apologies. Not anymore. His hands, which had been spread in supplication, dropped to his sides. He spoke quietly this time, and I strained to hear. "We'll leave tomorrow, then," he replied. "But if... if you change your mind, I'll be spending the morning ashore gathering supplies."

This last part was for me, I knew, because his gaze sought mine as he said it. Was he offering me passage home? Or something more? Despite the horrid timing and my own harrowing experience, I thought of our kiss. His declaration. *I had to know what that was like. Just once.*

Peter didn't bother with any final words or parting insults. Moving more quickly than I'd ever seen him do, he snapped around and sped into the gloom. As we rushed headlong to shore, I wondered if he remembered that I was clutched in his arms. He did, because he set me down as though I were like the window I'd escaped through. Fractured. Damaged. Irreparable.

Now that the danger was past, the pain announced itself. I winced, plucking bits of glass from my palm. "Well, then. I suppose I should thank..."

Peter stumbled toward a tree. He flattened his palm against it. Sounds tore from him, strangled and muffled. Wherever his tears fell, a flower bloomed. It started to rain, as well, fat drops that dampened everything in their path. Then, without warning, Peter's arm moved in a blur, and he hit the tree so hard that bark dislodged from its trunk. In the dark, the pieces looked like fleeing bats.

I didn't think about how, just an hour ago, I'd been kissing his brother. I didn't think about how he would always love Bell. I didn't think about my injuries or my battered heart. I didn't think about anything; I just went to him.

The boy fought me. Pushed me away. Flinched from my touch. Refused to speak. I didn't relent, merely wrapping my arms back around him every time he managed to get free. His skin was slick and difficult to hold onto, but I did. In the end, Peter succumbed. I pressed my forehead to his temple and tasted the salt of tears, along with the bitter rain. Together, we sank to the dirt.

And wept.

CHAPTER 16

HUMMING. Someone was humming.

The sound became louder and louder, insistent as a train whistle on a busy platform. Eventually it forced me to open my eyes. I expected to see the rain-drenched ground where Peter and I had fallen asleep. When I saw where I really was, my mind could not accept it. It rejected the four walls, the wide window, the unyielding door. *Oh, no. God, please, anywhere but here.*

I was aboard the *Jolly Roger*.

Once again I stood in the captain's quarters, water swirling around my ankles. No, it was impossible! I'd escaped this place, I was certain of it. Had it all been a dream? The mermaid breaking the window, the crocodile, Aurora? Had I died here instead?

Right now, the truth didn't matter—soon this room would be at the bottom of the ocean. I tried to move, tried to run for that window again, but I couldn't. It was as if my feet had become part of the floor. And where was that blasted humming coming from?

I looked down again. This time I noticed there was a gilt picture frame clutched in my hands. Or maybe it hadn't been there before. I frowned, unable to ignore the feeling there was something naggingly familiar about the image. I brought it closer to my face, squinting in the dying light. A memory triggered; this frame had floated past me the first time I was standing in this spot, ignored in my desperate bid for survival.

It was a younger version of Captain Bainbridge, standing behind two other people. A man and a woman, who were undeniably his parents. He had the man's jaw, the woman's eyes.

And as I watched, the woman turned her head to fix those grainy eyes directly on mine. I stopped breathing.

"Did you really think I would be so easily forgotten?" she taunted. The humming had been her doing; it ceased the moment she spoke. Paying no mind to my shock, the woman continued. "How quaint. Not to mention foolish. I'm coming for you, Miss Davenport, make no mistake."

It was her voice that did it.

Memories came screaming back like a train through a tunnel, bursting forth on the other side.

"Lady Bainbridge," I whispered. She smiled, and in that single action, I was reduced to the girl I had been. Small, quiet, afraid. My tongue felt numb. It was like a forgotten word or a bubble struggling to the surface. Suddenly I remembered the offer she'd made me... and that I had accepted it.

Peter. She wanted me to kill Peter.

This time, I couldn't lie to myself. The truth was that I could no more kill Peter than I could Slightly, or Freckles, or Bashira.

But my failure meant my family would pay the price. It was all coming back now. The lady had threatened to expose the truth about our lost fortune and my ruined virtue. Another jolt of fear went through me. I gripped the frame painfully tight and croaked, "You'll never find us."

She wagged her finger and crooned, *"Second star to the right, and straight on 'til morning. A few thoughts with some dust, and soon you'll be soaring."*

As that last note rang in my ears, the window shattered. My head snapped up. Once again I tried to run, but the lady was laughing, using whatever power she possessed to keep me there. Water poured in, rushing every which way, claiming my calves, my knees, my thighs, and I opened my mouth to scream—

"Wake up. Wendy, open your eyes."

Someone was tapping my nose. It was enough to tear me out of the pirate ship and back into the halfway state of sleep and awareness. So it had been a dream. Only a dream. In the vast darkness, I curled on my side. But whoever had spoken was determined; when I only mumbled incoherently, still begging Lady Bainbridge for my life, they kept at it. Tap. Tap. Tap.

Finally I awakened, pushing the hand away, and Peter's

gleaming teeth were all I could see. It was a welcome sight. I sat up, rubbing the sleep from my eyes. Gradually, the nightmare faded and reality ebbed back. It seemed as though Peter's cries still echoed through the trees. The rain had stopped, but there were still shadows and moonbeams surrounding us. I rubbed my arms to bring warmth into them. "How long—"

"Only a few hours. Morning hasn't come yet."

Leaves and mud were caked to my skin. I peeled and scratched the mess off, asking, "Should we return to camp?"

"No. We're going somewhere else."

I examined Peter from beneath my lashes, and there was no evidence of the inner turmoil I'd witnessed hours before. It was as if we'd drifted to sleep, rather than capitulated to it, and I hadn't held him in my arms all night. Oblivious, Peter looked at me with raised brows and waited for me to ask about this newest place. My hand was aching where the glass had punctured it, and the memory of having seawater in my lungs was all-too fresh. My body longed for more sleep and relief. But I just sighed. "Where?"

"Glad you asked. Please, Wendy, calm yourself. To answer your question, I want to show you this island's heart. Considering I've already shown you mine." Peter winked. I didn't have a retort; the sight of his grin was more wonderful than soaring on the back of a Neverbird or swimming through a cave of stars. While I gaped, Peter turned and dove into the jungle. I closed my mouth and hurried after him, not bothering to argue—wherever this heart was, I knew it was nearby, because we hadn't taken to the sky.

I was right. We ran like deer, light and silent, swift and sure. Ducking beneath branches and weaving through vines. Until finally, next to an ordinary-looking tree, Peter halted. At its base, there was a hole. It would be impossible to find, if the boy hadn't brushed aside a curtain of moss that acted as a door. *Not a door,* I thought. *A guardian.* He gestured that I should enter first. Warily, I approached the rim and peered down. There was a narrow flight of stairs, descending deep into the ground.

"What is this?" My voice instinctively emerged as a whisper.

Peter's expression was solemn. There was no hint of his usual mischief as he said, "Neverland's greatest secret."

My pulse was an erratic, feathery thrum. Feeling his eyes on me, I reached down with my toe, onto the first step. Peter was close behind, his breath stirring wisps of my hair. The way was dark and our progress slow. Water squelched inside my boots. I cautiously explored the ceiling and sides, still straining to see even though the air was painted black.

"Almost there," Peter said.

Before he finished uttering the words, a light appeared in the distance. My chest loosened with relief. It flickered and guided the rest of our journey down the treacherous path. Then we rounded a corner, and the tunnel ended with great fanfare. It opened into a cave, although calling it so seemed lacking. Awed, I drank it in. The walls were jagged and obsidian, glistening with water and untouched gems. The roof seemed so high, so far, that I imagined myself dizzy, swaying from the thin air in my attempt to touch the stalactites. I never believed a place could be more than a place, but there was *power* here. It lived in the air, more substantial than swirling leaves or flitting hummingbirds.

Peter came to stand beside me, and his hand brushed mine. A jolt from the simple touch traveled up my arm. Normally, this would lead to forbidden thoughts and memories. Now all I could think was that Peter would be dead soon and he'd never cause that jolt of desire again.

Oblivious to how my mood had darkened, he gestured toward the figures milling about the gigantic space. "They've been wanting to meet you."

And now I noticed them. Beings so poised and quiet that it had been easy to lose myself in the cave first. "Faeries," I breathed.

In my imaginings, they looked quite different. Tiny, winged creatures with pointed ears and gossamer gowns. These faeries were nearly human in appearance, although there was something... long about them. Their hair, their limbs, their features. Their cheeks were hollow, as though they'd been locked in a forgotten room for weeks on end. They wore things like what Bashira had lent me on the night of the ceremony, made of materials I'd never seen used for clothing. Bark, petals, grass. A few faeries cast curious glances my way, but none approached.

Peter noted my confusion. "They've learned to be wary of strangers. They went into hiding here after Bell..."

He didn't finish the sentence, but he didn't need to—I knew how it ended. With the death of the person he'd loved most. With a bond between brothers shattered forever.

Someone said Peter's name, then, and it was a gentle sound, similar to a breeze in your ears. We shouldn't have been able to hear it, and it occurred to me that I knew nothing about these people or what abilities they possessed. Peter left the mouth of the tunnel without hesitation. But I remained, clinging to the darkness like it was my mother's skirt. Realizing this, Peter paused. He backtracked a few steps to hold out a hand. He offered no promises or reassurances. Still, I found comfort in the steadiness of his blue gaze.

My fingertips curled into his. Bound by what happened the night before, and the simple act of holding onto each other now, we walked toward a cluster of faeries at the center of the cavern. The lot of them were so unmoving, so quiet, it betrayed the years they'd had to perfect such habits. Dozens. Hundreds. Thousands. However long the world had existed, so had faeries.

Perspiration beaded over my upper lip.

As we drew closer, I saw they stood around a strange, brilliant light. A fire, of sorts, but it hung midair without tinder or oil to give it life. Its movements were soundless. The flames were varying hues of blue and green and violet, the same strange colors that hovered above the Torch Bearer's staff. I knew I could stare at it for hours. Doubtless, this was the gift from Bashira's story, and these people were the original inhabitants she'd mentioned.

Peter noticed my enthrallment. "They call it an aura," he said, with some reverence of his own. "A bit of magic that reflects Neverland's state of well-being."

"Then the island must be happy, indeed," I murmured, following the blaze up, up, to where it almost reached the ceiling.

"It is," a new voice replied, made of old tree roots and flowers after a summer storm.

Startled, I turned quickly, and I noticed Peter's demeanor shift from the corner of my eye. He wore an expression I had never seen upon his face before. Not meekness, I decided. Respect.

"This is Illeryial, oldest of the fae," he said as I focused on the faerie coming toward us.

As it had been with Mr. Starkey, Illeryial was not particularly noteworthy for someone of his ilk, with features nondescript and an unassuming manner. Then he stopped beside us. There was no crown nestled atop his gleaming hair—which was longer than I was accustomed to seeing on a man—but authority and time rolled off him like a scent. My mouth went dry.

He was ancient. The ocean had been a puddle when he came to be. The sun was a faint, distant light. And I was only a blink in his eye compared to the millennia he had lived through.

I realized that he was speaking, saying something directly to me.

"...of Neverland speaks of your triumph today," the formidable being remarked, seemingly unaware of how I gaped. His English was careful but flawless. "You sank the humans' ship and gave them a wound like no other they have experienced. They will leave these shores and finally allow us to emerge from the hollow. You have proven your-self as a person we can trust, Wendy-bird."

Hearing my name on his lips was thrilling and disori-enting all at once. I was on the verge of asking if the pirates were truly making preparations to leave, as Captain Bain-bridge promised, when a girl joined us. Her bare feet slapped against the stone.

If time wafted from the other faerie, this one emanated serenity. She had the thickest hair I'd ever seen, even more so than Bashira, tumbling in black ropes and braids. Her bones were pronounced, painfully so. With a dreamy smile she said, "I am Donella, daughter of Illeryial. Will you come with me?"

I looked at Peter, and he just shrugged. Illeryial's face was smooth and impenetrable.

Nodding in assent, and some curiosity, I trailed after his daughter toward the far side of the cavern. Fairies parted for us and revealed another tunnel, even narrower than the first, not much bigger than my own frame. Donella ducked inside. I hesitated an instant before following. My eyes once again adjusted to smothering darkness. Almost immediately, the path curved upward. We were going back to the surface. Our breathing was loud in my ears.

An owl hooted as we emerged. I could feel Neverland stirring, beginning to wake like a person in a warm bed, morning spilling across a windowsill.

Something gave a sudden, mighty belch. I imagined a creature, bloated with its latest meal. Donella and I didn't falter; she walked with purpose down a well-trodden path.

Her destination was obvious the moment I saw it.

The tree was embraced on all sides by a tight wall of green, and the air felt different as we entered. As if we were not just on a magical island, but in another realm. While not as massive as the tree Peter and I sat atop of the other night, this one was more overwhelming. The same power I felt in the cavern was here, tenfold. The trunk was gnarled, like an old, old man. The bark and leaves and roots glimmered, as though covered by a fine sheen of dew. Upon closer inspection I saw that it was slightly gold.

And there was Bell, waiting beside it.

Donella left us soundlessly, a subtle scent of berries fading with her. I was too busy staring to manage a farewell.

Bell's age was impossible to discern—at one angle, she seemed younger than me. But like Illeryial, her expression was serene in a way that no young person could ever achieve.

Regardless of however long she'd been alive, the faerie was beautiful in every sense of the word. High cheekbones, full lips, smooth skin. She was dressed in a gown of white. Like the rest of the faeries, her feet and fingers were bare. No adornments, no trinkets, no distractions. That silvery hair spilled down her back like the moon had turned to liquid and drained out of the sky, onto her.

"You are Wendy," she said by way of greeting.

"You are Bell."

She tilted her head. Now that I wasn't being taken by pirates, or spying on her and Peter in the Neverwood, we were able to inspect each other in a way we couldn't before.

Few people had ever looked at me so closely, so thoroughly. I returned the favor. This was the infamous girl who had captured the wildest of hearts and put an everlasting rift between brothers. She had no visible wounds or ethereal glow, and my mind struggled to accept that she was dead. The tree beside us seemed to shift. Could it understand us? Was it offering encouragement?

"You don't love him yet, but you could. I see it," Bell said softly.

It had the effect of something hard and sharp—pain lodged beneath my ribs. So she didn't know. Whatever magic this faerie had, it hadn't revealed Peter's fate. Only I and Tootles knew that to love him was to embrace the wholly unique agony of loving someone who wasn't long for this world.

I couldn't bring myself to meet Bell's gaze anymore. I fixed mine on anything and everything else. The tree, the fireflies, the flowers. "Why have you been helping me?" I asked a particularly vibrant bloom with yellow-streaked petals.

"For him."

The faerie said it without pause or speculation, as if nothing was more simple. Peter's voice responded in my head, saying *I will always love her* again and again. I suspected it was the same for Bell. So much was becoming clear, more of the pieces forming a picture.

"You left that map for James Bainbridge. Back in London, on the floor of his rented room," I said abruptly, a detail that had bothered me for weeks.

Her silence was as good as an answer. Bewilderment tugged at the corners of my mouth, and I speculated out loud, "The island can only be found if the person has been allowed to find it. How was the captain able to come here? Terrible things have happened because of him."

Finally, there was a flicker of emotion in her face; a shadow passing over the moon. Perhaps Bell was not as tranquil as she appeared. "Neverland may love Peter, but it also loves chaos and change," she told me. "And their family has a bond with this place. A history that was never written down or put into song, so no one but the island remembers."

Lady Bainbridge's song, I thought. She'd said the lullaby had been passed down to her.

Laughter echoed from the tunnel, distracting both of us. The sound was followed by a faint swell of music, and the instruments were like nothing I'd ever heard before. As I listened, I knew I wore an expression of awe. Bell watched me and smiled. "They will tell your story for the rest of time, you know."

Her entire countenance emanated sincerity, along with a hint of admiration, and suddenly it felt like someone had poured a jar of thorns down my throat. "I only did it out of spite," I mumbled. "I was angry."

"Anger is a powerful thing. Even Illeryial has been swayed by it—he once spoke of peace." She seemed more saddened by this than her own death. I'd spent so long resenting Bell, loathing the idea of her, that it was a bolt of lightning, the realization *I liked her.*

"Even if you can't touch each other, why should that

matter so much? Why not continue to enjoy each other's company?" I forced myself to ask. Fearing the answer and needing it all the same.

"For him," Bell repeated. "I am leaving soon."

I frowned and started to ask where she planned to go. Thankfully, I understood her meaning before I actually said the words. *Of course.* She was a spirit. It stood to reason that she would long for the place other spirits went, and the peace that awaited there. Here in Neverland, she was constantly reminded of all she had lost. I couldn't think of anything to say except, "I'm sorry."

Bell lifted her head to respond, but her focus shifted to something behind me. Her luminous eyes changed, just a little, and I knew she was looking at Peter. My own heart quickened, as well.

"I'm glad I met you, Wendy Davenport," Bell said, refocusing on me.

"And I you," I replied, surprised to discover that it was the truth. We looked at each other some more, and though I felt no threat from her, something coiled between us. An awareness, perhaps, that had our circumstances been different, we might not be meeting in such a cordial manner.

Suddenly Bell moved, and it seemed she was in front of me within the blink of an eye. I was about to step back when she put her hand on my shoulder—I felt nothing, not the pressure of her fingers or the slightest shift in temperature—and put her lips beside my ear.

"Maybe you were sent here to *save* Peter. Not destroy him," she whispered, the words meant only for me. I frowned into her lovely face, my thoughts already churning like a vat of butter. Before I could say anything else, Bell faded into nothing.

I wondered if it was the last time I'd ever see her.

The sounds of the jungle swelled in the faerie's absence. Monkeys, birds, and insects called and clicked into the humidity. After a few moments, Peter approached me. His scent, which had become more familiar than my own, like sleep easing through you unawares, wafted past. I closed my eyes, wanting him so much it was a physical ache. My longing felt even more wrong after speaking with Bell.

"It's called a Pan Tree," he said, his breath tickling the back of my neck. Apparently we weren't going to acknowledge the fact that I'd just met his former lover. "Fae term, of course. It means 'soul.' They say that if you stand close enough, you can hear the voices of those who have died in Neverland since the beginning."

All I heard was the wind. Frogs and crickets chorused together, reminding me of carolers at Christmastime, and I experienced a surge of longing for a place I couldn't quite remember. "It's beautiful," I murmured.

"This tree... this tree is what allows Bell to walk among us. Should it be destroyed, we would never see her again. Or the others." There was tension in Peter's voice; he was trusting me with another secret. When I unthinkingly touched his arm, his expression intensified. Peter stepped away and knelt in front of a smaller, less imposing tree. He pulled a knife from the sheath on his leg. He used the tip and started to scrape away small pieces of bark. When he didn't offer an explanation, I crept closer and peeked over his shoulder to see what he was carving.

Peter and Wendy, it said in a boyish, uneven scrawl.

"So all of Neverland will know," Peter said. He didn't say anything else, but I understood that it was for me to know, too. My thoughts went in every direction. Nervous, happy, confused. What did this mean? What did I *want* it to mean?

Nonsensical babble left my mouth. It felt like I could hear the flowers and bugs laughing. "But what about Bell? Can she read English? She's smart, even I know that, and we just met. I'd wager she knows how. Bell will see it and she—"

"—will be glad. It's true, she was the jealous sort once. As one would expect, death changes people. It would be an awfully big adventure, don't you think?"

At this, the wonder Peter's words had sparked in me faded, and my heart broke instead. I felt it, like a fissure in the earth, a crack opening through its very center.

"I hope neither of us finds out," was all I could think to say. I turned from him, the carving, and pretended to be occupied by the Pan Tree again.

Peter must have sensed something amiss, but he didn't press for answers. This time, he let me decide. We stood there in the dell, with joyous faeries below and a lightening sky above. Our fingers entwined, and he was wonderfully warm. It was the most content I'd ever been in Neverland.

Suddenly, though, I was painfully aware of time passing. There was something I was supposed to be considering, a choice that arrived with the sun. *We'll leave tomorrow*, Captain Bainbridge had said, his eyes boring into mine over sea and discord. *But if you change your mind, I'll be spending the morning ashore gathering supplies.*

If I left with the captain in a few hours, I knew I would never see Peter again. But if I stayed, I would see him die.

We were so close I could feel Peter's breath on my cheek now. Beyond him, those engraved names caught my eye. Even when the wood healed, they would linger, like a spirit in the Pan Tree.

I returned my focus to Peter. On the curve of his cheek, the star-shaped birthmark on his jaw, his disheveled hair, the indents around his mouth, marks his smile had left behind, more detailed than footprints in wet sand.

As the subject of my scrutiny stared back with undeniable feeling, the grief in my heart was overpowered. Something else inside me unfurled and stretched, like the petals of a flower after a long winter experiencing spring. Fireflies winked and dimmed. Peter laced the rest of our fingers together, and his thumb rested on my wrist, the gentlest of touches. My heart was a drum, so loud and forceful that I knew he could feel it. I wasn't worried about his shadow, close as it was to dark—no, this fear was of something else entirely.

"Wendy," he whispered. No one had ever said my name like that before, as though it was pain and ecstasy all at once. And I understood it.

That was the moment, despite everything, I began to love the boy called Peter.

Slowly, he bent his head. My heart beat in my ears and I didn't move. Our lips brushed so hesitantly I hardly felt it.

When I uttered no protest, Peter returned, coaxing my mouth open. We tasted each other again, more deeply now, and his tongue was sweet. Though we'd kissed before, something felt different this time. As if it meant more to both of us.

Then we were moving and turning and stumbling, our passion ignited once again, spreading like the hungriest of flames. My back hit the tree Peter had carved. He raised my arms and pressed them against the bark, running his fingertips down my skin. I tipped my head back and lost myself in the sensation of his lips skimming my neck and my collarbone. I murmured Peter's name and pushed my body into his, thrilling at the feel of his arousal. It pulsed against me, so long and hard.

Just as I reached to open his trousers, Peter put his hands on my waist. He shifted away a bit, then tipped forward to press our foreheads together. Though I blinked in surprise, I didn't question him. I knew he was trying to say something. Communicate something. I just wasn't entirely certain what.

The urgency between us eased until I could breathe again. Slowly, Peter tugged me to the ground, and if it was hard or uncomfortable, I didn't notice—every fiber of my being was focused on him. Slowly, Peter pulled my gown up, his fingers skimming my ribs along the way. Tiny bumps raced across my skin. Once the dress had gone over my head, the night air kissing my bared breasts, I did the same for Peter. As if it was the first time we'd seen each other like this, my fingers trembled slightly. I wondered if Peter could hear the riot of butterflies inside me.

He didn't say a word, and that was unnerving in itself. The air was fraught with meaning. Mist hovered around us, thick with floral aromas, and it hadn't been there a few moments ago. Peter and I went on to remove each other's undergarments, as well. At times, our movements weren't completely graceful—my ankle got caught, and Peter had to sit up in order for me to pull his off—but when I caught sight of the twinkle in his eye, I found myself smiling, too.

On our knees, both of us completely naked, Peter began to kiss my neck, my shoulders, my chest. I tentatively explored his back, his stomach, his thighs. Every part of him was hard and honed, including, I noted with a rush of hot desire, that wicked length between his legs. I wrapped my hand around it slowly, and Peter made a soft sound, his grip tightening on my waist.

Something about that sound drove me wild. My apprehension forgotten, I gave Peter's chest a light push. He acquiesced to the silent request and shifted until his back rested against the jungle floor. Thinking of a passage from *The Lustful Turk*, I tucked myself between his legs. I'd never done such a thing before, but the notion of performing this act incorrectly didn't seem quite so terrible anymore. Perhaps Peter would tell me what he liked.

Feeling his eyes on my naked body, I began to lick and suck my way down his. Startling me, Peter gathered my hair in his hand, keeping it out of the way as I moved. When I finally reached his eager cock, I felt that rush of boldness again, and I couldn't resist torturing him a bit. I nipped and kissed Peter's inner thighs, the light dusting of hair tickling my mouth. His hand fisted in my hair, and his manhood was so hard now that it rose into the air like a flag.

"Fuck," Peter breathed, slightly tipping his head back. His expression was almost... helpless. As if he was utterly at my mercy. No one had ever looked at me like that before. I met his gaze again and held it as I grasped his cock with one hand.

Still taunting him, I ran my tongue along the sides of it, licking over the top and then back down, caressing his length with my palm at the same time. The muscles in Peter's stomach clenched and his head fell back, his throat moving as he swore softly under his breath.

Then, between one breath and the next, I took him completely into my mouth.

The change in him was instantaneous—Peter made a sound I'd never heard before, and his hips started moving subtly, almost involuntarily, plunging deeper into my mouth. His grip on my hair was even tighter now, and his chest rose and fell more forcefully. I smiled as I continued to kiss and suck him. Seeing Peter at my mercy, how he groaned from my touch, made the place between my own legs dampen and throb. But I didn't stop, not for a moment. Instead, with the hand I wasn't using, I reached down and stroked myself, too. Peter saw what I was doing and it only made his eyes burn brighter. Heat rose inside me, along with a tingling sensation that threatened to derail what I was doing. I kept going, even as my own hips began to undulate.

Just as it seemed he was about to come undone, though, Peter sat upright. The suddenness of it made me lean back, and I asked a question with my expression. The boy moved in a blur, a whisper of air moving over my skin, and suddenly I was the one resting against on the mossy ground. I stared up at Peter, my lips wet and swollen, and waited for him to claim me in a burst of fervor and rough need.

Nothing happened. For a moment or two, Peter did nothing but stare, as if he were committing the sight of me to memory. Suddenly I remembered another night we had shared. *You are magic*, he'd said then, and he'd been wearing the same expression he was now. Appreciation. Desire. Anticipation. Despite the similarities, it felt as though we were entirely different from the ones who'd met in that shadowy bedroom.

At least one thing hadn't changed, however—I *ached* for him.

Burying my fingers in the hair at the base of his neck, I pulled Peter close and gave him a kiss that consumed both of us. Our bodies crushed together, skin to skin, and Peter shifted to position his cock at my entrance. Inflicting some torment of his own, he rubbed himself up and down my slick folds. "Please," I said, the words almost a whimper. "*Please*."

With a lock of hair dangling over one eye, lending him a particularly roguish look, Peter flashed his infamous grin. "I like it when you beg."

I scowled. "You arrogant—"

Peter captured my mouth with his, and an instant later, his cock nudged at my opening. Its long length was still wet from my mouth, and inch after inch of him slid inside effortlessly, until he was buried up to the hilt. As he filled me, I bit my lip to contain a blissful moan and linked my ankles behind his back.

With his elbows on either side of my head, Peter began to move, pulling out and driving back in again. There was nothing gentle about our joining, but I still felt the connection between us, shining as forcefully as one of those compass stars. My fingers dug into his back, and I began meeting him thrust for thrust. If Peter felt any pain from my nails, he gave no sign. In an attempt to muffle my cries, I bit his shoulder. Peter seemed to like this, because he made another sound deep in his throat.

Suddenly I felt his hand between us, his knuckles brushing against my lower stomach. Then it moved down farther, even farther, until he was touching that part of me where so many sensations had gathered.

He kissed me at the same time his thumb began to make perfectly pressured circles. I moaned again, this time into Peter's mouth. His hips moved faster and harder, along with his thumb, which never strayed from that bundle of nerves at the apex of my thighs.

Suddenly Peter pulled back, abruptly ending our kiss, but the rhythm we'd created never paused or faltered.

"Say you're mine," he breathed. There was something desperate in his eyes. The slapping noises our bodies made echoed through the jungle.

"I'm yours," I said, and there was a helpless note in my voice, too. What he was doing felt so good, I knew I probably would've agreed to anything. It felt like we were climbing a summit together, going higher, higher, almost touching the sun.

Seconds or minutes later, Peter gave a shout. He threw his head back and his rhythm became something mindless, as if he were at its mercy. But somehow, even in the throes of pleasure, he never ceased to move his thumb. I reached the peak a moment later, and anything else I felt was lost in the avalanche of light, pleasure, and release. My core clenched around Peter's cock, again and again, and I heard his low curse. My lips curled into a small, satisfied smile.

Later, I wouldn't remember falling asleep. I wouldn't be able to recall either of us moving so that Peter's chest pressed against my back, his body curled around me like a warm shell. If I had, I might've thought to put some clothes back on or climb into the canopy to avoid any hungry beasts. But the air was balmy, the Pan Tree hovering over us like an ancient protector, and I slept more peacefully than I had in weeks. Not a single dream visited me and I didn't wake at any point during the night.

It seemed as though only a few minutes had passed when light coaxed me from my blissful slumber.

Dawn shone through the leaves, and the colors were more lovely than any others I'd seen during my time in Neverland. But neither of us paid it any mind—Peter was already reaching for me, his manhood hard and eager for more.

Gradually, tenderly, he pushed his way inside again. I grasped his firm backside and silently urged him onward with my hands. Peter whispered my name, then everything quickened. He rocked more forcefully. Our sounds became louder. *I will never grow tired of this,* I thought amidst the blinding surges of pleasure. Driven once more by that deep, mindless instinct, I clawed Peter's back and clenched around him.

"Fuck," he gasped, and a familiar tremor went through him.

Afterward, we lay on the bed of moss, drowsy and content once more. Sunlight caressed our gleaming bodies, and I wished we could pass the entire day in such a fashion. In spite of all the rest we'd just achieved, Peter's eyes fluttered, then closed completely. A line deepened between his brows. Smiling, I traced the indentation with my finger. I repeated the motion, almost absently. Within minutes, Peter was asleep again.

It was the first time I had seen him in this state. His face went slack, and he seemed younger. Free. Things that I had always assumed he was, but now, I wasn't so sure. His hair lifted slightly in a breeze, settling back down. Maybe Peter thought it was a part of a dream, that the gentle air was someone brushing their fingers over his skin, because the tension in his body ebbed. A breath escaped between his lips, almost a sigh. Another half-smile hovered at my lips—I liked being able to stare at Peter without worrying he would catch me.

Still half-asleep, he nuzzled my neck and inhaled my scent, humming that achingly familiar song.

Maybe it was due to the closeness we'd shared these past several hours, but in that moment, I couldn't bear the lie anymore. My deceit became a physical pain, as if hundreds of needles had sprouted from the tender flesh of my heart.

"*Second star to the right, and straight on 'til morning,*" I heard myself sing, a terrible waver in the words. It was the only piece of his mother Peter had, the piece he'd never known the truth of—he still believed it was from James. I did it partly on impulse and partly as a result of the agonizing weeks leading up to this moment. Because of the tossing and turning, the guilt, the indecision, the obstinance of memories that refused to be banished. And because I loved him. "*A few thoughts with some dust, and soon you'll be soaring.*"

Peter's eyes snapped open. Any lingering lethargy moved away like parting clouds. Speechless, he stared at me. "Did the captain—"

The words kept spilling out of me. "No. Not him. Your mother came to my house shortly after you and I met. She isn't dead, Peter, and she's known about you for quite some time. They were just waiting for an opportunity."

"They?" he repeated tightly.

"Yes. Your mother and Constable Collingwood. When he spotted you watching me from a rooftop, it led her to me. They're siblings, you see. They would do anything to avoid a scandal, and if London discovered she'd had an illegitimate child, the entire family would be ruined. The lady implied that if I didn't kill you, she would spread rumors about my virtue and my family's fortune."

His expression pierced my soul as if it were made of paper. I forced myself to go on. "But even her threats weren't enough to make me agree. Then... then Michael became ill and I needed money to pay the physician. I didn't have a choice, Peter."

As I spoke, an odd smell wafted past. It made me think of a toad I found in Hyde Park once, dead and rotten on the ground, skin shriveled and eyes eaten by flies. I knew it wasn't my imagination when I saw the flowers around us wither.

"There is always a choice. You just didn't like yours," Peter replied, his voice flat. He stood and pulled his clothes on. Every movement was sharp and methodical.

Watching him, I bit my lip. I sat up and wrapped my arms around my knees. "Really? What about the choice you made? When Captain Bainbridge came to Neverland and explained the misunderstanding, then offered to take you and the others back to London?"

"I'm not going to talk about that."

I wanted to scream. How could we go so quickly from an intimacy I'd never known to acting like dissonant strangers? The sense of safety and togetherness was long gone. The sun felt obtrusive now. I scrambled up to avoid its glare and reached for my own pile of clothing. "Why? Because then you'd be forced to face the fact that Neverland isn't as grand as you make it out to be? That those children don't have to kill and starve and fight every day? That all of this is your own—"

"Shut up!" Peter hissed. Venom filled his eyes.

Unnerved, I took a step back. My heel sank into a fallen log and it broke open. Fat, black beetles poured out. I swallowed the shriek rising inside me and moved out of their path.

"You may have had some bad luck with your parents, I'll give you that," I said, matching his clipped tone. "But you insist on blaming James for how you live here because you can't endure the thought of having any responsibility."

"James, is it?" he mocked.

I flushed. "He came back for *you*, Peter. I know it ruined everything when his men killed Bell, but he still cares. I care for you, as well. You're so afraid to trust someone, to be—"

"I'm afraid of nothing."

"You're the biggest pretender of us all." I took a shuddering breath. And, despite how my stomach quivered and the ground rumbled, continued on. "You're selfish. You're cruel. And most importantly, you *are* afraid."

"I'm afraid of nothing," Peter said again, with enough force that a blast of wind tore at my shirt, whipping it against me.

I raised my voice so he would hear over the flurry. "Everyone is afraid of something! Everyone has a weakness. I've found yours!"

As swiftly as it grew, the wind quieted.

"Oh? And what's that?" he purred. It sounded like he'd said it directly in my ear. Yet somehow Peter had put so much distance between us that he was on the path, ready to burst into the sky at any moment. His voice was cold. It sent a shard of ice through my heart, and I swallowed, answering in spite of the ache.

"Me."

Peter hooted with laughter. Humiliation spread up my

neck and into my cheeks, a prickling heat. "You're more arrogant than I am! Quite a feat, Miss Davenport."

"Why else would your shadow despise me, Peter?" I retorted. "I make you want to *care* again. To be something more than a boy of Neverland. You're so *lost*—all of you are —and I awaken the part of you that wants to be found."

The vehemence I felt made it difficult to breathe; my chest heaved. For an instant, Peter and I just stared at each other. There was no trace of the adoration or awe that had been in his face earlier. Now there was only a cruel sneer.

Then he said, "You were nothing more than a good fuck."

Any love lingering within me was crushed beneath the weight of my pure, incandescent rage. *He's lying,* reason tried say. But I wasn't feeling reasonable anymore. There was another beat of silence between the two of us, his blue eyes boring into mine, and I wanted to hurt Peter as badly as he'd just hurt me.

"I kissed your brother," I heard myself say.

The quiet became choking. Peter's expression was inscrutable, and somehow, that was worse than how he'd just been looking at me. A moment later, he rose off the ground and disappeared into the heavens.

Slowly, the jungle noises resumed, as if every creature on the island had felt Peter's ire. I looked up and saw the colorful dawn had turned to gray. As quickly as it had come, my anger departed. Now I searched the roiling sky and wished I could take it all back—every truth spoken, every word spat. I covered my face and whispered, "Don't cry. Don't you dare cry."

Defiant tears softened the glen, smearing at the lines and edges of everything. My shadow drew closer. It seemed more hesitant this time to make its offer, but it still reached for me with timid, incorporeal fingers. More tears plopped to the grass while I considered.

This pain I would not keep. Nor these memories. Nor this love.

"Take it all," I said through my teeth. The same moment I stretched my hand toward the shadow, something startled the birds seeking refuge in the Pan Tree. They took flight all at once and the sound of beating wings filled the air.

My hand jerked away.

"Peter?" I called, hope wavering in the sound of his name. Something moved to my left. I spun around and saw a flash of long, dark hair. "Bashira? Is that you?"

No reply. I scanned the jungle and eventually spotted her, a silhouette in the darkness. Thinking that my friend was playing a game, I wiped away any evidence of the exchange with Peter. I started to move toward her, mustering a feeble smile.

But it was Lily who emerged.

"Wendy-bird," she spat. I reared back in surprise, and my heel slipped on a damp leaf. The Pan Tree caught me. Ridges of its bark dug into my spine, and I straightened, noting the gold that now covered my palm. Lily noticed the rest, my mussed hair and hastily-donned clothes. Her knuckles whitened around the hilt of the sword she held. Her eyes were bright.

I saw the truth then, as naked as a newborn babe. *She's in love with him,* I realized.

Helplessly I wondered what I could say to reason with the younger girl. But what words could bring her peace? After all, I knew from experience that the young felt things more intensely than any adult. In the end all I could say was, "I didn't know. I'm sorry. There will... there will be others, Lily."

"Not like him," she said. Then she dove at me.

It was so unexpected I had no chance to react. I hit the ground and pain flared through my head, sudden as a smattering of color traveling across one's vision as it adjusted to light. Lily's face loomed above me, hard and calculating.

Then, nothing.

CHAPTER 17

EVERYTHING WAS RED.

So violently red. Was this death? No. Only the sun streaming through my eyelids, I concluded with relief, when I was able to feel the hard rock beneath me. But my eyes had crusted shut during the night. For a few moments, I couldn't open them.

Seconds later, the pain announced itself and a groan escaped my lips. Still blind, I lifted a shaky hand and pressed it to my forehead. Dried blood sprinkled down. Where was I?

As I attempted to gather my wits, rough hands grabbed me. I felt a burst of fright, and at last, managed to wrench my eyes open. A girl I didn't recognize was tying my hands together. My ankles were already secured by the same tight loops of rope. Whimpering, I began to struggle, but I was too weak and dizzy. Images and sounds began clomping through my memory, artless as wobbly heels on a wooden floor. The faeries, the Pan Tree, the argument with Peter, Lily's attack.

How long had I been unconscious? I arched my neck to peer upward. The sun smirked from its perch. It was afternoon, then.

There were others on the rock besides me and the girl— a blurred shape moved next to us. When it turned at the same moment my vision cleared, I gasped. Or tried to, anyway, but the hot sun had apparently absorbed every last drop of moisture within my mouth and throat. "Captain Bainbridge?" I rasped.

"Hello, there," he said weakly. His hair was caked with an alarming amount of blood. Bashira was tying him up, as well, and a shock went through me at the sight of her. She didn't raise her gaze. Sweat gleamed on my friend's forehead. I was about to say something to her when the captain added, "I was wondering if you'd wake. Haven't been able to listen for a heartbeat."

The girl who'd been securing my bonds was finished now. She put her back to us and moved to the edge of the rock.

"How—" My voice was hardly more than a whisper. I stopped and swallowed several times before trying to speak again. "How did they capture you?"

Though Bashira's hands didn't slow, I knew she could hear every word. Instead of answering, Captain Bainbridge coughed. Lily must have dealt him a hearty blow, too, because he squinted at me as if I might be a mirage. "I was waiting by the Neverwood. Hoping you'd come back with me to England," he said after a long pause.

Now that I had some of my wits about me, I felt the beginnings of panic, like claws sinking into the tender flesh of my stomach. I twisted in an effort to discern where we were. Water surrounded us on every side. Seagulls cried overhead—they circled our small gathering, wings wobbling on currents of air.

"Bashira, help us," I begged. My husky plea rolled off the girl like dew on a leaf, and I knew she was following the orders of her Torch Bearer. Bashira had always spoken of her home, her people, and her traditions with such reverence and devotion. Even if she might not completely agree with Lily's orders, it was in her nature to trust. To believe. That was what Neverland had taught her, and it was why I couldn't depend on her now.

Finished with the captain's bonds, Bashira knelt behind me and tugged at the rope to be sure it was knotted adequately. The other girl waited for her with the same stony expression. I thought of what I had learned about the geography here and concluded this must be Marooners' Rock. It was within the Mermaid Lagoon. The bloodthirsty creatures would soon sense our presence, if they hadn't already.

Horror gripped me with sharp, black claws as I comprehended why we'd been brought to this particular spot.

Lily was going to let the mermaids do her dirty work.

We watched the two Neverlanders return to shore in

their boat. There was no sign of Lily amongst them or on the island—she was undoubtedly with Peter, distracting him, talking over the whispers of the trees.

Captain Bainbridge spoke lightly, as if we were sipping tea and nibbling on *petit fours*. "No matter. That brother of mine is bound to swoop in and rescue you soon enough."

"Peter won't be saving us," I said past cracked lips. His name tasted like dirt and ash. I pictured the hollow look in his eyes from that morning, heard the icy depths of ocean in his voice. No, I couldn't depend on him, not even if Lily were to fail in her efforts at diversion. Aurora couldn't intervene, either—my voice was too weak to shout and she wouldn't come at the captain's call.

Despite the direness of our circumstances, I continued to examine the possibilities. The feeling was beginning to leave my arm, and I shifted to relieve some weight. In doing so, my fingers brushed something. It was cool and smooth to the touch. My breathing went shallow. Was that a knife? *Bashira,* I thought in a rush of gratitude. She must've set it within reach when she was supposedly testing the rope around my wrists. She hadn't completely forsaken me! She'd defied the Torch Bearer in the only way she could. If Lily ever discovered what she'd done...

"We're getting off this rock," I said urgently, contorting my body to grip the knife's handle.

The captain must have seen it. There was now a bit of strength in his voice as he said, "You are full of surprises, Miss Davenport."

"Call me Wendy, please. We're far past such formalities."

"Then you must call me James." A fly landed on his neck, but he was too weak to fuss at it. Whatever blows Lily had given me, she had given him and more. Perhaps even a poke with her sword, if the round stain on his shirt was any indication. I concentrated on every movement, trying to saw at the rope without severing my arm along with it.

The heat, desperation, and thirst collided. Spots marred my vision. The knife dropped from my grip and bounced. It slid, landing dangerously close to the edge of the rock. I swayed and uttered every curse I knew. James followed the knife with his eyes. "Can you reach it?" I rasped.

In response, the captain adjusted himself so that he sat with his back to the water, and scooted closer to our salvation. His proximity to the edge made me nervous; the mermaids could reach him. In fact, it seemed odd they hadn't come yet.

The instant I thought this, the breeze arrived, carrying a sound with it. James was too preoccupied to notice. It started faintly, but grew louder. *Tick. Tick. Tick.* What *was* that? I frowned, searching the air and the waves. There was nothing to explain the ticking.

When I faced forward again, my heart stopped. It felt as if seagulls fell dead from the sky and the sun exploded and colors darkened into gray.

A crocodile was making its way up the side of the rock.

It couldn't be. But yes, it was the same one that I'd confronted on the *Jolly Roger*—there were deep gouges in its side from Aurora's talons. The clock I'd thrown at it must have survived the journey down that long throat; the ticking was indisputable. James was still reaching, stretching his fingers out for the knife. He didn't see the animal, couldn't with his back turned. I opened my mouth to cry out a warning, but it was too late.

The crocodile's jaws closed, and James released a scream so agonizing that it didn't sound human. He tore free of the beast's teeth. There was nothing left below his wrist other than a scarlet, ragged stump. *Tick. Tick. Tick.* I was moving on instinct, lashing out with my bare feet. They pounded harmlessly against the crocodile's scaled side. It retreated a bit to swallow the hand it had claimed. My stomach lurched when I caught a glimpse of the beast's huge tongue, smeared with James's blood. I lost my place on the rock, scraping my way down to the water, leaving James unprotected.

The crocodile's black eyes gleamed as it swung in the captain's direction once more—it seemed to have no interest in me whatsoever. James had enough sense to climb higher. *Tick. Tick. Tick.* I realized the knife was within reach now and snatched it with my bound hands. I pushed myself up and hopped, slipping once, slamming face-first on the rock. My ears rang and a metallic taste filled my mouth. James shouted, and I used the last shred of endurance inside me to stand again. The horizon tilted. *Tick. Tick. Tick.*

With a shout, I leaped onto the crocodile's back. I gave it no time to react. Using both hands, I raised the knife high and brought it back down, jammed its entire length into the top of the beast's head. It made a strange half-grunt, half-growl sound, moving back and forth as if it could shake the knife out, which I still needed to cut my bonds. After several attempts to pull the knife free, it eventually popped out with a wet sound.

I didn't wait for the crocodile to die before throwing myself off it. I'd barely landed back onto the rock when I started hacking at the ropes still hindering me. There was blood everywhere, making the rope and my skin slick. I spared no more thoughts for the crocodile. I didn't even think to listen for it. There was only the pain, the desperation, the knife in my wet hand.

It felt like an hour had gone by once I finally broke free and scrambled to James's side.

"Let me see," I panted, pushing his remaining hand out of the way. When I did, everything went red again. But my eyes weren't closed this time—they were wide, wide open. Unstoppable tears streaked down my cheeks, salt joining blood.

Not even leaves of the Fire Tree could fix this.

Don't let him see your horror, Wendy-bird. I schooled my expression into a neutral mask and tugged the rope off him, easily accomplished now that it only encircled one wrist. Then I bent to do the same for the length of rope around his feet.

"Wendy."

The captain's enlarged pupils were peering over my shoulder. Expecting the worst, I turned. The crocodile had left a trail of blood as, unbeknownst to us, it slinked back to the sea. I watched it slip beneath the surface before I could decide whether to go after it again. Ripples expanded, then it was gone. The ticking finally silenced.

I cut part of my skirt into a strip and set to work binding James's arm. It reminded me of the night Slightly was bitten by the Pink Lady. Blood everywhere, terror in my trembling fingers, pain in the folds of his pinched skin. Unlike that night, though, I didn't speak during my efforts. I knew there was nothing I could possibly say that would comfort James. The sun beat us mercilessly with its luminescent fists and I leaned back, trying to think of what else I could do. Frustration burrowed deep into my heart.

"You should..." James grimaced, started again. "You should swim back to shore while that vile creature nurses its wound."

The makeshift tourniquet was as effective as a bucket with holes. Blood pooled on the rock all around us now. Desperate to stop the flow, I grabbed the bandaged stump and pressed down as hard as I could. James moaned. The color had drained from his face. *He looks dead*, I thought distantly.

The truth of it struck me. Like his brother, James's soul was bound for the mysterious place all souls go.

He knew it, too. Wheezing, James put the hand he had left over mine. "It's all right."

"It doesn't end here," I told him thickly, releasing my hold. The bandage was soaked through, but I didn't prepare a fresh one. "Even if we don't survive this, we shall see each other again."

"Are you speaking of Heaven?" he asked. His voice was so faint, I had to lean close to hear it.

An inexplicable calm had stolen over me. I brushed a strand of hair out of James's eyes and attempted to smile. "I suppose it's a matter of perspective. There's a place on the island—oh, you can't imagine until you've seen it—the most beautiful spot I've ever been. It's a tree. The roots themselves are embedded in magic."

James couldn't keep his eyes open anymore. I shifted so that he was propped against me, uncaring of the mess or the dull pounding in my skull.

"Tell me another story," James said. His voice lost its usual crispness, making him sound like a child.

I froze. Those words. Those four words. They were a shower of sparks, an exploding sun, a shattering lantern. In my mind's eye I saw him, a boy, sitting upright in bed with an excited smile, patting the spot beside him with a small, frail hand. *Tell me a story, Wendy.*

"Oh, God," I said hoarsely, smashing my blood-spattered fist against my mouth. What had I done? "*Michael.*"

My brother.

During this painful revelation, James had slumped lower. His head lolled in the crook of my elbow. "What did you say?" he whispered.

The veins in his eyelids were prominent and blue. Without the Fire Tree leaves, he had minutes left. His heartbeat was already slowing.

I had to get back to London. Had to set things right. Had to save Michael's life, which was the only reason I'd come here in the first place. Fresh determination surged through me. "We're not dying today, James," I said through my teeth. "Hold on just a bit longer."

If Aurora or Peter weren't options, there was only one left. I squinted out at the water and began to chant under my breath, fingers tightening on James with every syllable, "Serafa. Serafa. *Serafa.*"

By the time she appeared, the sun was well on its way to the other side of sky. I'd kept at it until my voice was nearly gone, and James had lost consciousness. I was beginning to succumb to the thirst and pain, too, when a splash alerted me. I lifted my head bleakly, thinking that if the crocodile or anything else had come for us again, I had no strength left to fight it.

And there she was. With a playful air, Serafa gripped Marooners' Rock, hiding most of her face behind the ledge. Curiosity emanated from her milky eyes. "What does the Wendy-bird want, hmmm?" she asked. Her sultry tones felt like fingers trailing over my skin. James stirred.

"I understand blood is powerful in Neverland," I said, numb to her, to everything.

She cocked her head with interest and pulled herself up. Rivulets streamed down her breasts. "You wish to make a bargain?"

Ice formed in my veins. It would be the third arrangement I'd made since all this began, and I had yet to fulfill one of them. What did I even have to bargain with? I looked down at the captain's pale face. Michael pervaded my thoughts, as well. Nothing but magic would help them now.

Resignation crept through me, tenacious as any illness. "Very well," I managed. "I offer you my life in exchange for—"

Scorn swelled in the air. The mermaid clicked her tongue. "Tsk, tsk. Serafa doesn't want Wendy's blood. No, no, no. Not hers."

There could be no mistaking who she meant. Who she truly wanted. Peter believed the aura was the heart of Neverland, but it was him. The center, the source. Every creature, light and dark alike, was drawn to the boy who could fly. It was undoubtedly why he was fated to die.

It was why I had to betray him now.

This was different than the first time. I had agreed to Lady Bainbridge's terms when I hardly knew Peter. But as the words left my mouth in this moment, I uttered them knowing that I was condemning someone I loved in order to save another. There would be no going back. My shadow stepped closer as I said, "For our safety—no, for our safety and the grant of a wish—I will swear on my own life to give you a taste of the one you want so badly."

Serafa's brow rose at my impulsive addendum, but she didn't argue. At her nod, I picked up the knife and sliced it across my palm. The sting was nothing compared to the chaos in my head and my heart. I hardly reacted. Red beads seeped through the opening like flowers in springtime. The mermaid didn't move from her place in the water, so I clumsily set the captain down and crawled to her. At the edge, I had no more strength for caution. My hand flopped palm-up on the rock in an apathetic offering, and Serafa was smug and deliberate in licking it clean. I didn't even have the strength to shudder.

Then, using the same preternatural power she'd displayed upon our first meeting, the mermaid yanked me toward her. I screamed and swallowed a mouthful of water. It closed over my head, shockingly cool after the relentless sun. I floundered in the depths while Serafa vanished. Had it been a trick? Was our bargain that meaningless to her? I grappled for a handhold, intending to climb out and rescue James from the mercurial creature. But at that same instant, a body fell into the water beside me, and I caught a glimpse of a bandaged arm just before we were both seized again.

She moved at a speed I didn't know was possible beneath the sea. I couldn't breathe, couldn't think—there was only fear and drowning. Waves crashed in my lungs. Silver fish and blue water blurred past. Seconds later, Serafa tossed James and me onto the shore as if we were nothing more than a handful of pebbles. *We've struck a blood bargain, Wendy-bird,* her voice said. *It cannot be undone. Cannot, cannot. I will know what Peter tastes like.*

I was incapable of a response, and she gleefully retreated. I didn't think to ask for my wish until she was already gone. *To be collected at a later time, then.*

The captain and I lay there on the flat, wet shore, gasping in mouthfuls of sand. Pain also throbbed through my face now, a reminder that I'd smashed it against the rock. I'd stopped feeling anything during the battle with the crocodile. James and I were damaged, bruised, and bleeding, but we'd survived. I started to tell him this, to buoy his spirits in any way I could.

Peter arrived before I could say anything.

There was no gust or scent, but still, I sensed him. Shuddering and coughing, I rolled onto my side. Peter stood nearby, lovely as the sunset. At first glance, he seemed devoid of feeling, but the way he held himself belied this. He was too completely and unnaturally still. He didn't quite meet my gaze. He focused on my forehead and said, "I didn't know, Wendy."

James came alive.

His head jerked up, he spotted Peter, and somehow he got to his feet. Chunks of damp sand fell off. What was left of his arm dangled uselessly. Serafa must have lent him strength, or some sort of magic, because he was faring better than he had been before her arrival. I hurried to support the captain, and his weight made every injury of my own twinge and burn.

Swaying, James opened his eyes and looked directly at Peter. In that moment, I didn't recognize the man I'd come to know. Something dark and maniacal had entered him, his face ravaged by rage and pain. His next words sounded like a curse. "The islanders did this for you. This loss... is because of you. Whatever existence I lead from this point forward will be a half-life *because of you*. Oh, how I wish I hadn't found you in that orphanage. You'll regret it as much as I do. Soon."

Peter said nothing, but his nostrils flared and his eyes

were too bright. When the silence became too long, too strained, I hesitated. "James, it was—"

The captain shook me off, and I almost lost my balance from the roughness of it. Peter took a threatening step forward. I shook my head at him, and he surprised me by halting.

"You saved my life today, Miss Davenport," James said as though we were strangers. He didn't quite achieve his usual mask of pleasant detachment, though. His eyes were too glassy and his face too pale. "That's the only reason I shan't wrap my remaining hand around his throat. But mark my words, I'll return. And you'd best not be at his side when I do."

He stumbled away, and knots formed in my stomach as I watched him go. For a moment, I considered accompanying James back to *The Fountain*. Perhaps I could attempt to reason with him as we went. But my legs would no longer function, and before I could panic, the beach rushed up to meet me.

Peter didn't offer help or even move. Within moments, I forgot his presence anyway—that mind-numbing pounding had returned. My face was half-buried in sand. I could still see part of the sky, though. Neverland had decided to end this day, close its curtains over the play we'd provided.

I was about to drift into a dream when numerous pairs of feet appeared all around me.

"Come along, Wendy-bird," someone murmured. "Else we'll have to build a house around you. And where would be the sense in that?"

They lifted me. Carried me. Their grips were gentle and their voices kind. We went up the hill and into the jungle. I watched the canopy above, drowsily captivated by the glimpses. Glimpses of creatures that hid from daylight, even in a place like this. A bird with backward wings. A lizard with veins that glowed. A monkey with two heads.

At camp, the children whisked me into my usual tree, setting me upon the leaf that I'd spent so many nights in. That was when I finally recognized Nibs. Another girl—Alice, I'd named her after the play, though she hadn't been given one yet—held me up while they removed the ruined gown. A fresh shirt was dropped over me. Tootles and Slightly climbed up with a bowl of soaked rags. They washed off the filth and blood. I could hear murmurings below. My name. Something about a broken nose.

Soon the boys departed. Nibs tucked me under the leaf as though I were a child, humming an odd tune. While she was preoccupied with this, I saw it—the cat. It was balanced on a branch disconcertingly close to mine. I could make out the flecks of blue in those yellow eyes and feel the growl at the center of its chest. Her tail flicked.

Why are you following me? I wanted to ask. The day I'd asked Peter, he'd mentioned change. What sort of change had occurred today to bring this creature to my feet? To make it regard me as a threat?

I tried to say something to Nibs, warn her.

"Sleep, Wendy-bird," she ordered, hearing my croak. Her raven brows drew together and she patted me. "Just sleep."

Perhaps Nib had some magic in her, too, because the

words had the effect of a spell. My eyes fluttered. I resisted, wanting to make sure the beast didn't come any closer. It was futile. The girl, the island, and the great cat faded. My old friend darkness was waiting again, and now I went willingly into its arms.

Part of me hoped it would never let go.

CHAPTER 18

I SLEPT all through the night and the following day.

The sound of snoring disturbed my dreams. I was reluctant to wake; Slightly was nestled against me, better than the ceramic hot-water bottle from back home. But the snoring didn't relent, and I noticed four things upon opening my eyes. The first was Nose, who sat with his back to the tree trunk, chin dipped against his chest in deep slumber. He had his bow resting across his lap, an arrow partially notched against the string. Protecting me from Lily, no doubt. I wondered whether he'd been assigned to this duty or had chosen it. Whatever the reason, the weary lines in his face were there all the same. Grateful tears flooded my sight.

After blinking them away, the second thing I noticed was that the yellow-eyed cat was gone. The place it had been resting was empty, and the only sign it had visited at all was a bit of fur caught on the bark. I knew it was not the last I'd seen of the creature, and next time, it would not come merely to watch. *Change*, Peter had said. That was the key. And I wasn't done changing yet.

The third detail was that my wounds had healed, even the sunburns. My face no longer hurt to touch, either. Someone must have put pieces of the Fire Tree on each one. Remnants of its dried leaves fluttered off me when I sat up. There were scars left behind on my arms and legs, so faint they were only visible if the marks were truly searched for.

And the fourth element was more important than all the rest—a wondrous *smell*. Oh, God, that smell. My mouth watered.

Grease. Fat. Meat.

Leaving Slightly to his dreams, I crawled from our cocoon and made my way past Nose. There was no soreness or discomfort as I moved; I'd been remade. My journey to the ground was swifter than it had ever been. I hurried into cover to relieve myself. When I returned to the clearing, Peter's children were already staring and whispering. I heard one of them say Lily's name.

My heart was a trunk with a broken latch, and it had tipped over on Marooners' Rock, making all the contents inside fall out. I couldn't bear any feeling besides hunger, so I focused solely on finding the source of that smell. House-keeper had anticipated me; he came bearing a platter.

"Good evening," he rumbled. He left it at that, which I appreciated. I took the burden and plunked down next to the fire.

Steam rose from my meal. There were no knives or forks, but I didn't care. I held the hot meat with bare fingers. As soon as the flavor touched my tongue, any self-consciousness or worry faded. This was no mealy, bitter piece of fruit. I was ravenous, tearing at it with my teeth and barely tasting the pieces before they slid down my throat. Housekeeper brought a jug. I fumbled with it frantically. Water dripped off my chin as I gulped. Just a minute later, it was gone.

My stomach gurgled with contentment. I slumped, sighing, and finally perceived the envious glances. At some point, Tootles had settled beside me. "Peter has asked me to bring you to him," he said. "He's at the faerie hollow."

Since waking, I hadn't allowed myself to wonder where he was or where we stood, Peter and I. There was a faint memory, at the back of my head, of being carried and tended to by the other children. Had they done so because he told them to?

None of that mattered, I reminded myself. Not anymore. Though part of me yearned for a romp through the Neverwood or a ride on Aurora's back, the other part was in London, with Michael. Seeing as Peter and I were not exactly on good terms, and James Bainbridge was in no state to helm a ship—if he was making the voyage at all, anymore —the fae might be my only hope of returning to England.

"Is it far?" was all I said.

At that moment, Nose climbed down and spotted us. I tried to convey my thanks for his diligence in a smile. The gangly boy nodded, and though his expression didn't change, there was kindness in the gesture. He turned from me and approached Housekeeper, who was already preparing another platter.

Tootles and I began our journey to the cavern.

"Do you ever see good things?" I asked him. Through breaks in the treetops, moonlight brushed my cheek with gentle fingers.

The boy grinned over his shoulder. It was a painful reminder of how young he was. "Of course," he replied. "If there's anything we can depend on in this world, it's balance. Whenever I see something awful, something good comes along, too. Eventually. 'Tis no easy thing, knowing the future. There are days I'd give it back if I could. The good is what makes it bearable."

"What good can come of Peter dying?" The question emerged more harshly than I intended, with the force of throwing knives. But Tootles was unruffled.

"I've seen *you*, miss," he said truthfully, doing a nimble hop over something in the dark. A vine, I saw once I drew closer. "Back in England. You miss him, but you're happy, too. His death leads to choices that you wouldn't have made otherwise."

A shriek echoed through the tangle of green surrounding us—out there, beyond our reach, something else was dying. I absorbed this latest revelation. "Tell me. Have you ever been wrong?"

Tootles must've heard the hope in my voice, because there was regret in his. "Not yet, miss. Not yet."

The entrance to the hollow was closer than I realized.

This was how I was able to see the nameless boy lurking near it. He was so startled by our appearance that he tripped over a branch in an attempt to retreat.

"Sorry," he blurted, eyes obscured by riotous curls. Before either of us could speak, the boy leaped into the jungle. He moved as soundlessly as Nose—handy trait for a spy.

"He was looking for the faeries," I said grimly, staring after him. "Do you think he found the hollow? Or the Tree?"

But Tootles's attention was elsewhere; he gazed at something above. There was nothing I could see, when I twisted to look. Nothing other than a wistful crescent moon. Tootles refocused on me a moment later, his smudged face somber. "Forgive him, if you can," he advised.

It took me a moment to understand. "Do you mean Peter? It hardly matters—"

"Might I have a word?" a familiar voice cut in.

Slowly, I turned to him. He'd come from the sky, no doubt, like all beautiful things. Snow, rain, stars. He stood in the shadows. Despite everything, I did want to speak to him. But this was not a conversation I wanted to have in the place where our names were carved in wood. Where I would look at the ground and see us there, lying on the moss, slick with sweat and dew.

As if Peter could hear my thoughts, he said, "Not here. I have someone guarding the Pan Tree, in case James comes into the Neverwood looking for me, and I don't want to be overheard."

I started to thank Tootles for acting as my guide and

discovered that Peter and I were alone. Nervously, I stepped toward him, and Peter shocked me by offering his arm. He seemed more solid than usual; I didn't have the urge to hold as fast and hard as possible, to keep him at my side. There was an air of uncertainty around us, and I tried not to breathe, bring it into my lungs. "Why don't the fae have one of their own watching over the Tree?" I asked, delaying the difficult exchange ahead.

"Violence is not their way. They make no effort to protect themselves. Careful, there's an animal that camouflages with the ground. It keeps its mouth open and waits for prey to walk over."

Now I searched for the glint of teeth or eyes. However grisly the reason, it was a relief to have something to concentrate on, and I was so consumed by it that I couldn't interact with Peter. Then we arrived at a wall, of sorts. It seemed someone had begun to build a house. The structure was not destroyed; it had never been finished. Time must've done the rest, and it was reduced to a pile of crumbling stones. I toyed with a bit of ivy, wondering who these people had been and whether they'd survived this place.

His voice came from behind, soothing and composed, like the turn of a page. "Lily will never touch you again. I spoke to her. I made sure of it."

Why bother? I wanted to ask snidely. I was thinking of our argument now, remembering the cruel words he'd thrown at me. But I had said some cruel words of my own. I didn't want to keep hurting each other. No more betrayals. No more lies.

"I made a bargain with Serafa," I said flatly, snapping an ivy stem in half. "In exchange for her assistance, I promised her a taste of you. Although I suspect she wants a little more than that."

Silence. Heat brushed my back as Peter closed the distance between us. I stiffened, expecting the same fury as when I'd told him about Lady Bainbridge. But instead he said, "She's been trying to lull me into the water for years. A bargain might make things more interesting."

Confusion sent my thoughts scattering, like a gale lifting fallen leaves into the air. Was this kindness a trick? Was it guilt for Lily's brutality?

In the midst of my conjecture, Peter circled me. He stopped beneath a spot of moonlight, the truth of what he felt written upon his face. I drank him in—his eyelashes, his lips, his remorse, his love. Peter still didn't try to reach out. For an instant, I wanted to forget again, to rush into his arms like one of the women in those novels.

It was the thought of forgetting that caused me to harden again. "You made me forget him," I said flatly.

At first, Peter's brow lowered in confusion, but he understood my meaning within seconds. I could tell from the way his gaze cleared. "You *wanted* to forget, Wendy," the boy told me.

A fire flared to life inside me. It climbed higher, almost painful in its intensity, and this time the heat had nothing to do with lust or desire. "No. You wished for it and made it so!" I said hotly.

"As did you. Or some dark, secret part of you."

As quickly as I'd lashed out, I went still. As always, my shadow was nearby. It hid behind the wall, observing us with obvious fear. I looked at it and slowly shook my head. "I wouldn't do that to my brother."

But the words were weak, and we both knew it. Peter didn't bother responding. He let me sink, sink, sink into a swamp of self-loathing and realization. Memories ran through the gate that had been shut for too long. I saw myself turning away from Slightly again and again, wanting nothing to do with him, while my shadow clung to the boy like soggy clothes. All its fascination with dancing, curtseying, Bashira's dress, while I'd wanted nothing to do with them. Everything motherly or feminine—what I'd been in London, the things that had gradually forced me to give up my own interests or secret hopes, and allowed Lady Bainbridge to gain the upper hand—had gone to the darkness.

Peter waited. I stared at my hands, stretching fingers out, watching the way the skin around my knuckles stretched and thinned. "There *was* a part of me that wanted to forget," I whispered. "That liked living without the burden. Maybe I've been angry at my brothers. No, not them. Not really. Angry at my parents. It was so hard, Peter. Being the strong one, taking care of everyone when I wasn't finished being taken care *of*."

A sob escaped. I covered my mouth and tried to turn away, but Peter tugged me back. His thumb rested against the tip of my chin and brought it up. His eyes had become flinty. "That's when you learn to take care of yourself," he said.

Shame buried in my chest like a dagger. Of course Peter knew better than anyone what it was to be alone. To worry. Neither one of us had chosen our circumstances, but it didn't excuse what we'd done as a result. We hadn't lost those parts of ourselves—we'd stepped away from them and turned our backs.

"Is there a way? To know whether or not he's still alive?" I asked, the question tearing from me like a piece of skin. Peter hesitated. I hadn't said Michael's name, but there could be no mistaking who I meant. "You can tell me. I'm not fragile," I added.

His mouth tightened. A small creature scuttled across the path, chittering loudly, but neither of us looked away. "I've never thought you were fragile," Peter said. "You're one of the strongest people I know. But I can't tell you if Michael still lives; there's no magic like that. No matter how much I want to."

Another silence fell, and the words I'd been meaning to say all along gathered on my tongue. They would hurt more than confessions or truth, and my shadow twitched, wanting to take this from me, too. Still, I said them, because I'd learned that the hardest things were the ones you shouldn't avoid. "I'm going home, Peter."

There was a slight flickering in his eyes; he'd been expecting this. "I can't take you back," he muttered. "Not right now, at least. With everything that happened on Marooners' Rock and Lily—"

"I know. I'll find my own way."

Peter nodded, and he transferred his focus to the sky, lifting a hand to rub the back of his neck. Unbidden, the memory of our last night together flooded my mind. I started reaching for him, wanting to touch his face, but I resisted. Like the crocodile, I could feel my internal clock ticking. Peter didn't know it, but a question he'd once asked in the Neverwood had stayed with me ever since. It had become my compass and, despite my doubts, it was also what guided me home now, in addition to Michael.

What would make you happy?

So I lowered my arm and cleared my throat instead. "There's something else. I wanted to say how grateful I am to you, Peter. For bringing me here, for teaching me how to tame a Neverbird, for showing me that cave, for... everything. Even the painful parts. You taught me how to play again, how to *laugh* again, and such a lesson is beyond price. It might've saved my life, in a way. But I also wanted to stress that I'm not going back just for Michael. It's also because I need to grow up. I *want* to. To become the person I'm supposed to be, to make more choices and mistakes, to leave a mark on this world. No one can be a child forever."

"I can," the boy said softly. His response filled me with an incredible sadness. All of this felt like an argument we'd already had. We were talking in circles, repeating every-thing, saying nothing.

"Goodbye, Peter." This last bit sounded strangled, like someone had their hands wrapped around my throat and were squeezing, squeezing, squeezing. After a moment, I stepped around him and began walking in the direction of the faeries' doorway. After borrowing a bit of magic from them, I'd leave this place. God willing, Michael would still be alive. Time worked differently in Neverland; maybe only a week had passed in London.

"The day of Lily's ceremony," Peter called, sounding very much like the child he insisted on being, "why did you kiss me in the cottage? Did you feel sorry for me?"

The question seemed random, but somehow I knew my answer was important to him. Knew that it had the potential to haunt Peter like a spirit, live in his shadow, pounce like the great cat during an unguarded moment.

Lingering there, I thought about that heady moment we'd shared at the village. It had not been out of overwhelming pity or blind desire. Just something deep in me, hearing something deep in him. I smiled back at Peter, knowing this was the last time we would ever see each other. "No. Not at all. You—"

A scream clawed the night.

As one, Peter and I bolted, following the sound through darkness and danger. It brought us in the direction of the Pan Tree. Halfway there we drew up short, breathless.

It had been Nibs standing guard. She stood outside the dell now, eyes so wide I could see whiteness and veins even from a distance. Peter and I halted a short distance away, waiting for her to speak. But the girl didn't say anything, didn't move or blink, and my instincts shrieked. The air was thick with terror. The three of us were frozen, like an ominous, dusty painting hanging on the wall. Something about the girl's stance was stiff and odd, and I couldn't pinpoint what it was.

Not until Mr. Starkey revealed himself.

He'd been hiding behind her. The pirate moved like a snake, slithering off so quickly that I didn't comprehend anything had happened until Nibs crumpled. Then I saw the blood and I knew—he'd put a knife in her back, and it had been the only thing holding her upright.

With an enraged shout, Peter gave chase. I was already at Nibs's side, struggling to push her over. She was heavier than she looked. On the third attempt, I succeeded. Leaves stuck to the places on her person that were wet, but I saw her eyes flutter.

"She's alive!" I cried, fumbling to lift the hem of her shirt. There was no one to hear, and I prepared to help the girl with nothing but my own shoddy skills. When I saw her wound, though, the fragile bud of hope within me shriveled.

I hid my dismay, but not quickly enough. Perceptive as ever, Nibs managed, "That bad, is it?"

Nose burst into view, saving me from a response. He spoke in a rush. "The faeries are under attack. The pirates found the door. They..."

The boy halted at the sight of us. Slowly, his bow lowered until its tip brushed the ground. There a flash of anguish in his face.

"Please..." Nibs's feeble voice returned my attention to her. Hair fell over her eyes in greasy strands and I smoothed them away. She reached toward me with ruby-dipped fingers, and I understood what she wanted.

Complying with her voiceless request, I put my ear next to the girl's mouth. "I'm listening, Nibs."

"My name is Maud," she whispered. "Not Nibs. Maud."

"I'll remember," I swore. And those were the words she died hearing.

Nose knelt on her other side. He closed her eyes, then clenched both fists around the bow. He bowed his head to say a prayer. Something else I didn't expect from him. During his murmurings, my own thoughts wandered, hazy and detached. *She'll become just another rotting corpse in the Neverwood,* that inner voice sorrowfully predicted.

Our chance to mourn was disrupted—a red-orange light touched the foliage around us. A light that didn't belong. Nose's earlier words came back to me. *The faeries are under attack. The pirates found the door.* James was attacking the fae?

Suddenly everything felt like a dream. I set Maud's body down as gently as I could and went toward that colorful shimmer. The nimble tread of Nose's footsteps disturbed the eerie stillness. Then came crackling and a billow of heat. We passed the door to the cavern and entered the dell instead. Dread was heavy in my stomach.

The Pan Tree was on fire.

There were people everywhere, standing in the jungle or perilously close to the flames. *No, not people,* I thought slowly, remembering what Peter had told me about this place. Spirits. All these figures were spirits.

They watched as the single thing tethering them to existence burned away. Not just faeries, but humans, too. Old and young, tall and slight, pale and dark. While some did appear distressed, most seemed... peaceful. Peter was among them, trying to stop something as inevitable as an ocean wave or a sunrise.

"*No! No!*" he was screaming. He beat at the flames with his bare hands. Bell also stood by, watching helplessly. Her mouth formed a silent word—his name. Nose leaped into action, trying to pull Peter away, but the other boy was having none of it. I wanted to shout at him, tell him to seize these last moments with the one he loved, but I knew Peter would fight the blaze to its last ember.

If Bell left this world, left him without saying goodbye, he would never forgive himself. I got as close as I dared to the inferno, wincing. She noticed me and materialized at my side.

"Tell him to be brave," she yelled over the chaos. Tears streaked down her cheeks. I jerked my head to let her know I'd heard. Bell looked at Peter again, her body fading and reappearing in spurts. The Tree continued to burn. Nose gave up on Peter and plunged into the jungle with an arrow notched and ready. The faeries would need all the help they could get. But I wasn't leaving Peter, not for one second.

I sat down to wait.

When it was over—every spirit gone, the Tree a charred shell—Peter dropped to his knees, making sounds that weren't sobs or words. Quiet prevailed in the dell. Smoke stung my eyes. Morning should have arrived, but Neverland saw fit to make this night as unending as it was agonizing. My bones creaked as I crossed the space to embrace Peter.

"Don't," he whispered. I just rested my head against his

and breathed in his scent. He was rigid, but he didn't push me away this time. A tear dripped off the end of his chin. I wiped it away. There were no cries or lamentations, his despair so absolute that I couldn't bring myself to tell him Maud's body was nearby, abandoned in the dark.

Minutes passed. Peter didn't move or speak. Maybe he was hoping Bell would come. Maybe he didn't have the will to do anything else. But we had no idea what James had ordered his men to do, and they were still in the hollow, doing only God knew what to creatures that had done nothing to deserve such violence.

Battling reluctance and guilt, I finally ventured, "We should go to the faeries, Peter."

He didn't indicate that he'd heard. I was steeling myself to force him when something moved within the edges of the dell. Peter was too stupefied by grief to notice. I frowned, staring hard into the dim spaces between leaves. A pair of familiar, gray eyes peered back, and a shock went through me when I realized who was standing in the jungle.

James and I stared at each other.

I knew I should alert Peter, shout a warning to the others, run at him. But he was still the man who put a sword in my hand and asked for a story on a blood-covered rock. I heard that ticking clock, as if the crocodile were coming for us again. *Tick. Tick. Tick.*

I turned away.

In my peripheral vision, I saw James meld with the shadows. My heart didn't slow or calm. I tried not to consider the repercussions of allowing him to go free. Within seconds, though, I turned back to the place he'd been standing, as if I could undo the choice I'd made.

What had I done?

Before I could confess to Peter, a horde of pirates appeared at the end of the path, singing victoriously at the top of their lungs. They had a captive in tow. The silhouette was not struggling, but its hands were clearly bound.

Peter was still on his knees, and I rushed to him now, praying the pirates didn't notice the movement.

"Peter," I whispered, my voice shaking with urgency. I gripped his shoulder and dug my nails in, shaking him. "Peter, we must go—James's men are here. *Peter.*"

They were almost upon us, and it was a wonder we hadn't been seen. In a burst of panic, I rushed into the jungle, using its darkness to conceal my presence. My heart rioted in my chest as I peeked through the underbrush, hoping to see that Peter had hidden, as well. But he'd stayed right where he was, on his knees, head bowed. The remains of the Pan Tree still filled the air with smoke, making Peter look like a spirit himself.

"What 'ave we 'ere?" a gravelly voice drawled from the clearing.

I'd never known such fear.

I bit back a curse and my mind raced. My first instinct was to rush forward and throw my body over Peter's, for all the good it would do. *Be smart, Wendy. Be strong.* Right. I didn't have a sword or anything else to use as a weapon. Aurora was on the other side of the island, even if she heard my cry. That left me with absolutely no course of action that wouldn't immediately result in my own capture or murder.

The men had recognized Peter, of course. I heard one of them say his name. My fingertips dug into the bark of a tree —the very tree he'd carved our names on, I realized faintly —so hard that it hurt.

I could only watch, helpless, as they descended upon him.

CHAPTER 19

THE FAERIES SAT around the aura.

The flames had changed color, and it was significantly smaller. Fainter. There were red-rimmed eyes and grave expressions everywhere I looked. The room was so thick with emotions, they seemed to take the air with them. Every sound was cacophonous, all the sniffles, hushed words, and sobs. Strange to think these people had been celebrating less than an hour ago.

While the faeries keened the loss of their Tree, I couldn't stop agonizing over Peter. The pirates' song still echoed through me. In my mind's eye, I saw the scene over and over. I relived the moment they spotted Peter, then moved in dark blurs, their teeth gleaming in firelight.

He hadn't even fought. When they took him, Peter hadn't even *fought*.

Nose found me in the crowd. "They say the only thing

that made the pirates leave was an order from Captain James Bainbridge," he said quietly.

We both knew they would be back, with or without his blessing.

There was a dais at the far end of the cave, with a circle of ornately-carved chairs. Illeryial sat silently, fingers steepled in stormy contemplation. The faeries claimed to have no leaders, and yet his seat had many similarities to a throne. Twelve figures filled the other spots, and everyone else was on the floor. I was pressed against a far wall and Nose stood beside me.

One of the faeries dared to speak, his voice slightly wavering. "It's no longer safe here. We should leave this place."

Illeryial snapped.

"But *how did they know*?" he bellowed, lifting his great chair with inhuman strength. It crashed against the ground and shattered into a hundred splinters. And it became clear what his calm had been concealing in the brief time I'd known him—a deep, terrifying rage.

"Me," I whispered. "It was me."

All heads turned in my direction. Never had I felt so small or alone. Somehow I straightened and approached the half-circle of chairs. Startling me, Nose stayed close behind.

"Explain yourself," Illeryial ordered, his bland mask back in place. He stood in the center of all those chairs, an imposing figure in his long robes, with eleven faces behind him.

Like I was walking on coals, I said the words step by step,

one by one. "I didn't think we would survive, when the captain and I were left on Marooners' Rock. He had just lost his hand. I told James—Captain Bainbridge—a story about the Tree as he lay dying."

At the mention of him, a muscle ticked in my jaw. I may have let James go, but the resentment in my heart had become black, searing hatred. He'd gone too far by taking Peter.

The ancient faerie listened to my halting explanation without interruption or reaction. Afterward, his green eyes roamed the chamber. "One of my kind is missing," he noted.

My thoughts came to a screeching halt. Oh, God. In all the chaos, I'd forgotten about the captive. The pirates had been carrying a squirming sack. Doubtless they intended to bring their prize to Mr. Ashdown, and once he claimed his immortality, the man would probably allow his crew to tear apart whatever was left of the faerie. Soon the skies of Neverland would be full of airborne pirates.

"I'd wager that one of ours is missing, too," Nose mumbled. He glanced at me sidelong. His expression and the fact that he didn't go on spoke volumes. *The nameless boy.* Tootles and I had seen him outside the dell. James must've sent him to find the Tree, knowing it would eventually lead him to Peter and the faeries.

Agitation spread through the fae like fog. They whispered amongst themselves, and someone said a name. Illeryial heard it, too. He approached the very edge of the dais and towered over me. I couldn't help noticing the sword at his hip, not only because of how its jewels that caught the light of the aura, but also due to the blood clinging to that long blade.

Slowly Illeryial said, his voice darker than the stains in the dirt, "They've stolen my daughter. They've stolen Donella."

Nose shuffled even closer. I swallowed. "I'll bring her back, sir, I swear to you."

"Do you know what they intend to do to her?"

"Not for certain."

His ire was affecting the cavern around us—loose stones shook and the aura flared. But fear wasn't my sovereign. Not anymore. I raised my chin and envisioned riding beneath the clouds on a giant bird's back, where I always felt invincible. Limitless. Untouchable. "There's a man who believes her blood holds eternal life. They also know that she's the key to flight," I added.

Illeryial didn't question how they knew this. Maybe he didn't want to know.

"What makes you so certain they're alive? Either of them?" he asked instead, his voice still low and controlled. It seemed the angrier he became, the firmer he smashed that mask down. Instinct urged me to leave the cavern *now*. I didn't know what the fae were capable of, but for the first time, I wasn't curious about the unknown.

"The pirates won't kill her for a while, not until every one of them can fly," I answered, using every bit of the training I'd received at Miss Parker's cruel hands. "And the captain has... business with Peter. I believe he plans on taking his time with it."

A faerie in the crowd had started wailing at my blunt response. Illeryial kept his gaze on me. "Then go, Wendy-bird," he bid. "May Neverland be in good humor during your efforts."

Nose was quick to comply, but I didn't move. I took deep breath and said, "Peter told me violence is not your way."

"Wendy," Nose said. There was no inflection in his voice, but it held a warning all the same.

I ignored him, my focus entirely on Illeryial. "It's not mine, either. But there comes a time when a choice needs to be made. A change. It's not all right to kill. However, it *is* all right to defend your family. And we may need more than a few children to do it."

The cavern was hushed now, and Illeryial studied me. It felt as though he was watching every sin I'd ever committed or every good act I'd ever done. I was a window he could see through. What if he concluded I was untrustworthy? What if he decided I was better off dead than able to betray them again? Suddenly it was difficult to breathe.

"We shall discuss it amongst ourselves," he replied at last.

It was more than I'd hoped for, and I tried not to sag. Instinct kept me from showing these creatures any fear. With a brief, respectful nod, I spun and headed for the tunnel. Faeries hurried to clear a path.

It wasn't until we reached the surface that Nose dared to speak again. "The pirates can still do a lot of harm, in the time our rescue takes," he said.

I looked at the boy bleakly, expecting to see reproach in

his face, but there was no trace of it. Nose observed the jungle around us, his manner relaxed as ever. He didn't seem to hold me as responsible as the faeries. "It may take even longer than you're thinking," I told him. "We need the children, in case that lot can't be depended on. There's also the obstacle of reaching the ship without boats. Even if the faeries were to lend us a bit of flight, it's not certain that all the children will be able to do it. I'm proof of that."

My boots turned toward camp without guidance. There must have been a pack of wild dogs hunting, because their excited yips bounced off the moon. I hardly noticed. My mind mulled over how to rescue Peter as if it was a row of numbers in my father's ledger.

"We don't need magic or boats," I blurted. An idea had started to form, and it was so reckless that I knew Peter would approve.

"We don't?" Nose said.

The rush of hope was so heady, so wonderful, that it was what I imagined opium to feel like. I looked to the sky and smiled. "I might not be able to fly... but I know someone who can."

The Neverbirds were more wild than I'd ever seen them.

Morning had arrived like my father coming through the front door—reluctantly and distantly. The horizon was the color of a bruise. Now that Bell was truly dead and Peter was in the pirates' clutches, I'd braced myself for storms, cyclones, earthquakes. But he was either numb or oblivious to the world. Worse, perhaps, if James had truly gone mad. I refused to consider the possibilities.

Almost everyone from camp accompanied me through the jungle. I was still surprised that so many had chosen to come, especially considering the brief speech I'd given back at camp. It felt like I could still taste the hard, sour words on my tongue. *Allow me to be very clear. What we are about to do is dangerous. You could be harmed or killed.*

I'd given them the hardest stare I could manage. The faces that looked back at me were unafraid, and I worried they didn't fully understand the risk. I was on the verge of pressing my point when my gaze landed on Freckles, who wore such a serious expression that it made him look ten years older.

For Peter, he said. The others nodded their assent, a dozen thin voices rising into the air.

Yes, for Peter.

Anything for Peter.

Once we reached the cliffs, the children lined up and made it a game, as they did with everything else. They dared and taunted, seeing how far their chums would be willing to put their feet over. Tootles had stayed behind with Slightly and the others that were too young for such things. House-keeper and Nose were there, standing apart from the group, and patiently awaited my next course of action.

I tipped my head back and screamed her name to the heavens.

She came straightaway, landing so hard that the gust

nearly knocked us over. Narrowly avoiding Aurora's cruel beak, I swung onto her back. The children gaped, their game forgotten.

"These creatures can sense fear," I said, raising my voice to be heard over the wind and crying seagulls. I gripped Aurora's feathers harder to stop her from snatching Freckles. "But that isn't what will make them tear you to pieces. It's any sign of retreat, of cowardice, of giving in to the terror. You must conquer it as thoroughly as you conquer your creature. After that, you are equals. Treat them as such."

They were timid at first, just as I had been. But as the afternoon wore on, each child successfully overpowered their winged mounts. The worst injury among them was a gash from a beak. At the end, we had ten young soldiers sitting atop their chittering Neverbirds. Smiling triumphantly, I turned to Nose. He was appraising our army with a creased brow.

"What is it?" I questioned, turning back, trying to see what he saw. Gray clouds roiled behind the solemn-faced riders. Their delight had faded now that the hour of Peter's rescue drew nearer.

"We need more. More people, more weapons. The pirates outnumber us three to one and they'll be fighting with swords, not cooking knives and clubs. We won't make it past the deck if we attack with this many, and we shouldn't depend on the faeries."

He was right—I'd witnessed what Mr. Starkey was capable of. Ready as these children were, they wouldn't stand a chance against him. Not without true, experienced warriors at their side.

Nose followed my gaze toward the plains. He didn't hide his surprise. "Lily will never agree. And time is short."

She also loves Peter, I almost said. But it seemed wrong to reduce all she was, her decisions and choices, to the single act of loving a boy.

"She deserves to know what's happening," I said simply. Nose was a boy of few words, and he'd already voiced his thoughts, so he set about obtaining a Neverbird while I shared my flying techniques with everyone. Some, of course, paid me no mind. They would be the ones who'd have a difficult time in the sky.

Once I'd finished and Nose was prepared, I raised my fist and bellowed, *"To the plains!"*

"To the plains!"

Off we went. Aurora was fervid, surging to the cliff's edge with such speed that I nearly toppled over. Her talons rapidly touched the rock—*click-click-click*—and then we were between sea and sky.

In the wake of everything that had happened today, I wanted to be immune to the thrill of flight. But even the coldest heart would thaw from soaring atop a warm Neverbird. I leaned closer to Aurora, daring to rub my cheek on the soft, downy feathers at the scruff of her neck. We approached the islander camp, ocean spray making a valiant effort to reach us. Some of the islanders were on the water, nets in their hands, the boats beneath them rocking with every wave. Nose cupped his mouth and shouted for them to follow.

The loss of the Pan Tree had affected the islanders, as well. They were in mourning, obvious from the unbridled wails and unrestrained tears. Some held each other, some knelt in the dirt, some stared quietly at the horizon. It was such a contrast from what I knew. In my old world, we were not to show desire, ambition, or misery. But I looked at their pain and I only saw humanity.

Lily wasn't difficult to find—she was among her people, comforting a woman with a gentleness I hadn't seen in her before. A few had noticed our arrival and, little by little, conversations stopped. Whether they were unnerved by the sight of our Neverbirds or Peter's absence, I couldn't be certain.

The other children remained on their birds, but I jumped down. I strode forward without hesitation, and Aurora startled me by remaining close behind. Lily also seemed taken aback, just before the shutters closed within her.

I stopped a few yards away, close enough to hear each other, but not so close that Aurora could impale Lily if the urge struck her. Once, I may have treated the Torch Bearer with deference—now all I could muster was detachment. I took stock of who stood nearby and immediately spotted Bashira, who stood with several girls. Our gazes met, and hers was dark with guilt. All I could do was nod before facing Lily.

Scorn twisted her young face. There would be no apologies taking place today. "Do you think to impress me, flying here on the Neverbirds?" she demanded.

Aurora jabbed at my shoulder. I dodged the blow and put a soothing hand to her side. She calmed, but fixed her eyes on Lily. Though I appreciated the shared dislike, it didn't bode well for my purposes.

"The pirates burned down the Pan Tree. They've taken Peter, along with Illeryial's daughter," I announced. Gasps erupted, but I didn't give anyone a chance to speak. There was no time for questions. "They shall kill Donella for her immortality and do worse to Peter. After they've learned how to fly, of course."

The islanders were frantic. I heard some talk of rescue while others wanted to flee. Many called for revenge. Lily put up her hand for silence. They obeyed instantly; even after Marooners' Rock, they respected her. Her gaze pierced me, and a rumbling began in Aurora's breast.

"I won't risk my people's lives," Lily replied evenly, showing no fear. "Even if what you say is true, we have no quarrel with the pirates. Involving ourselves would surely begin one."

Frustration boiled in my belly. I was tired and desperate and frightened, and the insult rose to my lips without any forethought. "Coward."

We were dry tinder and the word was a single spark— Lily was upon me in an instant.

Aurora reared, and both Freckles and Housekeeper seized her feathers to hold her back. The Torch Bearer was equally feral, fighting with none of the calculation or control

James had exhibited in his lessons. I felt her nails rake through my skin. She yanked at my hair, bit my shoulder. She was so fast that I couldn't get a handhold. As we scuffled, I caught a flash of Nose, reaching for his bow uncertainly.

"Don't," I blurted. He froze.

At that moment, I managed to get Lily underneath me, my back to her chest. Before she could use the opportunity to clamp her arm down, barring life and air, I bent my arm and slammed it back. Elbow struck throat. Lily choked. I'd anticipated that she would jerk and had already straightened. While she coughed, I slung my head against hers. *Thud.* Pain shuddered through my skull, but it couldn't be anything compared to Lily's.

I rolled to my feet, breathing hard but steadily. Cuts bled freely where Lily had scratched me and I'd have many more bruises by morning. The discomfort was nothing compared to the pride I felt. My opponent was still sprawled, though she managed to shake her head at the warriors rushing for us. I offered her a hand, knowing as I did that she wouldn't take it. Lily stood—an impressive feat, considering how my head was smarting—and regarded me with a frosty expression. I sensed her surprise again.

Aurora was livid. At the sound of her squawk, I turned from Lily to give her my attention. Her wide, golden eyes darted to my wounds and brightened with another blast of outrage. Every person on the cliffs clapped their hands over their ears when she shrieked. Freckles and Housekeeper continued to restrain her, and I recklessly wrapped my arms around Aurora's massive beak, humming all the while. The bird's fight diminished. There was cautious curiosity in those eyes now.

"*Second star to the right, and straight on 'til morning,*" I crooned. The Neverbird huffed, but her feathers settled.

Lily had watched the exchange with an unfathomable expression. Turning from Aurora again, I raised my brows in a silent question.

Slowly she said, "Peter has long been a friend of this village. And if the pirates grow any stronger, they may do more than burn or fly. For these reasons, it is worth the risk."

After that, the Torch Bearer said something in Spanish. A few members of the village replied, including Bashira and Juan. Shouts clashed and battled in the air. All the children and I could do was stroke our birds and wait.

In the midst of everything, Lily looked to a tall woman with a square jaw. *Her mother*, I thought, seeing the resemblance straight away. The straight-backed figure seemed to be on the outside of things, yet within them, as well. I hadn't noticed her during the conflict. Deep lines traveled from the corners of her eyes and her long hair had streaks of gray. But no one aged in Neverland, did they?

What if, on this island, you appeared however old you felt? By how much wisdom you'd gained? By how many misfortunes you'd lived through?

Musings for another time. Bashira appeared at my side. "This decision is yours to make," she said.

I frowned at her, but my face cleared a moment later when I realized she was translating. Lily must have looked to her mother for guidance. I glanced back at the young ruler.

In a brief, unguarded moment, Lily's shoulders slumped—it reminded me how young she was and how heavy a burden she carried.

Then I remembered that this was the girl who left me and James on Marooners' Rock and caused a man to lose his hand.

She straightened, and I hardened my heart.

The new Torch Bearer continued to deliberate. Besides the restless noise of the Neverbirds and a lonely breeze, the entire village was still. When this stillness went on and on, the children began to fidget. We wouldn't be able to keep the birds on the ground much longer. I glanced at Nose, and he was stoic as ever.

With every second that passed, Peter might be suffering. We couldn't waste any more time. Just as I was about to ask Lily what her choice would be, she declared, "We leave at nightfall."

There was no great cheer, as there had been with my children. Everyone instantly began preparations, with the exception of a woman. She sat outside her cottage, scowling and clutching at a grown man who I guessed to be her son. Tension filled the village like smoke. The islanders sharpened weapons and fitted armor over themselves, even the women.

They gifted us with swords, as well. I accepted mine gratefully, balancing the blade in my palm, acquainting myself with the weight and feel of it. Élise brought me a breastplate. She didn't linger—there was little time for that —but she smiled warmly and gave my arm a brief, encouraging touch before moving away.

Shortly after that, the sun came to a bitter end, its blood soaking cotton clouds. Bashira found the courage to approach me. She wore a bracelet of shells around her ankle, and it jangled when she shifted. She held a bowl in her left hand, a fine-tipped brush in the other. "Would you like some?" she offered, staring at the grass.

"Yes." The answer was instant; I didn't need to think about it.

Bashira raised her gaze and indicated with her chin that we should begin. I hadn't realized how much taller I was than her. For an awkward moment or two, we both bent and stretched, deterring the other. Bashira giggled. It made my mouth twitch, too. Finally I sat, crossing my legs, and she did the same. We were still smiling.

After another moment, she dipped the brush into the bowl. Using the fire for light, she began to paint my eyes. Her touch felt like lashes fluttering against my cheek. We didn't speak, at first. Her lips were pinched in concentration. She eventually closed my eyes to paint the lids and I heard her ask, "Are you nervous?" Puffs of air teased my senses.

"Neverland has taught me what an awful liar I am," I said dryly, blind to her reaction. "So I suppose I may as well admit that I'm absolutely terrified."

Bashira smiled again, this one faint and distracted. She said nothing to offer comfort, but I supposed there wasn't much comfort to be had—it was why I hadn't minced words as I'd been enlisting the children. The commotion around us began drawing away, heading for the sea and the battle ahead. Now I was the one who fidgeted, anxious to find Aurora and the children.

"You are ready, Wendy-bird of the Neverwood, She Who Tames Beasts and Girl That Sinks Ships. Would you like to see?" Bashira asked. I could only nod. She left briefly and returned with a gilt-edged mirror.

The reflection staring back was no shadow or beautifully-written passage of who I wished to be. It was me. Fierce and frightened and powerful. I'd claimed it, and I would never let it go. Not even in whisper-filled tearooms or the cobblestoned streets, with nothing else to me but the clothes on my back and the name I'd denied for so long. My eyes were lined with black kohl and my lips painted red. 'Twas difficult to see on a night dark as this, but the face in the glass was so vicious it would accept nothing else.

I looked up from the mirror and met Bashira's gaze. "Thank you," I told her.

My tone was heavy with meaning, and Bashira's eyes flickered as she understood I was also thanking her for her bravery on Marooners' Rock. She nodded and said, "If we should fall tonight, there is no Pan Tree to catch us. Live well and die better, Wendy-bird."

A quake of fear went through me as I realized this could be the last time we spoke to each other, but I lifted my chin, refusing to submit to it. "The same to you, Bashira of the Golden Plains. She Who is Kind and Girl That Speaks Truth."

My friend didn't give me a chance to respond—instead, she ran to her family, hair flying and feet barely touching the ground. I watched her go, then sighed. It was time to gather Peter's small band of rescuers and fly to *The Fountain*. But just as I took a step toward the cluster of restless Neverbirds and riders, I felt eyes on me, and I turned in the direction the prickle of awareness seemed to come from. There was Lily, pausing near the fire. We gazed at each other until she gave me a solemn, unexpected nod. Then she also ran to join her people at the boats.

Nose and the rest of our ragtag army had returned to the cliff. They were armed and dressed, grim expressions all around. This was no game. Housekeeper released Aurora, who managed to nick my arm as I climbed onto her back. I didn't care—they were all watching me, awaiting the order.

I was not one for speeches, but there was no need for it. They loved Peter, too. And anyone who came to Neverland had known death in one way or another. The secret no one told. It was the silent presence in an empty room, the thing that moved in complete darkness, the tightness in your chest during a solitary moment. It would be breathing down our necks aboard that ship. Some of us, it would take.

Aurora must've felt my acceptance. Without movement or sound from me, she flapped her giant wings and carried us into night's embrace. My stomach dropped. I could hear the other children laughing, and it seemed extraordinary they still could after everything they'd endured, both in their old lives and this one.

"We're coming for you, Peter," I muttered. I urged the Neverbird to go faster, and she was happy to oblige.

We rounded another cliff, and *The Fountain* came into

view. Lanterns lit the deck and moonlight shone down on it. Wind attacked us with a ferocity that burned my skin. I grinned in surprise—Peter was definitely here, and he was rousing at last. The islanders were swiftly closing the distance between them and the ship, so I didn't delay, and we landed onboard with several dull thuds. The flock of Neverbirds left us to our own devices. As they vanished into the night, I prayed any pirates who heard their cries would dismiss them.

Most of the men would be sleeping belowdecks, but I saw three of them had been assigned to keep watch. While our soldiers cut them down, Nose acting as a general, I stole toward where the captain's quarters should be. Housekeeper was at my back. He must've had some familiarity with a ship's layout, because he whispered, a frown in his voice, "Are you certain they'd keep a prisoner up here?"

He asked more questions than Nose, I observed distantly. My eyes adjusted to the dark and I walked with more certainty. "No," I said.

"Then why aren't we going to the hold?" he asked next.

"Because we need leverage," I answered, my tone indicating that it was the last question I would answer, for we had reached the door I'd been seeking.

There was a lone pirate sitting guard—he slept with his head tilted back and mouth wide open. Harmless enough, but he was blocking the knob. Housekeeper noticed the same time I did, and he resolved the matter by clasping his hands together and bringing them down on the man's unsuspecting head. The pirate's muscles slackened even more, and he slid to the side. We left him there, a puddle of drool and dreams.

The door was unlocked, and I strolled in with my sword raised, prepared for resistance. But only one man awaited on the other side. He was weedy and pale, his eyes so wide I could see the whites around his irises, though they were more yellow than most people's.

James had been telling the truth—his financier was dying.

Mr. Ashdown whimpered and trembled, hands splayed against the wall next to the bed. He took in the sight of us and squeaked, "Who are you?"

I bared my teeth at him and spun the sword I'd been gifted. It caught the light and gleamed silver. "I am Wendy."

He screamed.

CHAPTER 20

BOUND AND GAGGED, Mr. Ashdown walked before us as we returned to the main deck.

I stepped into the light, bracing myself for chaos or bloodshed. But all the children were lined up, their captives wriggling and making muffled sounds of protest. One boy was beaming. So far, we'd been met with little resistance— this was going too well. Where were James, Mr. Starkey, Mr. Jukes, or any of the other dozens of pirates?

"What next?" Freckles piped up.

"Lower ropes to the water for the islanders to climb," I ordered, glancing at the sea. There was no sign of Lily or her people yet. No Illeryial or faeries, either. Did we dare go to the hold? What if we woke the men and the battle began without the Neverlanders?

There was no telling what my hesitation was costing Peter and Donella. Saving them was worth the risk. I jerked my head at Housekeeper, and he tightened his grip on Mr.

Ashdown. Snot and tears ran down the man's gag. We moved toward the stairs, and Nose stayed behind again to command the others.

We crept down a flight of stairs. The cargo hold was on the steerage deck, which was a level lower, so we eased past doors on either side, toward the cargo doors on the floor. They were wide and heavy.

Grunting, Housekeeper opened them, his arms bulging with effort. I lowered myself into the ship's murky bowels. Mr. Ashdown followed like a sack of potatoes, and then a more graceful Housekeeper. I glared at the sickly man—if there were any crew members sleeping down here, they were probably aware of our presence now, thanks to him.

Before I could conjure a threat, the *smell* hit me. It was so powerful that my eyes watered. I faltered, trying not to cough.

"Wendy," Housekeeper warned.

He was referring to the man standing guard. Mr. Smee, I realized when he lifted the lantern in his hand. The smell of unwashed body wafted from him. His expression was as bland as the first time we'd met, but my instincts insisted there was more than met the eye with him. Confirming this, I spotted a book nestled in the hay, beneath the chair he'd been sitting on.

"Let us pass, or we slit your financier's throat," I snarled.

His voice startled me. It was rich and smoky, much like the food he cooked. "I want no trouble, lass."

"Nor do I. I am just here for Peter, and you happen to be

the one standing between us. For both our sakes, step aside, sir."

A second passed. Two. Three. Then, never taking his gaze from mine, the pirate obeyed. Boards creaked beneath his weight, and my grip instinctively tightened on my sword. I forgot to breathe, terrified the other men on the ship had heard the sound, but nothing stirred or awakened. Air returned to my lungs. I regained enough sense to take the lantern from Mr. Smee before I moved to go in search of Peter.

"You'll want to give me a nice, hard lump," Mr. Smee interjected quietly. I stopped again, uncertain what to do. Had I heard him correctly? He stared straight ahead, seemingly unconcerned with the fact that Mr. Ashdown was listening to everything.

Housekeeper was not so uncertain. With a proficiency that was disconcerting, he swung his fist. It audibly collided with Mr. Smee's skull. He swayed for a few seconds, then crumpled.

His body hadn't yet hit the ground when I spun around and lifted the lantern, straining to see beyond its flickering light. The room was brimming with crates and barrels. All I wanted was to shout Peter's name, run frantically from corner to corner. The possibility of slumbering pirates was the only thing from keeping me from doing just that. Housekeeper went off in another direction, dragging Mr. Ashdown with him. The lantern's handle whined with every lurch. A few minutes later, when I'd explored every nook and cranny to no avail, despair rose inside me. Was Peter being kept with the crew, perhaps?

"Wendy!" came a hiss. "Over here!"

I hurried toward it. A cry lodged in my throat at the sight of Peter—somehow Housekeeper had found him without a light. He was chained to the wall, and there was nothing nearby except a lone bucket. *Even animals are treated better than this*, I thought tightly. Had James truly fallen so far from the kind brother I'd once known?

There was no sign of Donella.

Setting the lantern down on top of a barrel, I knelt and cupped Peter's face. His skin was cold. "Peter. Wake up, dearest. Open your eyes. We're here, all of us, and we're taking you home."

Nothing. Finally I resorted to slapping him. Peter gasped and blinked up at me. Dried blood ran from a cut on his temple.

"Tink?" he gasped. There was such raw hope, such stark pain in his voice.

My joy fizzled. "No. It's Wendy."

Peter rested against me for the briefest of moments, his ruined hands shaking. There was a vivid cut across his wrist, as though someone had taken a knife to it, intending to cut off his hand. Disbelief and fury clogged my throat. Housekeeper knelt and applied Fire leaves to the wounds, something I hadn't even thought of bringing—they must've been in his pocket. Peter moaned as he healed. His eyes opened fully, but there was no life in them. Not yet.

For once, I had a little magic of my own.

"I have a message for you. From Tink," I whispered. Peter's nostrils flared at her name. I put my lips next to Peter's ear for the next part, and Housekeeper took a respectful step back. "She said to be brave."

There was a faint sound from above. A moment later, the children started shouting. Housekeeper and I looked at each other in silent, mutual agreement. He pushed the financier toward the doors and I looped Peter's arm around me. The lantern guided us, and with every step, I felt him regaining strength. Together our small company emerged onto the main deck.

The scene that awaited us was not the same as we'd left it.

James and Mr. Starkey stood in the middle of the children, whose weapons were pointed at their throats. Nose had his bowstring pulled taut. The round, white moon made everything bright.

The captain showed no fear, despite how the tip of a sword scraped his throat as he spoke. "I'm impressed, Miss Davenport," he said by way of greeting. Peter let go of me.

"How..." I swallowed, trying not to glance at the bandage where his hand had once been. "How have you been faring, since we escaped Marooners' Rock?"

His eyebrows rose. "Quite busy, actually. You've been keeping secrets from me, Miss Davenport. Looking back, I do believe I allowed myself to be distracted by your many, shall we say... *attributes*."

Peter stiffened at the reminder that I'd kissed his brother. Noting this, James smirked. I'd never seen him do that.

There was something in his eyes that hadn't been there before, either, like a fine stallion that had been violently treated and, beneath the spurs and saddles, had succumbed to an empty sort of madness.

As I constructed a response, the captain's focus shifted toward the stern. Every person on deck turned, myself included.

Lady Julie Bainbridge stood above us, her gown looking resplendent against the backdrop of stars. Her voice floated down a moment later. "You disappoint me, Miss Davenport."

I couldn't move, couldn't speak. My throat was too dry. Peter heard the mangled sound I was making and asked a question with his gaze that I couldn't answer—his mother had become an unknown entity in my mind, an ominous, shrouded threat. To be so forcefully reminded of her existence was enough to yank me back toward the girl I had been.

Some details were different from the woman who had stood in my foyer, though. I latched onto these to maintain balance. There was a scratch through her eyebrow, and wisps of her hair had escaped from their pins, doubtless due to her long journey. There were wrinkles in her skirts and her face was splotchy, the red so vivid that not even powder could hide it. "How?" I managed.

It was James who responded.

"The timing was uncanny," he said. "You came aboard while we went ashore to receive Lady Bainbridge. Rough flight, it was—Curly hasn't quite mastered his new skill and he struggled with the weight. You see, after we obtained a faerie, I sent the boy to London to fetch Mother."

"Curly?" I echoed blankly. Then the boy himself appeared, his head poking out from behind her fluttering skirt. Of course. The nameless traitor.

"He's just come back from waking the men, I expect," James added cheerfully.

I was scared to look at Peter. He was no fool; he must've put the puzzle pieces together and discerned that his mother had arrived. But if the men were coming, we needed to get off this ship *now*. I hadn't anticipated it taking so long for the artillery to arrive, and there weren't enough of us to fend off every pirate belowdecks. I could call for Aurora, but that would mean abandoning the children, whose birds may not come so soon after their taming. Most of them probably hadn't been named, since I hadn't thought to mention it. That might affect the likelihood of depending on Neverbirds, as well.

With our wings gone—and the water full of crocodiles and mermaids—we could only hope the islanders or faeries would arrive. Where *were* they?

There was nothing left to do but stall for time.

"Why bring her here?" I asked James, desperate to fill the silence. Peter was unnervingly still. "I know how much she hurt you."

The captain clenched his jaw, and I knew he was likely remembering every time his mother had made him feel ashamed of who he was. It was as if he had a knife in his gut and I'd pushed it in deeper.

Behind him, still too far away to participate in our conversation, Lady Bainbridge lifted her skirts and started down the stairs.

"It's simple, really," James said. "I've long known of her attempts to destroy Peter, and I wanted him to feel a modicum of the loss I experienced on Marooners' Rock. What better way to match that pain than by forcing a boy to hear his own mother say she doesn't want him?"

I shook my head so hard it felt like my mind was slamming against the walls of my skull. "You don't want this, not really. I saw his wrist, James. You *stopped*. You're a good man."

"Perhaps you didn't notice, but my shadow has grown distant of late." James glanced down to where the black shape of himself was. Or where it was supposed to be.

Like mine, the captain's shadow had separated from his body. He'd spoken truthfully. I couldn't seem to stop staring at it, as if looking at it long enough would make reality change. The other half of James Bainbridge was leaning toward Peter... and it still had both hands. Pity swelled inside me, a flower in a tiny cave, nowhere else to grow.

Though the shadow had no face, I sensed that it only wanted to be near Peter. Not harm him. The man it belonged to, however, did. Very deliberately, he inclined his head at the woman rounding the cluster of children and swords. "Peter, may I present our mother?"

Peter held his breath—I felt it. And she wouldn't even look at him. She was pretending, even now, that he didn't exist. Tears quivered down to my lips. Oh, James had chosen the perfect revenge. This was a pain sharper than losing a limb. If I hadn't allowed him to slip away last night, none of this would be happening.

Suddenly Peter's words chimed through my head. *There's a high price for morality and sentiment. It's going to cost you someday.*

I hadn't known it would cost him, as well. I hadn't known.

A bevy of shouts interrupted the strained reunion and pirates began to fill the deck. We'd foolishly left our backs exposed, and the three of us—me, Peter, and Housekeeper—were seized. My sword clattered to the deck during the scuffle. I tried what I'd learned from Lily, fighting with nails and teeth, growls and kicks. During the struggle, I glimpsed the face of the pirate holding me, and lo and behold, it was Mr. Jukes. My jaw clamped down on his finger, and he yowled.

He wrenched free, leaving the bitter taste of blood in my mouth, and got his arms around me before I could move. "You're going ter regret that," he hissed in my ear.

Then four other men were there. One of them slapped me, and the world started ringing. I landed on hands and knees, tracing the patterns in the wood with my eyes. *Lines, so many lines...*

All the children were yelling again, and beneath the dull throbbing that held most of my focus, I knew something was happening. Something I needed to stop.

After another moment of struggling, I got my head up. Once my vision cleared, I saw that Mr. Starkey had escaped the children's circle of swords. The quartermaster now stood amongst a throng of his comrades, smugness radiating from his slight smile. Captain Bainbridge hadn't managed to follow him, though. *We can use his capture as leverage until our aid makes an appearance*, I thought. But I was too dizzy to stand, and Peter had still said nothing.

As the chaos continued, Lady Bainbridge raised her eyebrows at Mr. Starkey. Her meaning was so clear even the children who noticed the gesture understood it—they aimed their rage at her now.

"Whore!"

"Rot in Hell!"

"Peter will 'ave your 'ead for this!"

The insults were no more to her than a beggar asking for coin or someone crying out in pain, and Lady Bainbridge walked away from the scene without a trace of feeling in her expression. As the vibrations of her footsteps faded, Mr. Starkey plucked a knife from his boot and started walking toward Peter.

Panic filled every face and voice. I looked to James, ready to plead with him again, but he was off to the side with Lady Bainbridge. Her back was to me. She made harsh gestures as she spoke, and James's lips pursed. Whatever she said prompted him to eventually give a reluctant nod.

The din grew louder. I turned to see Mr. Starkey holding the blade to the corner of Peter's jaw, who even now, was strangely subdued. "Release the captain, or I slit this boy's throat," Mr. Starkey told the children pleasantly.

Ferocious as they were, they loved Peter more. One by one, they raised their swords. Freckles made a gesture that would've shocked me once. Captain Bainbridge sauntered to his mother's side, but his shadow remained near the children.

"You would murder your brother? Your son?" I spat at them, struggling in vain. The imprint on my cheek tingled.

Lady Bainbridge only shrugged, an elegant movement. "I came to finish this. 'Twould have been far easier if you'd just kept your word, dear girl. As it is, I've made certain that the Davenport name is forever tarnished. Your family won't be able to move in London circles again."

"Neither will yours, once I'm done with those pretty faces," a familiar voice said from behind.

Never had I been so glad to see Lily. She vaulted over the side of the ship, followed by Drystan and Élise's daughter, Simone. Although their armor was mismatched and their weapons dented, chipped, or rusting, there was something wild about the Neverlanders. Even to me, they were terrifying.

It still didn't cause the pirates hesitation. They charged.

With curled lips and glittering eyes, the islanders threw themselves into battle. More were pouring onto the ship. Swords and shields clashed. The children were everywhere, too. It happened so quickly that I lost sight of Peter. No, there —he was by the captain's quarters, talking to Lady Bainbridge. What could she be saying to him?

"Miss Davenport," James called. Following the sound of his voice, I turned and saw the captain step over a body near the stairs. Blood pooled beneath the dead man's chest. James bent, took the sword from the pirate's limp fingers, and tossed it. I stepped back just in time, and the stained weapon landed at my feet. James unsheathed his own blade and positioned himself.

My nails bit into my palms, leaving fresh half-moons in my skin. "I don't want to fight you."

His only reply was a smile and a small, playful twitch. Apparently he knew how to fight left-handed. Seeing no other alternative, I retrieved the sword he'd thrown and found my stance.

Quick as that, I was fighting for my life. Even with the loss of his hand, James was skilled and relentless. I hardly had time to block one blow when another came at me. I parried, I spun, I winced. James seemed tireless, and my arm began to ache. This was different from our lessons—he didn't hold back or pause for instruction. Everything around us ceased to exist. There was only the two of us and the sounds of our swords, our lungs.

Finally, I saw my opening. I changed tactics mid-thrust and caught James off guard, using a move he'd never taught me. It was something I'd thought up during one of my long nights in that unbearable tree. With a blurred, desperate move, I sent James's sword skittering down the deck. Mine was at his throat before he could go after it.

"Is that all?" I panted, trying not to grin.

James didn't smile back. His eyes caressed me so unexpectedly, so intimately, that my grip loosened.

"Look at you," he murmured. "What a sight you are, Wendy Davenport. When we first met, I saw a girl torn between worlds. Confused about who she was and what she wanted. Now I see someone so fierce and certain she could shake the very foundation of whatever world she chooses to be in."

Flattery. His words were flattery and nothing more. At least, that's what I told myself in an effort to stop my sword from trembling. The hum in my veins was quieting. This was my chance; if I cut Captain James Bainbridge down, part of the threat against Peter and the faeries would be eliminated. His vicious pursuit would end. I told myself I was unfeeling as a statue, willed my heart to become stone.

James and I stared at each other. As he waited for me to take his life, I saw my shadow draw nearer. I knew it was waiting for me to make a decision, too. If I wanted, I could give it all the guilt churning in my belly, along with whatever good things I felt toward James. With all of that gone, I'd be able to kill him quite easily.

One girl is more use than twenty boys.

"No. I can't." I lowered my sword, swallowing. James's brows rose in a silent question and I searched his eyes, praying for a glimpse of the kind man I might have given my heart to, if Peter hadn't gotten to it first. "You were my friend."

The captain had me before I could gasp or blink.

"And now I'm disappointed." He crushed my hand around the sword's handle and forced me to hold the edge against my own throat. He used the length of his other arm to pin our bodies together. I felt one of my fingers begin to slip onto the blade and couldn't hold back an agonized cry. James was unmoved. "What did I tell you during our lessons, Miss Davenport?"

I was stiff with pain and rage, but I knew instantly what he referred to. The memory was as permanent in my mind as the spiderweb on Mr. Jukes's skin. *There will be opponents who fight without honor. Never forget that,* James had said that day.

Before I could respond, someone else growled, "Release her."

From the corner of my eye, I saw a knife slip beneath James's chin. I couldn't see who held it, but his scent surrounded us a moment later. No one else had such a unique, wonderful aroma about them. A tremor went through me.

Peter was *back.*

I dared to twist my head, for no other reason than to lay eyes on him. It was worth the risk. Gone was the shell that had been standing in Peter's place earlier. He was alive once again. Unfortunately, there was no joy in his face—just pure, unadulterated anger.

"Absolutely. In exchange for you, of course," James replied. Despite his words, the weapon at his throat must've made him nervous, because he turned to fully face his brother. I was between them now. Peter still held the knife and I still had an unwilling grip on the sword.

James's gaze flicked toward Mr. Ashdown, who had somehow avoided all the action and was hovering nearby to eavesdrop. "I would also like a few faeries. In fact, I think I'll keep Miss Davenport as incentive. You'd best make a deal with the fair folk—better they come willing than bring all of them down on our heads. Return here for surrender. Only then will your lady be released."

My finger was embedded on the sword's edge now. Blood dripped from it like tears. But I was still about to tell Peter not to worry, James wasn't a killer, when he pulled away. What was he doing?

"Not a chance," Peter said calmly. "But I can promise that if you harm a single hair on her head, I won't rest until you've paid for it in blood."

The captain laughed, a hysterical sound. "You're gambling with Miss Davenport's lovely fingers, brother. She won't thank you for that when this is over."

Peter ignored this. His clear gaze met mine. "Do you trust me?" he breathed.

Without hesitation, I looked him in the eye and nodded. Peter moved in a flurry, and I was free within seconds. He held James at bay long enough for me to stumble out of reach. The brothers instantly locked in battle, which I was able to glimpse as I slipped on a pool of blood and hit the side of the ship.

I couldn't even scream before I fell into the water.

CHAPTER 21

I HEARD someone cry my name as I went overboard. Then the ocean was all around.

It was a shock—this was no balmy swim in a cave. Neverland was cold with rage. I floundered in the depths, all thoughts and instincts frozen in place. The ice in my brain cracked, however, when a shadow whispered past. I whirled, barely containing another scream. Like a vine, desperation grew inside of me and rose into my throat until I was nearly choking. Everything was so dark, so bottomless. Anything could live down here.

My imagination produced images of crocodile hordes, an immense kraken, and countless other hungry things beneath my feet. Coming closer. Opening their mouths. In jerky, frantic strokes, I aimed for the surface.

Halfway there, something touched me. I recoiled and choked on saltwater. My heartbeat faltered as a face emerged from the blackness. Comprehension made it speed up again.

The mermaids had come.

It wasn't clear whether this was better or worse than what I'd been picturing. They approached from every direction, and I saw a pale cheek, a strand of hair, the curve of a hip. Their scaled tails were silvery, like Peter's eyes. Once in a while, there was a shimmer of color in them. The women didn't attempt seduction or devouring; they only surrounded. Once there were no glimpses of the sea left— just mermaids and bits of moonlight—I felt an undeniable tingle of magic.

See, a chorus of voices said in my head. I was helpless as a leaf in a current.

They showed me a memory. Not mine, because it was one I'd never seen before. Peter was in the lagoon. Night trickled from the sky and into the water. This must've been near the date of my arrival to the island, because his hair was shorter, as it had been during that time. Peter knelt on a rock that loomed above the glassy surface. There was no trace of fear in his face or his voice as it echoed over the tepid waves. "You will never harm Wendy again," he called.

Silence met him. Unperturbed, Peter revealed the small knife he always carried, and proceeded to cut his hand. Drops fell soundlessly to the sea, and hisses erupted through the lagoon. The mermaids had been there all along. Like sharks, they thrashed, turning on each other for a mere taste.

"There is plenty more in my veins," Peter told them, watching coldly from his perch. "I'll share, when I've a mind to. If you agree to my terms. Do we have an accord?"

Yes!

An accord!

Enthusiastic splashes sounded across the water. As they faded, Peter set about cleaning his blade, as though he had no further interest in the conversation. When the mermaids realized that he would give them nothing more, they gradually returned to their wet hovels. Until only Serafa remained, peering up at him with her black eyes.

Why does Peter do this for her? she asked. Peter was not so distant as he acted; the question made him hesitate. Serafa's voice lilted with sudden knowing. *Ah. He loves. That is why.*

The scene faded without warning, and I had no opportunity to think about what I'd just witnessed. No time to consider the fact that perhaps, every time it had felt like Peter abandoned me, there might have truly been a purpose to his absences. *I had other matters to attend to*, he'd said that first night when I demanded why he hadn't been there. So cavalier. So distant.

That was how Peter guarded his heart.

Bubbles trembled around me as a new memory crowded in. Air wasn't an issue, it seemed. Now I was in a different part of the Neverwood, enveloped by trees rather than mermaids. Bark was rough against my palms and a leaf tickled my cheek. Through the tangles and branches, there were Peter and Bell. He held her to him, or tried to, his expression one of pain and conflict. This was familiar, as well.

"...have grieved," she was telling him. The faerie was so

vibrant that it was easy to forget she was dead. "But it's time for change. That's the way of humans."

Peter was just as obstinate with her as he'd been with me. "I'm not human."

"Your mind and body remain young, yes. But your heart, your aura, your soul? They *ache* with humanity, Peter. And so does hers."

The lump in Peter's throat bobbed. It took him several attempts to respond, but just as he said Bell's name, a sound startled them. Their gazes shot toward my hiding place.

"Is that you?" Peter demanded, tensing to give chase.

He didn't see me—just the trembling leaves I'd left behind. He'd go on to blame Curly, I knew.

Apparently that was all I'd be privy to; the bubbles rushed in again. My own eyes snapped open, slow to understand that Serafa's lips were pressed to mine. She'd been lending me whatever magic, whatever breath she had. The instant I became aware of it, I moved to crush her against me. She evaded my grasp with a giggle and a wink.

Why show me this? I shouted at them as the haze cleared. Yet a single word never left my mouth.

They gave no reply. Even if they had, I was drowning and wouldn't be able to hear it. My lungs shrieked and gurgled. The surface beckoned, and instincts, slow but strong, guided me. Then Serafa wrapped her arms around my body and wriggled her tail, projecting us upward. I reached open air and coughed water out.

We showed you our secrets-secrets because Serafa likes you, the mermaid murmured in my ear. *Don't forget our bargain.*

I struggled back to *The Fountain*. Sounds of battle corrupted the serenity of stars upon waves. Somewhere, Peter was laughing. Water lapped at my chin as, relieved, I saw that the ropes we'd lowered for Lily's people were still there. Just as I started climbing, the world brightened. I glanced up and saw soaring, glowing shapes vanishing over the ship's edge. Dust floated down from them like a fine mist, tiny bits of gold catching the moonlight.

Faeries.

I renewed my efforts. The skin on my palms wept and tore, unheeded. Thanks to my time living in the jungle and sleeping in trees, I was hardly bothered by the exertion. By the time I rolled onto the ship, landing painfully on my shoulder, the deck was littered with bodies. With the arrival of Illeryial, the fighting was nearly over. The pirates were vastly outnumbered, and most of them knew it. Swords were thrown down. As I stood, I saw that Donella had been freed —they must've been keeping her in another room. From this distance she looked like a doll, porcelain and breakable.

Some of the crew were not so easily defeated, though. On the opposite end of the deck, Peter and James had found their way back to each other. "I admire your bravery, but this is a fight you can't win, Peter," I heard the elder brother said. "Surrender."

Peter spun his sword in a playful movement, then pointed it at him. "I'd rather die bravely than live a coward."

They swung their weapons so hard, the resulting clash rose above all the other shouts and clangs. I started to interfere, to keep Tootles's prophecy from coming true, but a familiar glint of red hair caught my eye—a man had Freckles cornered and was about to stab him. Gasping, I yanked a knife out of an inert chest and threw it with the precision James had taught me. The tip sank into the giant's hand, and he dropped his sword with a bellow. His wild eyes met mine, and he charged like a bull. I braced myself for impact.

Lily cut him down less than a yard away. Blood hit my face like ocean spray.

A nod of thanks was all I could manage. The *thud-thud-thud* of another foe made the boards shudder. I grabbed a sword that probably belonged to one of the fallen, ducked a pirate's unchecked swing, and popped up in front of him. Without hesitation I jammed the sword in and out of his throat. Wetness spurted from the wound but I didn't linger to watch him fall.

There was no time to absorb the fact that I'd just killed someone. It had all happened in a matter of seconds, and another pirate was already closing in. I was too late in jumping back, and swore as a fresh cut opened on my thigh. But the man was too big, too slow, and soon his blood splattered my face. I whipped around to face a third.

It was Mr. Starkey.

"I see you have some skill with the blade," he said in his oily tones. After everything, he still remained clean and composed. Even his hair was properly tied.

In that moment, I knew I going to lose. There was something about the way Mr. Starkey stood, or perhaps the way he held his sword, that hinted he was far more skilled than I. It was an extension of him, even precious to him, as if the pirate adored his weapon for the blood he'd spilled with it.

Knowing I would not survive this fight did not mean I would go quietly. I adjusted my grip on my own sword and taunted him with the crude gesture Freckles had recently taught me. "Let's get on with it, then."

The quartermaster took a single step closer, and that's when Donella snuck up from behind. For a petrifying moment I was convinced he would sense her presence. He didn't.

Despite Mr. Starkey's agility and malice, it was over before it began. Donella slit his throat and watched him die with unveiled relish. *Peaceful, indeed.* While the light left his eyes, she glanced at me and started to say something. In the same instant, horror ripped through the air and made us both stiffen.

Peter.

Screaming, I bolted across the deck and caught him. James's sword clattered to the deck, and I dropped beside it. Peter was a ragdoll in my arms and a red flower bloomed across his chest. I looked up, thinking to call for help, and I spotted Lady Bainbridge vanishing into the chaos. I pieced together what had happened—while the brothers fought, she must've slinked up and stabbed him.

"No, no, no," I chanted, pressing my hand against the wound. Blood gushed into the gaps between my fingers, and Serafa's voice chose that moment to float cruelly through my head. *He loves. That is why.*

I glared wildly at the crowd of onlookers. The sheen of tears in my eyes made them blurry. "Someone go to the Fire Tree, damn it!" I snarled.

None of them moved. Then Peter made a wet sound, and my focus snapped back to him. Pain burrowed in my own chest, as if I was the one who'd been stabbed. Trying not to look frantic, I patted Peter's cheek a tad too hard. "No, Peter, look at me. *Look at me.*"

His glazed eyes focused on my face. After a moment, he smiled faintly. "Shall I become one of your stories, now?"

"Stop it!" I glared and held him tighter. "Peter, I love you. To *live* will be an awfully big adventure, don't you see? There's so much we can learn together. So much we can do. It's not time to say goodbye, all right?"

I didn't recognize the expression on Peter's face, because it was one I hadn't seen from him before. The boy skimmed his finger along the edge of my jaw, staring as though I were some rare creature he'd stumbled upon in the Neverwood. "Never say goodbye, because goodbye means going away... and going away means forgetting," he murmured.

"I could never—" I started, but Peter coughed and sent more blood spattering down the front of his shirt. His eyes left mine, seeking someone else. James stepped into our line of vision. His expression was dazed, and I saw that his shadow was plastering itself against him. Not quite attached, but touching. Peter mouthed his name.

"Forgive me," the elder brother whispered.

Peter's throat moved. "Only if... only if..."

Somehow James understood what he was trying to say.

Only if you forgive me. He responded without hesitation. "Done."

As if this had been all he was holding on for, Peter's eyes fluttered. I held him tighter and lowered my voice, bending to put my mouth beside his ear. "Please don't. This isn't goodbye, Peter. It isn't time for your grand adventure. Tootles was *wrong*. Prove him wrong. We'll get some bandages and you'll be right as rain. There might even be enough time to fly back to London. Yes! There's a physician that attended to my brother when he had the fever. Dr. Waghorn. Odd name, isn't it? He'll have the proper tools and medication—"

A hand settled on my shoulder. Whoever was touching me had dirty fingernails. "He's gone, lass," Mr. Smee said.

My mind could not accept it. But Peter had become utterly, unbearably still. He wasn't blinking anymore. It felt as if someone had reached inside my chest and taken a fistful of everything bloody and vital. One of the younger boys sobbed.

Then I wrenched away from Mr. Smee's grasp and stood. My vision had gone red and it felt as though my veins were on fire. There was a ringing in my ears, worse than any slap. I searched the tearful crowd.

"You," I hissed.

Lady Bainbridge's eyes widened. She snatched her gown up and ran, shrieking for James. No one tried to restrain me as I took a knife from a dead pirate's hand and thundered after her. She trapped herself at the stern and spun.

"It had to be done," she argued shrilly, a loose strand of

hair slipping into her mouth. When I said nothing, still advancing, her desperation increased. "He would have ruined me! I had no choice!"

"There is always a choice," I said flatly, raising my weapon. "And by the way, his name was *Peter*, you heartless bitch."

The woman threw her hands up and cowered. I didn't move. No one did.

The silence embraced us with its thick arms, and it felt like every person here was holding their breath. A Neverbird called, its wild cry echoing off the cliffs. I kept my focus on Lady Bainbridge, thinking of all the reasons I should kill her. There were many. Why, then, couldn't I bring myself to end her life?

After a minute, the knife slipped from my limp fingers, slick with blood. Vomit surged up my throat. I bent and gagged. Apparently there wasn't anything left in my stomach —it slipped out of a corner of my mouth and down my chin in a thin stream. When I was able to raise my head again, Lady Bainbridge gave me a triumphant, serpentine smile. "You can't do it."

"I can," James said, who'd followed us. He touched my wrist before I could snatch it away, then lifted his sword once again.

But I didn't want the captain to lose anything else. He'd lost a hand, a shadow, a brother. If his soul departed, nothing would save him. So I used both hands and pushed Lady Bainbridge squarely in the chest.

She tumbled off the ship and tried to take me with her by seizing my hair. At the last second, I grabbed hold of the edge. A chunk ripped from my scalp, clutched in her fingers as she hurdled into the sea. I was leaning over, forced to see the dozens of hands that grasped Lady Bainbridge by her flailing arms and legs. Her screams ended abruptly.

Every person on *The Fountain* waited to see what I would do. They would be disappointed; I was only capable of inhaling and exhaling. Over and over. I closed my eyes and was content to remain like that, with my hands wrapped around the side.

Only when light seeped through my eyelids did I open them and ease into an upright position again.

It was one of the shortest nights I'd experienced since coming to Neverland—we couldn't have left camp more than two hours ago and the sun was already rushing back. The brilliant sky allowed me to look at the faces of those lying still and silent. Nose was among the dead. As were Drystan and Illeryial. And many others whose names I never learned. Now I wished I had. Peter was still there, lying in the center. It was fitting, somehow. That odd smile lingered on his lips.

I had no more tears to shed.

Something would need to be done about Mr. Ashdown and the rest of the pirates. Not my concern, thankfully. Donella seemed to be taking charge, along with Lily. They'd both suffered losses, obvious by the darkness in their eyes, and I admired their endurance. Good manners dictated that I acknowledge their part in today's battle. But I couldn't bring myself to go near them or the shells of my former friends.

Before the thought was completely formed, James joined me. I was glad to see that his shadow had reunited with him. It stretched out, firmly attached at the boots, as it should be. The meanness had left James's expression, too. At least something good had come of Peter's death.

"I heard it, you know," he said suddenly. The way he squinted at the horizon, avoiding my gaze, made it seem as if he were conversing with the sun. "On the rock, when you made a bargain with that mermaid. I confess to some curiosity. What would you have wished for?"

I wanted to blame him. Hate him. James had brought Lady Bainbridge here and played a part in all the death. It was too exhausting, though. If the evil didn't end here, we were no better than his mother.

"Honestly, I didn't know at the time," I sighed. "But now... I'd wish for him. Just him."

"I'm sorry, Wendy. I'm so sorry."

It was his use of my Christian name that caught my attention. Not the catch in his voice or the sheen in his gaze. I shifted, facing him fully, and James no longer hid his feelings for me. They lived in his eyes, bright and hopeful as glowworms in a cave. There was also regret, which would stay there until the day he died.

I had learned that everyone could be cruel, under the right circumstances. Impulsively, I cupped the captain's jaw and pressed a brief, light kiss to his cheek. The surprised sound he made rippled through me. "Thank you," I said.

He blinked, and I'd laugh under any other circumstance. "For what?"

"You didn't mock me. You put a sword in my hand and believed I was as capable as any man."

"Because you are," he whispered. It was a good ending.

I left him there to contemplate the morning.

PART THREE

WENDY

CHAPTER 22

THE ISLANDERS BROUGHT us back to shore.

The quiet was full of a thousand things unsaid. Our numbers were fewer, and soon the faeries would arrive with the children we'd lost, along with the rest of the dead. Though I longed to summon Aurora, it didn't seem fair to the others—all of us were bonded now, whether we liked it or not, and I accompanied them until the moment our feet touched land.

Freckles found me as the islanders pushed off again, probably returning to *The Fountain* to assist with the bodies. "No point heading back to camp just yet," he said. "Last time we lost this many, Peter had us burn 'em right here on the beach. If we made a pile in the jungle, it would draw the beasts right to us."

"Right," I murmured, deciding not to ask how those children had died.

As Freckles sank to the ground, I searched the beach for

Slightly. There no sign of him—it seemed the children who'd stayed behind from the battle hadn't arrived yet. With a sigh I felt in my soul, I settled onto the sand beside Freckles and prepared to wait. The humming that had lived in my veins during the battle finally faded to nothing, leaving me feeling hollow and weary.

Many of the children laid down and closed their eyes, even Housekeeper, and those who didn't sleep found ways to pass the time. Nimble went about building a sandcastle. Freckles stared out toward the horizon, its buttery light making his skin glow.

Though the beasts that hunted at night had gone silent, I kept watch. It wasn't difficult to stay awake—every time I closed my eyes, I saw the blood spreading across Peter's shirtfront, and I felt a pain so enormous that it felt too big for my body.

Birds chirped into the stillness. The ever-brightening sun began to drive out the cold. Eventually Housekeeper roused and went into the jungle with Nose's bow. From an outsider's perspective, it may have been deemed disrespectful to take it, but nothing went to waste in Neverland. Doubtless the boy was off to secure breakfast for everyone, using the bow Nose no longer had need of.

Suddenly a strange urgency came over me, and I couldn't sit there a moment longer. I yanked my boots off and jumped up. There was a shock of cold as I sloshed through the sea, then plunged my feet deep into the wet sand. Freckles didn't move or speak from his spot. Squinting out at the water, I wriggled my toes. The action reminded me of childhood holidays at the coast. After a while, I looked down and became absorbed in how the waves reflected off the sand in glassy shimmers. The fish grew accustomed to me and got bolder, swimming so close that I felt them brush against my ankles.

I was still watching them dart between my legs when the bodies were carried in.

It was my first time seeing the faeries fly in daylight, and it was akin to spotting something out of the corner of your eye. Translucent and fluttering, like a dandelion on the wind. There was more of that coveted dust, as brightly golden as Peter's hair.

Watching the faeries drew my attention to a lone dinghy on the water. The individual inside it was unexpected— maybe I'd been anticipating James. The sun was to his back, but that round shape was familiar. Mr. Smee dragged the dinghy to safety and brushed his hands off. He spotted me and approached. There was a cut over his eyebrow and someone had ripped a piece of his beard off. Strangely enough, I suspected that his injuries were not inflicted by our side. So much had happened during the fighting, but I had a fleeting memory of him turning on one of his brethren to protect a child.

Up and down the beach, faeries were setting down the dead. One of them was Peter, I noted dimly, spotting that familiar golden hair.

I wondered what the fae would do with their own fallen warriors. Soon, they would be finished and gone, and we'd have graves to dig. The islanders hadn't returned. Perhaps they were making sure the pirates didn't try any tricks, or they'd just taken their dead to another part of the island.

"Do you have business here?" I asked Mr. Smee. There was a large lump on his forehead now, courtesy of House-keeper's none-too-gentle knock while we'd been rescuing Peter.

Mr. Smee paid no mind to the goings-on behind us. On the horizon, *The Fountain* floated, all white sails and painful memories. "Just wanted to visit this place one more time," he answered, gazing at it. "Come tomorrow morning, I won't be feeling land beneath my feet for weeks."

So they were leaving. I thought I would be outraged knowing those wicked men wouldn't be punished for their dark deeds, but I felt nothing. "I trust Captain Bainbridge will be making the journey, as well?" I asked.

The portly man shoved his hands in his pockets. "He will, but Mr. Bainbridge formally stepped down as captain. Since Mr. Starkey is dead and I'm second mate, *The Fountain* is my responsibility now. I'm taking her back to England, along with that wretched lot. There are one or two good ones that'll help me keep the order."

His words came from a distance—I couldn't respond. Looking at the ship was making me remember, and Peter was dying in my arms again. *Shall I become one of your stories, now?*

I must've made a sound, because Mr. Smee's head bowed. "I'm sorry," he said at last. "That feelin' will never truly go away, I can tell you that. But you'll survive it. We all do."

Farther down the beach, a girl started wailing. She'd flung herself across one of the bodies. I couldn't stand here, with a pirate, and disregard them. But there was something soothing about Mr. Smee. Reluctant to face the funerals ahead, I cleared my throat and met his kind eyes. "Do you—"

"Wendy!"

We turned. Tootles and Slightly were coming out of the Neverwood. Letting out a relieved breath, I swept the child into a tight embrace. He was surprised, at first, but swiftly recovered and hugged me back. It was a pain I welcomed, along with his scent, which was positively wretched. Gracious, when was the last time Slightly had *bathed*?

I hugged Slightly even tighter and thought of another small boy. A boy who'd been waiting for me long enough.

A boy who might very well have passed into the next world while his sister dallied on a tropical island with her lover.

Mr. Smee allowed us a few moments. A breeze ruffled the gray tufts of hair around his ears. Then he drew close again to say, "While Miss Donella was being held prisoner, she told me that faeries burn their dead. I know the lad was fond of their kind. Farewell, Miss Davenport."

He went back to the dinghy. Instead of following Mr. Smee's progress as I was, Slightly was looking at the prone figures lying in the sand.

"Where is Peter?" he asked in a small voice.

Grief hit me like a fist to the stomach. I let go and knelt in front of him. Slightly's face was so open, so trusting, even after the way I'd treated him. I couldn't bring myself to answer, to tell him the truth. But the child wasn't paying attention to me anymore—he'd noticed my hands, which forced me to take note of them, too. They were covered in blood. Peter's blood. Why hadn't I noticed it?

Now my insides heaved, threatening once again to upend whatever was left. Slightly's bottom lip quivered.

Before I could tell him that Peter wasn't coming back, someone else took hold of my red fingers. I started to pull away, but then I raised my gaze and saw it was Tootles. The tension seeped from me.

"The tide pools are nearby," he informed the younger boy, a tuft of his brown hair lifting in a breeze. "Have a look, won't you?"

Perhaps Slightly hadn't wanted to hear the truth any more than I wanted to say it. He nodded and scampered off. Tootles seemed unbothered by the sight of his friend's blood on me. He tried to wipe it away with his own sleeve. When that was ineffective, he bent, pulling me with him. The sea washed off all remnants of the battle.

"Shouldn't I be taking care of you?" I asked faintly.

"We're a family, miss. We take turns caring for each other."

Emotion swelled in my throat. Apparently Tootles hadn't seen my departure in a vision, and I wasn't certain if I should be nervous about that. "That's—"

He frowned and glanced toward the trees. Something made his eyes widen. I turned, my heartbeat accelerating.

Tootle's voice had dropped to a whisper as he said, "The she-beast."

Now I saw her, too. She moved through the leaves, peeking out at me, a beast of hard muscle and flashing gold. Her unmistakable intent sent goosebumps racing over my skin. I told myself that as long as there were people everywhere, the cat wouldn't leave the Neverwood. Why did she keep appearing wherever I went? Was she hunting me? Why allow me to live every time we encountered each other, then?

I didn't realize I'd been wondering all of it out loud until Tootles looked at me just as Peter had. With surprise, speculation, and a bit of awe. After a moment he answered, "She lives on the mountain, and nothing else dares to join her there. She only hunts for one reason, so we know that when she leaves the peak, she's sensing a creature that is like her. Not creatures who are the most beautiful, or the most violent, or the most certain. No, the she-beast battles the biggest threat of all—those who fear the dark but step into it all the same."

The words resonated deep within me, like a stone dropped into a well.

So there were beasts inside us all. A wildness that was just waiting for a chance to come out. I'd been keeping mine in a muzzle, caged, with a blanket over the bars.

This place had taught me how to free it. How to stretch its legs and feel the sun on its fur. And though my beast couldn't do so all the time, especially when I returned to London, there were occasions that a little wildness was forgivable. No, not simply forgivable, but necessary.

I think Neverland may change you as much as you change Neverland, Peter had said to me once.

Yes, I've changed. More than any Neverbird or jungle. Are you happy? I asked the island silently. It didn't answer, of course, but I imagined its silence as sympathetic and, most likely, a bit smug. Like Peter himself. Perhaps he wasn't completely gone, as I'd thought. Even without the Pan Tree, a part of him would live on.

Tootles cleared his throat, and I jumped. Sheepishly, I realized that he'd been standing next to me during my reverie.

"You'll be needing these," he told me, pressing something into the center of my palm, then closing my fingers around it. I looked down and glimpsed a violent color that could only be a Fire Tree leaf. Tootles acknowledged my grateful smile with a solemn nod, then he moved to join the others.

I pocketed the leaves and took stock of the beach again. The faeries and islanders were gone. Peter's children had given up their antics and sat near the bodies. Lost and listless, they waited for orders from someone. Anyone. Housekeeper hadn't returned yet.

I glanced at the trees again. The she-beast had retreated, for now, but my own was here and strong, which was how I knew I could survive what came next. Taking a deep, fortifying breath, I went to the children. Peter's prone form rested beside them.

Some noticed me coming and stopped talking. Gradually, they all fell silent, until our small gathering stood on the beach like strange, sad statues.

"Gather your strength," I said finally, hiding my own bone-deep weariness. "There's work to be done."

Freckles lifted his head. It was the first time he'd moved since landing on shore, and I felt another pang of sorrow at the loss of his relentless cheer. "What sort of work?" he asked.

I finally looked at the bodies, and my gaze fell on the one closest to me. It was Nose. Not even in death did he reveal any emotion—his features were gray and solemn as ever. I thought of the first time I'd seen him. He would always be that tall figure on a distant shore, a bow clenched in his dirty hands.

Suddenly I missed being numb. Swallowing, I lifted my head and met Freckle's gaze. He was still waiting for a reply.

"We need to build a pyre," I said.

Far below, the water was sluggish and dark.

It hadn't been easy, getting the bodies up to the cliffs. But it was worth it. We were so high that smoke from the flames was sure to brush against the sky. If the souls of the dead couldn't find peace in the Pan Tree, perhaps they would find it up there.

Peter was all that was left. We'd been at it all day, performing so many funerals that it was tempting to climb onto the pyre with them. The children were nearly undone, too. When they saw it was Peter's turn, though, spines straightened and gazes cleared. Housekeeper adjusted his hold on Slightly, who was perched on the large boy's hip. Truth be told, we probably should have brought him back to camp, but he'd loved Peter, too. He had a right to say goodbye with the rest of us.

Now the boy who'd changed all our lives lay on a narrow pile of wood and rocks, just like the others had. The ground beneath it was dirt, so there was no risk of the blaze spreading. It was why I'd chosen this spot, despite how far it was from anything living or familiar.

The only sound among us, save the ones coming from the darkening jungle, was a single cough. No one knew how to begin, I realized. I felt several of the children glancing in my direction, but I couldn't move. I didn't want to get any closer to that body than I had to.

Then, to my relief, Freckles shuffled forward. He faced us but kept his gaze downcast. "I met Peter next to the Thames. I was going to drown myself, I was. Dear old Dad liked to knock me around, and there was no food. I didn't see much point in trudging on. But then Peter showed up. Everything was quiet, seeing as no one else was awake yet, not even the bakers. We were standing on that bridge, and Peter looked at me, all solemn-like. He just asked one question. 'If you end it all now, you'll never see it.' 'See what?' I asked him. That was when he told me about Neverland."

Freckles stopped and ducked his head down. His throat worked. *Help him, Wendy,* I thought to myself, urging my body to move forward. But even now, I couldn't do it. Being near that body, seeing Peter's pale face, would force me to relive his death.

"I've got a story about Peter," someone blurted. I turned to see Nimble making his way to the front. With a grateful nod, Freckles returned to my side. Nimble looked out at us, and there was no trace of fear in his face. In spite of what he'd enduring the night of the drawing, Neverland had changed him for the better, I thought.

The anecdotes brought smiles to tear-stained faces. The stories caused sprinklings of laughter. I had no desire to speak—I guarded our shared moments selfishly, like a dragon over its treasure—but I kept thinking about Peter's smile, how his eyes would crinkle at the corners, so alive anything otherwise seemed impossible. He Whom We Loved, The Boy Who Wouldn't Grow Up.

My mind chose that moment to picture our names carved into that tree, and I heard Peter's voice again as he told me, *So all of Neverland will know.*

"Well, at least there's no chance of him growing up now," I murmured, tasting the salt of my own tears. If it had survived, would I be able to hear his voice within the Pan Tree?

The instant it occurred to me, I fought the temptation to run there. All that place held now was ashes and wisps of fading memory. Just like this one.

Freckles wiped his nose roughly with the back of his sleeve. "No," he agreed, the word muffled. "Perhaps it's better this way."

"Perhaps."

All this time, we'd been alone on the cliff. I'd assumed the faeries and islanders were probably too busy mourning their own. But now the sound of footsteps reached my ears, and when I looked again, there stood most of Neverland. Not just the inhabitants I'd met, but people I had never heard of. Beings with branches growing out of their limbs, a cluster of naked people who held seal skins in their hands, a girl with claws and fangs. Lily was at the front, eyes downcast in respect and, I knew, heartbreak.

It must've all been too much for Slightly, because the toddler began to cry without warning. He was still lodged on Housekeeper's hip, so the older boy walked away with him. Snatches of a lullaby drifted back to us—Housekeeper had a lovely singing voice, I noted with faint surprise. No one else moved toward Peter, and we all knew there was only one thing left to do.

Once again making the decision for all of us, Freckles squatted to start the last fire. I stared at the crude pyre we'd labored over, and in that instant, I knew I could not stay to watch the flames consume Peter's body. Whatever they left behind would bear no resemblance to Peter, and it would be my last memory of him. There were so many sorrows and difficult things in our stories. Beauty faded, secrets emerged, life ended. But this was not something I could face. Not this. I skirted the gathering, which was so large now that it put me at the spot where land began to slope.

I wished I'd thought to say goodbye to Bashira on *The Fountain*, and even to Lily, but our final words would have to suffice. At least they had been words with meaning. *Live well and die better, Wendy-bird.*

"I have to go now," I said, raising my voice slightly to draw their attention. Everyone turned toward me, their expressions varying from surprise to indifference. I searched for Freckles, Housekeeper, and Nimble, making sure to meet their gazes one by one. "Anyone who wishes to accompany me is welcome."

No one stepped forward, but I was not surprised. Housekeeper adjusted his grip on Slightly again. "Will you tell anyone? About the island, I mean?" he asked.

This was a question everyone wanted to know the answer to, obvious in how they went still and their small sounds ceased.

Looking at all of them, I imagined a world that knew about this strange and magical place. There would be treasure hunters, fortune seekers, world destroyers. They would take every bit of magic there was and leave a dried husk, like all the deserts I'd read about.

"Never," I said.

The tension leaked into the ground and disappeared. A few of the children had started to turn away when tiny, white things filled the air. It wasn't ash or some kind of hail. No, this was something else entirely. Alarmed, Slightly buried his face into the curve between Housekeeper's neck and shoulder.

"What's happening?" I heard one of the children whisper.

I put my palm out. The spots of cold only lasted an

instant before dissolving onto my skin. "It's snow," I remarked.

Exclamations immediately followed my words, some of them coming from behind, and I whirled to see that every person in Neverland had come to pay their respects to Peter, villagers and faeries alike. They, too, were astonished by this turn of events. I caught sight of Bashira and Juan, their faces raised toward the gray sky.

While the Neverlanders marveled amongst themselves, catching snowflakes of their own, I finally acknowledged my shadow—since Peter's death, it had been restless and demanding, waiting for me to do what I'd made of habit of doing, and hand over anything unpleasant or difficult. Indeed, it would be so easy to let the grief leave me, seep into that roiling darkness like blood from a wound.

Instead, I stepped on it.

For a few moments, the shadow writhed. Fought me. Tried to remain separate. But it was as simple and difficult as that, and eventually, it lost whatever sense of free will or unique thought it had possessed. I closed my eyes as every part of myself I'd lived so long without settled back into place. The woman, the sister, the daughter, the human. There was pain, but there was joy, too. I'd forgotten about that. A sigh left me.

"Wendy?" Nimble ventured. "Are you going home now?"

I smiled at him, and I saw my sorrow reflected in his brown eyes. "Yes. Michael is waiting."

Slightly's chin dropped to his chest. I knelt before the young boy, recommitting his dear face to a memory rusty with disuse. No matter how badly I wanted to, I knew I couldn't take him with me. I had no way to support him, and an unmarried mother would have even bleaker chances of securing work or lodging.

"Are you walking down to the ship, then?" Housekeeper asked as I straightened.

I shook my head. "No. I won't be sailing back."

The boy's brow furrowed. Tootles was smiling—maybe he *had* seen me in one of his visions. "Then how..." Housekeeper started.

In response, I turned and searched the throng of fae. Donella felt my gaze. She'd been sticking her tongue into the air, trying to get her first taste of snow. When I didn't look away, she left the other faeries.

Somehow Donella knew exactly what I wanted, and once she reached me, she cupped my face with feather-like fingers. Her rosebud lips parted to let out a breath. I saw a cloud of gold dust just before I closed my eyes. It settled onto my skin much like the snowflakes falling all around us.

Donella's hands fell away, and after a moment, it seemed safe to look at her again. "Thank you," I said, meeting her gaze.

Without a word, Donella floated back to her people. What was there to say, really?

The crowd watched as I went to the cliff's edge. The snow was coming down even harder now, but it wasn't thick enough to obscure the Neverbird swooping and shrieking overhead. Her cries pierced the frigid wind moaning past. Even if my shadow had taken everything, I'd recognized

Aurora. Her sounds vibrated through my bones; maybe she knew we would never see each other again. Tears stung my eyes. "Goodbye, friend," I murmured, hoping she would hear me.

I spread my arms and stared into the sun. A snowflake tangled in my eyelashes.

Behind me, people started muttering about the she-beast. I glanced over my shoulder. I saw the great cat in an instant. She was running in my direction. She'd be here within seconds. I had finally become worthy, dangerous, capable. She yowled her intent to kill—her teeth flashed—and I faced the horizon again. The sound of her approach was like thunder.

But I only cared about Peter's voice in my head, urging me on. *The trick is to think of something meaningful. It doesn't have to be particularly happy or important. Just a thought that makes you feel as though there's more to the world than what everyone sees.*

Peter, I thought.

And my feet left the ground.

CHAPTER 23

LEAVES SKITTERED DOWN THE STREET.

The house was the same as I'd left it—somehow I had expected it to be different. I allowed myself a minute to look at everything. The brick exterior, the red trim, the slate roof. Dawn cast a yellow tint to it. My family's home appeared so ordinary and calm. I knew what awaited inside was anything but.

A cold gust sent the leaves swirling. London was bracing for winter, and I wasn't dressed properly. If anyone looked out their window, they'd see a filthy, ragged girl, with clothes a bit too big and weapons she shouldn't know how to use. And, unlike the house, there was a wildness within me I worried would show on the outside. Neverland may have been an ocean away, but it was also beneath my skin. Just as Peter had predicted.

I think Neverland may change you as much as you change Neverland.

Slurred singing disrupted the night—a drunkard was clinging to a lamppost nearby. It seemed a good time to face the life I'd run away from, and I hastened up the steps. Thankfully the door was unlocked.

Every curtain was drawn, the air still. There was only furniture to watch my nervous progress. A hulking shape made me jump, before I realized it was the piano. Papa had been planning on selling it, before he succumbed to the drinking. The instrument sat in the corner with a forlorn air, as if no one had touched it in a long, long time. Shaking myself, I aimed for the bedrooms. My shadow slanted over the floor, firmly attached to my person.

Then came the sound of nails, rapid on the stairs. In an instant, I knew Nana was loose. I turned at the same time she reached me.

"Good girl," I whispered, kneeling in front of her. I scratched her ears while she huffed and sniffed my face. Her damp nose left spots of cold where it touched. "Oh, you're such a good girl. I missed you, smelly thing."

The dog let out a low, happy whine and her tail wagged so hard it made her whole body shake. Though I would've liked to throw my arms around her, I patted Nana's head and continued on, still hearing that relentless tick, tick, tick of time working against me. Against Michael.

Upstairs, there was a strong smell of decay. Fear and shame perched on my shoulders and hissed in both ears. The door to Michael's room was slightly ajar. It was plain there had been enough delays, so I pushed it open. The hinges moaned.

An oil lamp burned on the table. Dust motes floated through the air. There were two people sitting vigil. The man looked like he hadn't eaten in weeks; his cheeks were gaunt and unshaven. The woman beside him looked no better. Her hair was tangled, her eyes sunken. Her hands fluttered over the bed like mad birds, useless and desperate.

My parents.

The figure they hovered beside seemed smaller than the last time I'd seen him. Slowly, I went to his other side. Michael's lips were cracked and unbearably dry. His hair was matted to his head and his eyelids were nearly translucent. But his face was tranquil, and I wondered if whatever beckoned was so wonderful that he didn't want to return to us.

He was dying.

"Wendy?" Papa stared at me as if I was a mirage. A vein throbbed in his temple. He said nothing else.

Mama was not so speechless. She flew to her feet and cried, "Where have you been? You've been gone for *days*! How could you? When we needed—"

Before I could speak, the fever dug its claws deeper into Michael. He tossed his head and moaned. It was a miracle he was still alive.

My vision blurred with tears. I got on my knees and grasped his hand. It was cold and clammy.

"I have a present, little brother," I whispered. "Something I brought back from the island. Just for you."

Tootles's parting gift was still in my pocket, the texture of the leaves rough and strange. Slightly damp, but not from rain—Housekeeper said they were like that when you plucked them off the Fire Tree. If they'd been any other kind, they wouldn't have fared well after such a rough flight and a long journey. As my hand unfurled, a new terror ripped through me. I'd only seen the leaves applied to injuries... what if they didn't work for illnesses?

I couldn't entertain the thought. Mama said something that I didn't hear while I crushed one of the precious leaves into tiny fragments. After a breath of deliberation, I retrieved a glass of water from the nightstand and dropped them in. Then I tipped Michael's head forward and carefully made him drink. His sickly scent washed over me, but it was no match for my determination. The floorboards creaked—John coming in, Nana close behind—but I didn't turn, despite how much I longed to greet them. My other brother must have sensed the tension in the air, because he didn't say a word, either.

Michael leaned back again, unchanged. He'd barely stirred during any of it. Mama and Papa couldn't have known what was happening, but they remained silent. As we waited, I described the landscapes of Neverland to him. The golden plains, the jagged cliffs, the misty mountain. *It must work, it must,* I kept thinking.

I knew the instant the magic of the Fire leaves began to take hold; Michael's muscles seemed to turn to liquid, and his breathing became so faint that the only sign he still lived was the slight flaring of his nostrils. Then, so subtly I almost missed it, his eyes cracked open.

"Wendy?" he said sleepily.

My knees went weak. For a moment, I could do nothing but breathe.

Papa exhaled in disbelief. "Is he...?"

"How?" Mama cried, fraught with joy and incredulity. Weeping, she flung herself across Michael's chest. Nana barked. They were going to wake Liza and Mrs. Graham. No matter; they'd want to see this.

"Magic," I said, as John leaped onto the bed and whooped. Nana followed suit. It was beautiful chaos.

Michael blinked up at me with obvious interest, and our parents were breathlessly intrigued, as well. They wouldn't believe it. Any of it. Neverland, Peter, the islanders, the mermaids, the pirates, the faeries, the Pan Tree. But it was the truth, and I'd learned the truth was the grandest adventure of all.

Smiling, I opened my mouth and told them a story.

EPILOGUE

One month later

THE *SS MAJESTIC* was a flurry of activity.

A woman shrieked instructions at the poor fellows carrying her trunks aboard. A child screamed as she was carried away from a couple huddled on the street. Servants seemed to be everywhere, their movements frantic, their expressions harassed. Seagulls circled overhead and cast small shadows upon the deck. Meanwhile I stood at the railing, a silent spectator to it all. My own luggage was safely stored away in a cabin and I'd said every goodbye yesterday, in another city altogether.

Someone mentioned my name, their tone dripping with derision. I glanced toward a family standing near the stairs —one of the faces was familiar. Gwendolyn Adney. In another lifetime, we had come out together. She'd made her curtsey to the queen just before I did. The instant our gazes met, she turned away, a deliberate snub. So she was the reason none of the well-dressed people here had deigned to make introductions. The wildness in me was tempted to approach, say something vulgar enough to make them faint. Peter would've appreciated it, no doubt.

Days ago, the thought might have caused my smile to fade. Now, it caused a twinge, but the small smile remained.

As the sun continued to rise, I stayed where I was. I faced the pink horizon and watched its progress. My nostrils flared. The air in Liverpool smelled different. Cleaner. The hubbub went on behind me, but my mind traveled to where the air was familiar.

Back in London, what few belongings the Davenports had left were being packed away, prepared for a journey out of the city. Father had found a cottage with low rent, and Mrs. Graham had kindly secured him a valet position in an esteemed household. Though they would not be living in luxury, my family would not starve, especially now that Michael was strong and healthy. As I wouldn't be going with them, this was a worry I could slide off my shoulders and leave on the road behind me.

"Will this be your first time in America?"

I jumped, more startled by the fact that someone was addressing me than actual surprise. A gentleman stood in the space that had been created by society's cruelty. I'd begun to think of it as a moat, and here someone was, without a boat or a way back.

The gentleman tugged at the bottom of his waistcoat as he waited for my reply. It was unclear why he was opening himself to rumors and ridicule. Perhaps he was a rare breed, and favored kindness over appearances. Perhaps he sensed Neverland in me and couldn't help it. Perhaps he didn't know of me at all, and had only wandered over here for a polite conversation with a stranger.

Whatever the reason, I inevitably thought of his yearly salary. Mama's voice also sounded in my head, faint and despairing. *Our only hope is for an advantageous marriage, Wendy. You must find someone before word gets out and all of society knows about our misfortune.*

"Yes, it will. I'm also excited to spend a week on this ship; I do so enjoy my solitude." I softened my pointed words with a smile. There was a path at my feet and nothing would lead me away from it.

The rejection took him so off guard that, for a moment, the gentleman said nothing. He recovered, replied with polite words, and withdrew. I could have exchanged a few niceties with him, I supposed as I watched him go, but I'd had little patience for such things since coming back from Neverland.

Once again, I could feel others staring in my direction. I didn't acknowledge them, but the need arose in me for exhilarating heights and star-kissed wind. I strolled away from their prying eyes, hands behind me, neck arched back. A wistful urge remembered how it felt to fly. Perhaps someday I would again—no one knew what the future held. Well, one person did, but he was far from here.

"Don't be frightened."

I froze.

The sound of his voice opened a yawning hole inside of me. Nothing about it had changed, I thought in a detached sort of way. It was still warm, as if we shared some secret, and still boyish, as if he hadn't experienced the sort of pain that would destroy even the strongest person.

In the secret places of my head, I'd been expecting him. Hoping for him. Had I finally gone mad?

Breathing shallowly, I turned. He stood behind me, legs spread apart in his usual stance, looking exactly as I remembered him. My voice was barely audible as I breathed, "Peter?"

"We never had the opportunity to dance again, after Lily's ceremony, did we?" he asked with that impudent glint in his eye. "Shall we put on a show for your friend back there? She seems like a jolly good time."

"I'm dreaming," I whispered, devouring the sight of him. It couldn't be real... he was wearing a *suit*. But more alarming than that was his shadow, which was properly attached to him and slanted over the deck, moving only when Peter moved.

Peter took a step closer, and his demeanor became tender. "Or perhaps you're finally awake, and you've been asleep until this moment."

"It can't be," I insisted, shaking my head so hard pain radiated through it. My bun loosened and tendrils of hair fluttered. I was crying, too, not from pain, but from desperate hope. "You *died*. I couldn't stop it. I held you in my arms and watched you slip away."

"You also made a bargain with the mermaids," Peter

countered, still approaching steadily. I hit the railing and he planted his hands on either side of me. When I didn't respond, my mind slow to comprehend what he was saying, Peter bent. He brushed his lips over my forehead, my closed eyes, the corner of my mouth. He was warm, oh, so warm. "If you gave them a taste of my blood, they would grant you a wish."

"But I didn't give them..." I trailed off. The events of that day flipped through my head like the pages of a book. And in a burst of clarity, I knew. I saw her falling into the water and all those white hands dragging her down. "Lady Bainbridge."

"Apparently she was a satisfactory substitute—turns out, the mermaids have been wanting Mother dearest for years. They were a bit unclear on the details about that. Anyway, Serafa heard you tell my brother that if you'd had a wish, it would have been for my life. Soon after you left, I awoke. I find it quite upsetting that you didn't bother to stay for my entire funeral," he added.

We stared at each other for an instant. Then, with a cry, I launched myself at him. Peter caught me and stumbled back. When he hit the wall behind him, I was already kissing him.

It was a reunion equal to every story or legend. We were delirious with joy, almost to the point where we were rough with each other. He buried his fingers in my hair and I dug mine into his back. Our passion had never been extinguished, only smothered by circumstance. It flared into being and was, for however long we were against that wall, all that existed.

A wonderfully familiar jolt of heat went through me, and as if he sensed it, Peter reached beneath my skirts. I felt the warm roughness of his fingertips just before I jerked away.

"We can't," I protested, breathless. "We're in broad daylight, Peter."

Heaving a sigh, he bent his head and pressed it against my shoulder. His voice was husky as he said, "You smell so good."

A shiver went through me and my toes curled. After a few minutes, getting the words out between kisses, Peter whispered to me. "I understand congratulations are in order. You've been accepted to university?"

I was so exhilarated by the reminder that I pulled back. Peter's face was still clutched between my hands. "Yes! The Women's Medical College of Pennsylvania. It was my time in Neverland that helped me realize. All those wounds, all the occasions I could do so little. The rest of the world doesn't have Fire Trees, you know. Mother is scandalized. She's taken to bed again."

"Well, who wouldn't be appalled at the notion of their child pursuing such a noble profession? Dr. Davenport, indeed. Perish the thought." Peter gave a mock shudder.

I would've swatted at him, but the excitement was tumbling out of my mouth. "Best part of it all is the traveling. After all, physicians are needed in every part of the world, aren't they? I'll be able to visit the places in my father's atlas and learn about the things I've only been able to read about. The Northern Lights, Peter! Your clothes..." Quick as that, I forgot my news and touched his lapels. I felt dizzy with happiness. "You look so different."

He smirked. "I think you mean dashing."

Now my hands clenched into fists, wrinkling the material. This was all happening so fast. I was still inclined to believe it wasn't real. Levelly I said, "Peter, it seems as though… if you intend to make a life here, I know it's because of me. I can't ask you to do that. To stay and be someone you aren't."

"What if I want to stay and be someone I am?" he countered.

His dear face blurred through a sheen of tears. I shook my head again. "But it's *not*. You're the boy who flies. The boy who finds lost children. The boy who saves faeries. The boy who doesn't grow—"

"I'm the boy who loves Wendy," he interrupted, acting as if it truly was that simple.

"I won't be enough," I argued. "What about the *sky*, Peter? Your favorite place?"

"You were right, you know. When I left London all those years ago, I *was* afraid. The island seemed like the answer to every question I'd ever had. Never would I grow up to become a parent that would leave their child, never would I be forced to curb my impulses or desires, never would I be vulnerable again. But after meeting you, I don't belong there anymore. Even if you were to say that you don't want to be with me, I wouldn't go back."

In searching for something to say, my gaze fell upon a commotion on the docks. Crates were being carried onboard. But most of the luggage had already been tended to, which meant those crates probably belonged to a late arrival. "Are those... yours?" I asked, glancing at Peter with raised brows.

To my surprise, the light in his eyes had dimmed. A muscle worked in his jaw. He nodded without looking away from the line of men. "I brought funding to commission some headstones. One for every child that died in the drawings."

Pain swelled in my chest, and I thought of that terrible night I'd witnessed Nimble slaughter another boy. However much I longed to comfort Peter, I couldn't tell him he was blameless. I couldn't tell him he'd been forgiven, because the ones he'd wronged no longer had a voice to speak with.

"This is what it means to grow up, Peter," I said finally. "To recognize our mistakes and bear the weight of them. All we can do is try to be better."

He remained silent. I watched him, hesitating, because there was something else he needed to know. Another hard truth I had to acknowledge. My gaze fell as I tried to think of how to say it, and in doing so, I saw his shadow. It struck me all over again, the strangeness of how still it was. After a moment, I refocused on the shadow's owner and said, my words ringing with absolution, "I'm going to America, Peter. Nothing will tempt me to get off this ship. Not even a boy coming back from the dead."

There was a second pause, this one even longer, and the silence terrified me. Peter squinted at the sky and pinched his lips in thought. "I've heard a lot about Americans.

They're rumored to be a brash bunch. I think I'd fit in rather well, don't you?"

"Hello? Is someone there?" a familiar voice called before I could answer.

"Oh, blast!" I dove down a flight of steps and dragged Peter with me. Behind us, I heard heels clipping against the boards. "It's that wretched Gwendolyn. No, Peter, don't!"

He'd hopped into view with that roguish grin I thought I'd never see again. Hurriedly I fixed my gloves and fanned my face, hoping to make the color and swelling retreat. Scowling, I shuffled into the open, as well.

Gwendolyn spotted us instantly, of course. Her expression cleared. "Oh, Miss Davenport! I see you've met Mr. Pan."

I was on the verge of replying when the name sank in. Did she say Pan? I avoided looking at Peter, but my mind traveled to an island, the only means of which could be reached by flying toward a second star to the right and straight on 'til morning, where there was a dangerous wood and a magical tree residing within it, with our names carved along its bark.

I smiled, and it was a wonderful thing, that smile. Completely free of the sadness that had been following me for weeks. "Yes, we just met."

"Did he tell you about his exciting adventures in the West Indies?" Gwendolyn said with a coquettish glance in his direction. "He and his brother just arrived to London with boatloads of gold. It's all anyone can talk about. How thrilling it must have been, making such a discovery!"

"Quite," Peter agreed, barely suppressing a grin.

Gold didn't interest me in the least. Not compared to the other information she'd just supplied. "Brother?" I inquired, resisting the urge to elbow Peter. James was *here*?

Gwendolyn beamed, though it was all for the man at my side, of course. "Yes, Captain James Pan. A very handsome man and perfectly charming! Would you like to meet him? I'd be delighted to make the introductions."

For a moment, I was confused that James had taken on a new identity, as well. But it made sense, really—he'd been hidden away from society most of his life, and no one in the city knew him as Lady Bainbridge's son. It stood to reason that he could begin anew, just like the rest of us. That he could leave behind a legacy of shame and secrets to create one that was entirely his own.

"I think I *would* like to meet the captain," I decided. Peter offered his arm, and I took it. We exchanged blissful, conspiratorial smiles. The sunlight was warm on my skin. A salt-laden breeze pushed at our backs, as if to say, *Go, go.*

And so we went.

ACKNOWLEDGMENTS

The person I must acknowledge first is none other than Ben Alderson. If it weren't for our FaceTimes and writing sprints, this manuscript would probably still be sitting on my hard drive. Thank you for being such a great writing partner, Ben!

Next, of course, I need to thank Jessi Elliott, my dear friend who is relentlessly supportive and encouraging. This past year was infinitely more bearable because of you. Thank you for every kind word, every thoughtful gift, and every day of friendship. I am so lucky to have you in my life.

Thank you, as well, to my agent Beth Miller. The feedback you provided for *Straight On 'Til Morning* is a huge part of how it became this final product, a book I can feel proud of. Reading an entire manuscript in its roughest stage is no small feat, and I'm eternally grateful for the time you dedicated to this story.

My eternal love and appreciation to Ashleigh from A Frolic Through Fiction and Becca from Becca and the Books.

Your perspectives were invaluable for this book's blurb, in addition to your proofread, Becca. Both of you have been a much-needed source of light and laughter during this past year! Here's to more buddy reads, drunk livestreams, and insightful conversations in the year to come.

I'd also like to express gratitude to my copy editor, Kate Anderson, along with Dani, who responded to my Instagram post calling for outside readers. Thank you for lending me your time and your sharp eyes, not to mention reading it in such a short amount of time!

Finally, I need to mention Jane and August. They can't read, but the world should still know the integral part they played in the creation of *Straight On 'Til Morning*. Without their cuddles, the afternoons they forced me to leave the house and actually step into the sunlight, and the joy they bring each day, I'm not sure I would've had the drive to accomplish anything. I love you, you spoiled beasts.

TURN THE PAGE
FOR A SNEAK PEAK OF

FORTUNA SWORN

AVAILABLE NOW

CHAPTER ONE

They put me in a cage.

After that, they loaded it into the back of a van. I tilted with the container and slammed hard onto my elbow, but I didn't give them the satisfaction of crying out. The doors closed, leaving me in darkness. I sat there and shook with rage as the engine rumbled to life. I could hear my captors talking and laughing. One made a lewd joke.

I didn't bother demanding to know our destination; they had been talking about the market for the three days I'd been in their grasp. More often than not, it was a place Fallen went to die.

Fallen. I hadn't had to use that term in ages. Every species—faeries, werewolves, shapeshifters, nymphs—were descended from angels. No one knew whether it was mutation or evolution that had separated us.

My captors thought I was a werewolf or a faerie, both of which would fetch a high price. Some buyers would pay even more if they intended to kill the creature and sell its parts. It was well-known that the muscles of a werewolf gave you unparalleled strength. The hands of a faerie lent you their magic. The lungs of a nymph brought the ability to breathe underwater.

The heart of my kind would eliminate all the eater's fears.

I didn't allow myself to wonder what would happen if I caught the attention of a buyer; I'd find a way to escape before then.

It was still hard to believe this was happening. I kept replaying the kidnapping in my head, cursing my own recklessness. A few nights ago, I'd been in the woods. During my exploration of those hills, a splash of color had caught my notice. A flower, nestled in the grass, beneath the sky's luminous glow. As I'd knelt to admire it, something struck me from behind.

And here I was.

Hours later, my muscles were screaming. Just when I thought I would finally open my mouth and give the pain a voice, the van lurched to a halt. The engine died again. My captors got out, still talking, and the doors opened. Brightness poured inside. I squinted, so disoriented that I forgot to curse at them as they took hold of the cage.

The selling hadn't begun yet. It was mid-morning and everything was awash in soft, yellow light. Dew still clung to the grass. Every time someone spoke, white puffs of air accompanied the words. The men—although I suspected they were goblins, based on the greed that shone from their dark eyes—carried me along a row of stalls, platforms, and cages. Vendors and merchants unpacked their wares or lined up their prisoners. Chains clinked, undoubtedly dipped in holy water. The stories of iron or silver holding us had been fabricated for humans.

The holy water also made it difficult to maintain any glamour—a powerful but subtle magic that disguised a Fallen's true form. In passing, I caught a glimpse of wings. Those were worth a fortune, as well.

As my captors found a place for their prize, I couldn't resist looking at the rest of those for sale. A boy stared back at me with his watery blue gaze. He stood on a small, wooden platform, a sign around his neck that displayed his species and price. Vampire. They could be out in the sun, of course; they simply preferred the night. He looked like a boy of twelve or thirteen. If he was lucky, he'd be sold to a family that wanted someone in their kitchen. If he was unlucky, he'd be sold for his incisors—their teeth were useful for witch spells and poisons. But a vampire without his fangs would soon die of starvation.

Within seconds, we were out of each other's line of sight. My captors had found an open spot toward the end of the row, and as they set the cage down, it brought me within reach of them. But even if my powers weren't dormant in the daylight, my bound hands prevented me from touching anyone through the bars. I leaned back to wait for another opportunity. With every second that passed, one thought screamed louder than the rest. Torturing me, taunting me.

Is this what happened to Damon?

"I smell coffee," one of the men said, rubbing his hands together for warmth. "Want to find it?"

The other nodded, and they walked away, leaving me there. The cage was so small that I could only stand bent over or remain seated. I chose the latter. A lovely smell teased my senses, and I saw that an old woman selling herbs and flowers had set up nearby. She noticed me and bared pointed, yellow teeth. I quickly looked away.

While the market filled, I took stock of what I had in my possession for the umpteenth time. Jeans, a plaid button-up, and hiking boots. The men had taken the laces, though, and the rest of my gear. They'd also found Dad's pocket knife after I'd been knocked unconscious.

I began searching the ground for a rock, but my skin prickled in that way it did when someone was watching. Tensing, I lifted my head. There was a male standing in front of me. Not a man, for I knew instantly this was no human.

"Hello there," he said the moment our eyes met.

His hair rested against the back of his neck in soft, brown curls. His cheekbones were sharp and his jawline defined. His irises were gray, or hazel, I couldn't tell from a distance. He wore a wool coat to ward off the chill in the air. He appeared human, but that was the work of a glamour— power rolled off him like perfume. I studied his ears, his eyes, his fingers. Nothing gave him away. He was appealing, yet not so much that he attracted attention.

"What is your name?" the stranger asked. I realized I'd been staring. His voice was crisp and unhurried, like a dead leaf falling from a tree.

"Fuck," I answered, hiding my embarrassment. "Would you like to guess my last name? I'll give you a hint. It rhymes with 'shoe.'"

To my surprise, a faint smile curved his lips. "How refreshing. A slave with spirit left in her."

Though there was no point in engaging with him, the word made my stomach churn with fury. I longed to be free of the rusty bars. "I'm not a slave," I hissed.

He tilted his head. "You're in a cage. You can be purchased. Isn't this the definition of a slave?"

"I'll show you the definition," I purred. "Find the key and let me out."

"Something tells me it's in my best interest to leave you there," the stranger remarked. His tone was dry but his eyes twinkled merrily.

Just I started to respond, my captors returned, cups of coffee in hand. The stranger slipped away soundlessly. I watched him go, noting that he walked as though his feet didn't quite touch the ground. *Faerie*, I thought darkly. Of course, there were any number of things he could be, but my gut told me I was right.

So far, I had yet to meet a faerie I could trust. Once, one came into the bar where I worked and stole tips from my apron while I wasn't looking. Another tried to sexually assault me in the street after a closing shift.

And then there had been Sorcha. Vivacious, lovely, intriguing Sorcha. We'd sensed each other at the movie theatre one night, during my freshman year of high school. Our friendship had been immediate and all-consuming. For me, someone who didn't make friends easily, it had been everything. Then Sorcha seemed to fall off the face of the earth. She stopped texting, stopped coming by, stopped showing up at the local haunts. My theories had ranged from her being killed by a faerie hunter to something with her parents' jobs going wrong.

Weeks later, though, I saw her again at a pool party.

The image was still vivid in my mind. Her laying there on that lounge chair, wearing a neon orange bikini. My stricken face reflecting in the darkness of her sunglasses. When I asked her why she hadn't called me back, she said in a bored tone, "Oh, you didn't know? I'm done with you now."

It had been years since that conversation, but the effect of it hadn't faded.

"...so beautiful. But what is it?" a woman was asking. I tore my focus away from the faerie's retreating back. A couple now stood before the cage. It seemed my captors had found some prospective buyers. The woman studied me like I was a side of meat or a charmed necklace. Insults and taunts rose to my lips.

"Not entirely sure," one of the men replied, giving me a warning glare. His fingers idly brushed against the cattle prod at his hip. I ground my teeth together and stayed silent. "We found it on a mountain, kneeling in some moonlight. It has a lot of power, though. Makes my hair stand on end."

I had never bothered telling these morons the truth; I'd been on the mountain for a purpose, yes, but not to change form or draw power from the moon.

That night, I'd been looking for my brother.

There was still some small, unconquerable part of me that couldn't accept he was gone. Really, though, going into the woods had been more for myself than Damon. Two years had passed since I'd come home from work and found his note on the kitchen table. *Went out to check the garden*, it said in my brother's nearly illegible handwriting. It wasn't out of the usual for him to go out in the middle of the night; I felt the restlessness, too, when the moon was bright and high. His vegetable patch was in the backyard, visible through the kitchen window, but I'd been so tired from a shift at Bea's that I didn't even look out the glass before heading to bed.

When I woke up the next morning, his room was still empty.

The sheriff's department went through all the motions. Search parties, missing posters, phone calls to hospitals. Eventually, everyone reached the same conclusion.

Damon Sworn was dead.

The night my captors found me was the anniversary of his disappearance.

Unsurprisingly, the two of them had trouble selling something they couldn't advertise. Guess that hadn't occurred to them in all the excitement of discovering me. The couple moved on, and farther along the row, a young shapeshifter caught their interest. She was so frightened that she couldn't keep hold of one skin, switching from girl to cougar to bird between one breath and the next. She was in a glass box so she couldn't fly away. Anyone who bought her would have to know a spell or possess a bespelled item to keep her from escaping. I watched the couple negotiate with a black-haired woman standing beside the box, but couldn't stomach seeing how it ended. I leaned my temple against the bars and closed my eyes.

More time went by. Mist retreated and sunlight crept

forward. The fools trying to sell me grew bored. They got lawn chairs out of the van and started playing a game of cards. Somewhere in the market, an auction began, and the auctioneer was louder than the crowds. I'd barely slept in three days, and I began to drift off, his bellowing voice a bizarre lullaby. "Ten thousand dollar bid! Do I hear fifteen thousand? Now fifteen thousand, will you give me twenty thousand?"

Suddenly there was a clinking sound near my head. I jerked upright so quickly, I nearly collided with the bars. Something glittered on the metal floor, and the breath caught in my throat when I saw what it was.

Keys.

I snatched them up, terrified that my captors had noticed. But they'd started drinking hours earlier, and they saw nothing but their bottles and cards. I looked around for whoever had left this unexpected gift. There were only merchants, buyers, and slaves. No one looked in my direction.

I'd asked one person for a key—the faerie. Why would he help me? What did he stand to gain from my escape?

Questions that I would ask myself later. I tucked the keys into my pocket and waited. Everything inside of me longed to take action, but sunlight still touched the market, keeping my abilities dormant. Any escape attempt would fail.

Night was slow in coming. Though I continually started to tap and fidget, I forced myself to be still again. Eventually the sky darkened and part of the moon turned its face toward us. Feeling its effects, some of the other captives began to whine and pull at their chains. Fortunately for the slavers, it wasn't a full moon. While werewolves weren't forced to change, as the humans believed, they were stronger then. We all were.

My captors had been careful to avoid physical contact these past three days. It was the only intelligence they'd displayed. At their cabin, they'd kept me tied up in a storage room, with just a bucket for company. I'd had to eat food from a bowl like a dog. When they decided to switch to the cage, they'd used tranquilizer darts. Several, in fact, since they weren't certain what I was. And if I happened to be allergic or have a bad reaction to the drugs, well, too bad.

I remembered all of this as dusk faded, and the fire crackling within me climbed higher and hotter. Starlight shone serenely upon the market. My captors put away their chairs, talking about possibilities for tomorrow. The small-eyed one suggested using torture to find out what I was. The other mentioned displaying me naked. Every word only stoked the flames.

Luck was finally on my side. Slavers and vendors were so preoccupied packing up their wares, no one saw me use the key and slip out of the cage. Well, no one but the shapeshifter, whose eyes met mine for a brief moment before she fixed hers pointedly on her feet. She'd been sold earlier, so I had no idea why she was still here. Maybe her new owners had gone to get another vehicle. Couldn't have a dirty slave on their sleek leather upholstery, now, could they?

Like the rest of my kind, I moved silently, creeping upon the kidnappers like a dream. My heart pounded harder as I edged around the van. I would only have one chance to do this right; goblins possessed enhanced speed, strength, and healing abilities. The men were lifting the empty cooler inside when my time came. Quickly, giving them no chance to react, I opened the door on the other side. They were just lifting their heads when I reached across and grasped their wrists—no easy task with my own hands tied. That was all it took. I had hold of their minds now, and before they could seize me or shout an alarm, I disappeared in a burst of black smoke. To them, anyway. Anyone else would still see me, standing there, smiling like a cat with its paw in a bowl of dead mice.

I allowed my voice to slither around them, echo a thousand times, as though I were a legion instead of one. "You will regret the night you took me. You will repent for these last three days."

"What are you?" the small-eyed goblin whimpered. For goblins they were. A single touch had told me so much.

It wasn't enough to answer. Instead, I let go of their wrists and circled the van—Nightmares don't sit on our victims' chests as they sleep, like it describes on Wikipedia or in books; once I touch someone, there's no need to maintain physical contact—until I was right behind them. I leaned close and pressed the side of my chin against the trembling goblin's temple. I stroked the back of his head with my still-bound hands. He probably would've bolted right then, but I'd made them believe they couldn't move. "I am the last of my kind," I whispered. "Does that mean anything to you?"

His breathing was ragged. There were only a few deadly

possibilities, and everyone paid attention to endangered species. Especially slavers. Better selling value, of course. The thought made my nails dig into his scalp. The goblin made another sound, deep in his throat. Now that I had finally touched him, I could taste his terror. Everyone's had a unique flavor and most were decidedly unpleasant. This one had the tang of chicken fat, and it coated my tongue.

I hardly noticed, however, as images flickered across my closed eyelids; I'd found his fears. Not all of them, not the ones that kept him awake at night. But the phobias that hovered just beneath his skin, ready to come out at a moment's notice, those were mine. The small-eyed goblin had typical ones. Spiders, heights, death.

His companion was a bit more interesting. Above all, he dreaded being alone.

Now that's exactly what he was.

All the goblin saw was whiteness. There was no ground and no sky, no walls and no surroundings. He wrapped his arms around his knobby knees—no glamour, because this was his own mind, after all—and began to rock back and forth. His pointed teeth flashed as he sang a song his mother had taught him. Meanwhile, the other was slapping at his own arms and legs, believing himself to be covered in spiders. Cliché, maybe, but there was no time for ingenuity.

I held out my wrists, making the goblin believe they were his. He couldn't very well slap at any spiders if his hands were tied, so he desperately yanked Dad's knife out of his boot and hacked at the ropes. I tried to jerk back, but he was too fast. The blade nicked my arm. I hissed at the pain. The ropes fell away, though, and I ended the illusion before the goblin could cut my entire hand off. He returned to slapping at the spiders, dropping Dad's knife, and I bent to retrieve it. It was a welcome weight in my hand.

He'd loved this thing. The blade was Damascus steel, made by a hand-forged process of folding and refolding layers of hot high-carbon steel and iron. There were beautiful swirls and contours along its length. The handle was made of dyed wood, which I rubbed affectionately with my thumb before tucking the knife away.

Despite an ever-increasing sense of urgency, I lingered to observe my handiwork. The other goblin was already soaked in his own urine. Satisfaction curled around my heart. Smirking, I climbed into the van to reclaim my belongings. Everything was scattered, presumably from when they'd dug through everything on the day of my capture. They must have gotten rid of my phone—no doubt it was back at the cabin. I didn't know where that was, and not even an expensive iPhone could tempt me to find the place again. Seething, I slung my bag on and got out of the van. I planned on driving it back home, but I couldn't leave. Not yet.

Outside, the goblins were both crying now. I still put more power into their visions. More spiders, more echoes. They wouldn't be free of me until dawn, if the terror didn't kill them before then.

I hurried into the aisle of crushed grass and straggling buyers. Using my power after so long—I hadn't touched it even before the goblins took me, so it had been a few weeks since the last time, probably—made the blood in my veins feel like champagne. My head felt fuzzy, too. It was better than any drink or drug. Striding through the market, I cracked my neck in an effort to stay alert. At the same time, I noticed someone standing a few yards away. My steps slowed.

The faerie stood in a slant of moonlight, and in that moment, he truly looked like the angels we were all descended from. The corners of his mouth tilted up in a half-smile. I scowled in return, still distrustful, regardless of the fact that he'd aided my escape. Was he coming to collect a debt? Did he want me for his own?

Apparently not, because once again, he turned and walked away.

I suspected it wasn't the last I'd see him. Shaking myself, I continued on through the market. My progress didn't go unnoticed; Nightmares always drew stares. Whenever someone looked at me, they saw whatever face they believed the most beautiful. Like the nightmares that came at night, we were meant to be seductive. We were designed to lure our victims in. Then, when it was too late to draw back, we struck.

I couldn't find the keys for each and every cage. I also couldn't take on all the slavers here. But there was one thing I could do.

The woman who had sold the shapeshifter was preoccupied with a game on her phone. It was impressive she even got a signal up here. I knelt in front of her. "Hello."

"What do you want?" she asked without looking up. She looked entirely human and there was no trace of glamour.

Her hair was gray at the roots. The rest was an unnatural, black dye.

I wrapped my fingers around her ankle, the closest patch of bare skin within reach. The woman's head snapped up, but it was too late. She was afraid of small spaces, shrinking walls, being locked in the dark. With another wicked grin, I made her believe she was the one in a glass box. The woman jumped up, gasping, and fumbled with a chain hanging around her neck. A key appeared at the end of it. She fit it into the lock, and the door swung open. The shapeshifter scrambled out so quickly that she tripped on her skirt. She took a few steps, paused, and faced me again.

"Thank you," she whispered. Hair hung over her eyes, hiding them from view, but there was gratitude in her voice.

Before I could reply, she transformed into an owl and flew away.

ABOUT THE AUTHOR

K.J. Sutton lives in Minnesota with her two rescue dogs. She has received multiple awards for her work, and she graduated with a master's degree in Creative Writing from Hamline University.

When she's writing, K.J. always has a cup of Vanilla Chai in her hand and despises wearing anything besides pajamas. K.J. Sutton also writes young adult novels as Kelsey Sutton.

Be friends with her on Instagram, Facebook, and Twitter. And don't forget to subscribe to her newsletter so you never miss an update!

Printed in Great Britain
by Amazon